文学翻译

——大文学，小翻译

WENXUE FANYI

—— DA WENXUE, XIAO FANYI

黄伟珍 ◎ 著

四川大学出版社

SICHUAN UNIVERSITY PRESS

U0666710

项目策划：梁　平　陈克坚
责任编辑：陈克坚
责任校对：杨　果
封面设计：璞信文化
责任印制：王　炜

图书在版编目（CIP）数据

文学翻译：大文学，小翻译 / 黄伟珍著．— 成都：
四川大学出版社，2022.3（2024.6 重印）
　　ISBN 978-7-5690-5177-3

　　Ⅰ．①文… Ⅱ．①黄… Ⅲ．①文学翻译—研究 Ⅳ.
① I046

中国版本图书馆 CIP 数据核字（2021）第 240239 号

书　名	文学翻译——大文学，小翻译

著　　者	黄伟珍
出　　版	四川大学出版社
地　　址	成都市一环路南一段 24 号（610065）
发　　行	四川大学出版社
书　　号	ISBN 978-7-5690-5177-3
印前制作	四川胜翔数码印务设计有限公司
印　　刷	永清县晔盛亚胶印有限公司
成品尺寸	185mm×260mm
印　　张	14.25
字　　数	397 千字
版　　次	2022 年 4 月第 1 版
印　　次	2024 年 6 月第 2 次印刷
定　　价	78.00 元

◆ 读者邮购本书，请与本社发行科联系。
　　电话：(028)85408408/(028)85401670/
　　(028)86408023　邮政编码：610065
◆ 本社图书如有印装质量问题，请寄回出版社调换。
◆ 网址：http://press.scu.edu.cn

四川大学出版社
微信公众号

前　言

　　"大文学"之"大"有两方面含义。首先是指文学概念的转变。英国著名文学和文化评论家特里·伊格尔顿（Terry Eagleton）在《文学事件》（*The Event of Literature*，2012）中花不少笔墨探讨"何为文学"的问题。在伊格尔顿看来，文学作品常常具有以下一些特征：虚构的（fictional）、道德的（moral）、语言的（linguistic）、非实用的（non-pragmatic）和规范性的（normative），但他同时又用"苏格拉底式"的质疑法逐步分析，最后得出结论：这五个因素中的任何一个因素，都不是一部作品成为文学作品的充分条件，也非必要条件，任何一种试图准确定义"文学"的做法，最终都可能作茧自缚，维特根斯坦的"家族相似法"也无可奈何。不仅如此，"文学"的范畴，还受到具体的时代背景和文化环境影响，一些过去未被纳入文学的作品，随着时空的转换，可能成为另一个文化下或时代里的经典之作。"文学"也成了一种不断"生成"的概念。此外，"大"还有另一层意思。随着"跨学科""交叉学科""去学科"和"新文科"等概念的提出，文学的外延也不再仅仅局限于文本内部，大有溢出之势。文学除了与史学、哲学和科技等传统学科相互融合，还与图像、视频和音乐等其他艺术形式有了交集。本书使用"大文学"这一表述，也是出于这样的考虑，即它不仅涉及传统的文学类型，如诗歌、小说和戏剧等，还涵盖了戏曲、影视和歌曲等非传统意义上的文学类型。

　　需要指出的是，本书的标题中的"大文学　小翻译"，绝无贬低"翻译"的意味，只是基于目前教学实践的反思，指出"文学翻译"不仅仅是翻译的问题，更是对文学文本解读能力的综合考量。在日常教学过程中，我们常重视翻译技能，忽略了文本的解读，使得译文只是在语言表层达到某种貌似的"忠实"。在文学翻译课程上，"读不懂"成了一个重大的瓶颈。于此，很有必要重提文学文本的鉴赏能力。正所谓"磨刀不误砍柴工"，对文学文本内涵的深入理解，不仅可以提高译文的准确性，还可以提升个人的素养和审美趣味。本书书名里所说的"大"，便是针对当下具体教学语境考量，有"重视""重要"之意。

　　与传统的文学翻译书籍相比，本书有以下几个方面的不同。

　　1. "读＋译"：既注重文学文本的翻译，同时也结合相关文学或文艺理论，注重文学文本阅读能力的提升。

　　2. "大文学"：不仅分析了传统诗歌、小说等文学类型的翻译问题，还探讨了戏曲、儿童文学、电影、歌曲等"大文学"的翻译。

　　3. "中＋西"：在讲解西方的文学现象的时候，也特别注重中文文献的对照阅读和比较分析，加深理解。

　　在编排上，本书主要按照文学体裁类别进行分章讨论。每一章又分为"文体特征""赏·译·评"和"翻译练习"三个小节，兼顾阅读、翻译、评析和实训等多方面的需求。在"文体特征"方面，每一章都有相应的侧重点，注重文本性、图像性和视听性等多种文本内部因素和文本外部因素，选择名家的权威之说进行阅读和讨论。在"赏·译·评"模块里，"赏"的部分主要是联系本部分选文的作者的其他作品，解读该作者的写作风格及特色，"译"的部分提供选文的一个或多个中文译本，"评"的部分则比较灵活，虽然都涉及对译文的评析，但形式比较多样：有些是针对原文的特征进行点评，有些是针对某一个中、英文版本进行对照解读，还有一些则主要对选文的几个不同译文进行比较，有时还会对同一译者不同年代的译文进行解析，透视译文变化的原因及各自的优点和缺点。在"翻译练习"部分，则主要根据前两部分的探讨，选择代表性的文本，进行翻译实训，考察并巩固学生的文学阅读和翻译能力。

　　本书可供高等院校英语专业作为文学翻译用书或参考书，也可供广大中学教师及具有一定英语水平的英语自学者和文学翻译爱好者作为进修读物。在编写过程中，曾参考了国内外出版的许多文学创作、文学批评理论书籍和名家译作，由于著者水平有限，书中错误和考虑不周之处在所难免，恳切希望读者和专家批评指正。

目　录

1

第一章　诗歌的翻译

　　诗歌，是最古老的文学形式之一。在很长的一段时间里，"诗"（poetry）跟"文学"（literature）几乎是可以画上等号的。古代许多对诗歌的专论，如《诗学》《诗品》等，日后也成了文学评论的佳作。本章选取《文心雕龙》《论修辞》和《诗论》等著作中的文章，对诗歌的基本特征展开介绍，之后再选取若干中英文诗歌译作进行评析。

第一节　文体特征

　　本节主要从风格、意象和格律三个维度，选取古今中外名家名篇，介绍诗歌的主要特征。

一、风格

　　夫情动而言形，理发而文见，盖沿隐以至显，因内而符外者也。然才有庸俊，气有刚柔，学有浅深，习有雅郑，并情性所铄，陶染所凝，是以笔区云谲，文苑波诡者矣。故辞理庸俊，莫能翻其才；风趣刚柔，宁或改其气；事义浅深，未闻乖其学；体式雅郑，鲜有反其习：各师成心，其异如面。

　　若总其归途，则数穷八体：一曰典雅，二曰远奥，三曰精约，四曰显附，五曰繁缛，六曰壮丽，七曰新奇，八曰轻靡。典雅者，熔式经诰，方轨儒门者也；远奥者，复采曲文，经理玄宗者也；精约者，核字省句，剖析毫厘者也；显附者，辞直义畅，切理厌心者也；繁缛者，博喻酿采，炜烨枝派者也；壮丽者，高论宏裁，卓烁异采者也；新奇者，摈古竞今，危侧趣诡者也；轻靡者，浮文弱植，缥缈附俗者也。故雅与奇反，奥与显殊，繁与约舛，壮与轻乖，文辞根叶，苑囿其中矣。

　　若夫八体屡迁，功以学成，才力居中，肇自血气；气以实志，志以定言，吐纳英华，莫非情性。是以贾生骏发，故文洁而体清；长卿傲诞，故理侈而辞溢；子云沉寂，故志隐而味深；子政简易，故趣昭而事博；孟坚雅懿，故裁密而思靡；平子淹通，故虑周而藻密；仲宣躁竞，故颖出而才果；公干气褊，故言壮而情骇；嗣宗俶傥，故响逸而调远；叔夜俊侠，故兴高而采烈；安仁轻敏，故锋发而韵流；士衡矜重，故情繁而辞隐。触类以推，表里必符，岂非自然之恒资，才气之大略哉！

夫才由天资，学慎始习，斫梓染丝，功在初化，器成采定，难可翻移。故童子雕琢，必先雅制，沿根讨叶，思转自圆。八体虽殊，会通合数，得其环中，则辐辏相成。故宜模体以定习，因性以练才，文之司南，用此道也。

赞曰：

才性异曲，文体繁诡。辞为肌肤，志实骨髓。

雅丽黼黻，淫巧朱紫。习亦凝真，功沿渐靡。

（刘勰《文心雕龙·体性》）

Let the matters just discussed be regarded as understood, and let the virtue of style be defined as "to be clear" (speech is a kind of sign, so if it does not make clear it will not perform its function) —and neither flat nor above the dignity of the subject, but appropriate [prepon]. The poetic style is hardly flat, but it is not appropriate for speech.

The use of nouns and verbs in their prevailing [kyrios] meaning makes for clarity; other kinds of words, as discussed in the Poetics, make the style ornamented rather than flat. To deviate [from prevailing usage] makes language seem more elevated; for people feel the same in regard to word usage as they do in regard to strangers compared with citizens.

As a result, one should make the language unfamiliar; for people are admirers of what is far off, and what is marvelous is sweet. Many [kinds of words] accomplish this in verse and are appropriate there; for what is said [in poetry] about subjects and characters is more out of the ordinary, but in prose much less so; for the subject matter is less remarkable, since even in poetry it would be rather inappropriate if a slave used fine language or if a man were too young for his words or if the subject were too trivial, but in these cases, too, propriety is a matter of contraction or expansion [of what is being said].

As a result, authors should compose without being noticed and should seem to speak not artificially but naturally. (The latter is persuasive, the former the opposite; for people become resentful, as at someone plotting against them, just as they are at those adulterating wines.) An example is the success of Theodorus' voice when contrasted with that of other actors; for his seems the voice of the actual character, but the others' those of somebody else.

The "theft" is well done if one composes by choosing words from ordinary language. Euripides does this and first showed the way. Since speech is made up of nouns and verbs, and the species of nouns are those examined in the Poetics, from among these one should use glosses and double words and coinages rarely and in a limited number of situations. (We shall later explain where; the reason has already been given: the usage departs from the appropriate in the direction of excess.)

A word in its prevailing and native meaning and metaphor are alone useful in the lexis of prose. A sign of this is that these are the only kinds of words everybody uses; for all people carry on their conversations with metaphors and words in their native and prevailing meanings.

Thus, it is clear that if one composes well there will be an unfamiliar quality and it escapes notice and will be clear. This, we said, was the virtue of rhetorical language.

The kind of words useful to a sophist are homonyms (by means of these he does his dirty work), to a poet synonyms. By words that are both in their prevailing meaning and synonymous I mean, for example, go and walk; for when used in their prevailing sense these are synonymous with each other. Now what each kind of word is and how many species of metaphor there are and that metaphor has very great effect both in poetry and speeches has been said, as noted above, in the Poetics.

In speech it is necessary to take special pains to the extent that a speech has fewer resources than verse. Metaphor especially has clarity and sweetness and strangeness, and its use cannot be learned from someone else.

One should speak both epithets and metaphors that are appropriate, and this will be from an analogy. If not, the expression seems inappropriate because opposites are most evident when side-by-side each other. But one should consider what suits an old man, just as a scarlet cloak is right for a young one; for the same clothes are not right [for both].

And if you wish to adorn, borrow the metaphor from something better in the same genus, if to denigrate, from worse things. I mean, for example, since they are opposites in the same genus, saying of a person who begs that he "prays" or that a person praying "begs", because both are forms of asking, is composing in the way described; as also when Iphicrates called Callias a "begging priest" rather than a "torchbearer" and the latter replied that Iphicrates was not initiated into the Mysteries or he would not have called him a begging priest but a torchbearer; for both are religious epithets, but one is honorable, one dishonorable. Then there are the "parasites of Dionysus", but the persons in question call themselves "artistes". These are both metaphors, the former one that sullies, the profession, the latter the contrary. Pirates now call themselves "businessmen". Thus, one can say that a criminal "has made a mistake" or that someone making a mistake "has committed a crime" or that a thief both took and "plundered". A phrase like that of Euripides' Telephus, "lording the oar and landed in Mysia", is inappropriate [in prose], since lording is too elevated; there is no "theft" [if the metaphor is too flagrant].

There is a fault in the syllables if the indications of sound are unpleasant; for example, Dionysius the Brazen in his Elegies calls poetry "Calliope's screech" because both are sounds; but the metaphor is bad because it implies meaningless sounds.

Further, metaphor should be used in naming something that does not have a proper name of its own and [it should] not be far-fetched but taken from things that are related and of similar species, so that it is clear the term is related; for example, in the popular riddle [ainigma], "I saw a man gluing bronze on another with fire", the process has no name, but both are a kind of application; the application of the cupping instrument is thus called "gluing". From good riddling it is generally possible to derive appropriate metaphors; for metaphors are made like riddles; thus, clearly, [a metaphor from a good riddle] is an apt transference of words.

And the source of the metaphor should be something beautiful; verbal beauty, as Licymnius says, is in the sound or in the sense, and ugliness the same; and thirdly there is what refutes the sophistic argument: for it is not as Bryson said that nothing is in itself ugly, since it signifies the same thing if one word is used rather than another; for this is false; one word is more proper than another and more like the object signified and more adapted to making the thing appear "before the eyes". Moreover, one word does not signify in the same way as another, so in this sense also we should posit one as more beautiful or uglier than another; for both signify the beautiful or the ugly, but not solely as beauty or ugliness. Or if they do, [it is] only in degree.

(From *On Rhetoric*: *A Theory of Civic Discourse*)

二、意象

诗的理想是情趣与意象的欣合无间，所以必定是"主观的"与"客观的"，但这究竟是理想。在实际上"主观的"与"客观的"虽不是绝对的分别，却常有程度上的等差。情趣与意象之中有尼采所指出的隔阂与冲突。打破这种隔阂与冲突是艺术的主要使命，是把它们完全突破，使情趣与意象融化得恰到好处，这是达到最高理想的艺术。完全没有把它们突破，从情趣出发止于啼笑嗟叹，从意象出发止于零乱空洞的幻想，就不成其为艺术。这两极端之中有意象富于情趣的，也有情趣富于意象的，虽非完美的艺术，究仍不失其为艺术。

克罗齐否认"古典的"与"浪漫的"分别，在理论上自有特见，但是在实际上，古典艺术与浪漫艺术确各有偏重，也毋庸讳言。意象具有完整形式，为古典艺术的主要信条，拿这个标准来衡量浪漫艺术则大半作品都不免有缺陷，例如19世纪初期诗人柯尔律治和济慈诸人，有许多好诗都是未完成的断简零编。情感生动为浪漫派作品的特色，但是后来写实派作者却极力排除主观的情感而侧重冷静的忠实的叙述。"表现"与"再现"不仅是理论上的冲突，历史事实也很明显地证明作品方面原有这两种偏向。

姑就中国诗说，魏晋以前，文风以浑厚见长，情感深挚而见于文字的意象则如叶燮在《原诗》里所说的"土簋击壤穴居俪皮"，仍保持原始时代的简朴。有时诗人直吐心曲，几乎仅如嗟叹啼笑，有所感触即脱口而出，不但没有在意象上做功夫，而且好像没有经过反省与回味。我们试玩味下列诸诗：

彼黍离离，彼稷之苗。行迈靡靡，中心摇摇。知我者谓我心忧，不知我者谓我何求。悠悠苍天，此何人哉！

——《诗经·王风·黍离》

······

骄人好好，劳人草草。苍天苍天！视彼骄人，矜此劳人。

——《诗经·小雅·苍伯》

······

公无渡河，公竟渡河。堕河而死，当奈公何！

——《箜篌引》

这些诗固然如上文所说的"痛定思痛"，在创作时悲痛情绪自成意象，但与寻常取意象来象征情绪的诗自有分别。《诗经》中比兴两类就是有意要拿意象来象征情趣，但是通常很少完全做到象征的地步，因为比兴只是一种引子，而本来要说的话终须直率说出。例如"关关雎鸠，在河之洲"，只是引起"窈窕淑女，君子好逑"，而不能代替或完全表现这两句话的意思。而"昔我往矣，杨柳依依；今我来思，雨雪霏霏"，情趣恰隐寓于意象，可谓达到象征妙境，但在《诗经》中并不多见。汉魏作风较《诗经》已大变，但运用意象的技巧仍未脱比兴旧规。就大概说，比多于兴，例如：

薤上露，何易晞！露晞明朝更复落，人死一去何时归！

——《薤露歌》

皑如山上雪，皎如云间月。闻君有两意，故来相决绝······

——卓文君《白头吟》

翩翩堂前燕，冬藏夏来见。兄弟两三人，流宕在异县。

——《艳歌行》

朝云浮四海，日暮归故山。行役怀旧土，悲思不能言······

——应场《别诗》

以上都仅是"比"。"兴"例亦偶尔遇见，但大半仅取目前气象，即景生情，不如《诗经》中"兴"类诗之微妙多变化。例如：

大风起兮云飞扬，威加海内兮归故乡，安得猛士兮守四方！

——汉高帝《大风歌》

青青河畔草，郁郁园中柳。盈盈楼上女，皎皎当窗牖······

——《古诗十九首·青青河畔草》

明月照高楼，流光正徘徊。上有愁思妇，悲叹有余哀······

——曹植《七哀诗》

开秋兆凉气，蟋蟀鸣床帷。感物怀殷忧，悄悄令心悲······

——阮籍《咏怀》

这些诗的起句，微有"兴"的意味，但如果把它们看作"直陈其事"的"赋"亦无不可。在汉魏时，诗用似相关而又不尽相关的意象引起本文正意，似已成为一种传统的技巧。有时这种意象成为一种附赘悬瘤，非本文正意所绝对必需，例如：

> 鸡鸣高树巅，狗吠深宫中。荡子何所之，天下方太平……
>
> ——古乐府《鸡鸣》

> 月没参横，北斗阑干。亲交在门，饥不及餐……
>
> ——古乐府《善哉行》

> 孔雀东南飞，五里一徘徊。十三能织素，十四学裁衣……
>
> ——《孔雀东南飞》

> 蒲生我池中，其叶何离离！傍能行仁义，莫若妾自知……
>
> ——古乐府《塘上行》

起首两句引子，都与正文毫不相干，它们的起源，与其说是"套"现成的民歌的起头，如胡适所说，不如说是沿用《国风》以来的传统的技巧。《国风》的意象引子原有比兴之用，到后来数典忘祖，不问它是否有比兴之用，只戴上那么一个礼帽应付场面，合不合头也不管了。

汉魏诗中像这样漫用空洞意象的例子不甚多，但从另一方面看，这时期的诗应用意象的技巧却比《诗经》有进步。《诗经》只用意象做引子，汉魏诗则常在篇中或篇末插入意象来烘托情趣，姑举李陵《与苏武诗》为例：

> 良时不再至，离别在须臾。屏营衢路侧，执手野踟蹰。仰视浮云驰，奄忽互相逾。风波一失所，各在天一隅。长当从此别，且复立斯须。欲因晨风发，送子以贱躯。

中间"仰视浮云驰"四句，有兴兼比之用，意象与情趣偶然相遇，遇即欣合无间。此外如魏文帝《燕歌行》在描写怨女援琴写哀之后，忽接上"明月皎皎照我床，星汉西流夜未央，牵牛织女遥相望，尔独何辜限河梁"四句，也有情景吻合之妙。这种随时随景用意象比兴的写法打破了固定地在起头几句用比兴的机械文法，实在是一种进步。此外汉魏诗渐有全章以意象寓情趣、不言正意而正意自见的风格，班婕妤的《怨歌行》以秋风弃扇隐喻自己的怨情是著例。这种写法也是《国风》里所少有的。

中国古诗大半是情趣富于意象。诗艺的演进可以从多方面看，如果从情趣与意象的配合看，中国古诗的演进可以分为三个步骤：首先是情趣逐渐征服意象，中间是征服的完成，后来意象蔚起，几成一种独立自足的境界，自引起一种情趣。第一步是因情生景或因情生文；第二步是情景吻合，情文并茂；第三步是即景生情或因文生情。这种演进阶段自然也不可概以时代分，就大略说，汉魏以前是第一步，在自然界所取之意象仅如人物故事画以山水为背景，只是一种陪衬；汉魏时代是第二步，《古诗十九首》、苏李赠答及曹氏父子兄弟的作品中意象与情趣常达到浑化无迹之妙，到陶渊明手里，情景的吻合可算登峰造极；六朝是第三步，从大小谢恣情山水起，自然景物的描绘从陪衬地位抬到主要地位，如山水画在图画中自成一大宗派一样，后来便渐趋于艳丽一途。如论情趣，中国诗最艳丽的似无过于《国风》，乃"艳丽"二字不加诸《国风》而加诸齐梁人作品者，正以其特好雕词饰藻，为意象而意象。

转变的关键是赋。赋偏重铺陈景物，把诗人的注意渐从内心变化引到自然界变化方面去。从赋的兴起，中国才有大规模的描写诗；也从赋的兴起，中国诗才渐由情趣富于意象的《国风》转到六朝人意象富于情趣的艳丽之作。汉魏时代赋最盛，诗受赋的影响也逐渐在铺陈辞藻上做功夫，有时运用意象，并非因为表现情趣所必需而是因为它自身的美丽，《陌上桑》《羽林郎》和曹植《美女篇》都极力铺陈明眸皓齿艳装盛服，可以为证。六朝人只是推演这种风气。

一般批评家对于六朝人及唐朝温、李一派作品常存歧视。其实诗的好坏绝难拿一个绝对的标准去衡量。我们说，诗的最高理想在情景吻合，但这也只能就大体说。古诗有许多专从"情"出发而不十分注意于"景"的，魏晋以后诗有许多专从"景"出发，除流连于"景"本身外，别无其他情趣借"景"表现的。这两种诗都不能算达到情景欣合无间的标准，但也还可以成为上品诗。我们姑且举几首短诗为例：

公无渡河，公竟渡河，堕河而死，当奈公何！

——《箜篌引》

奈何许！天下人何限，慊慊只为汝！

——《华山畿》

昔我往矣，杨柳依依；今我来思，雨雪霏霏。

——《诗经·小雅·采薇》

结庐在人境，而无车马喧。问君何能尔，心远地自偏。采菊东篱下，悠然见南山。山气日夕佳，飞鸟相与还，此中有真意，欲辨已忘言。

——陶潜《饮酒》

江南可采莲，莲叶何田田！鱼戏莲叶间，鱼戏莲叶东，鱼戏莲叶西，鱼戏莲叶南，鱼戏莲叶北。

——《江南》

敕勒川，阴山下，天似穹庐，笼盖四野。天苍苍，野茫茫，风吹草低见牛羊。

——《敕勒歌》

这六首诗之中，只有三、四两首可算情景吻合，景恰足以传情。一、二两首纯从情感出发，情感直率流露于语言，自然中节，不必寄托于景。五六两首纯为景的描绘，作者并非有意以意象象征情趣，而意象优美自成一种情趣。六首都可以说是诗的胜境，虽然情景配合的方法与分量绝不同。不过它们各自成一种新鲜的完整的境界，作者心中有值得说的话（情趣或意象）而说得恰到好处，它们在价值上可以互相抗衡，正是因为这个缘故。

我们的着重点在原理不在历史的发展，所以只就六朝以前古诗略择数例说明情趣与意象配合的关系。其实各时代的诗都可用这个方法去分析。唐人的诗和五代及宋人的词尤其宜从情趣意象配合的观点去研究。

（选自朱光潜《诗论》）

Concreteness—the image of person, scene, action, or object—is, as we have earlier insisted, at the very heart of poetry. But we have also insisted that the image, in poetry, is never present merely as description, as report, as documentation; it has, at the very least, some aura of significance, and it may have, as we have already seen, rather complex meanings. A poet, it is sometime said, "thinks" by means of his images, or in his images. It might be said, too, that the feels by means of images, and in them. This density, this interpresentation, this fusion of thought, feeling, image, and, as we must add, rhythm and verbal texture, is of the essence o poetry and is the source of its power.

We now turn to explore some instances more complex and subtle than most of those that have engaged us thus far; or at least, we now bring more concentrated attention to bear on their qualities as imagery. What function, we must ask ourselves in each case, is being served by imagery? And in what particular fashion?

...

She Dwelt among the Untrodden Ways
William Wordsworth (1770—1850)

She dwelt among the untrodden ways
Besides the springs of Dove,
A Maid whom there were none praise
And very few to love:

A violet by a mossy stone
Half hidden from the eye!
Fair as a star, when only one
Is shining in the sky.

She lived unknown, and few could know
When Lucy ceased to be;
But she is in her grave, and oh,
The difference to me!

...

In the present poem, the basic structure is a discourse; the poet tells us various things about Lucy, but no image appears until the second stanza. To understand the importance of imagery here we may try the experiment of omitting the second stanza. What have we left? The "poem" remaining (Stanza 1 and 3) tells us that since Lucy live remote from the great world, her death passed unnoticed. Few people knew her, and any way there were simple, unlettered folk who lacked the means to set forth to the world the tributes due her. Yet, though Lucy's passing made no difference to the great world, it had made all the difference to her lover, who speaks the poem.

So much for a summary of the content of Stanza 1 and 3. But isn't this all the poem has to say anyway? What is lost if we leave out the images of the violet and the evening star? We may be tempted to answer: just some ornamentation—two comparisons that are meant to enhance Lucy's charm by associating her with such attractive objects as flowers and stars.

Yet, if this is all the imagery does, one might properly wonder why the poem would be just as valuable (or vapid) if Wordsworth had never written Stanza 2. Or if we feel that the poem would seem intolerably bare if it contained no comparisons at all, wouldn't another flower have done just as well? For example, the poet might have written:

A full-blown rose of glorious hue,
Bright'ning a garden wall.

Clearly, the rose will not do—and the fact that it will not proves that the imagery in Stanza 2 does more than supply a vague enhancement to the girl. Lucy's natural charm, like that of the violet, was derived from her modesty. She, too, was "half-hidden from the eye", obscure and unnoticed. Yet, if this is really the point the poet has attempted to make with his violet-comparison, then doesn't another problem arise? Doesn't the poet confuse matters by offering the star-comparison that immediately follows? Doesn't his emphasis on the prominence of the star—it must almost certainly be Venus as evening star, normally the first star to shine forth after sunset—involve a contradiction? How can Lucy be at once too easily overlooked and yet impossible to miss?

There is, of course, no contradiction. The second stanza enacts through its imagery the very "statement" made in the third stanza—and it is a somewhat paradoxical statement: though Lucy was, to the world, as completely obscure as the modest flower in the shadow of the mossy stone, to the eye of her lover she was the only star in his heaven, shining like the planet of love itself.

We are perhaps now ready to answer the question asked earlier: what is the importance of the imagery in this poem? In an important sense the imagery is the poem. It is not simply a fancy way of illustration what the poet might have said in abstract terms; that is, the imagery is not something "additional"—merely decorative. If poetry does bring together idea and emotion, rendering an experience dramatically in concrete terms, then Stanza 2 is the core—the very heart—of the poem.

(From *Understanding Poetry*，有删减)

三、格律

节奏是宇宙中自然现象的一个基本原则。自然现象不能彼此全同，亦不能全异。全同全异不能有节奏，节奏生于同异相承续，相错综，相呼应。寒暑昼夜的来往，新陈的代谢，雌雄的匹偶，风波的起伏，山川的交错，数量的乘除消长，以至于玄理方面反正的对称，历史方面兴亡隆替的循环，都有一个节奏的道理在里面。艺术返照自然，节奏是一切艺术的灵魂。在造型艺术则为浓淡、疏密、阴阳、向背相配称，在诗、乐、舞诸时间艺术则为高低、长短、疾徐相呼应。

在生灵方面，节奏是一种自然需要。人体各器官的机能如呼吸、循环等等都是一起一伏地川流不息，自成节奏。这种生理的节奏又引起心理的节奏，就是精力的盈亏与注意力的张弛，吸气时营养骤增，脉搏跳动时筋肉紧张，精力与注意力亦随之提起；呼气时营养暂息，脉搏停伏时筋肉弛懈，精力与注意力亦随之下降。我们知觉外物时需要精力与注意力的饱满凝聚，所以常不知不觉地希求自然界的节奏和内心的节奏相应和。有时自然界本无节奏的现象也可以借内心的节奏而生节奏。比如钟表机轮所作的声响本是单调一律，没有高低起伏，我们听起来，却感觉它轻重长短相间。这是很自然的。呼吸、循环有起伏，精力有张弛，注意力有紧松，同一声音在注意力紧张时便显得重，在注意力松懈时便显得轻，所以单调一律的声音继续响下去，可以使听者听到有规律的节奏。

这个简单的事实可以揭示节奏的一个重要分别，节奏有"主观的"与"客观的"两种。我们所听到的钟表的节奏完全是主观的，没有客观的基础。有时自然现象本有它的客观的节奏，我们所听到的节奏不必与它完全相符合。比如一组相邻两音高低为1与3之比，另一组相邻两音高低为1与5之比，同-1音在前组听起来较高，在后组听起来较低，因为受邻音高低反衬的影响不同，这正犹如同一炮声在与枪声同听时和与雷声同听时所生的印象有高低之别一样。

主观节奏的存在证明外物的节奏可以因内在的节奏改变，但是内在的节奏因外物的节奏而改变也是常事。诗与音乐的感动性就是从这种改变的可能起来的。有机体本来最善于适应环境，而模仿又是动物的一种很原始的本能。看见旁人发笑，自己也随之发笑，看见旁人踢球，自己的腿脚也随之跃跃欲动；看见山时我们不知不觉地挺胸昂首；看见杨柳轻盈摇荡时，我们也不知不觉轻松舒畅起来。这都是极普遍的经验。外物的节奏也同样逼着我们的筋肉去适应它，模仿它。单就声音的节奏来说，它是长短、高低、轻重、疾徐相继承的关系。这些关系时时变化，听者所费的心力和所用的身心活动也随之变化。因此，听者心中自发生一种节奏和声音的节奏相平行。听一首高而急促的调子，心力与筋肉亦随之做一种高而急促的活动；听一曲低而柔缓的调子，心力与筋肉也随之做一种低而柔缓的活动。诗与音乐的节奏常有一种"模型"（pattern），在变化中有整齐，流动生展却常回旋到出发点，所以我们说它有规律。这"模型"印到心里就成了一种心理的模型，我们不知不觉地准备着照这个模型去适应，去花费心力，去调节注意力的张弛与肌肉的伸缩。这种准备在心理上的术语是"预期"（expectation）。有规律的节奏都必能在生理、心理中印为模型，都必能产生预期。预期的中不中就是节奏的快感与不快感的来源。比如读一首平仄相间的诗，读到平声时我们不知不觉地预期仄声的复返，读到仄声时不知不觉地预期平声的复返。预期不断地产生，不断地证实，所以发生恰如所料的快慰。不过全是恰如所料，又不免呆板单调，整齐中也要有变化，有变化时预期不中所引起的惊讶也不可少。它不但破除单调，还可以提醒注意力，犹如柯勒律治所比譬的上楼梯，步步上升时猛然发现一步梯特别高或特别低，注意力就猛然提醒。

从上面的分析看，外物的客观节奏和身心的内在节奏交相影响，结果在心中所生的印象才是主观的节奏。诗与乐的节奏就是这种主观的节奏，它是心物交感的结果，不是一种物理的事实。

（朱光潜《诗论》节选）

英语最小的发音单位为音素，音素构成音节（syllable），音节又构成音步（foot）。音步（也被称为韵步）是一个或两个重读音节和一个或两个非重读音节的排列组合，即一般至少由一个轻音、一个重音构成。英语中常见的几种音步有以下四种：

抑扬格（the iamb）：一个轻读音节后面紧跟着一个重读音节，标记为"_ /"，如"between""a pear""of life"等。

扬抑格（trochee）：一个重读音节后面紧跟着一个轻读音节，标记为"/ _"，如"treasure""tyrant"。

抑抑扬格（the anapest）：两个轻读音节后面紧跟着一个重读音节，标记为"_ _ /"如"overhead""as I breath"。

扬抑抑格（the dactyl）：一个重读音节后面紧跟着两个轻读音节，标记为"/ _ _"，如"tenderly""scornfully""take her up"。

此外，还有一些不太常见的音步，如抑抑格（the pyrrhic），一个轻读音节后面紧跟一个轻读音节，标记为"_ _"；还有扬扬格（the spondee），即一个重读音节后面紧跟着一个重读音节，标记为"/ /"等。

上述各种主要音步在诗歌中的应用，可参见下述例子：

1. 抑扬格

_ / _ / _ / _ / _ /
So long | as men | can breathe | or eyes | can see,

　　_　／　_　／　_　／　_　／　_　／

So long | lives this | and this | gives life | to thee.

(William Shakespeare, "Shall I Compare Thee to a Summer's Day")

以上三个诗行，每行都有5个抑扬格音步，这样的诗行也就叫"五步抑扬格"（five feet pentameter）或"抑扬格五音步"（iambic pentameter）。

2. 扬抑格

　　／　_　　／　_　　／　_　　／

Twinkle, | twinkle, | little | star

　　／　_　／　_　／　_　_　／

How I | wonder | what you | are.

　　／　_　／　_　　／　_　／

Up a | bove the | world so | high,

　　／　_　　／　_　_　／

Like a | diamond | in the | sky.

(Jane Taylor, "Star")

以上这首诗除了最后一个音步，其他全部都是扬抑格，前三个诗行都是由四个音步构成，因此就称作"四音步扬抑格"（four feet trochee）或"扬抑格四音步"（trochaic tetrameter）。

3. 抑抑扬格

　_　_　／　_　_　／　_　_　／　_　_　／

In the morn | ing of life | , when its cares | are unknown,

　_　_　／　_　_　／　_　_　／　_　_　／

And its pleas | ures in all | their bright lus | tre begin.

(Thomas Moore, "In the Morning of Life")

以上两个诗行都是由抑抑扬格构成的，每个诗行都有四个音步，因而也被称作"抑抑扬格四音步"（anapaestic tetrameter）或"四音步抑抑扬格"（four feet anapaest）。

4. 扬抑抑格

　　／　_　_　／　_　_

Touch her not | scornfully;

　　／　_　_　／　_　_

Think of her | mournfully.

(Thomas Hood, "The Bridge of Sighs")

以上两个诗行都是由扬抑抑格构成的，且每个诗行都是两个音步，因而称作"扬抑抑格两音步"（dactylic dimeter）或"两音步扬抑抑格"（two feet dactyl）。

上述各种音步种类中，最为常见的是五步抑扬格，这种诗也叫作英雄体诗行（the

heroic meter)。在莎士比亚的十四行诗中，大多使用这种音步。为加强节奏和音响效果，虽然诗歌从头到尾可能会有一种基本的音步，但千篇一律不免呆板，为了加强某些特定的修辞意义，音步可能发生变化。这种变化分为两种，一种是音步数目的变化，另一种则是音步本身发生变化，如从抑扬格变成扬抑格或抑抑扬格等，即"变格"（variation）。[①] 这种变格常常可以起到一些特定的效果。下文将主要从变格的角度，说明诗歌形式与内容之间的关系。

例子一

Romeo	If I profane with my unworthiest hand
	This holy shrine, the gentle fine is this:
	My lips, two blushing pilgrims, ready stand
	To smooth that rough touch with a tender kiss.
Juliet	Good pilgrim, you do wrong your hand too much,
	Which mannerly devotion shows in this;
	For saints have hands that pilgrims' hands do touch,
	And palm to palm is holy palmers' kiss.
Romeo	Have not saints lips, and holy palmers too?
Juliet	Ay, pilgrim, lips that they must use in prayer.
Romeo	O, then, dear saint, let lips do what hands do;
	They pray, grant thou, lest faith turn to despair.
Juliet	Saints do not move, though grant for prayers' sake.
Romeo	Then move not, while my prayer's effect I take.
	Thus from my lips, by yours, my sin is purged.
Juliet	Then have my lips the sin that they have took.
Romeo	Sin from thy lips? O trespass sweetly urged!
	Give me my sin again.
Juliet	You kiss by the book.

(William Shakespeare, *Romeo and Juliet*, Act 1, Scene 5)

以上是罗密欧与朱丽叶见面时的对话，正好构成一首十四行诗，主要由五步抑扬格构成，但上面黑体标出的这一句话的音步却发生了变化：

$$/ \quad \_ \quad \_ \quad / \quad \_ \quad / \quad \_ \quad \_ \quad /$$

Thus from | my lips, | by yours, | my sin | is purged.

规律的抑扬格在这里变成了扬抑格，读起来需要在"thus"上稍作停留，然后又轻

---

① 总体看来，英语诗歌在音步方面的变化，常常被中国学生忽略。这一方面和时代的背景有关，英语诗歌在20世纪早期大量进入中国文人的视野，当时中国正在进行新文化运动，对传统的格律持否定态度，而英美现代主义思潮的影响下，英语现当代诗歌也多以自由诗或素体诗为主，不太讲求严格的韵律。此外，受到中国不可"因文害义"的传统思想的影响，读英语诗歌的时候主要关注的是它的文字意义，对形式则不那么在意。诗歌是最讲究音乐性的文类，其节奏、押韵往往与意义密切关联。在翻译中，如果忽视了这一点，就会影响我们对作品的理解，也势必影响翻译标准的"信"的原则。

读 "from" 和 "my" 两个词，重心便落到 "lips" 一词上，从声音上强调这是罗密欧第一次亲吻朱丽叶。

例子二

Doubtful it stood,

As two spent swimmers that do cling together

And choke their art.

The merciless Macdonwald

Worthy to be a rebel，for to that

The multiplying villainies of nature

Do swarm upon him from the Western Isles

Of kerns and gallow glasses is supplied；

And Fortune，on his damned quarrel smiling，

Showed like a rebel's whore．But all's too weak；

For brave Macbeth（well he deserves that name），

Disdaining Fortune，with his brandished steel，

Which smoked with bloody execution，

Like valor's minion，carved out his passage

Till he faced the slave；

Which ne'er shook hands，nor bade farewell to him，

Till he unseamed him from the nave to th' chops，

And fixed his head upon our battlements.

(William Shakespeare, *Macbeth*，Act 1，Scene 2)

上面黑体标出的这一句话的音步如下：

　_　　/　　_　　/　　/　_　　_　　/　　_　　/

For brave | Macbeth | well he | deserves | that name.

此处的扬抑格在诗行中间出现，在读完 "well" 这个副词之后，重点就到了 "deserves" 这个动作上。这个词本来就有两个意思——"值得" 或 "活该"。格律的变化使这个程度副词被强化了，就像汉语里 "你真好" 这个短语，不同的口气朗读，会产生截然相反的效果。如果是用一般的口吻读，是真的表扬，但如果轻读 "你" 之后，重读 "真" 或 "好" 字，表扬很可能就变成了讽刺。在英语诗歌中，由于抑扬格和扬抑格的交替使用，便产生了类似汉语语气一样的功能。被强调的 "deserve" 一词，产生一种反讽的效果：表面上看，说话者是在称赞麦克白勇敢，但实际上叙述者很可能在影射他名不副实。

例子三

Iago　　　　My lord，you know I love you.

Othello　　　I think thou dost；

　　　　　　And for I know thou'rt full of love and honesty

　　　　　　And weigh'st thy words before thou giv'st them breath，

Therefore these stops of thine fright me the more.

For such things in a false, disloyal knave

Are tricks of custom; but in a man that's just,

They're close dilations working from the heart

That passion cannot rule.

Iago: For Michael Cassio,

I dare be sworn I think that he is honest.

Othello: I think so too.

Iago: Men should be what they seem;

Or those that be not, would they might seem none!

Othello: Certain, men should be what they seem.

Iago: **Why then, I think Cassio's an honest man.**

(William Shakespeare, *Othello*)

最后这句话主体为抑扬格，但中间出现了一个变格。两个连续的弱读音节后，重音落到了"honest"（诚实的）一词的前半部分，如下：

_ / _ / / _ _ / _ /

Why then I think Cassio's an honest man

这大概是说话者特意提醒奥赛罗注意，貌似诚实的卡西欧其实并不诚实。莎士比亚利用格律上的一个小变化，让这句话有了反讽的意味。

第二节 赏·译·评

一、《诗经》节选

《周南·关雎》

关关雎鸠，在河之洲。窈窕淑女，君子好逑。

参差荇菜，左右流之。窈窕淑女，寤寐求之。

求之不得，寤寐思服。悠哉悠哉，辗转反侧。

参差荇菜，左右采之。窈窕淑女，琴瑟友之。

参差荇菜，左右芼之。窈窕淑女，钟鼓乐之。

《小雅·采薇》

采薇采薇，薇亦作止。曰归曰归，岁亦莫止。

靡室靡家，猃狁之故。不遑启居，猃狁之故。

采薇采薇，薇亦柔止。曰归曰归，心亦忧止。

忧心烈烈，载饥载渴。我戍未定，靡使归聘。

采薇采薇，薇亦刚止。曰归曰归，岁亦阳止。
王事靡盬，不遑启处。忧心孔疚，我行不来！

彼尔维何？维常之华。彼路斯何？君子之车。
戎车既驾，四牡业业。岂敢定居？一月三捷。

驾彼四牡，四牡骙骙。君子所依，小人所腓。
四牡翼翼，象弭鱼服。岂不日戒？猃狁孔棘！

昔我往矣，杨柳依依。今我来思，雨雪霏霏。
行道迟迟，载渴载饥。我心伤悲，莫知我哀！

赏

《诗经》是我国一部诗歌总集，对后世的诗歌有深远的影响。我们经常提到的"诗有六义"，即"风、雅、颂"和"赋、比、兴"。其中，"风、雅、颂"指的是诗歌体裁。"风"主要是民间地方性的有关风土、风俗之记载，按地区分为《周南》《召南》《邶风》《鄘风》《卫风》《王风》《郑风》《齐风》《魏风》《唐风》《秦风》《陈风》《桧风》《曹风》《豳风》，共160篇，合称"十五国风"。"雅"分《大雅》和《小雅》，主要是朝廷之诗，是表现君主和诸侯关系的，有些是宴会上的乐歌；"颂"则是庙宇之诗歌，分为《周颂》《鲁颂》和《商颂》。

"赋、比、兴"则是创作手法，"赋"有铺陈之意，直陈其事，"比"类似今天的比喻，"兴"则是由一物触发联想并摹写另一物的表达手法，二者未必有直接的关联。简单而言，"赋"是叙物以言情，以情尽物；"比"是索物以托情，以情附物；"兴"触物起情，因物动情。无论是赋、比，还是兴，均关乎"情"和"物"两个方面，描述的是物，阐发的却是情感，即融情于景。

在写情方面，《诗经》可谓写尽各种爱情婉转微妙，有表达思慕之情的：[①]

关关雎鸠，在河之洲。窈窕淑女，君子好逑。

有表达爱而不得的：

---

① 《诗经》中的《国风》涵盖了爱情的种种婉转曲折，后世也有各种总结，基本不出其右。1919年在哈佛大学的陈寅恪曾对友人吴宓阐述自己的"五等爱情论"：第一，情之最上者，世无其人，悬空设想，而甘为之死，如《牡丹亭》之杜丽娘是也；第二，与其人交识有素，而未尝共衾枕席次之，如宝、黛是也；第三，曾一度枕席而永久纪念不忘，如司棋与潘又安；第四，又次之，则为夫妇终身而无外遇者；第五，最下者，随处接合，惟欲是图，而无所谓情矣。陈寅恪先生提到的"五等爱情"，在《诗经》中基本都能找到范本。

> 蒹葭苍苍，白露为霜。所谓伊人，在水一方。
> 溯洄从之，道阻且长。溯游从之，宛在水中央。

还有表现热情奔放、大胆求爱的篇章：

> 摽有梅，其实七兮。求我庶士，迨其吉兮！
> 摽有梅，其实三兮。求我庶士，迨其今兮！
> 摽有梅，顷筐塈之。求我庶士，迨其谓之！

表现父母之命不可违的无奈：

> 将仲子兮，无逾我里，无折我树杞。岂敢爱之？
> 畏我父母。仲可怀也，父母之言亦可畏也。

也有表现夫妻思念之情的：

> 采采卷耳，不盈顷筐。嗟我怀人，寘彼周行。
> 陟彼崔嵬，我马虺隤。我姑酌彼金罍，维以不永怀。

还有两情相悦或祝贺新嫁娘的：

> 投我以木瓜，报之以琼琚。匪报也，永以为好也。
> 桃之夭夭，灼灼其华。之子于归，宜其室家。

另一些表现夫妻生活乐趣的对话：

> "鸡既鸣矣，朝既盈矣。"
> "匪鸡则鸣，苍蝇之声。"
> "东方明矣，朝既昌矣。"
> "匪东方则明，月出之光。"

对于爱情的讨论，在古代中国常被嫁接到"后妃之德""求贤"等问题上。从本质上看，不过是因为对理想的追求和对恋人的渴慕在情感上有相通之处。然而，在儒学占主导地位的时代，这种理想多表现为入仕求学、齐家治国和闻达于天下的政治抱负。例如，在屈原的《楚辞》里，关于香草美人的譬喻，多暗含诗人的政治理想和抱负。后世也有不少诗继承了这一传统：表面上看似写情，实际上则是写对仕途的志忑和抉择。朱庆馀的"洞房昨夜停红烛，待晓堂前拜舅姑。妆罢低声问夫婿，画眉深浅入时无"，看似写情，实际上却是自比新妇，试探主考官对自己的作品是否满意。这从诗的标题

《近试上张籍水部》上，也可管窥。而张籍的《节妇吟·寄东平李司空师道》一诗中，作者也是以"节妇"自喻，婉拒当时炙手可热的藩镇人物李师道的拉拢：

> 君知妾有夫，赠妾双明珠。
> 感君缠绵意，系在红罗襦。
> 妾家高楼连苑起，良人执戟明光里。
> 知君用心如日月，事夫誓拟同生死。
> 还君明珠双泪垂，恨不相逢未嫁时。

此外，还有一些读书人将对恋人的追求比作读书理想的实现过程，如王国维提到的读书三境界：

> "昨夜西风凋碧树，独上高楼，望尽天涯路。"此第一境也。"衣带渐宽终不悔，为伊消得人憔悴。"此第二境也。"众里寻他千百度，蓦然回首，那人却在灯火阑珊处。"此第三境也。

这三个境界都引用了古诗词中写情的名句，来表达读书过程中追求真理的三个不同阶段。

其实，这种将爱情与个人理想相结合的思路，并非中国文学传统里所特有的。在西方的基督教传统里，由于个人的生命意义被安置在彼岸世界里，儒家那种注重现世生活的"齐家、治国、平天下"的此岸理想，对于基督徒而言并没有太大的吸引力。在虔诚的基督徒看来，此岸世界不过是一个赎罪的过程、一种通往彼岸世界的方式和手段罢了。得到上帝的宽恕和眷顾，才是其生命的终极意义。[①]

在不同的文化里，由于整体蓝图（blueprint）的不同，理想的具体形态也有所变化，但人类的情感却是共通的，尤其是爱情与理想，二者都会让当事人在某一阶段为之奋斗不息，同时又常产生一种"所谓伊人，在水一方"，若即若离、患得患失的感觉。即便在同一文化渊源里，理想的具体形态也会因时代的不同而发生变化。例如，在西方前现代时期，宗教伦理占很重要的地位，但到了现代社会，随着宗教的式微和工业资本家的崛起，前者以特殊的形式渗透到后者的血液之中。在马克斯·韦伯（Max Weber）看来，西方现代社会一个最大的转变，就是成功地将宗教伦理转变成了资本主义工作伦理，把要努力侍奉上帝、为上帝做工的精神，转化为在现世中勤勉工作的现代价值理念。

总体而言，不同时代的理想的具体形态，本质上都和爱情的发生有着微妙的相通之处。因此，当20世纪心理学鼻祖弗洛伊德将"性"看作是个人行为的主要驱动力的时候，或许我们不太赞同他把人性的本质降格为动物生物性的做法，但却不得不承认他的解释，无论放到古今中外都具有一定的合理性。

---

① 在《圣经》的《雅歌》篇里，新郎与新娘互相称颂的爱情之歌，就常常被转译为天堂与教会的关系和上帝与世人的关系，也就不足为奇了。

译

《周南·关雎》 译文一

Kwan kwan go the ospreys.

On the islet in the river,

The modest, retiring, virtuous, young lady:—

For our prince a good mate she.

Here long, there short, is the duckweed,

To the left, to the right, borne about by the current.

The modest, retiring, virtuous, young lady:—

Waking and sleeping, he sought her.

He sought her and found her not,

And waking and sleeping he thought about her.

Long he thought; oh! Long and anxiously;

On his side, on his back, he turned, and back again.

Here long, there short, is the duckweed;

On the left, on the right, we gather it,

The modest, retiring, virtuous, young lady:—

With lutes, small and large, let us give her friendly welcome.

Here long, there short, is the duckweed;

On the left, on the right, we cook and present it.

The modest, retiring, virtuous, young lady:—

With bells and drums let us show our delight in her

(James Legge 译)

《周南·关雎》 译文二

Merrily the osprey cry,

On the islet in the stream.

Gentle and graceful is the girl,

A fit wife for the gentleman.

Short and long the floating water plants,

Left and right you may pluck them.

Gentle and graceful is the girl,

Awake he longs for her and in his dreams.

Filled with sorrowful thoughts,

He tosses about unable to sleep.

Short and long the floating water plants,

Left and right you may gather them.

19

Gentle and graceful is the girl,

He'd live to wed her，the qin and se playing.

Short and long the floating water plants,

Left and right you may collect them.

Gentle and graceful is the girl,

He'd like to marry her，bells and drums beating

（杨宪益、戴乃迭译）

《小雅·采薇》选 译文一

At first，when we set out,

The willows were fresh and green；

Now，when we shall be returning,

The snow will be falling clouds.

Long and tedious will be our marching；

We shall hunger；we shall thirst.

Our hearts are wounded with grief,

And no one knows our sadness.

（James Legge 译）

《小雅·采薇》选 译文二

When we set out,

The willows were drooping with spring,

We come back in the snow,

We go slowly，we are hungry and thirsty,

Our mind is full of sorrow，who will know of our grief?

（Ezra Pound 译）

《小雅·采薇》选 译文三

When I left here,

Willows shed tear.

I come back now,

Snow bends the bough.

Long，long the way；

Hard，hard the day.

Hunger and thirst,

Press me the worst.

My grief overflows,

Who knows? Who knows?

（许渊冲 译）

评

上面三个版本的译文，詹姆斯·理雅各（James Legge）用的是散文体，忠实于原文每个词的意思。许渊冲的翻译，每一行都控制在四个词以内。确切地说，除了"Willows shed tear"和"Hunger and thirst"两句为三个词，其他的均为四个词，且每个诗行均为四个音步。可以看出，译者试图在节奏上与中文版《诗经》的四字格相照应，且也是三个版本唯一有押韵的版本。从形式上看，许的翻译实现了他提倡的"音美、形美"原则，无疑也是三个版本中最忠实于原文的。

庞德的译文是最简洁的，可看作一种意译。虽无逐字逐句翻译，但整个意境都译到了。庞德本人的诗人身份让他在翻译中文诗歌的时候，也具有一般人难以企及的高度。"杨柳依依"一句，历来有着不同的解释。有的解释为"杨柳在风中摇摆，似乎在向离人道别，一副依依不舍的神态"。这是诗人在"托物言志"，自己也舍不得离去，一切景物也染上他的情绪了。许渊冲的翻译即采取这种理解。也有的解释说，春天柳树发芽了，青翠欲滴，是一种快乐心情的写照，与下文的"雨雪霏霏"形成对此。理雅各即采用这种解释，因而翻译为"The willows were fresh and green"。相比之下，庞德的翻译为"The willows were drooping with spring"（"春天挂在柳枝上"），只是平平道来，是"乐"是"苦"都没有点破，保存了原诗的含蓄意味，留下了多重解释的可能。在中国古典诗词中，"青草""垂柳"是常见的意象，涵义十分丰富。"忽见陌头杨柳色，悔教夫婿觅封侯"，是惊喜之后恨意生；"记得绿罗裙，处处怜芳草"，是叮嘱，也是不舍；"枝上柳绵吹又少，天涯何处无芳草"，则是情感受挫后的自我宽慰……《采薇》原诗古典含蓄，在情感上节制有度。在这个意义上，庞德的翻译，无疑是最贴近原文风格的。

熟悉庞德诗歌的人，不难想到他在诗中运用过类似的表达：

A Virginal

No, no! Go from me. I have left her lately.

I will not spoil my sheath with lesser brightness,

For my surrounding air hath a new lightness;

Slight are her arms, yet they have bound me straitly

And left me cloaked as with a gauze of ḗther;

As with sweet leaves；as with subtle clearness.

Oh, I have picked up magic in her nearness

To sheathe me half in half the things that sheathe her.

No, no! Go from me. I have still the flavour,

Soft as spring wind that's come from birchen bowers.

Green come the shoots, aye April in the branches,

As winter's wound with her sleight hand she staunches,

Hath of the trees a likeness of the savour:
As white their bark, so white this lady's hours.

(不，不！离开我。她刚走。

我不希望自己的外套被暗淡的光玷污，

周围有了新的光泽，

她娇小的臂膀将我围住，

好像薄纱把我包裹，

像甜美的树叶，又像微妙的清新

哦，在她身边我有了魔力，

包裹她的那一半也将我包罗。

不，不！离开我。我还带着芬芳，

像春天的柔风拂过白桦树梢，

树叶鲜嫩，四月上了枝头，

冬天袭来，她坚定不移

带着树的芬芳

树干洁白，纯洁无瑕的她。)

上面这首诗中，有一句为"April in the branches"，直译为"枝头的四月"，其实是说"春天来了，草木怒发，枝头一片欣欣向荣，充满活力"。此处与上文提到的庞德将《诗经》中的"杨柳依依"一句翻译为"The willows were drooping with spring"有着异曲同工之妙，都是用一个时间（季节或月份）与具体的自然物放在一起，生动地创造出一种春天到来、万物复苏的景象。

不可否认，庞德在翻译中文诗歌的时候，不仅仅只是翻译，而是一种再创作。比如下面这一首班婕妤的诗《怨歌行》：

新裂齐纨素，鲜洁如霜雪。

裁为合欢扇，团团似明月。

出入君怀袖，动摇微风发。

常恐秋节至，凉飚夺炎热。

弃捐箧笥中，恩情中道绝。

翟理斯的版本如下：

O fair white silk, fresh from the weaver's loom,
Clear as the frost, bright as the winter snow-
See! Friendship fashions out of thee a fan,
Round as the round moon shines in heaven's above,

At home, abroad, a close companion thou,
Stirring at every move the grateful gale
And yet I fear, ah me! that autumn chills,
Cooling the dying summer's torried rage,
Will see thee laid neglectd on the shelf, All thoughts of bygone days, like them bygone.

而庞德的"翻译",则只剩下了三行：

O fan of white silk,
Clear as frost on the grass-blade
You also are laid aside
(扇，致陛下
哦，白绸的扇，
洁白如草叶上的霜
你也被搁在一边。)

译文中，除了最核心的几个意象，如"白扇子""草叶"，诗歌的其他内容则全部被省略了。对意象的情有独钟，让庞德在"翻译"中文诗的时候，不再亦步亦趋，而是大胆创新，让一切为他所用，为意象派诗歌增色。

二、《楚辞》节选

浴兰汤兮沐芳，华采衣兮若英。
灵连蜷兮既留，烂昭昭兮未央。
蹇将憺兮寿宫，与日月兮齐光。
龙驾兮帝服，聊翱游兮周章。
灵皇皇兮既降，猋远举兮云中。
览冀州兮有余，横四海兮焉穷。
思夫君兮太息，极劳心兮忡忡。

赏

《楚辞》里呈现的世界，与《诗经》不太相同，二者属于不同的文化与美学体系。后者是朴素的、古典的和含蓄的，而前者则是相对外放的、浪漫的和激越的。它们构成了我们生命中两种不同的力量，需要借助我们自己的生命力慢慢去平衡。刘勰曾在《文心雕龙·辨骚》一文中，给予《离骚》很高的评价：

《国风》好色而不淫，《小雅》怨诽而不乱，若《离骚》者，可谓兼之；蝉蜕秽浊之中，浮游尘埃之外，皭然涅而不缁，虽与日月争光可也。

《楚辞》还以其瑰丽奇美的特点闻名于世，刘勰也对各篇特点做了概述：

> 故《骚经》、《九章》，朗丽以哀志；《九歌》、《九辩》，绮靡以伤情；《远游》、《天问》，瑰诡而惠巧；《招魂》、《招隐》，耀艳而深华；《卜居》标放言之致，《渔父》寄独往之才。故能气往轹古，辞来切今，惊采绝艳，难与并能矣。

在语言特点上，《楚辞》以三言为基础，"兮""些"等语气助词与二言、四言配合使用。《楚辞》中句法的扩展和语气词的使用，形成了一种飞扬飘逸之美，加上南方民族神话的气氛、丰富的想象，在战国时代常被看作是"风雅寝声"之后"奇文郁起"的一种新诗体。

在主题上，《楚辞》抒发了诗人郁郁不得志、报国无门的无奈。例如，在《离骚》中，诗人以种植芳草为比喻，说明自己精心培养的贤能之士，希冀他们有朝一日能报效朝廷，不料他们却志气不坚，为了满足一己私欲，"众皆竞进以贪婪兮，凭不厌乎求索"，阿谀奉承，贪婪成性，正如诗中所写：

> 余既滋兰之九畹兮，又树蕙之百亩。
> 畦留夷与揭车兮，杂杜衡与芳芷。
> 冀枝叶之峻茂兮，愿俟时乎吾将刈。
> 虽萎绝其亦何伤兮，哀众芳之芜秽。
> 众皆竞进以贪婪兮，凭不厌乎求索。
> 羌内恕己以量人兮，各兴心而嫉妒。
> 忽驰骛以追逐兮，非余心之所急。
> 老冉冉其将至兮，恐修名之不立。
> 朝饮木兰之坠露兮，夕餐秋菊之落英。
> 苟余情其信姱以练要兮，长顑颔亦何伤。

即便最后形容枯槁，众叛亲离，诗人依然不愿改变初衷。在《渔父》篇中，面对渔父的不解和困惑，诗人再次表明自己的志向：无论面对怎样的污浊和不幸，绝不"以皓皓之白，而蒙世俗之尘埃"：

> 渔父曰："圣人不凝滞于物，而能与世推移。世人皆浊，何不淈其泥而扬其波？众人皆醉，何不餔其糟而歠其醨？何故深思高举，自令放为？"
> 屈原曰："吾闻之，新沐者必弹冠，新浴者必振衣；安能以身之察察，受物之汶汶者乎？宁赴湘流，葬于江鱼之腹中。安能以皓皓之白，而蒙世俗之尘埃乎？"
> 渔父莞尔而笑，鼓枻而去，乃歌曰："沧浪之水清兮，可以濯吾缨；沧浪之水浊兮，可以濯吾足。"遂去，不复与言。

在古代中国，不得志的文人，大体可以分为两大类。其中一类可谓"君子固穷"，屈原可视作这类代表之一。他们对政治理想坚贞不渝，宁可忍受痛苦也不肯放弃，明知无济于事也要坚持，态度令人肃然起敬。这从他们的诗句中可以管窥，如：

安得广厦千万间，大庇天下寒士俱欢颜。

——杜甫《茅屋为秋风所破歌》

春蚕到死丝方尽，蜡炬成灰泪始干。

——李商隐《无题》

妾拟将身嫁与一身休，纵被无情弃，不能羞。

——韦庄《思帝乡》

寄意寒星荃不察，我以我血荐轩辕。

——鲁迅《自题小像》

另一类则继承了庄子旷达洒脱的传统，看任何问题都保持着一种历史的眼光和通达的态度，无论遇到什么样的苦难，总能从精神上解脱出来。最典型的代表就是宋代的苏轼，无论是"莫听穿林打叶声，何妨吟啸且徐行""云散云明谁点缀，天容海色本澄清"，还是"问汝平生功业，黄州惠州儋州"，总能感受到他内心的释然。这些人虽在政治上无丰功伟绩，但在钱穆先生看来，中国的历史恰恰是因为他们，才得以绵延不绝：虽然论其事业不够载入历史，但在其无表现之背后，则卓然有一个大写的人的存在，这便是一大表现了。[1]

译

译文一

We have bathed in orchid water and washed our hair with perfumes,
And dressed ourselves like flowers in embroidered clothing
The god has halted, swaying, above us,
Shining with a persistent radiance.
He is going to rest in the House of Life.
His brightness is like that of the sun and moon.
In his dragon chariot, dressed in imperial splendour.
Now he flies off to wander round the sky.
The god had just descended in bright majesty,
When off in a whirl he soared again, far into the clouds.
He looks down on Ji-zhou and the lands beyond it;
There is no place in the world that he does not pass over.
Thinking of that lord makes me sigh.

---

[1]　钱穆：《中国历史研究法》，北京：九州出版社，2017年，第99页。

And afflicts my heart with a grievous longing.

(Frow David Hawkes, *The Songs of the South*: *An Ancient Chinese Anthology of Poems by Qu Yuan and Other Poets*)

译文二

Hot baths of thoroughwort, hair washed in fragrant herbs,

In robes of many colors, hung with galangal.

A shamanka dances writhing—she has made him stay,

His aura spreads in rays clear and unending,

Yes, he will take his ease in the Temple of Longevity,

Mate of sun and moon, his light as bright.

Driving a dragon chariot, dressed in the colors of the Sky Lords,

He soars now, wandering everywhere.

For as soon as the spirit descends in his splendor

He rushes away, rising into the clouds.

To look down on Jizhou here and beyond.

To go where he pleases over the four seas—what limit has he?

The Lord in our thoughts, we sigh long sighs,

Our hearts at the limit of sorrow, weary, weary.

(From Gopal Sukhu, *The Shaman and the Heresiarch*: *A New Interpretation of the Lisao*)

评

《云中君》选自《九歌》。《九歌》共有十一章，乃祀神祭辞。里面的神灵大抵可分为天神、地祇和人鬼三类。其中，"天神"包括东皇太一（天神之贵者）、云中君（云神）、大司命（主寿命的神）、少司命（主子嗣的神）和东君（太阳神）。"地祇"包括湘君与湘夫人（湘水之神）、河伯（河神）和山鬼（山神）。"人鬼"即为最后一章《国殇》里提及的阵亡将士之魂。

上述两个版本，大卫·霍克斯（David Hawkes）的翻译中，前两句的主语是"我们"（we），也就是"我们"在"浴兰汤兮沐芳，华采衣兮若英"，等待云中君的到来。中间七行诗句都是描述云中君的动作、服饰和神态等。最后一句诗行则是写"我"的思念之情。

在戈帕尔·苏克（Gopal Sukhu）的译文里，则是采取第三方的视角，描述"她"与"他"的关系，译文的第三句出现第一个主语"她"，前两句的主语为"她"，（她）"浴兰汤沐芳，华采衣若英"等待云中君的来临。接下来的七行诗也是写云中君的动作，最后一句诗则是写"我们"因思念云中君而沉痛。

从人称的角度来看，霍克斯的翻译更加统一，苏克的翻译有些跳跃，前面写的是"她"在等待"他"，到最后却成了"我"在思念"云中君"。此处的"思夫君"的主语，应当照应上文中的"她"，即"她"在等待，"她"在想象，"她"感到失落。在《九歌》

中，叙述者的口吻因时因地而变。如《湘夫人》里，叙述者就是用湘君的口吻，而在《湘君》里，叙述者又采用了湘夫人的口吻。在上面这篇《云中君》里，叙述者采用一位女性或"我们"的声音，描述云中君的变幻莫测、瑰奇奥妙，表达对他的思念之情。

《楚辞》的翻译，除了人称指代不明产生的歧义外，另外一个难点就是对"兮"这个词的处理。语气词"兮"字是言语停顿处发出的"余声"，有着拖长声音、表示停顿和抒发情感的用途。在《楚辞》里，"兮"字把诗句分成前后两部分，形成了下列七种句式：

"oo 兮 oo"
"ooo 兮 oo"
"ooo 兮 ooo"
"ooo 兮 oooo"
"ooo 兮 ooooo"
"oooo 兮 oo"
"oooo 兮 oooo"

在具体的翻译实践中，可以使用格律、添加英语语气词"oh"或语义停顿的方式进行处理，如《九歌·东皇太一》中两句诗中的"兮"，可以有以下几种不同的处理方式：

吉日兮 辰良，穆将愉兮 上皇。
抚长剑兮 玉珥，璆锵鸣兮 琳琅。

Lucky the Hour，auspicious is the day，
When Homage to our Lord on high we pay.
He grasps his long Sword's Hilt in Jasper bound，
The clanging Pendents wrought in Jade resound.

(杨宪益夫妇　译)

Auspicious hour，‖ oh! ‖ of lucky day!
With deep respect，‖ oh! ‖ we worship our lord.
His jade pendants，‖ oh! ‖ chime on display;
He holds the hilt，‖ oh! ‖ of his long sword.

(许渊冲　译)

On this lucky day，‖ good in both its signs，
Let us in reverence give pleasure ‖ to the Monnarch on high.
I hold my long sword ‖ by its jade grasp;
My girdle-gems tinkle ‖ with a ch'iu-ch'iang.

(Arthur Waley　译)

可以看出，无论哪一种方式，都是权宜之计，很难达到与原诗完全一致的意境。

三、《声声慢》

寻寻觅觅，冷冷清清，凄凄惨惨戚戚。乍暖还寒时候，最难将息。三杯两盏淡酒，怎敌他、晚来风急！雁过也，正伤心，却是旧时相识。

满地黄花堆积，憔悴损，如今有谁堪摘？守着窗儿，独自怎生得黑！梧桐更兼细雨，到黄昏、点点滴滴。这次第，怎一个愁字了得！

译

译文一	译文二
So dim, so dark, So dense, so dull, So damp, so dank, so dead! The weather, now warm, now cold, Makes it harder than ever to forget. How can thin wine and bread Serve as protection Against the piercing wind of sunset? Wild geese pass overhead— That they are familiar Makes it more lamentable yet! The ground is strewn with staid And withered petals; For whom now should they be in vases set? By the window shut, Guarding it alone, To see the sky has turned so black! And on the cola nut To hear the drizzle drone At dust: Pit-a-pat, pi-a-pat! Is this a mod and moment Only to be called "sad"? （林语堂　译）	Tune: "Slow, Slow Tune" I look for what I miss; I know not what it is. I feel so sad, so drear, So lonely, without cheer. How hard is it To keep me fit In this lingering cold! Hardly warmed up By cup on cup Of wine so dry, Oh, how could I Endure at dusk the drift Of wind so swift? It breaks my heart, alas! To see the wild geese pass, For they are my acquaintances of old. The ground is covered with yellow flowers Faded and fallen in showers. Who will pick them up now? Sitting alone at the window, how Could I but quicken The pace of darkness which won't thicken? On parasol-trees leaves a fine rain drizzles As twilight grizzles. Oh! What can I do with a grief Beyond belief? （许渊冲　译）

评

李清照的《声声慢》中，最难翻译的是"寻寻觅觅，冷冷清清，凄凄惨惨戚戚"一句。语词的重复在古典诗词中并不少见，例如王维的诗《栾家濑》：

> 飒飒秋雨中，浅浅石溜泻。
> 跳波自相溅，白鹭惊复下。

Rapids by the Luan Trees
The moaning of wind in autumn rain,
Swift water trickling over stones.
Leaping waves strike one another—
A white egret startles up, comes down again.

(宇文所安　译)

又如《积雨辋川庄作》一诗中的"漠漠水田飞白鹭，阴阴夏木啭黄鹂"一句，宇文所安在翻译的时候，依然只是把两个叠词意思翻译出来，而没有考虑形式上重叠的艺术手法：

> *Over the mists of watery fields*
> *a white egret flies.*
> *In the shade of a summer wood*
> *a yellow oriole warbling.*

在李白的《黄鹤楼》一诗中，"晴川历历汉阳树，芳草萋萋鹦鹉洲"一句，宇文所安也是用同样的手法进行意译，将"历历"翻译成"clear and bright"，"萋萋"翻译为"lush and green"，具体如下：

> *Clear and bright in the sunlit stream*
> *the trees of Han-yang,*
> *Springtime's grasses, lush and green,*
> *all over parrot Isle.*

这种以意义为中心的翻译，若能使英文译文明晰和晓畅，也无大碍，尤其是对于那些已经约定俗成的汉语修饰语的叠词，如刘勰在《文心雕龙·物色》中所说：

> 是以《诗》人感物，联类不穷；流连万象之际，沉吟视听之区。写气图貌，既随物以宛转；属采附声，亦与心而徘徊。故"灼灼"状桃花之鲜，"依依"尽杨柳之貌，"杲杲"为出日之容，"瀌瀌"拟雨雪之状，"喈喈"逐黄鸟之声，"喓喓"学草虫之韵。……虽复思经千载，将何易夺？[①]

---

① 刘勰：《文心雕龙》，北京：中华书局，2012 年，第 520 页。

在摹拟物状的时候，这类叠词已经成为汉语中的固定表达，精练而形象。在顾随先生看来，因为汉语音节较短，叠词正好可以弥补这方面的缺憾，起到平衡声音的效果。在英语中，其实也有一些类似的表达，不过不是体现在字词的重复上，而是主要体现在音节的重复上，如，"pitter-patter"（啪啪哒哒）中的/p/和/tʒ/两组音的重复，"tittle-tattle"（喋喋不休）中的/t/和/tl/的重复，以及"niddle-noddle"（点头不已）中的/n/和/dl/等等。

不过，在汉语古典诗词中，不是所有的字词重复都可以纳入上述叠词的范围。有一些重复是特殊的修辞手法，如李商隐的"春日在天涯，天涯日又斜"便是一种顶针手法。另有一些重复，则完全是一种诗意的表达了，如下面这首唐代诗僧寒山的《杳杳寒山道》：

> 杳杳寒山道，
> 落落岭涧滨。
> 啾啾常有鸟，
> 寂寂更无人。
> 淅淅风吹面，
> 纷纷雪积身。
> 朝朝不见日，
> 岁岁不知春。

诗歌表达了山林中的空寂与静谧，花开花谢，年年岁岁都相似。每句诗都以相同的两个字开始，形式上的整齐和重复更说明山间千年如一日、亘古不变的境况，与诗歌的涵义可谓相得益彰。寒山的另一首诗《独坐常忽忽》也是如此，不同的是，重复的词从每句诗的前两个字移到了最后两个字：

> 独坐常忽忽，
> 情怀何悠悠。
> 山腰云缦缦，
> 谷口风飕飕。
> 猿来树袅袅，
> 鸟入林啾啾。
> 时催鬓飒飒，
> 岁尽老惆惆。

> *I was sitting alone,*
> *Feeling at ease.*
> *The clouds were wandering around the mountain,*

The wind howling across the valley.
The apes climbing and trees waving,
Birds chirping,
My hairs rustling in the air,
The best days are gone.

　　翻译成英文之后，虽然意义基本保持一致，但要想在形式上做到"信"则不太容易。毕竟，中英文的句法构成有较大的差异。对于诗歌而言，形式与内容常常是一体的，甚至可以说"形式即内容"。上面这个例子的中英文对比之下，对重复不做处理的英语译文的况味减了不少。如果从形式的角度，上面这首《杳杳寒山道》可以做如下翻译：

Long, long the pathway to Cold Hill;
Drear, drear, the waterside so chill.
Chirp, chirp, I often hear the bird;
Mute, mute, nobody says a word.
Gust by gust winds caress my face;
Flake on flake snow covers all trace.
From day to day the sun won't shine;
From year to year no spring is mine.

　　但这样的表达在英文中是否合理呢？事实上，利用语词重复表达心境的诗歌，可谓是中国古典诗词的一大重要艺术手法，早在汉代的时候就有了，其中最著名的就是《青青河畔草》，它出自有"诗母"之称的《古诗十九首》：

青青河畔草，郁郁园中柳。
盈盈楼上女，皎皎当窗牖。
娥娥红粉妆，纤纤出素手。
昔为倡家女，今为荡子妇。
荡子行不归，空床难独守。

诗的前几句连用"青青""郁郁""盈盈""皎皎""娥娥"和"纤纤"六个叠词，形容春色迷人和女子的青春靓丽。这一类作者有意使用的词，在翻译成英文的时候，若只是简单转换为对应的英文形容词，而不考虑形式上的特点，原诗的韵味必将大打折扣。
　　在《声声慢》的英文译文中，可以看到，以"脚踏中西文化，一心做宇宙文章"为写作志向的林语堂先生，在处理重复的问题上，可谓独具匠心，既考虑原诗的意蕴，又充分考虑了英语中对等的表达习惯，尽可能使译文在形式和内容上保持一致，保留原诗的况味。在句意上，林语堂译文利用同义反复的方式，试图把原诗中那种惆怅、无奈和苦闷的感觉用英文表述出来。用了"dim""dark""dense""dull""damp""dank""dead"七个表示"暗淡""无聊""死气沉沉"的词表达诗人的心情。虽然每个词的意思不一定完全对应，但整体的意境是比较接近的。在形式上，林的英文译文中也用了重复的手法，只不过把重点落在了"so"（"如此，多么"）这个程度词上。此外，林译文还以辅音/d/开始的英文单词来表现汉语中的"寻寻觅觅，冷冷清清，凄凄惨惨切切"七个叠音词。这样处理的妙处就在于它符合英文中拟声词的构词方式，即以发音接近的单词构成。下文中的"点点滴滴"，林译文更是直接使用英文中现成的"pit-a-pat"（哒哒声）这一拟声词。相比之下，许的译文则主要注重意义与原文的对等，形式上的对等就显得相对弱了一些。

事实上，英文自身的句法结构决定了它很难像中文这样灵活，也很少有类似的表述。不过，在一些经典的语言大师笔下，倒是不乏连续性的语词重复。这些词不仅仅是为了满足发音的拟声需求，而是同一个词的反复强调，如莎士比亚的《麦克白》中就有一句连续三次出现"tomorrow"一词：

> *Tomorrow, and tomorrow, and tomorrow,*
> *Creeps in this petty pace from day to day*
> *To the last syllable of recorded time.*

此外，在美国诗人爱伦·坡（Allan Poe）的"The Bells"（1849）诗中，也在不断重复一些词，如"时间"（"time"）、"铃"（"bells"）：

> **Keeping time，time，time，**
> *In a sort of Runic rhyme,*
> *To the Paean of the bells—*
> *Of the bells: —*
> **Keeping time，time，time，**
> *In a sort of Runic rhyme,*
> *To the throbbing of the bells—*
> *Of the bells, bells, bells—*
> *To the sobbing of the bells: —*
> *Keeping time, time, time,*
> *As he knells, knells, knells,*
> *In a happy Runic rhyme,*
> *To the rolling of the bells—*
> *Of the bells, bells, bells: —*
> *To the tolling of the bells—*
> *Of the bells, bells, bells, bells,*
> *Bells, bells, bells—*

To the moaning and the groaning of the bells.

那么，汉语古典诗词在翻译成英文的时候，是否可以采取上述的形式？如将《声声慢》的第一小节翻译为：

Xun xun mi mi,

Leng leng qing qing,

Qi qi can can qi qi.

The lingering cold,

Most difficult to endure.

Cups of wine would utterly fail to cope with the evening gale.

It breaks my heart to see the wild geese pass,

For they are my old acquaintances.

上面提到的莎士比亚和爱伦坡的英语诗歌例子中，重复的词多为名词。汉语古典诗词中许多词性灵活的词，能否也做同样的处理？而且重复之后会给英语读者怎样的感受？这些都有待我们进一步观察和实践。

四、*Paradise Lost* 节选

Nine times the Space that measures Day and Night

To mortal men，he with his horrid crew

Lay vanquisht，rowling in the fiery Gulfe

Confounded though immortal：But his doom

Reserv'd him to more wrath；for now the thought

Both of lost happiness and lasting pain

Torments him；round he throws his baleful eyes

That witness'd huge affliction and dismay

Mixt with obdurate pride and stedfast hate：

At once as far as Angels kenn he views

The dismal Situation waste and wilde，

A Dungeon horrible，on all sides round

As one great Furnace flam'd，yet from those flames

No light，but rather darkness visible

Serv'd only to discover sights of woe，

Regions of sorrow，doleful shades，where peace

And rest can never dwell，hope never comes

That comes to all；but torture without end

Still urges, and a fiery Deluge, fed
With ever-burning Sulphur unconsum'd:
Such place Eternal Justice had prepar'd
For those rebellious, here thir prison ordained
In utter darkness, and thir portion set
As far remov'd from God and light of Heav'n
As from the Center thrice to th' utmost Pole.
O how unlike the place from whence they fell!
There the companions of his fall, o'rewhelm'd
With Floods and Whirlwinds of tempestuous fire,
He soon discerns, and weltring by his side
One next himself in power, and next in crime,
Long after known in Palestine, and nam'd
Beelzebub. To whom th' Arch-Enemy,
And thence in Heav'n call'd Satan, with bold words
Breaking the horrid silence thus began.
If thou beest he; But O how fall'n! how chang'd
From him, who in the happy Realms of Light
Cloth'd with transcendent brightness didst out-shine
Myriads though bright: If he whom mutual league,
United thoughts and counsels, equal hope
And hazard in the Glorious Enterprize,
Joynd with me once, now misery hath joynd
In equal ruin: into what Pit thou seest
From what highth fall'n, so much the stronger prov'd
He with his Thunder: and till then who knew
The force of those dire Arms? yet not for those,
Nor what the Potent Victor in his rage
Can else inflict, do I repent or change,
Though chang'd in outward lustre; that fixt mind
And high disdain, from sence of injur'd merit,
That with the mightiest rais'd me to contend,
And to the fierce contention brought along
Innumerable force of Spirits arm'd
That durst dislike his reign, and me preferring,
His utmost power with adverse power oppos'd
In dubious Battel on the Plains of Heav'n,
And shook his throne. What though the field be lost?

All is not lost；the unconquerable Will,

And study of revenge，immortal hate,

And courage never to submit or yield：

And what is else not to be overcome?

That Glory never shall his wrath or might

Extort from me. To bow and sue for grace

With suppliant knee，and deifie his power,

Who from the terrour of this Arm so late

Doubted his Empire，that were low indeed,

That were an ignominy and shame beneath

This downfall；since by Fate the strength of Gods

And this Empyreal substance cannot fail,

Since through experience of this great event

In Arms not worse，in foresight much advanc't,

We may with more successful hope resolve

To wage by force or guile eternal Warr

Irreconcileable，to our grand Foe

Who now triumphs，and in th' excess of joy

Sole reigning holds the Tyranny of Heav'n.

赏

上文选自约翰·弥尔顿（John Milton，1608—1674）的《失乐园》（*Paradise Lost*）。弥尔顿在年轻的时候，就展现出写史诗的才华，并立志要成为英格兰民族的骄傲，还留下不少这样的签名：约翰·弥尔顿，英国人。他的生活经历与当时英国的重大问题和政治危机紧密相关，不时地卷入新科学、言论自由以及宗教等社会问题的讨论中去。

《失乐园》讲述了当时人们所熟知的亚当和夏娃背叛上帝的故事，但手法与《圣经》却有很大的区别。通过丰富的心理刻画，弥尔顿赋予这两个主要角色更多人性化的特征，使得他们更加生动、具体。此外，这部史诗还充满想象力地描绘了地狱和天堂的图景，成功地塑造了撒旦这个叛逆的形象，尤其是它的雄辩和决心，给读者留下了深刻的印象。与托马斯·霍布斯（Thomas Hobbes）等推崇强权的政治主张不同，弥尔顿强调个人的独立和自由，赞成离婚，倡导诗歌的变革和言论的自由。《失乐园》中的撒旦是勇于抵制强权统治的一个象征并成为英国文学史上一个重要母题。在后世许多文学作品中，都能找到它的影子，如拜伦笔下的许多英雄人物（"Byronic Heros"），艾米丽·勃朗特（Emily Brontë）的小说《呼啸山庄》（*Wuthering Heights*）中的赫斯克利夫（Heathcliff）等等。在风格上，《失乐园》是一种无韵体史诗。诗中使用大量长句，有些段落可以连续 10 行、20 行，从句之中又套着从句，应用大量倒装、典故等手法，形成一泻千里、气势磅礴的特殊效果。这从上面关于撒旦的选文中，可以得以管窥。

当然，我们也要看到，任何伟大的作家都是多维的。弥尔顿虽然看到了撒旦反抗的意义，正如他本人一样，一生都在和各种强权作斗争，但他也很清楚，有时候顺从命运的安排，未尝不是一种美德。在双眼失明的时候，弥尔顿也曾经历心理的挣扎和困惑，并写下《失明》（"On his Blindness"）一诗：

> When I consider how my light① is spent
> E're half my days, in this dark world and wide,
> And that one Talent② which is death to hide,
> Lodg'd with me useless, though my Soul more bent
> To serve therewith my Maker, and present
> My true account, least he returning chide,
> Doth God exact day-labour, light deny'd,
> I fondly ask；But patience to prevent
> That murmur, soon replies, God doth not need
> Either man's work or his own gifts, who best
> Bear his milde yoak, they serve him best, his State
> Is Kingly. Thousands at his bidding speed
> And post o're Land and Ocean without rest：
> They also serve who only stand and waite.

> 想到自己未到半生就双目失明，
> 眼前的世界是一片茫茫的黑暗，
> 想到那不用将招致死亡的才干
> 在我手里却无用武之地，尽管
> 我的灵魂更愿意侍奉我的造主
> 并献上真心，免得算账时遭斥；
> "神要人白天做工，竟不给光明？"
> 我愚蠢自问；但忍耐阻止抱怨
> 抢先做了应答："神既不要人的
> 工作也不收回他的礼物；谁最
> 能轻松地背稳神轭，谁就最能
> 侍奉。"他君临天下，差遣千万
> 万天使，越疆跨海，忙碌不停：
> 那些只站立等候的，也在侍奉。

(黄宗英　译)

---

① eyesight，life

② The word "talent" signifies an intellectual gift (here Milton's poetic gift) as well as the silver coin, a talent, in the biblical parable of the talents.

在诗的前半部分，叙述者似乎心有怨气，想向上帝讨回公道：自己那么努力服侍上帝，但上帝却无情地剥夺了他的光明，让他成为"无用"之人，无端蒙受了巨大的冤屈。在诗歌的后半部分，叙述者却换了一种语气，告诉自己要有耐心：那些翻山越岭、终日忙碌的天使在给上帝做工，而那些接受命运的安排，安静地站在一边等待的人，未尝不是一种做工。这里我们看到，那位金刚怒目的弥尔顿，也有了温顺的一面。在一番理性的自问自答之后，他决定服从上帝的安排，接受"无为也是做工"的观点。

除了对个人的失明思考外，弥尔顿还写过感人肺腑的《致亡妻》（"To His Deceased Wife"），表达了对第二任妻子凯瑟琳·伍德科克（Katherine Woodcock）的深切思念。

Methought I saw my late espoused saint
Brought to me like Alcestis from the grave,
Whom Jove's great son to her glad husband gave,
Rescued from death by force though pale and faint.
Mine as whom washed from spot of childbed taint,
Purification in the old law did save,
And such, as yet once more I trust to have
Full sight of her in heaven without restraint,
Came vested all in white, pure as her mind:
Her face was veiled, yet to my fancied sight,
Love, sweetness, goodness in her person shined
So clear, as in no face with more delight.
But O as to embrace me she inclined
I waked, she fled, and day brought back my night.

我仿佛看到了去世不久的圣徒般的妻回到了我身边，像阿尔塞斯蒂斯从坟墓被尤比特伟大的儿子用强力从死亡中救出，苍白而虚弱，交给了她的丈夫，使他欢喜。我的妻，由于古戒律规定的净身礼而得救，洗净了产褥上斑斑的玷污，这样的她，我相信我还能再度在天堂毫无障碍地充分地瞻视，她一身素服，纯洁得和她心灵一样，肤上罩着面纱，但我仿佛看见爱、温柔、善良在她身上发光，如此开朗，什么人脸上有这等欢颜。但是，唉，正当她俯身拥抱我的当儿，我醒了，她逃逸了，白昼带回了我的黑天。

(杨周翰　译)

这首感人至深的诗歌，是在凯瑟琳去世后不久写的。全诗都在梦境中，意象模糊，有一种迷离神秘的气氛，那种"十年生死两茫茫，不思量，自难忘"的悲凉，跃然纸上。本诗的深刻之处还在于它有圣洁的一面，即诗中的妻子既是爱情、甜蜜的象征，更是犹如阿尔塞斯蒂斯般自我牺牲的象征，是神成肉身，是基督的具身化。因而，夫妻之爱成了凡人与上帝之间关系的隐喻。

译

失乐园（节选）
一下子天使极目远眺，但见
阴郁的景象，满眼尽莽莽苍苍
一座阴森森的地牢，四周熊熊
烈火像个大熔炉，可是这火焰
有焰无光，只见黑漆漆一片
足以窥见哀伤凄凉的情景
悲愁的地域，可怕的阴暗，那儿
和平、安谧从不驻足，希望
临万物，这儿却不来；而无尽痛楚
依然交加，烈火的洪流，添加
不断燃烧的硫黄，永无穷尽。

战场失利算什么？
没有完全丧失：不可征服的意志，
报仇的努力，永不熄灭的憎恨，
还有那绝不投降屈服的勇气：
这些在一起岂不是就不可克服？
那种荣誉，他的愤怒和暴力
都休想向我逼取。卑躬屈膝，
低头哈腰求恩宠，拜倒在他权力下，
不久前这次动干戈他还吓破胆，
对自己的权力丧失信心——真下贱；

那种无耻、下流比这次贬谪
更下等，因为凭天数、神力、
神注定不能失败，
因为经历了这次伟大的战事，
论武器不逊色，论预见大有增益，
我们更可以怀必胜的信念，决心
用武力或奸计，掀战争，无止无休，
对我们头号的敌人永不妥协，
他如今胜利了，兴高采烈很得意，
寡国统治，天庭施行暴政。

评

《失乐园》结构繁复、语言瑰丽，除了受到外来语的影响外，还和当时流行的巴洛克艺术之风有关。巴洛克风格最早与宗教有关，讲究绚烂豪华的造型美、雕琢美和具象美，是天主教会用来对抗新教提出的朴素简单的风格而提出的艺术理念。17世纪，这种风格始于罗马，后迅速扩大到法国、意大利北部、西班牙、葡萄牙和德国南部。巴洛克风格倾向于使用夸张的动作、复杂的细节描绘，以此产生戏剧效果并唤起人们心中的敬畏感，特别重视动态和情节的展现。在表现手法方面，经常使用对比、复杂的细节和深色调，强调宏伟和震撼的效果，如伦勃朗·梵·莱茵（Rembrandt van Rijn，1606—1669）的《夜巡》（*The Night Watch*，1642）就是巴洛克风格的绘画的代表作之一。在文学方面，巴洛克风格的作品往往使用华丽的语汇、繁复的修饰以及各种精致的修辞手法，如比喻、象征和夸张等，以此表现激烈的情感，如托马斯·布朗爵士（Thomas Browne，1605—1682）的《医生的宗教》（"Religio Medici"）一文：

> *Schollers are men of peace, they beare no arms, but their tongues are sharper than Actisu his razor, their pens carry farther, and give a lowder report than thunder; I had rather stand in the shock of a Basilisco than in the fury of a mercilesse Pen. It is not mere zeal to Learning, or devotion to Muses, that wiser Princes Patron the Arts, and carry an indulgent aspect unto Schollers, but a desire to have their name eternized by the memory of their writings, and a feare of the revengefull pen of succeeding ages.*
>
> *(译文：学者是爱和平的人，他们不携带武器，但他们的舌头却比阿克提乌斯的剃刀还锋利，他们的笔更厉害，比雷声还响；我宁肯忍受大炮的震撼，也不愿忍受一只无情的笔的怒袭。聪明的君主奖掖文学，不仅仅是因为他们热衷学术或敬重诗神，才以宽容的脸色对待学者，而是因为想借学者门第和著作垂名千古，并防后人的直笔。)*

这段话主要写学者的文笔比武器更加有力，布朗爵士在描写的时候，利用"剃刀""雷声"等比喻，还说自己宁可忍受大炮的袭击，也不要忍受作家的愤怒。整段话一共就两句话，第二句话为强调句型，"It is not ... that ... but ..."，前后共三行半，可谓一气呵成。

弥尔顿的《失乐园》中，也有大量这类长句。例如，上文中的"眼睛"一词除了前面的形容词"baleful"，后面又有定语从句"That witness'd huge affliction and dismay"，以及分词构造"Mixt with obdurate pride and stedfast hate"。此外，"he views"后面紧跟的10行诗句，都是形容撒旦此刻的所见所闻。内容上，一个景象紧接着一个景象；结构上，一个句子套着一个句子，陈陈相因，环环相扣，充分展现了地狱之火的无边无际以及撒旦即将面临的无涯的折磨，从而反衬出它誓不屈服的反抗精神。在具体的翻译活动中，要充分看到该诗篇的形式背后蕴藏的内涵，不能随意改变句式和结构，而应该在达意的同时，尽可能维持原文的形式架构，方不失其旨趣。

五、"A Valediction: Forbidding Mourning"

As virtuous men pass mildly away,
And whisper to their souls to go,
Whilst① some of their sad friends do say
The breath goes now, and some say, No:

So let us melt, and make no noise,
No tear-floods, nor sigh-tempests move;
'Twere② profanation of our joys
To tell the laity③ our love.

Moving of th'④ earth brings harms and fears,
Men reckon what it did, and meant;
But trepidation of the spheres,⑤
Though greater far, is innocent.

Dull sublunary⑥ lovers' love
(Whose soul is sense) cannot admit
Absence, because it doth remove
Those things which elemented it.

But we by a love so much refined,
That our selves know not what it is,
Inter-assured of the mind,
Care less, eyes, lips, and hands to miss.

Our two souls therefore, which are one,
Though I must go, endure not yet
A breach, but an expansion,
Like gold to airy thinness beat.

---

① While
② It were
③ ordinary people
④ the
⑤ "trepidation of the spheres" means "earthquake"
⑥ early, commonplace

If they be two，they are two so
As stiff twin compasses are two；
Thy soul，the fixed foot，makes no show
To move，but doth，if the other do.

And though it in the center sit，
Yet when the other far doth roam，
It leans and hearkens after it，
And grows erect，as that comes home.

Such wilt thou be to me，who must，
Like th' other foot，obliquely run；
Thy firmness makes my circle just，
And makes me end where I begun.

赏

本诗为英国诗人约翰·多恩（John Donne，1572—1631）所作。与那个时代许多文人一样，多恩也曾涉足多个领域，主要有经院哲学、数学、生理学、神学、炼金术和宇宙学（cosmology）等。对多学科领域的了解让多恩的诗歌里有了很多新颖的东西，尤其是他笔下许多奇特的比喻，或曰"奇思妙想"（metaphysical conceit）。对于那些老生常谈的譬喻，如"恋人的脸庞如玫瑰花般""爱神之箭穿心而过"等，多恩很不屑。他的笔下，出奇的比喻也随处可见，如"爱人的眼球系在一根绳上"（Lovers' eyeballs threaded on a string）、"一滴眼泪包含并淹没了整个世界"（A teardrop that emphases and drowns the world）。这些看似不自然的比喻，往往蕴含着深意。读者也能在解码的过程中，获得一种阅读的喜悦。

在多恩最重要的诗集《诗歌和十四行诗》（Songs and Sonnets）里，有许多描绘爱情的诗，其中有一首题为《去吧，去抓住一颗流星》（"Song：Go and Catch a Falling Star"，1633）的诗里，开篇就连用了八个"不可能做到的事"，其中六个用到了比喻，如"抓住流星""与曼德拉草生孩子""谁劈开了魔鬼的脚趾"和"听到美人鱼的歌唱"等，来说明真诚、美好的女性就像这些事物一样是很难找到的。

Go and catch a falling star,
Get with child a mandrake root,
Tell me where all past years are,
Or who cleft the devil's foot,
Teach me to hear mermaids singing,
Or to keep off envy's stinging,

And find

What wind

Serves to advance an honest mind.

If thou be'st born to strange sights,

Things invisible to see,

Ride ten thousand days and nights,

Till age snow white hairs on thee,

*Thou, when thou return'st*①, *wilt*② *tell me,*

All strange wonders that befell thee,

And swear,

No where

Lives a woman true, and fair.

*If thou find'st*③ *one, let me know,*

Such a pilgrimage were sweet;

Yet do not, I would not go,

Though at next door we might meet;

Though she were true, when you met her,

And last, till you write your letter,

Yet she

Will be

False, ere I come, to two, or three.

另外一首写爱情的诗，题为《跳蚤》（"The Flea"，1633），如果不看诗的具体内容，大概很难想到跳蚤与爱情能有什么关联，阅读的过程变成了揭示谜底的过程：

Mark but this flea, and mark in this,

How little that which thou deniest me is;

It sucked me first, and now sucks thee,

And in this flea our two bloods mingled be;

Thou know'st that this cannot be said

A sin, nor shame, nor loss of maidenhead,

Yet this enjoys before it woo,

---

① returned
② would
③ found

And pampered swells with one blood made of two,
And this, alas, is more than we would do.

Oh stay, three lives in one flea spare,
Where we almost, nay more than married are.
This flea is you and I, and this
Our marriage bed, and marriage temple is;
Though parents grudge, and you, w'are met,
And cloistered in these living walls of jet.
Though use make you apt to kill me,
Let not to that, self-murder added be,
And sacrilege, three sins in killing three.

Cruel and sudden, hast thou since
Purpled thy nail, in blood of innocence?
Wherein could this flea guilty be,
Except in that drop which it sucked from thee?
Yet thou triumph'st, and say'st that thou
Find'st not thy self, nor me the weaker now;
'tis true; then learn how false, fears be:
Just so much honor, when thou yield'st to me,
Will waste, as this flea's death took life from thee.

跳蚤在多恩生活的时代是一个常见的意象，以跳蚤为诗歌主题描写爱情也非多恩独创，只是这一首是流传最为广泛的。在《跳蚤》这首诗的第一小节里，多恩就点明这个小动物与爱情之间的关联：跳蚤的叮咬，让一对恋人的爱情在第三个生命体里有了交集；第二小节里，多恩戏拟了律师的口吻，对于是否该打死这只跳蚤这样微不足道的小事，煞有介事地摆事实、说道理，条分缕析，层层深入。叙述者还在奉劝他的恋人，委身于他并非什么罪过，就像跳蚤吸走一点血并不会让人丧生一样。

此外，下面这首离别辞一改在《去吧，去抓一个流星》中对爱情的不信任态度，用圆规这一不同寻常的意象，表现了叙述者对爱情的坚贞和矢志不渝。

译

离别辞：莫悲伤

有德之士安详地辞世
只轻轻对自己的灵魂说声：走吧
他那些悲伤的朋友，

43

有的说：他走了；
有的却说：不，还没有。

就让我慢慢逝去，不要喧哗，
不要泪如泉涌，不要叹息不已，
这样像凡人表达我们之间的爱，
是一种亵渎

地球的移动带来危害和恐惧，
人们都清楚这一点
天体的运动巨大得多
但却不为人知

世俗之爱，灵魂就是感官
容不得片刻分离
肉体一分离，爱也随之消逝

但是我们之间，爱得高贵
不知其为何物
只道是思想的交融
无心关注眼睛、嘴唇和双手

我们的灵魂是一体的
虽然我要离开了
但不是分离，而是延伸
就像金片打成空气般稀薄的金箔一样

若说是两个灵魂，
那该是圆规两只坚定的脚
你的灵魂是定脚，固定不移；
但若另一只脚起步，你便随之转动

尽管一只脚稳据中央，
但当另一只脚四周漫游，
定脚准会侧身倾听，
另一只脚归来时，便依然笔直。

你对我而言，就像这只圆规定脚，

我是另一只倾斜移动的脚
你坚定不移，我的轨迹浑圆，
并停止于起点之处。

评

《离别辞：莫悲伤》一诗大约写于 1611 年到 1612 年，发表在 1633 年的《诗歌和十四行诗》集中。当时恰逢妻子要到欧洲大陆旅行，多恩便用富有哲理性的语言平静地与爱人话别，并将两人的爱情与凡人之爱进行比较：凡夫俗子最忌别离，因为他们的爱是建立在感官基础之上的，一旦肉体分开，就以泪洗面，叹息不已；而诗人与他的爱人的感情超凡脱俗，不为肉体束缚，分离不仅不是爱情的终结，还是爱情的延伸。

该诗的第一节主要是说有德之人的死亡是平平静静、悄无声息的，就连身边的亲朋好友都不知道他何时停止呼吸。第二节则从死亡转到恋人的分离。在诗人看来，真正相爱的两个人的分离也该如有德之人面对死亡般平静、自然，而非像俗人那样大声喧哗、哭声震天。第三节是本诗较为难懂的部分，尤其是 "trepidation of the spheres" 一词。这个词与托勒密宇宙论（Ptolemaic cosmology）有关，是一种假想的天体运动。这种理论在公元 9 世纪到 16 世纪期间比较流行，此处用来指比地震大得多的一种运动。本小节的大意是说：人们能感觉得到地球的运动，但对于更高层面的天体运动的威力和意义却无动于衷，这就像人们能感觉到世俗之爱，但对于更加高尚的、超越肉体的灵魂之爱，却无法心领神会。接下来的两节——第四节和第五节——分别讲世俗之爱和诗人自己的爱，二者形成鲜明的对比。第四节讲述那些以感官为基础的俗人之爱，一旦两人肉体分离，爱也就无处附着，烟消云散了。第五节则写诗人与爱人的情感并不是以肉体为基础的。相反，肉体越分离，爱越是得以延伸，就像金片制成稀薄的金箔，越是拉伸，距离越开，就越能铺展开来，绵延不绝。最后三个小节，则主要围绕圆规的比喻展开，其中前两节主要说圆规的物理形态，最后一小节直接将其联系到诗人与恋人的爱情上。用圆规这个意象来比喻两人爱情的坚贞不渝：圆规的双脚，一方是定点，另一方无论走多远，都是围绕这个圆心展开，而且最终仍会回到定点。

玄学派诗歌中的奇喻实质是隐喻的延伸，其主要作用有两个：其一，奇喻能给读者以一种思想上的惊喜；其二，奇喻能给人以哲学上的启迪。奇喻往往把一些品质赋予其他原本毫不相干的东西，是一种 "和谐的不和谐"（harmonious discord）。在 17 世纪批评家塞缪尔·约翰逊（Samuel Johnson）看来，多恩的奇思妙想是把不同的东西强行拉扯在一起，虽然会引起惊奇，但却无法让人喜悦，但在当代著名批评家哈罗德·布鲁姆（Harold Bloom）看来，人们的品位会随着时代的不同而发生变化，虽然约翰逊不能从多恩那里享受阅读的快乐，但从塞缪尔·泰勒·柯尔律治（Samuel Taylor Coleridge）之后的整个 19 世纪以及 20 世纪，读者们都能在阅读多恩的作品中体会到快乐。

六、"A Red，Red Rose"

A Red，Red Rose

O my Luve is like a red, red rose
That's newly sprung in June;
O my Luve is like the melody
That's sweetly played in tune.

So fair art thou, my bonnie lass,
So deep in luve am I;
And I will luve thee still, my dear,
Till a' the seas gang dry.

Till a' the seas gang dry, my dear,
And the rocks melt wi' the sun;
I will love thee still, my dear,
While the sands o' life shall run.

And fare thee weel, my only luve!
And fare thee weel awhile!
And I will come again, my luve,
Though it were ten thousand mile.

赏

　　这首诗是有"以天堂为师的农夫"（Heaven-taught ploughman）之称的苏格兰诗人罗伯特·彭斯（Robert Burns）创作的。彭斯的诗歌主要来自两大传统：一是民间歌曲的口头传统，二是苏格兰的口语诗歌传统。如今，彭斯已成为苏格兰的一个文化和历史符号，甚至有这样的说法：当苏格兰忘记彭斯的时候，历史也忘记了苏格兰（When Scotland forgets Burns, then history will forget Scotland）。彭斯的诗歌充满活力，语言简朴，具有乡土气息，多为情感的自然流露，几乎没有来自学院派的东西。这个特征在下面这首《约翰·安德森，我的老头子》（"John Anderson My Jo, John"）上有很好的体现。

John Anderson my jo, John,
When we were first acquent,
Your locks were like the raven,
Your bonie brow was brent;
But now your brow is beld, John,
Your locks are like the snaw,
but blessings on your frosty pow,
John Anderson, my jo!

John Anderson my jo, John,
We clamb the hill thegither,
And monie a cantie day, John,
We've had wi' ane anither;
Now we maun totter down, John,
And hand in hand we'll go,
And sleep thegither at the foot,
John Anderson, my jo!

　　这首《约翰·安德森，我的老头子》主要以一位老妇人的口吻，描写了她和自己老伴的一生，第一小节写老伴年轻时与现在的外貌对比，年轻时候是英姿飒爽多福气，"头发乌黑亮黝黝，两道剑眉真叫个直"，现在"浓眉全掉光，头发像雪又像霜"。老人只平平地说，娓娓道来，没有任何哀婉叹息。第二小节先是以爬山的比喻，写两人的前半生携手同行，再用下山的比喻，讲述老年时候的光景：年纪大了，也要一起搀扶着，慢慢走完生命的最后历程，"在山脚下长眠"。诗歌运用苏格兰方言，口吻朴素自然，却触动人心。

　　此外，彭斯诗歌中往往使用大量重复手法，如《约翰·安德森，我的老头子》中的"John Anderson, my jo!"一句便重复了四遍，在《一朵红红的玫瑰》一诗中，除了诗句的重复，如"I will luve thee still, my dear"，还有不同诗节之间结构相对称，如第二小节和第三小节。重复的使用是民歌的一个重要特征，这样一唱三叹，回环复沓，朗朗上口，容易背诵，也容易在民间广泛传开来。这种手法在下面这首《我的心啊，在高地》（"My Heart's in the Highland"，1889）里也表现得十分突出。

My heart's in the Highlands, my heart is not here;
My heart's in the Highlands a chasing the deer;
Chasing the wild deer, and following the roe—
My heart's in the Highlands wherever I go.
Farewell to the Highlands, farewell to the North,
The birth-place of valour, the country of worth;
Wherever I wander, wherever I rove,
The hills of the Highlands for ever I love.

Farewell to the mountains high cover'd with snow;
Farewell to the straths and green valleys below;
Farewell to the forests and wild hanging woods;
Farewell to the torrents and loud-pouring floods.
My heart's in the Highlands, my heart is not here,

My heart's in the Highlands a chasing the deer;
Chasing the wild deer, and following the roe—
My heart's in the Highlands, wherever I go.

整首诗强调最多的就是"我的心啊，在高地"（"My heart's in the Highlands"）一句，呼应全诗的题目，第二节则以四个"Farewell to"的诗行开始，突出作者内心热烈的情感。

译

译文一

我爱如玫瑰，六月红蕾姣。

我爱如乐曲，妙奏声袅袅。

爱卿无限深，如卿绝世妍。

直至海水枯，此爱永绵绵。

直至海水枯，炎阳熔岩石。

但教一息存，爱卿无终极。

离别只暂时，善保千金躯。

终当复归来，万里度若飞。

（毕玆　译）

译文二

吾爱吾爱玫瑰红，六月初开韵晓风；

吾爱吾爱如管弦，其声悠扬而玲珑。

吾爱吾爱美而殊，我心爱你永不渝，

我心爱你永不渝，直到四海海水枯；

直到四海海水枯，岩石融化变成泥，

只要我还有口气，我心爱你永不渝。

暂时告别我心肝，请你不要把心耽！

纵使相隔十万里，踏穿地皮也要还。

（郭沫若　译）

译文三

我的爱人像一朵红红的玫瑰，六月里迎风初开；

呵，我的爱人像一曲甜蜜的歌，唱得合拍又柔和。

我的好姑娘，多么美丽的人儿！我呀，多么深的爱情！

亲爱的，我永远爱你，纵使大海干枯水流尽。

纵使大海干枯水流尽，太阳将岩石烧作灰尘，

亲爱的，我永远爱你，只要我生命犹存。

珍重吧，我唯一的爱人，珍重吧，让我们暂时别离。

但我定要回来，哪怕千里万里！

（王佐良　译，1959 年）

译文四

呵，我的爱人像朵红红的玫瑰，六月里迎风初开；

呵，我爱人像支甜甜的曲子，奏得合拍又和谐。

我的好姑娘，你有多么美，我的情也有多么深。

我将永远爱你，亲爱的，直到大海干枯水流尽。

直到大海干枯水流尽，太阳把岩石烧作灰尘，

我也永远爱你，亲爱的，只要我一息犹存。

珍重吧，我唯一的爱人，珍重吧，让我们暂时别离。

我准定回来，亲爱的，哪怕跋涉千万里！

（王佐良　译，1980 年）

评

译文一全部使用五言的构造，结构整齐、用词典雅，如"爱卿无限深，如卿绝世妍"。其中，不少地方的意象还化为我们所熟悉的传统诗词中的意象，如"善保千金躯"中的"千金"表示女性，而"万里度若飞"一句，则很容易让我们联想起《木兰辞》中的表示骏马奔驰、时光飞逝的那句诗："万里赴戎机，关山度若飞"。使用中文诗歌中一些对等的意象去翻译英文诗歌，从而达到一种"化境"的效果，让读者充分体会原诗的意蕴，是本译文的出彩之处。

译文二中，每一句诗都用七个字，节奏比较统一。语言上，有些地方比较文雅，如"六月初开韵晓风""吾爱吾爱美而殊，我心爱你永不渝"；有些地方则比较口语化，如"暂时告别我心肝，请你不要把心耽"，尤其是"只要我还有口气"一句，几乎是照搬日常生活中老百姓的发誓用词。译者是有意还是无意地融入这种口语化的语言元素，我们不得而知，但就整个译文而言，这样的句子跟一开始出现的"吾爱吾爱玫瑰红，六月初开韵晓风；吾爱吾爱如管弦，其声悠扬而玲珑"里较为文雅的口吻，显得不太相称。这种文白相杂的做法，把一篇赤诚、热情的爱情诗，译成了具有反讽意味的后现代诗歌，读起来难免有些滑稽，恐怕也不是英文原诗作者的本意。

上面两首译文，对每一行诗句的字数都有讲究，读起来都是朗朗上口。不过，这种整齐划一的七言或五言诗，因为着力痕迹过于明显，在某种程度上，反倒显得情感不够真挚。我们再来看一下王佐良先生的翻译。

王佐良先生在 1959 年和 1980 年两次翻译这首诗均未使用近体诗，而是采用通俗易懂的语言。在 1980 年的版本中，还特意在开篇添加了一个"呵"字，并把第二诗行的"甜蜜的"一词改为"甜甜的"，而最后一行的"我定"也变成了更加口语化的"我准定"。王佐良先生对这首诗歌的理解，源自他对彭斯的理解，正如他在《彭斯之乡沉思录》一文里，反复强调了彭斯最可贵的品质是使用来自民间的题材。在翻译过程中，王佐良先生也格外注重保留彭斯诗歌的民间特色，保持译文的通俗化、口语化特征。从这个意义上看，王佐良先生的翻译，无疑在韵味上是最接近彭斯原作的。

七、"A Bird, Came down the Walk—"

A Bird, came down the Walk—
He did not know I saw—
He bit an Angleworm in halves
And ate the fellow, raw,

And then, he drank a Dew
From a convenient Grass—
And then hopped sidewise to the Wall
To let a Beetle pass—

He glanced with rapid eyes,
That hurried all abroad—
They looked like frightened Beads, I thought,
He stirred his Velvet Head. —

Like one in danger, Cautious,
I offered him a Crumb,
And he unrolled his feathers,
And rowed him softer Home—

Than Oars divide the Ocean,
Too silver for a seam,
Or Butterflies, off Banks of Noon,
Leap, plashless as they swim.

赏

现代派诗人艾米丽·迪金森（Emily Dickinson）在诗歌形式方面的革新尝试以及其主题的丰富，使她成为美国最伟大的诗人之一。迪金森在世的时候由于深居简出，终生未婚，在她的邻居看来，不过是个过着隐居生活的怪异的老处女，但世俗的眼光并没有妨碍她成为伟大的诗人。迪金森是家中第二个孩子，她的家族在当地有着显赫的地位，迪金森几乎一辈子都在父母留下的房子里生活。她的诗歌题材十分广泛，宗教、科学、音乐以及时政，几乎无所不包。由于身边亲人好友的相继离世，迪金森对死亡有着深刻的思考，也留下了不少关于死亡的诗歌，其中最为著名的一首便是《因为我不能为死亡驻足——》（"Because I Could not Stop for Death"）

Because I could not stop for Death—
He kindly stopped for me—
The Carriage held but just Ourselves—
And Immortality.

We slowly drove—He knew no haste
And I had put away
My labor and my leisure too,
For His Civility—

We passed the School, where Children strove
At Recess—in the Ring—
We passed the Fields of Gazing Grain—
We passed the Setting Sun—

Or rather—He passed Us—
The Dews drew quivering and Chill—
For only Gossamer, my Gown—
My Tippet—only Tulle—

We paused before a House that seemed
A Swelling of the Ground—
The Roof was scarcely visible—
The Cornice—in the Ground—

Since then—'tis Centuries—and yet
Feels shorter than the Day
I first surmised the Horses' Heads
Were toward Eternity—

这首诗以倒叙的方式，描写死神驱着马车载"我"去看多年前的坟墓的情形。第一节、第二节主要写死神的彬彬有礼打动了"我"，"我"便上车了。第三节回顾了"'我'的一生"，"学校"是青少年时期的象征，"成熟的谷物"代表成年时期，而"落日"则表示老年时期。第四节写"我"在车上的感觉，穿着单薄，寒意袭人。第五节写马车到达了目的地——当年安葬"我"的坟墓。因为年代久远，墓的穹顶已经看不清楚了，飞檐也埋入泥土。第六节则写自己的生命得到了永生。全诗想象奇特，笔触极其冷静。除了想象死亡多年后的情形，迪金森还在诗作里写过死亡的现场景象，如下面的这首《感觉一个葬礼，在我的大脑里》（"I Felt a Funeral，in My Brain"）：

I felt a Funeral, in my Brain,
And Mourners to and fro
Kept treading—treading—till it seemed
That Sense was breaking through—

And when they all were seated,
A Service, like a Drum—
Kept beating—beating—till I thought
My mind was going numb—

And then I heard them lift a Box
And creak across my Soul
With those same Boots of Lead, again,
Then Space—began to toll,

As all the Heavens were a Bell,
And Being, but an Ear,
And I, and Silence, some strange Race,
Wrecked, solitary, here—

And then a Plank in Reason, broke,
And I dropped down, and down—
And hit a World, at every plunge,
And Finished knowing—then—

　　诗中的"我"刚刚离世，虽然已经不能动弹，却能清晰地感受周围人们的一举一动。葬礼上的鼓声、窸窸窣窣的脚步声，吵得"我"几乎失去感觉，脑子里一片空白。接着，"我"便听到开箱子的声音，靴子的声音像铅一样沉重，到处都是铃声，只有耳朵还有感觉，最后感觉不断下沉，应该是棺木被放到土里，"我"便完全没有知觉了。大概只有经历了太多生死并最终在精神上超越死亡的人，才可以用如此轻松、淡然的笔墨去描绘它吧。在中国文学史上，受孔子"未知生，焉知死"思想的影响，虽然有过不少悼亡诗，但对于死亡本身的讨论几乎是个禁忌，很少有诗人去描绘死亡的场景，有一个例外，那就是魏晋文人陶渊明的《拟挽歌辞三首》，与迪金森的这首诗似乎有着异曲同工之妙：

有生必有死，早终非命促。
昨暮同为人，今旦在鬼录。

魂气散何之，枯形寄空木。

娇儿索父啼，良友抚我哭。

得失不复知，是非安能觉。

千秋万岁后，谁知荣与辱。

但恨在世时，饮酒不得足。

在昔无酒饮，今但湛空觞。

春醪生浮蚁，何时更能尝。

肴案盈我前，亲朋哭我傍。

欲语口无音，欲视眼无光。

昔在高堂寝，今宿荒草乡。

一朝出门去，归来良未央。

荒草何茫茫，白杨亦萧萧。

严霜九月中，送我出远郊。

四面无人居，高坟正嶣峣。

马为仰天鸣，风为自萧条。

幽室一已闭，千年不复朝。

千年不复朝，贤达无奈何。

向来相送人，各自还其家。

亲戚或余悲，他人亦已歌。

死去何所道，托体同山阿。

　　诗人想象着自己去世的时候，亲朋好友在一旁哭泣，平日因家境贫寒，并无多少钱买酒喝，而此刻躺在棺木中，看到台上祭奠自己的各种美酒，"欲语口无音，欲视眼无光"，不免感到惋惜。紧接着诗人又想象了荒郊野外亲人送葬的情形——"荒草何茫茫，白杨亦萧萧"，而"幽室一已闭，千年不复朝"一句，与迪金森那句"棺木入穴，再无知觉"（"And hit a World, at every plunge, And Finished knowing—then—"）有异曲同工之妙。最后，陶渊明还写了葬礼仪式之后的情形："向来相送人，各自还其家。亲戚或余悲，他人亦已歌。"亲人把自己送走了，也该继续他们的生活了。这便是人生，作者没有责备，也没有怨言，人情世故大抵如此，而是坦然面对。对于死者而言，不过是回到青山的怀抱之中，正所谓"人生天地间，忽如远行客"，中国传统文人面对死亡的时候，有着自己的豁达和超脱。

　　在迪金森的死亡诗中，除了上面提到的比较严肃认真的，也会夹杂不同于东方的现代的西式幽默。比如下面这首《我听到苍蝇嗡嗡叫——在我死的时候——》（"I Heard a Fly Buzz—When I Died—"）：

I heard a Fly buzz—when I died—
The Stillness in the Room
Was like the Stillness in the Air—

Between the Heaves of Storm—

The Eyes around—had wrung them dry—
And Breaths were gathering firm
For that last Onset—when the King
Be witnessed—in the Room—

I willed my Keepsakes—Signed away
What portion of me be
Assignable—and then it was
There interposed a Fly—

With Blue—uncertain—stumbling Buzz—
Between the light—and me—
And then the Windows failed—and then
I could not see to see—

　　诗中写道：庄严肃穆的葬礼上，房间里一片寂静，气氛凝重，人们的眼睛都哭干了，死神即将到来，遗嘱得以宣读——就在这时，有一只苍蝇不识时务地"嗡嗡"飞来。庄严肃穆的死亡仪式上，为什么要插入这个格格不入的画面？在日常生活中，苍蝇是常见的小动物。但在诗歌中，尤其是死亡诗中，煞有介事地插入此情此景，就有些异常了。诗人是想追求一种诗歌的"真实性"（authenticity），如实描写生活？或是用反讽的语气，对有着"国王般尊严"的死亡之神表示不屑吗？还是想用依附腐烂物生存的苍蝇意象，提醒人们肉体腐朽之速吗？……总之，苍蝇与葬礼之间到底有怎样的关联，就像玄学派诗人多恩的诗歌一样神秘，留下了无限遐想。不过，单从诗学的角度看，迪金森却比许多玄学派诗人高明得多，因为后者习惯在诗歌中揭晓谜底，而迪金森却保持沉默，不透露任何答案。对读者而言，就在这苦苦思索的过程中，反倒获得了阅读的快乐和阐释的兴致。

译

小鸟沿着小径走来

一只鸟走过来——
我看到他了，他却不知道——
把蚯蚓咬断
然后吃下去，活生生地，

然后吸了一颗露珠

从近旁的草上
接着就跳到墙边
给一只甲虫让道

转动着灵活的眼睛
四下里打量——
宛若两颗受惊的珠子，我想
毛茸茸的脑袋晃了晃——

他小心翼翼——像遇到危险似的，
我投给他一块面包屑，
他却张开翅膀，
轻轻地飞回家了

比双桨划开大海的动作，还要轻盈
一片银辉，不留痕迹
比中午河堤的彩蝶轻盈
一跃，没溅起一点水花

评

迪金森的诗歌，涵义或许不好理解，但她所用的词和句式都是比较简单的。比如下面这首《我是无名小卒！你是谁——》（"I'm Nobody! Who Are You?"）。

Im Nobody! Who are you?
Are you—Nobody—too?
Then there's a pair of us!
Don't tell! They'd advertise—you know!
How dreary—to be—Somebody!
How public—like a Frog—
To tell one's name—the livelong June—
To an admiring Bog!

在翻译中，如果只是完成单词、语义上的对等，实现语言转换，倒不成问题。但是，如果要准确翻译出迪金森诗歌中那些大写的单词，还有满篇的破折号的言外之意或"对等形式"，就不容易了。迪金森写诗不单注重文字的使用，还讲究纸张、字体等的使用。她可以在任何纸片上写诗——信封的背面、巧克力包装纸、废纸的背面等（见图1.1），还会根据纸张的形状编排诗行（见图1.2）。

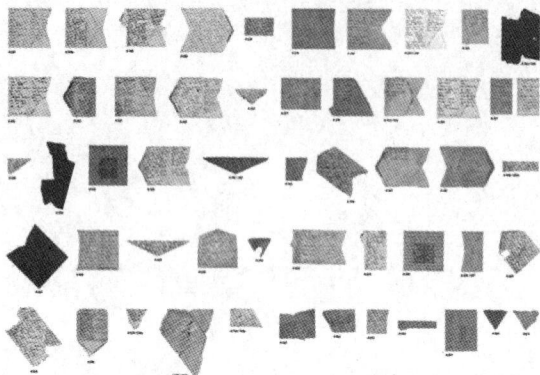

图 1.1　迪金森手稿一

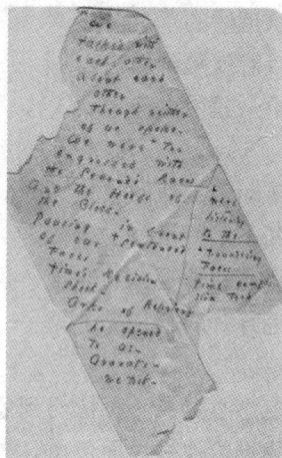

图 1.2　迪金森手稿二

迪金森还喜欢制作干花标本，从下图可以看出，除了注意花的品种，她对如何摆放不同的干花也很有考究。它们或按照原来的样子直接压制，或按照艺术的法则重新摆放。有的干花是带叶子的花朵直接制作，有的则是花和叶分别压制后再按一定的形状交错放在一起，还有一些则把花朵按照一定的形状摆开。

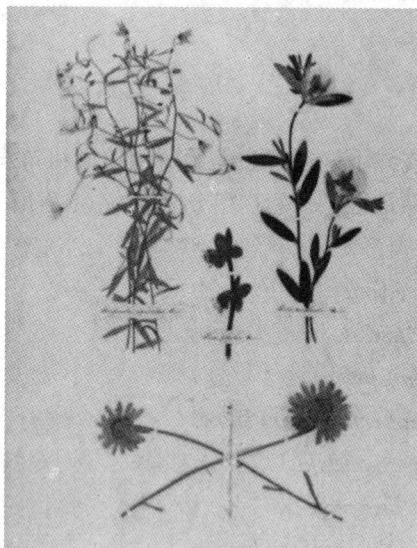

图 1.3　迪金森制作的干花标本

这些日常生活的细节，可以让我们更好地理解迪金森诗歌中对许多生活细节的描写以及许多看似微不足道的细小的形式方面的创新，如部分单词首字母的大写、破折号的使用等等。在《小鸟沿着小径走来》一诗中，大写的几个单词"小鸟""小径"和"蚯蚓"，第二节中有"露珠""草""墙""甲虫"，第三节中有"珠子""毛茸茸"，接下来的几节里还有"小心翼翼""面包屑""划""大海""彩蝶""河堤""中午"等，全部都是实词，其中大多数为名词，只有一两个是形容词。大写首字母后，就有了强调的意味，突出了意象。在中文诗歌传统中，这些词本身就可以构成诗歌了，如第二节的几个名词便呈现了一幅清新自然的夏日图景。在英语中，意象诗歌的传统要到 20 世纪的庞德才得以真正确立，而 19 世纪的迪金森似乎已经在无意识地使用这种方式创作诗歌了。迪金森诗歌中的破折号也起着强调或停顿的作用，因为翻译成中文，一些语序发生改变，破折号的位置也只能相应发生改变，这样的处理不免改变原文的蕴意，但为了意义的连贯，也是无奈之举。总体而言，迪金森诗歌中的形式创新，在翻译成中文的时候，很难保持意义和形式的双重对等。

　　事实上，这种形式上变换的转译的艰难，不仅发生在不同的语言之间，就是在同一种语言内部，也存在同样的难度。比如我国宋代诗人苏轼的这首《寒食帖》：

自我来黄州，已过三寒食。
年年欲惜春，春去不容惜。
今年又苦雨，两月秋萧瑟。
卧闻海棠花，泥污燕支雪。
暗中偷负去，夜半真有力，
何殊病少年，病起须已白。
春江欲入户，雨势来不已。
小屋如渔舟，蒙蒙水云里。
空庖煮寒菜，破灶烧湿苇。
那知是寒食，但见乌衔纸。
君门深九重，坟墓在万里。
也拟哭途穷，死灰吹不起。

从文字上，全诗意境萧索，凄凉惆怅，尤其是"苦雨""空庖""破灶""死灰"等意象的使用。如果能结合该帖的书法艺术（见图 1.4）来看，就更能体会诗人当时的心境。

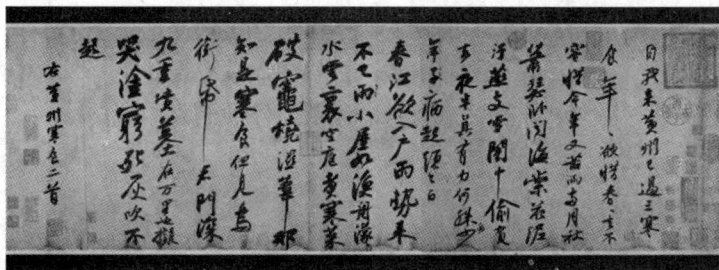

图 1.4　苏轼《寒食帖》（藏于国家博物馆）

　　从艺术上看，这幅帖是书法史上的名篇，整帖或正锋，或侧锋，转换多变，顺手断联，浑然天成。其结字亦奇，或大或小，或疏或密，有轻有重，有宽有窄，参差错落，恣肆奇崛，变化万千。从形式上看，"破灶烧湿苇"中的"苇"字的最后一竖，以及"那知是寒食，但见乌衔纸"一句中"纸"的最后一竖，都拉得很长、很细，成为视觉的焦点，深刻表达了作者内心的无奈和苦楚。而另外一些或粗或细的笔法，也让我们看到了诗人内心的起伏不平。将书法变化与诗歌内容放在一起解读，我们对诗人当时的心境，就会有更加深切的理解。书法形式上的这些特征，很少出现在流传广泛的苏轼选集里，也没有体现在上述的文字中。因此，要想更好地理解这首诗，就必须结合着苏轼当年的手稿一起看。同理，在解读迪金森这样注重形式创新的作家的时候，我们也要尽可能搜集各方面资料，细心体会她在这方面的不俗表现，从而保证我们的翻译能真正实现"化境"的目的。

第三节　翻译练习

一、《古诗十九首·明月皎夜光》

明月皎夜光，促织鸣东壁。
玉衡指孟冬，众星何历历。
白露沾野草，时节忽复易。
秋蝉鸣树间，玄鸟逝安适。
昔我同门友，高举振六翮。
不念携手好，弃我如遗迹。
南箕北有斗，牵牛不负轭。
良无盘石固，虚名复何益？

二、《登高》

风急天高猿啸哀，渚清沙白鸟飞回。
无边落木萧萧下，不尽长江滚滚来。
万里悲秋常作客，百年多病独登台。
艰难苦恨繁霜鬓，潦倒新停浊酒杯。

三、Sonnet 29

When, in disgrace with fortune and men's eyes,
I all alone beweep my outcast state,
And trouble deaf heaven with my bootless cries,
And look upon myself and curse my fate,
Wishing me like to one more rich in hope,
Featured like him, like him with friends possessed,

Desiring this man's art and that man's scope,
With what I most enjoy contented least；
Yet in these thoughts myself almost despising,
Haply I think on thee，and then my state,
(Like to the lark at break of day arising
From sullen earth) sings hymns at heaven's gate;
For thy sweet love remembered such wealth brings
That then I scorn to change my state with kings.

四、"Departmental"

An ant on the tablecloth
Ran into a dormant moth
Of many times his size.
He showed not the least surprise.
His business wasn't with such.
He gave it scarcely a touch,
And was off on his duty run.
Yet if he encountered one
Of the hive's enquiry squad
Whose work is to find out God
And the nature of time and space,
He would put him onto the case.
Ants are a curious race；
One crossing with hurried tread
The body of one of their dead
Isn't given a moment's arrest—
Seems not even impressed.
But he no doubt reports to any
With whom he crosses antennae,
And they no doubt report
To the higher-up at court.
Then word goes forth in Formic：
"Death's come to Jerry McCormic,
Our selfless forager Jerry.
Will the special Janizary
Whose office it is to bury
The dead of the commissary

Go bring him home to his people.

Lay him in state on a sepal.

Wrap him for shroud in a petal.

Embalm him with ichor of nettle.

This is the word of your Queen. "

And presently on the scene

Appears a solemn mortician;

And taking formal position,

With feelers calmly atwiddle,

Seizes the dead by the middle,

And heaving him high in air,

Carries him out of there.

No one stands round to stare.

It is nobody else's affair

It couldn't be called ungentle

But how thoroughly departmental

第二章　小说的翻译

小说是一种叙事性的文学体裁，通过人物的塑造、情节和环境的描述来表现社会生活的矛盾，一般分为长篇小说、中篇小说和短篇小说。

第一节　文体特征

本节通过名家名篇选读，主要从人物、视角和修辞几个方面探讨小说的基本特征。

一、人物

We may divide characters into flat and round. Flat characters were called "humorous" in the seventeenth century, and are sometimes called types, and sometimes caricatures. In their purest form, they are constructed round a single idea or quality: when there is more than one factor in them, we get the beginning of the curve towards the round. Flat character can be expressed in one sentence such as "I never will desert Mr. Micawber." There is Mrs. Micawber—she says she won't desert Mr. Micawber, she doesn't, and there she is. Or: "I must conceal, even by subterfuges, the poverty of my master's house." There is Caleb Balderstone in *The Bride of Lammermoor*. He does not use the actual phrase, but it completely describes him; he has no existence outside it, no pleasures, none of the private lusts and aches that must complicate the most consistent of servitors. Whatever he does, wherever he goes, whatever lies he tells or plates he breaks, it is to conceal the poverty of his master's house. It is not his *idée fixe*, because there is nothing in him into which the idea can be fixed. He is the idea, and such life as he possesses radiates from its edges and from the scintillations it strikes when other elements in the novel impinge. Or take Proust. There are numerous flat characters in Proust, such as the Princess of Parma, or Legrandin. Each can be expressed in a single sentence, the Princess's sentence being, "I must be particularly careful to be kind." She does nothing except to be particularly careful, and those of the other characters who are more complex than herself easily see through the kindness, since it is only a by-product of the carefulness.

One great advantage of flat characters is that they are easily recognized whenever they come in—recognized by the reader's emotional eye, not by the visual eye, which merely notes the recurrence of a proper name. In Russian novels, where they so seldom occur, they would be a decided help. It is a convenience for an author when he can strike with his full force at once, and flat characters are very useful to him, since they never need reintroducing, never run away, have not to be watched for development, and provide their own atmosphere—little luminous disks of a pre-arranged size, pushed hither and thither like counters across the void or between the stars; most satisfactory.

A second advantage is that they are easily remembered by the reader afterwards. They remain in his mind as unalterable for the reason that they were not changed by circumstances; they moved through circumstances, which gives them in retrospect a comforting quality, and preserves them when the book that produced them may decay. The Countess in *Evan Harrington* furnishes a good little example here. Let us compare our memories of her with our memories of Becky Sharp. We do not remember what the Countess did or what she passed through. What is clear is her figure and the formula that surrounds it, namely, "Proud as we are of dear papa, we must conceal his memory." All her rich humour proceeds from this. She is a flat character. Becky is round. She, too, is on the make, but she cannot be summed up in a single phrase, and we remember her in connection with the great scenes through which she passed and as modified by those scenes—that is to say, we do not remember her so easily because she waxes and wanes and has facets like a human being. All of us, even the sophisticated, yearn for permanence, and to the unsophisticated permanence is the chief excuse for a work of art. We all want books to endure, to be refuges, and their inhabitants to be always the same, and flat characters tend to justify themselves on this account.

All the same, critics who have their eyes fixed severely upon daily life—as were our eyes last week—have very little patience with such renderings of human nature. Queen Victoria, they argue, cannot be summed up in a single sentence, so what excuse remains for Mrs. Micawber? One of our foremost writers, Mr. Norman Douglas, is a critic of this type, and the passage from him which I will quote puts the case against flat characters in a forcible fashion. The passage occurs in an open letter to D. H. Lawrence, with whom he is quarrelling: a doughty pair of combatants, the hardness of whose hitting makes the rest of us feel like a lot of ladies up in a pavilion. He complains that Lawrence, in a biography, has falsified the picture by employing "the novelist's touch", and he goes on to define what this is:

It consists, I should say, in a failure to realize the complexities of the ordinary human mind; it selects for literary purposes two or three facets of a man or woman, generally the most spectacular, and therefore useful ingredients of their character and disregards all the others. Whatever fails to fit in with these specially chosen traits is eliminated—must be eliminated, for otherwise the description would not hold water. Such and such are the data: everything incompatible with those data has to go by the board. It follows that the novelist's touch argues, often logically, from a wrong premise: it takes what it likes and leaves the rest. The facets may be correct as far as they go but there are too few of them: what the author says may be true and yet by no means the truth That is the novelist's touch. It falsifies life.

Well, the novelist's touch as thus defined is, of course, bad in biography, for no human being is simple. But in a novel it has its place: a novel that is at all complex often requires flat people as well as round, and the outcome of their collisions parallels life more accurately than Mr. Douglas implies. The case of Dickens is significant. Dickens' people are nearly all flat (Pip and David Copperfield attempt roundness, but so diffidently that they seem more like bubbles than solids). Nearly everyone can be summed up in a sentence, and yet there is this wonderful feeling of human depth. Probably the immense vitality of Dickens causes his characters to vibrate a little, so that they borrow his life and appear to lead one of their own. It is a conjuring trick; at any moment we may look at Mr. Pickwick edgeways and find him no thicker than a gramophone record. But we never get the sideway view. Mr. Pickwick is far too adroit and well-trained. He always has the air of weighing something, and when he is put into the cupboard of the young ladies'school he seems as heavy as Falstaff in the buck-basket at Windsor. Part of the genius of Dickens is that he does use types and caricatures, people whom we recognize the instant they re-enter, and yet achieves effects that are not mechanical and a vision of humanity that is not shallow. Those who dislike Dickens have an excellent case. He ought to be bad. He is actually one of our big writers, and his immense success with types suggests that there may be more in flatness than the severer critics admit.

Or take H. G. Wells. With the possible exceptions of Kipps and the aunt in *Tono Bungay*, all Wells' characters are as flat as a photograph. But the photographs are agitated with such vigour that we forget their complexities lie on the surface and would disappear if it were scratched or curled up. A Wells' character cannot indeed be summed up in a single phrase; he is tethered much more to observation, he does not create types. Nevertheless his people seldom pulsate by their own strength. It is the deft and powerful hands of their maker that shake them and trick the reader into a sense of depth. Good but imperfect novelists, like Wells and Dickens, are very clever at transmitting force. The part of their novel that is alive galvanizes the part that is not, and causes the characters to jump about and speak in a convincing way. They are quite different from the perfect novelist who touches all his material directly, who seems to pass the creative finger down every sentence and into every word. Richardson, Defoe, Jane Austen, are perfect in this particular way; their work may not be great but their hands are always upon it; there is not the tiny interval between the touching of the button and the sound of the bell which occurs in novels where the characters are not under direct control.

For we must admit that flat people are not in themselves as big achievements as round ones, and also that they are best when they are comic. A serious or tragic flat character is apt to be a bore. Each time he enters crying "Revenge!" or "My heart bleeds for humanity!" or whatever his formula is, our hearts sink. One of the romances of a popular contemporary writer is constructed round a Sussex farmer who says, "I'll plough up that bit of gorse." There is the farmer, there is the gorse; he says he'll plough it up, he does plough it up, but it is not like saying "I'll never desert Mr. Micawber", because we are so bored by his consistency that we do not care whether he succeeds with the gorse or fails. If his formula were analysed and connected up with the rest of the human outfit, we should not be bored any longer, the formula would cease to be the man and become an obsession in the man; that is to say he would have turned from a flat farmer into a round one. It is only round people who are fit to perform tragically for any length of time and can move us to any feelings except humour and appropriateness.

So now let us desert these two-dimensional people, and by way of transition to the round, let us go to *Mansfield Park*, and look at Lady Bertram, sitting on her sofa with pug. Pug is flat, like most animals in fiction. He is once represented as straying into a rosebed in a cardboard kind of way, but that is all, and during most of the book his mistress seems to be cut out of the same simple material as her dog. Lady Bertram's formula is, "I am kindly, but must not be fatigued," and she functions out of it. But at the end there is a catastrophe. Her two daughters come to grief—to the worst grief known to Miss Austen's universe, far worse than the Napoleonic wars. Julia elopes; Maria, who is unhappily married, runs off with a lover. What is Lady Bertram's reaction? The sentence describing it is significant: "Lady Bertram did not think deeply, but, guided by Sir Thomas, she thought justly on all important points, and she saw therefore in all its enormity, what had happened, and neither endeavoured herself, nor required Fanny to advise her, to think little of guilt and infamy." These are strong words, and they used to worry me because I thought Jane Austen's moral sense was getting out of hand. She may, and of course does, deprecate guilt and infamy herself, and she duly causes all possible distress in the minds of Edmund and Fanny, but has she any right to agitate calm, consistent Lady Bertram? Is not it like giving pug three faces and setting him to guard the gates of Hell? Ought not her ladyship to remain on the sofa saying, "This is a dreadful and sadly exhausting business about Julia and Maria, but where is Fanny gone? I have dropped another stitch"?

I used to think this, through misunderstanding Jane Austen's method—exactly as Scott misunderstood it when he congratulated her for painting on a square of ivory. She is a miniaturist, but never two dimensional. All her characters are round, or capable of rotundity. Even Miss Bates has a mind, even Elizabeth Eliot a heart, and Lady Bertram's moral fervour ceases to vex us when we realize this: the disk has suddenly extended and become a little globe. When the novel is closed, Lady Bertram goes back to the flat, it is true; the dominant impression she leaves can be summed up in a formula. But that is not how Jane Austen conceived her, and the freshness of her reappearances are due to this. Why do the characters in Jane Austen give us a slightly new pleasure each time they come in, as opposed to the merely repetitive pleasure that is caused by a character in Dickens? Why do they combine so well in a conversation, and draw one another out without seeming to do so, and never perform? The answer to this question can be put in several ways: that, unlike Dickens, she was a real artist, that she never stooped to caricature, etc. But the best reply is that her characters though smaller than his are more highly organized. They function all round, and even if her plot made greater demands on them than it does, they would still be adequate. Suppose that Louisa Musgrove had broken her neck on the Cobb. The description of her death would have been feeble and ladylike—physical violence is quite beyond Miss Austen's powers—but the survivors would have reacted properly as soon as the corpse was carried away, they would have brought into view new sides of their character, and though Persuasion would have been spoiled as a book, we should know more than we do about Captain Wentworth and Anne. All the Jane Austen characters are ready for an extended life, for a life which the scheme of her books seldom requires them to lead, and that is why they lead their actual lives so satisfactorily. Let us return to Lady Bertram and the crucial sentence. See how subtly it modulates from her formula into an area where the formula does not work. "Lady Bertram did not think deeply." Exactly: as per formula. "But guided by Sir Thomas she thought justly on all important points." Sir Thomas' guidance, which is part of the formula, remains, but it pushes her ladyship towards an independent and undesired morality. "She saw therefore in all its enormity what had happened." This is the moral fortissimo—very strong but carefully introduced. And then follows a most artful decrescendo, by means of negatives. "She neither endeavoured herself, nor required Fanny to advise her, to think little of guilt or infamy." The formula is reappearing, because as a rule she does try to minimize trouble, and does require Fanny to advise her how to do this; indeed Fanny has done nothing else for the last ten years. The words, though they are negatived, remind us of this, her normal state is again in view, and she has in a single sentence been inflated into a round character and collapsed back into a flat one. How Jane Austen can write! In a few words she has extended Lady Bertram, and by so doing she has increased the probability of the elopements of Maria and Julia. I say probability because the elopements belong to the domain of violent physical action, and here, as already indicated, Jane Austen is feeble and ladylike. Except in her schoolgirl novels, she cannot stage a crash. Everything violent has to take place "off"—Louisa's accident and Marianne Dashwood's putrid throat are the nearest exceptions—and consequently all the comments on the elopement must be sincere and convincing, otherwise we should doubt whether it occurred. Lady Bertram helps us to believe that her daughters have run away, and they have to run away, or there would be no apotheosis for Fanny. It is a little point, and a little sentence, yet it shows us how delicately a great novelist can modulate into the round.

All through her works we find these characters, apparently so simple and flat, never needing reintroduction and yet never out of their depth—Henry Tilney, Mr. Woodhouse, Charlotte Lucas. She may label her characters "Sense", "Pride", "Sensibility", "Prejudice", but they are not tethered to those qualities.

As for the round characters proper, they have already been defined by implication and no more need be said. All I need do is to give some examples of people in books who seem to me round so that the definition can be tested afterwards:

All the principal characters in *War and Peace*, all the Dostoevsky characters, and some of the Proust—for example, the old family servant, the Duchess of Guermantes, M. de Charlus, and Saint Loup; Madame Bovary—who, like Moll Flanders, has her book to herself, and can expand and secrete unchecked; some people in Thackeray—for instance, Becky and Beatrix; some in Fielding—Parson Adams, Tom Jones; and some in Charlotte Brontë, most particularly Lucy Snowe. (And many more—this is not a catalogue.) The test of a round character is whether it is capable of surprising in a convincing way. If it never surprises, it is flat. If it does not convince, it is a flat pretending to be round. It has the incalculability of life about it—life within the pages of a book. And by using it sometimes alone, more often in combination with the other kind, the novelist achieves his task of acclimatization and harmonizes the human race with the other aspects of his work.

(From E. M. Forster, Aspects of the Novel)

二、视角

Who's in Charge Here?

Perhaps the novelist's hardest task is deciding who should tell the story. Main character? Secondary character? And what's his attitude toward others in the tale and the events therein? Is she speaking from within the events as they happen or long after? An outside voice? Limited to a single character or omniscient? Telling all or holding back? Amused, bemused, deeply involved, or bored with it all? It is sometimes said that a change of viewpoint is a change of religion, that an age without firm belief in an all powerful God cannot utilize the omniscient narrator. While that may or may not be true, this is: the course of the novel is set once the viewpoint is established. Moreover, readers' relationships to the action and characters of the book rest on this critical decision. We cannot imagine a Gatsby narrated by anyone but Nick Carraway, a *Moby Dick* without the voice of Ishmael, or a *The Fellowship of the Ring* told by Frodo. We will be spending anywhere from thirty thousand to two hundred thousand words with this voice, this creature; some of us will even share our bed. Small wonder that the choice of narrator and point of view is never undertaken lightly.

And all this angst over a very small range of possibilities. Here's pretty much the whole list.

Third person omniscient (sometimes listed as simply "omniscient"). This is the "godlike" option of immense popularity in the nineteenth century. This narrator can be everywhere in his creation at once, so he always knows what everyone is thinking and doing. The Victorian versions often had loads of personality, but it existed outside the story; if they used "I," it was in the context of talking directly to the reader.

Third person limited. Like the omniscient narrator, this one is an outsider to the action, usually unidentified as anything other than a voice. This one, however, only identifies with one character, going where she goes and seeing what she sees, as well as recording her thoughts. It provides a fairly one-sided view of the action, although this is not the impediment it might seem.

Third person objective. This one sees everything from the outside, thereby offering only external hints at the characters' interior lives. Since this is pretty much the state we find ourselves in regarding everyone we know, it's not all that inviting. I don't need a book to be clueless about other people, thanks.

Stream of consciousness. Not exactly a narrator at all, more an extractor that goes into characters' heads to pull out their own narration of their existence. More anon, in a separate chapter.

Second person. A true rare bird. You can count the novels you'll encounter in second-person in a normal reading life on one hand, not use the thumb, and still have digits left free.

First person central. The main character makes his own excuses. Think of *Huck Finn* or *David Copperfield*. Probably more popular in novels of growing up than in any other subgenre, with the possible exception of hard-boiled detective novels.

First person secondary. Oh, like you need me to explain this one to you. The sidekick, the second banana, the minor player, the guy standing right next to the hero when he took the bullet—you get the idea. The levels of subtlety and subterfuge are almost limitless here, which explains its perennial popularity with novelists.

That's the lot. Doesn't seem like such a big deal, does it? Of course, there are endless combinatory possibilities when the novelist starts dragging in reports, depositions, letters, statements from the involved, and birthday cards from Aunt Maude, but they still fall under one or another of these few headings.

On the other hand, maybe the scarcity of options is precisely why the choice is a big deal: in such a limited universe, how can I make my novel stand out? Will my Bildungsroman (a German jawbreaker applied to those novels about growing up from childhood to adulthood) look like every other Bildungsroman if I use a first-person central narration? On the other hand, will it be recognizable as what it is if I don't tell the story that way? After all, every novel ever written helps to define the universe of the Novel, and sometimes definition involves limitation. It's hard to write a novel about a fraud who comes to a bad end for a phony dream in the first-person secondary without seeming to ape The Great Gatsby.

I don't, however, think that's the main issue. Certainly novelists are aware of how their new creation may fit into that universe, but concern over narrative viewpoint is more basic than that. It will determine everything, from how well we know the main character to how much we can trust what we're told to how long the book winds up being.

Everything?

Consider this: what are the longest novels you've ever read? *Vanity Fair. Middlemarch. Bleak House. Tom Jones. The Bonfire of the Vanities.* What element do those eight-hundred-page monstrosities have in common, aside from chest-crushing weight? Omniscience. Third-person omniscient narration is uniquely well suited to novels of great length. Indeed, it almost invariably causes them. Why? Nowhere to hide. If the novelist plays fair, and if he sets up a universe in which his narrator can know everything, then that figure must show what he knows. He can't have someone moving surreptitiously in the shadows in another part of town and pretend not to know who is moving, what they're doing, and why they're doing it. He's omniscient, for crying out loud. All-knowing. Can't very well say, simply because it serves his purpose, oh, I don't know this one thing. That's not playing the game. That's also why you don't see a lot of omniscience in mysteries. They require secrets. And narrators who can see into everyone's mind can't pretend there are secrets.

So what does work for a mystery? Third person limited or objective shows up a good bit. Either we only know the detective's thoughts or we know no one's. First person is good. British mystery novels incline more toward first person secondary, American toward first person central. Why? Because of the stories being told. British mysteries tend to be ratiocinative (from the Latin, meaning having to do with working things out by means of reason). They rely on the brilliance of the detective. If he tells the story, we'll see where his brilliance is taking us and lose all surprise. So instead, the story is told by someone who is, well, slightly dim. Sherlock Holmes has his Dr. Watson, Hercule Poirot his Captain Hastings (sometimes) or another, delegated-just-for-this-once civilian. These narrators aren't stupid, or no more so than ourselves, and we're not stupid. But they're only ordinarily intelligent, whereas Holmes or Poirot are brilliant in a way that's not entirely human. American mysteries, on the other hand, tend toward the hard-boiled (from the American, meaning I'm tougher than you and will beat or shoot my way to the truth). The detectives aren't particularly brilliant, but they are tough, tenacious, cocky, and often good company. So they tell their own stories, from Raymond Chandler's Philip Marlowe to Mickey Spillane's Mike Hammer to Sue Grafton's Kinsey Millhone. For people in a tight-lipped line of work, they prove to be surprisingly loquacious, joking and threatening their way through life. The choice of first-person narration helps establish their personality, particularly when, as in the case of Linda Barnes's Carlotta Carlyle or Millhone, they ironically undercut their position with self-effacing wisecracks. The other really useful thing this viewpoint accomplishes in these novels is to let the main character make mistakes. One of the hallmarks of the American hard-boiled detective story is that periodically the baddies get the upper hand and the hero gets captured, misled, beaten up, shot, or otherwise snookered. When this happens in a third-person narration, as when Sam Spade gets drugged in *The Maltese Falcon*, it seems like he's letting down the side. After all, we spend most of the novel watching him be nearly infallible, and then this happens. Incredible. On the flip side, Kinsey Millhone splits her time between telling us how professional she is and noting her shortcomings, so we're not surprised when she gets herself in a pickle.

Okay, then, so what can first-person narration do and what else is it good for? It creates the illusion of immediacy. And we might as well stop here for a digression on illusion and reality. None of this is real, right? There is no boy Tom Sawyer, no Becky Thatcher he's sweet on, no pal named Huck. They're all built up out of words to trick the mind into believing, if just for a little while, that they exist. The mind, for its part, has to play along, not only believing (or at least not disbelieving) but actively taking the elements and adding to them in ways that render a more complete portrait than the one that actually exists on the page. But also, and this is key, no narrator. That creature who talks to us for all those pages is no more real than the rest of the fiction. In fact, it's a general truth: there is something like the Law of Look Who's Talking: The narrator of a fictional work is an imaginative and linguistic construct, every bit as much as the characters or events. The "omniscience" of omniscient narration is not that of God but of a godlike fictional construct, and the "person" of first-or third-person narration is not the author but a made-up entity into which the author sends a voice. (I have made a career of studying ephemera and shadows and things not really there; I could just as well be an economist.) So when we talk about what effects a certain technique produces, we're really speaking of creating certain sorts of illusion. There, I'm glad I got that off my chest.

NOW THEN, THE PROBLEM with first-person narration: here are the disadvantages that make it thorny.

1. The narrator can't know what other people think.

2. The narrator can't go where other people go when he's not around.

3. He's frequently mistaken about other people.

4. He's frequently mistaken about himself.

5. He can never get more than a partial grasp on objective truth.

6. He may be hiding something.

Given those limitations, why would a writer choose to employ such a shaky point of view? Consider the advantages.

1. The narrator can't know what other people think.

2. The narrator can't go where other people go when he's not around.

3. He's frequently mistaken about other people.

4. He's frequently mistaken about himself.

5. He can never get more than a partial grasp on objective truth.

6. He may be hiding something.

So what are the effects and functions of the first person?

...

You can push that identification-equals-sympathy equation one more step and use first-person narration to write about really awful creatures. There are a significant number of novels in which the main character is a monster, usually figuratively but once in a while literally, but in any case some being who in any other sort of book would be the villain. Think about it: would you be friends with Alex, from *A Clockwork Orange* (1962)? Would you even want to *know* him? The thing that makes most people lose sleep at night is the thought that there might be an Alex in their county—amoral, murderous, delighting in the aesthetics of violence, waiting for opportunity. But the thing is, in print, in his own voice, Alex is a charmer. Intelligent. Handy with a phrase. Witty. Clever. Sympathetic. Now how do you get from "amoral" and "murderous" to "sympathetic"? Words. Alex—or rather, his creator, Anthony

Burgess—spins a web of words to ensnare us in the more attractive elements of his personality while shielding us from a too—direct view of his more heinous actions. And "spinning a web of words" is exactly how the eponymous antihero of John Gardner's *Grendel* describes his self-conscious movement through the world. Gardner's task is even tougher than Burgess's: the teenage thug is a fairly recent development, but Grendel has been the byword for evil for more than a millennium. Nor does the novelist want to rehabilitate him or make him cute and cuddly. He's still a monster, still eats people, still revels in mayhem and blood. Not exactly best-buddy material. What Gardner wants to do is something trickier and more challenging, to keep him a monster and nevertheless make him sympathetic. So he makes him a good deal like us (except for the people-eating part): witty, observant, interested in language and what it can do for good or ill, interested in and critical of the shortcomings of the human society around him, alienated, aggrieved, and a little bit sorry for himself. As a result, readers are able to see the necessity of Beowulf's ultimate triumph while regretting the loss of Grendel's remarkable voice. And if you can do that for a twelve-hundred-year-old monster, you've really done something.

Now, the fact that there are only six options, and more like four for all intents and purposes, doesn't really limit the way stories are told very much. Novelists can mix and match, adjust, vary, and just plain abuse the options they're presented with. In his masterful *Snow*, Orhan Pamuk employs a kaleidoscopic point of view that seems for much of the novel to be nearly omniscient, then limited, and finally first person as a narrator from outside the story proper, called Orhan just to confuse the issue, reveals that he has been assembling this tale from documents left by the main character, a poet named Ka, as well as statements made about the now-deceased writer by friends and acquaintances. Both the apparent omniscience and objectivity are illusory; as a friend, Orhan is moved by feelings of loyalty and confusion in recounting the events of Ka's final trip home to Turkey. And here's the problem with categories: they're often fairly crude devices. Snow is a remarkably subtle narrative performance. Is it "first-person secondary"? Well, yes, sort of. That is, the narrator turns out to be a named character. who interacts with others in the story. Yet he's also a chameleon who imitates the devices of various third-person points of view. The definition doesn't really account for the changes a writer of Pamuk's ability can bring.

And if that's a problematic first-person novel, try John Fowles's The *French Lieutenant's Woman* (1969), in which the third-person narrator actually appears. Twice. The book takes the form of a Victorian novel, exploiting its conventions of omniscience (when it suits the narrative purpose) and reader-narrator intimacy. Two times, however, a person resembling Fowles himself (in different guises) turns up, once in a railway carriage where he observes the main character and once toward the end, when he sets his watch back fifteen minutes, thereby allowing for the book's famous two endings. There is only one person who can reset time in a novel, and he's not a character inside the story. Moreover, Fowles frequently uses "I" to refer to the narrator, although he never interacts with anyone or anything in the story. Even his ride on the train and walk outside the residence of Dante Gabriel Rossetti have a kind of stage artifice about them, suggesting he is metaphorically, rather than literally, present. So then, first person? Third? Third, pretty clearly, since the narrator isn't really a character in the novel, but like Snow, Fowles's book is far more subtle and sinuous in its use of point of view than any mere definition can ever hope to be.

So what? Why should we care about narrative POV? Does it really matter if it's first or third—or that the definitions don't always get the job done?

Well, yes and no. First, the no. You can get through most novels satisfactorily without paying much attention to who's doing the telling. You'll get the general drift of almost every novel, and everything there is to get with a lot of them. But also, yes. Who narrates matters in terms of trust. In general, third-person narration can be relied upon to be accurate. Narratives with "I" —as we shall see shortly—not so much. Real people lie. Misremember. Get confused. In one of history's most famous writers' tiffs, Mary McCarthy said of her former friend Lillian Hellman that "every word she says is a lie, and that includes 'and' and 'the.'" If persons in the real world have a tenuous connection to veracity, why should we expect those in made-up stories to be more truthful?

But differences can matter in other ways, too. What's our relationship to the story told? How far removed are we from it? How immersed in it? How are we being manipulated to see events one way or another? These things are often dictated by the choice of narrator. So we just might want to notice who that elusive creature is.

(From Thomas C. Foster, *How to Read Novels like a Professor*，有删改)

视角的伦理意义

对于视角的应用，虽然古已有之，但相关理论的探讨，最早则源自西方的一些小说研究者。因早期尚未形成一种清晰的概念，所以在称谓上，在不同的研究者笔下也有所不同。如美国作家亨利·詹姆斯（Henry James）称之为"意识中心"（center of consciousness），伯西·卢伯克（Percy Lubbock）则将其提炼为"戏剧化思想"（dramatize a mind），E. M. 福斯特（E. M. Forster）在《小说面面观》（*Aspects of the Novel*）中将其称作"视角"（point of view），韦恩·布斯（Wayne Booth）则称之为"angle of vision"，亦可译作"视角"。热拉尔·热奈特（Gérard Genette）则发展了"聚焦"（focalization）理论。其中，詹姆斯是最早在创作手法中自觉使用人物视角这个手法的。詹姆斯曾在《小说的艺术》（*The Art of Fiction*）一书中多次提到该创作手法，为了区分于传统的全知全能的叙述模式，他曾运用许多形象生动的比喻来说明这种以小说中一个人物的视角为中心的手法是如何运作的，如"把问题的中心放在少女本人的意识中……完全依靠她和她个人的心理变化，把故事进行下去，记住，这就需要你真正来'创造她'""用那个青年女子的肺部去呼吸""那方法就是只是用一个中心，而且始终保持在我的男主人公的意识范围之内"。①

特里·伊格尔顿（Terry Eagleton）是当代英国最有影响力的马克思主义文化评论家，在他看来，现实主义小说的结构本身，很多时候就是一种道德实践，他以全知全能的叙述为例进行说明：

> 通过这种神圣的力量（内在审美力）我们可以进入别人的内心世界，打碎自我是为了能无私地、设身处地去理解他人。因此，随着视角从一个意识中心转移到另一个意识中心，一个复杂的整体形成了。经典的现实主义小说的结构就是一种道德实践。文学在没有释放出道德情感的时候，就已经是一种道德实践了。②

伊格尔顿提出，传统的小说经常采用全知全能的叙述手法，叙述者可以无障碍地从一个视角进入另一个视角，这本身就象征着人与人之间相互理解的可能，象征着那时的社会总体看来依然是一个有机的整体。就像 J. 希利斯·米勒（J. Hillis Miller）认为的那样，全知叙述的前提是可操作社群（Operative Community）的存在，其中叙述者是这个群体意识的代言人，他的评论可以有效引导阐释。③

当詹姆斯提出的"意识中心"逐渐取代了全知视角，成为现代、后现代小说的重要叙述手法之一的时候，个人视角逐渐代替全知视角，这恰恰也意味着个人主义的崛起和对权威的质疑的时代的开启。在具体的小说创作中，视角本身的选择常常也成为一种道德实践。在詹姆斯看来，福楼拜的《情感教育》（*Sentimental Education*）最大的失败在于使用一个道德缺陷的男主人公作为意识中心。詹姆斯本人的创作对人物视角的选择颇有讲究。他笔下的主人公，除了《大使》（*The Ambassadors*）中采取了男性的意识中心，其他的大多数作品，如《一位女性的画像》（*The Portrait of a Lady*）、《鸽翼》（*The Wings of the Dove*）和《金碗》（*The Golden Bowl*）等，都采取了女性的"意识中心"。詹姆斯选取女性视角为中心，深入女性内心，以女性的眼光去看待周边的世界。从这个角度上看，无论作品的内容如何，在结构上已经表达了作者对女性命运的同情和关注，正如他在《一位女士的画像》的序言里写的那样："天天有千百万骄傲的少女，不论聪明的或不聪明的，在对抗着她们的命运，那么这对她们未来的命运究竟有什么影响，以致值得我们来为它呕心沥血？"④ 可见，作家在选择视角的时候，就隐含着对视点人物的同情了，而这已经是一种道德实践了。

在布斯看来，福楼拜的《爱玛》（*Emma*）中的女主人公爱玛有很多道德缺陷，但由于故事是通过她的内视点（inside view）呈现的，读者仍与她站在同一战线并喜爱

---

① 〔美〕亨利·詹姆斯：《小说的艺术》，朱雯等译，上海：上海译文出版社，2001 年，第 290～328 页。
② Terry Eagleton, *The Event of Literature*. New Haven and London：Yale University Press，2012. p. 60.
③ 赵毅衡：《当说者被说的时候：比较叙述学导论》，成都：四川文艺出版社，2013 年，第 142 页。
④ 亨利·詹姆斯：《小说的艺术》，第 287 页。

她。持续的内视点使读者希望与他共行的那个人有好运，无论其品质好坏。[①] 内视点最独特之处，在于它让读者对一个不那么完美的女主角产生了同情和理解。事实上，视点选择的道德性，还与人们的认知过程密切相关。人们对于不断出现在自己视线中的人物或事物，往往比对陌生人物或事物，更容易产生好感和认同。赵毅衡认为，视角引发同情的原因可能是美学上的"内模仿"，即从外到内的"移情"。谷鲁斯的"内模仿说"认为，审美主体在欣赏活动中，总能分享对象的姿态和运动，会有一种内模仿的运动神经活动，从而在主体的心灵中产生一种自觉或主动的幻觉，仿佛要把自我变形投射到旁人或外物中去，同时又把对象的审美情趣吸引到自身来。这一点类似于审美心理中的移情说。在具体的审美过程中，读者往往会同情视点人物，并认同其行为。关于这一点，我国梁启超先生曾有过生动而形象的论述：

> 凡读小说者，必常若自化其身焉——入于书中，而为其书之主人翁。读《野叟曝言》者，必自拟文素臣；读《石头记》者，必自拟贾宝玉；读《花月痕》者，必自拟韩荷生若韦痴珠；读梁山泊者，必自拟黑旋风若花和尚；虽读者自辩其无是心焉，吾不信也。夫既化其身以入书中矣，则当其读此书时，此身已非我有，截然去此界以入于彼界，所谓华严楼阁，帝网重重，一毛孔中万亿莲花，一弹指顷百千浩劫，文字移人，至此而极！然则吾书中主人翁而华盛顿，则读者将化身为华盛顿；主人翁而拿破仑，则读者将化身为拿破仑；主人翁而释迦、孔子，则读者将化身为释迦、孔子，有断然也。度世之不二法门，岂有过此？[②]

梁先生指出，文字具有"移人"之功效，在阅读中，读者常常会不自觉地内化主人公的意识，并受到影响，以小说主人公的角度去认识周边的事物。尽管电影和小说在表现媒介上有很多的不同，但同作为想象性的艺术，就其叙述手法而言，无论从叙述者和接受者的角度看，电影与小说都有诸多类似之处。如小说一样，电影视角的人物的所思所想、所闻所见，常常也会潜移默化地影响观众的看法。

三、修辞

Authorative "Telling" in Early Narration

One of the most obviously artificial devices of the storyteller is the trick of going beneath the surface of the action to obtain a reliable view of a character's mind and heart. Whatever our ideas may be about the natural way to tell a story, artifice is unmistakably present whenever the author tells us what no one in so-called real life could possibly know. In life we never know anyone but ourselves by thoroughly reliable internal signs, and most of us achieve an all too partial view even of ourselves. It is in

---

① Wayne C. Booth, *The Rhetoric of Fiction*. Chicago: The University of Chicago Press, 1983. p. 246.
② 梁启超：《论小说与群治关系》，《新小说》，1902 年第 1 卷第 1 期，第 24~31 页。

a way strange, then, that in literature from the very beginning we have been told motives directly and authoritatively without being forced to rely on those shaky inferences about other men which we cannot avoid in our own lives.

"There was a man in the land of Uz, whose name was Job; and that man was perfect and upright, one that feared God, and eschewed evil." With one stroke the unknown author has given us a kind of information never obtained about real people, even about our most intimate friends. Yet it is information that we must accept without question if we are to grasp the story that is to follow. In life if a friend confided his view that his friend was "perfect and upright", we would accept the information with qualifications imposed by our knowledge of the speaker's character or of the general fallibility of mankind. We could never trust even the most reliable of witnesses as completely as we trust the author of the opening statement about Job.

We move immediately in Job to two scenes presented with no privileged information whatever: Satan's temptation of God and Job's first losses and lamentations. But we conclude the first section with another judgment which no real event could provide for any observer: "In all this Job sinned not, nor charged God foolishly." How do we know that Job sinned not? Who is to pronounce on such a question? Only God himself could know with certainty whether Job charged God foolishly. Yet the author pronounces judgment, and we accept his judgment without question.

It might at first appear that the author does not require us to rely on his unsupported word, since he gives us the testimonial of God himself, conversing with Satan, to confirm his view of Job's moral perfection. And after Job has been pestered by his three friends and has given his own opinion about his experience, God is brought on stage again to confirm the truth of Job's view. But clearly the reliability of God's statements ultimately depends on the author himself; it is he who names God and assures us that this voice is truly His.

This form of artificial authority has been present in most narrative until recent times. Though Aristotle praises Homer for speaking in his own voice less than other poets, even Homer writes scarcely a page without some kind of direct clarification of motives, of expectations, and of the relative importance of events. And though the gods themselves are often unreliable, Homer—the Homer we know—is not. What he tells us usually goes deeper and is more accurate than anything we are likely to learn about real people and events. In the opening lines of the *Iliad*, for example, we are told, under the half-pretense of an invocation, precisely what the tale is to be about: "the anger of Peleus'son Achilleus and its devastation". We are told directly that we are to care more about the Greeks than the Trojans. We are told that they were "heroes" with "strong souls". We are told that it was the will of Zeus that they should be "the delicate feasting of dogs". And we learn that the particular conflict between

Agamemnon, "the lord of men", and "brilliant" Achilles was set on by Apollo. We could never be sure of any of this information in real life, yet we are sure as we move through the *Iliad* with Homer constantly at our elbow, controlling rigorously our beliefs, our interests, and our sympathies. Though his commentary is generally brief and often disguised as simile, we learn from it the precise quality of every heart; we know who dies innocent and who guilty, who foolish and who wise. And we know, whenever there is any reason for us to know, what the characters are thinking: "the son of Tydeus pondered doubtfully / ... Three times in his heart and spirit he pondered turning..."

In the *Odyssey* Homer works in the same explicit and systematic way to keep our judgments straight. Though E. V. Rieu is no doubt correct in calling Homer an "impersonal" and "objective" author, in the sense that the life of the real Homer cannot be discovered in his work, Homer "intrudes" deliberately and obviously to insure that our judgment of the "heroic" "resourceful" "admirable" "wise" Odysseus will be sufficiently favorable. "Yet all the gods were sorry for him, except Poseidon, who pursued the heroic Odysseus with relentless malice till the day when he reached his own country."

Indeed, the major justification of the opening scene in the palace of Zeus is not as mere exposition of the facts of Odysseus' plight. What Homer requires of us is sympathetic involvement in that plight, and Athene's opening reply to Zeus provides authoritative judgment on what is to follow. "It is for Odysseus that my heart is wrung—the wise but unlucky Odysseus, who has been parted so long from all his friends and is pining on a lonely island far away in the middle of the seas." To her accusation of neglect, Zeus replies, "How could I ever forget the admirable Odysseus? He is not only the wisest man alive but has been the most generous in his offerings ... It is Poseidon ... who is so implacable towards him ..."

When we come to Odysseus' enemies, the poet again does not hesitate either to speak in his own person or to give divine testimony. Penelope's suitors must look bad to us; Telemachus must be admired. Not only does Homer dwell on Athene's approval of Telemachus, he lays on his own direct judgments with bright colors. The "insolent", "swaggering", and "ruffianly" suitors are contrasted to the "wise" (though almost helplessly young) Telemachus and the "good" Mentor. "Telemachus now showed his good judgment." Mentor "showed his good will now by rising to admonish his compatriots". We seldom encounter the suitors without some explicit attack by the poet: "This was their boastful way, though it was they who little guessed how matters really stood." And whenever there might be some doubt about where a character stands, Homer sets us straight: "'My Queen', replied Medon, who was by no means a villain ..." Hundreds of pages later, when Medon is spared from Odysseus' slaughter, we can hardly be surprised.

The result of all this direct guidance, when it is joined with Athene's divine attestation that the gods "have no quarrel" with Telemachus and have settled that he "shall come home safe", is to leave us, as we enter upon Odysseus' first adventure in Book Five, perfectly clear about what we should hope for and what fear; we are unambiguously sympathetic toward the heroes and contemptuous of the suitors. It need hardly be said that another poet, working with the same episodes but treating them from the suitors' point of view, could easily have led us into the same adventures with radically different hopes and fears.

> *Jim had a great trick that he used to play w'ile he was travelin'. For instance, he'd be ridin' on a train and they'd come to some little town like, well, like, we'll say, like Benton. Jim would look out of the train window and read the signs on the stores.*
>
> *For instance, they'd be a sign, "Henry Smith, Dry Goods." Well, Jim would write down the name and the name of the town and when he got to wherever he was goin' he'd mail back a postal card to Henry Smith at Benton and not sign no name to it, but he'd write on the card, well, somethin' like "Ask your wife about that book agent that spent the afternoon last week", or "Ask your Missus who kept her from gettin' lonesome the last time you was in Carterville." And he'd sign the card, "A Friend."*
>
> *Of course, he never knew what really come of none of these jokes, but he could picture what probably happened and that was enough. Jim was a card.*

Most readers of Lardner's "Haircut" (1926) have recognized that Lardner's opinion of Jim is radically different here from the speaker's. But no one in the story has said so. Lardner is not present to say so, not, at least, in the sense that Homer is present in his epics. Like many other modern authors, he has effaced himself, renounced the privilege of direct intervention, retreated to the wings and left his characters to work out their own fates upon the stage.

> *In sleep she knew she was in her bed, but not the bed she had lain down in a few hours since, and the room was not the same but it was a room she had known somewhere. Her heart was a stone lying upon her breast outside of her; her pulses lagged and paused, and she knew that something strange was going to happen, even as the early morning winds were cool through the lattice ...*
>
> *Now I must get up and go while they are all quiet. Where are my things? Things have a will of their own in this place and hide where they like ... Now what horse shall I borrow for this journey I do not mean to take?. Come now, Graylie, she said, taking the bridle, we must outrun Death and the Devil .*

The relation between author and spokesman is more complex here. Katherine Anne Porter's Miranda ("Pale Horse, Pale Rider") cannot be simply classified, like Lardner's barber, as morally and intellectually deficient; the ironies at work among character, author, and reader are considerably more difficult to describe. Yet the problem for the reader is essentially the same as in "Haircut". The story is presented without comment, leaving the reader without the guidance of explicit evaluation.

Since Flaubert, many authors and critics have been convinced that "objective" or "impersonal" or "dramatic" modes of narration are naturally superior to any mode that allows for direct appearances by the author or his reliable spokesman. Sometimes, as we shall see in the next three chapters, the complex issues involved in this shift have been reduced to a convenient distinction between "showing", which is artistic, and "telling", which is inartistic. "I shall not tell you anything," says a fine young novelist in defense of his art. "I shall allow you to eavesdrop on my people, and sometimes they will tell the truth and sometimes they will lie, and you must determine for yourself when they are doing which. You do this every day. Your butcher says, 'This is the best,' and you reply, 'That's you saying it/ Shall my people be less the captive of their desires than your butcher? I can show much, but show only ...' You will no more expect the novelist to tell you precisely how something is said than you will expect him to stand by your chair and hold your book."

But the changed attitudes toward the author's voice in fiction raise problems that go far deeper than this simplified version of point of view would suggest. Percy Lubbock taught us forty years ago to believe that "the art of fiction does not begin until the novelist thinks of his story as a matter to be shown to be so exhibited that it will tell itself". He may have been in some sense right—but to say so raises more questions than it answers.

Why is it that an episode "told" by Fielding can strike us as more fully realized than many of the scenes scrupulously "shown" by imitators of James or Hemingway? Why does some authorial commentary ruin the work in which it occurs, while the prolonged commentary of Tristram Shandy can still enthral us? What, after all, does an author do when he "intrudes" to "tell" us something about his story? Such questions force us to consider closely what happens when an author engages a reader fully with a work of fiction; they lead us to a view of fictional technique which necessarily goes far beyond the reductions that we have sometimes accepted under the concept of "point of view".

(From Wayne Booth, *The Rhetoric of Fiction*，有删改)

Repetition

In the fall the war was always there, but we did not go to it any more. It was cold in the fall in Milan and the dark came very early. Then the electric lights came on, and it was pleasant along the streets looking in the windows. There was much game hanging outside the shops, and the snow powdered in the fur of the foxes and the wind blew their tails. The deer hung stiff and heavy and empty, and small birds blew in the wind and the wind turned their feathers. It was a cold fall and the wind came down from the mountains.

We were all at the hospital every afternoon, and there were different ways of walking across the town through the dusk to the hospital. Two of the ways were alongside canals, but they were long. Always, though, you crossed a bridge across a canal to enter the hospital. There was a choice of three bridges. On one of them a woman sold roasted chestnuts. It was warm, standing in front of her charcoal fire, and the chestnuts were warm afterward in your pocket. The hospital was very old and very beautiful, and you entered through a gate and walked across a courtyard and out a gate on the other side. There were usually funerals starting from the courtyard. Beyond the old hospital were the new brick pavilions, and there we met every afternoon and were all very polite and interested in what was the matter, and sat in the machines that were to make so much difference.

If you have the time and inclination, get some coloured pens or pencils and draw a ring round the words that occur more than once in the first paragraph of Hemingway's story, a different colour for each word, and join them up. You will reveal a complex pattern of verbal chains linking words of two kinds: those with referential meaning, *fall*, *cold*, *dark*, *wind*, *blew*, which we can call lexical words, and articles, prepositions and conjunctions like *the*, *of*, *in*, *and*, which we can call grammatical words.

It is almost impossible to write English without the repetition of grammatical words, so normally we don't notice it as such, but you can't fail to notice the extraordinary number of "*ands*" in this short paragraph. This is a symptom of its very repetitive syntax, stringing together declarative statements without subordinating one to another. The repetition of the lexical words is less evenly distributed, clustering at the beginning and end of the paragraph.

Lexical and grammatical repetition on this scale would probably receive a black mark in a school "composition", and quite rightly. The traditional model of good literary prose requires "elegant variation": if you have to refer to something more than once, you should try to find alternative ways of describing it; and you should give your syntax the same kind of variety. (The passage by Henry James discussed in Section 6 is rich in examples of both kinds of variation.)

Hemingway, however, rejected traditional rhetoric, for reasons that were partly literary and partly philosophical. He thought that "fine writing" falsified experience, and strove to "put down what really happened in action, what the actual things were which produced the emotion that you experienced" by using simple, denotative language purged of stylistic decoration.

It looks easy, but of course it isn't. The words are simple but their arrangement is not. There are many possible ways of arranging the words of the first sentence, but the one chosen by Hemingway splits the phrase "go to war" in two, implying an as yet unexplained tension in the persona of the narrator, a mixture of relief and irony. As we soon learn, he and his companions are soldiers wounded while fighting on the Italian side in World War I, now recuperating, but conscious that the war which nearly killed them may have made their lives not worth living anyway. It is a story about trauma, and how men cope with it, or fail to cope. The unspoken word which is a key to all the repeated words in the text is "death".

The American word for autumn, *fall*, carries in it a reminder of the death of vegetation, and echoes the conventional phrase for those who die in battle, "the fallen". Its juxtaposition with *cold* and *dark* in the second sentence strengthens these associations. The brightly lit shops seem to offer some distraction (an effect heightened by the fact that there is no lexical repetition in this sentence) but the narrator's attention quickly focuses on the game hanging outside the shops, further emblems of death. The description of the snow powdering in their fur, and the wind ruffling their feathers, is literal and exact, but tightens the association of *fall*, *cold*, *dark*, *wind*, *blew*, with death. Three of the repeated words come together for the first time in the last sentence with a poetic effect of closure: "It was a cold fall and the wind came down from the mountains." The mountains are where the war is going on. Wind, so often a symbol of life and spirit in religious and Romantic writing, is here associated with lifelessness. God is very dead in these early stories of Hemingway. The hero has learned from the trauma of combat to distrust metaphysics as well as rhetoric. He trusts only his senses, and sees experience in starkly polarized terms: cold/warm, light/dark, life/death.

The incantatory rhythms and repetitions persist in the second paragraph. It would have been easy to find elegant alternatives for "hospital", or simply to have used the pronoun "it" occasionally; but the hospital is the centre of the soldiers' lives, their daily place of pilgrimage, the repository of their hopes and fears, and the repetition of the word is therefore expressive. It is possible to vary the route by which the hospital is reached, but the terminus is always the same. There is a choice of bridges, but always you have to cross a canal (a faint suggestion of the river Styx in the underworld, perhaps). The narrator prefers the bridge where he can buy roasted chestnuts, warm in the pocket like the promise of life—except that Hemingway doesn't use that simile, he merely implies it; just as in the first paragraph he manages to make his description of the season as emotionally powerful as any example of the pathetic fallacy (see the preceding section) without using a metaphor. The line between charged simplicity and mannered monotony is a fine one, and Hemingway didn't always stay on the right side of it, but in his early work he forged an entirely original style for his times.

Needless to say, repetition is not necessarily linked to a bleakly positivist, anti-metaphysical representation of life such as we find in Hemingway. It is also a characteristic feature of religious and mystical writing, and is used by novelists whose work tends in that direction—D. H. Lawrence, for instance. The language of the opening chapter of *The Rainbow*, evoking a lost agrarian way of life, echoes the verbal repetition and syntactical parallelism of the Old Testament:

> *The young corn waved and was silken, and the lustre slid along the limbs of the men who saw it. They took the udder of the cows, the cows yielded milk and pulsed against the hands of the men, the pulse of the blood of the teats of the cows beat into the pulse of the hands of the men.*

Repetition is also a favourite device of orators and preachers, roles that Charles Dickens often adopted in his authorial persona. This, for instance, is the conclusion to his chapter describing the death of Jo, the destitute crossing-sweeper, in *Bleak House*:

> *Dead, your Majesty. Dead, my lords and gentlemen. Dead, Right Reverends and Wrong Reverends of every order. Dead, men and women, born with Heavenly compassion in your hearts. And dying thus around us every day.*

And of course repetition can be funny, as in this passage from Martin Amis's *Money*:

> *Intriguingly enough, the only way I can make Selina actually want to go to bed with me is by not wanting to go to bed with her. It never fails. It really puts her in the mood. The trouble is, when I don't want to go to bed with her (and it does happen), I don't want to go to bed with her. When does it happen? When don't I want to go to bed with her? When she wants to go to bed with me. I like going to bed with her when going to bed with me is the last thing she wants. She nearly always does go to bed with me, if I shout at her a lot or threaten her or give her enough money.*

It hardly needs to be pointed out that the frustrations and contradictions of the narrator's sexual relationship with Selina are rendered all the more comic and ironic by the repetition of the phrase "go to bed with" for which any number of alternatives were available. (If you doubt that, try rewriting the passage using elegant variation.) The final sentence also illustrates another important type of repetition: the recurrence of a thematic keyword throughout an entire novel—in this case, "money". It is "money" not "go to bed" that occupies the crucially important last-word space in the paragraph I have just quoted. Thus one kind of repetition, belonging to the macro-level of the text, functions as variation on the micro-level.

(From *The Art of Fiction*: *Illustrated from Classic and Modern Texts*)

Symbolism

"The fool!" cried Ursula loudly. "Why doesn't he ride away till it's gone by?" Gudrun was looking at him with black-dilated, spellbound eyes. But he sat glistening and obstinate, forcing the wheeling mare, which spun and swerved like a wind, and yet could not get out of the grasp of his will, nor escape from the mad clamour of terror that resounded through her, as the trucks thumped slowly, heavily, horrifying, one after the other, one pursuing the other, over the rails of the crossing.

The locomotive, as if wanting to see what could be done, put on the brakes, and back came the trucks rebounding on the iron buffers, striking like horrible cymbals, clashing nearer and nearer in frightful strident concussions. The mare opened her mouth and rose slowly, as if lifted up on a wind of terror. Then suddenly her fore-feet struck out, as she convulsed herself utterly away from the horror. Back she went, and the two girls clung to each other, feeling she must fall backwards on top of him. But he leaned forward, his face shining with fixed amusement, and at last he brought her down, sank her down, and was bearing her back to the mark. But as strong as the pressure of his compulsion was the repulsion of her utter terror, throwing her back away from the railway, so that she spun round and round on two legs, as if she were in the centre of some whirlwind. It made Gudrun faint with poignant dizziness, which seemed to penetrate to her heart. ROUGHLY SPEAKING, anything that "stands for" something else is a symbol, but the process operates in many different ways. A cross may symbolize Christianity in one context, by association with the Crucifixion, and a road intersection in another, by diagrammatic resemblance. Literary symbolism is less easily decoded than these examples, because it tries to be original and tends towards a rich plurality, even ambiguity, of meaning (all qualities that would be undesirable in traffic signs and religious icons, especially the former). If a metaphor or simile consists of likening A to B, a literary symbol is a B that suggests an A, or a number of As. The poetic style known as Symbolism, which started in France in the late nineteenth century in the work of Baudelaire, Verlaine and Mallarmé, and exerted considerable influence on English writing in the twentieth, was characterized by a shimmering surface of suggested meanings without a denotative core.

Somebody once said, however, that the novelist should make his spade a spade before he makes it a symbol, and this would seem to be good advice for a writer who is aiming to create anything like the "illusion of life". If the spade is introduced all too obviously just for the sake of its symbolic meaning, it will tend to undermine the credibility of the narrative as human action. D. H. Lawrence was often prepared to take that risk to express a visionary insight—as when, in another episode of *Women in Love*, he has his hero rolling naked in the grass and throwing stones at the reflection of the moon. But in the passage quoted here he has kept a nice balance between realistic description and symbolic suggestion.

The "spade" in this case is a complex action: a man controlling a horse frightened by a colliery train passing at a level crossing, while being watched by two women. The man is Gerald Critch, the son of the local colliery owner, who manages the business and will eventually inherit it. The setting is the Nottinghamshire landscape in which Lawrence, a coalminer's son, was brought up: a pleasant countryside scarred and blackened in places by the pits and their railways. One might say that the train "symbolizes" the mining industry, which is a product of culture in the anthropological sense, and that the horse, a creature of Nature, symbolizes the countryside. Industry has been imposed on the countryside by the masculine power and will of capitalism, a process Gerald symbolically re-enacts by the way he dominates his mare, forcing the animal to accept the hideous mechanical noise of the train.

The two women in the scene are sisters, Ursula and Gudrun Brangwen, the former a teacher, the latter an artist. They are out on a country walk when they witness the scene at the level crossing. Both identify sympathetically with the terrified horse. Ursula is outraged by Gerald's behaviour, and speaks her mind. But the scene is described from Gudrun's point of view, and her response is more complex and ambivalent. There is sexual symbolism in the way Gerald controls his mount—at last he brought her down, sank her down, and was bearing her back to the mark" —and there is certainly an element of macho exhibitionism in his display of strength in front of the two women. Whereas Ursula is simply disgusted by the spectacle, Gudrun is sexually aroused by it, almost in spite of herself. The mare "spun round and round on two legs, as if she were in the centre of some whirlwind. It made Gudrun faint with poignant dizziness, which seemed to penetrate to her heart". "Poignant" is a transferred epithet, which logically belongs to the suffering of the horse; its rather odd application to "dizziness" expresses the turmoil of Gudrun's emotions, and calls attention to the root meaning of poignant—pricking, piercing—which, with "penetrate" in the next clause, gives a powerfully phallic emphasis to the whole description. A couple of pages later, Gudrun is described as "numbed in her mind by the sense of indomitable soft weight of the man bearing down into the living body of the horse; the strong, indomitable thighs of the blond man clenching the palpitating body of the mare into pure control". The whole scene is indeed prophetic of the passionate but mutually destructive sexual relationship that will develop later in the story between Gudrun and Gerald.

This rich brew of symbolic suggestion would, however, be much less effective if Lawrence did not at the same time allow us to picture the scene in vivid, sensuous detail. The ugly noise and motion of trucks as the train brakes is rendered in onomatopoeic syntax and diction ("clashing nearer and nearer in frightful strident concussions"), followed by an eloquent image of the horse, graceful even in panic: "The mare opened her mouth and rose slowly, as if lifted up on a wind of terror." Whatever you think of Lawrence's men and women, he was always brilliant when describing animals.

It is worth noting that symbolism is generated in two different ways in this passage. The Nature/Culture symbolism is modelled on the rhetorical figures of speech known as metonymy and synecdoche. Metonymy substitutes cause for effect or vice versa (the locomotive stands for Industry because it is an effect of the Industrial Revolution) and synecdoche substitutes part for whole or vice versa (the horse stands for Nature because it is part of Nature). The sexual symbolism, on the other hand, is modelled on metaphor and simile, in which one thing is equated with another on the basis of some similarity between them: Gerald's domination of his mare is described in such a way as to suggest a human sexual act. This distinction, originally formulated by the Russian structuralist Roman Jakobson, operates on every level of a literary text, and indeed outside literature too, as my heroine Robyn Penrose demonstrated to a sceptical Vic Wilcox in *Nice Work*, by analysing cigarette advertisements. For more examples of how it operates in fictional symbolism, see the passage by Graham Greene, discussed under the heading of "The Exotic" in Section 35.

(from David Lodge, *The Art of Fiction: Illustrated from Classic and Modern Texts*)

第二节 赏·译·评

一、《史记》节选

沛公旦日从百余骑来见项王，至鸿门，谢曰："臣与将军勠力而攻秦，将军战河北，臣战河南，然不自意能先入关破秦，得复见将军于此。今者有小人之言，令将军与臣有郤。"项王曰："此沛公左司马曹无伤言之。不然，籍何以至此。"项王即日因留沛公与饮。项王、项伯东向坐；亚父南向坐，——亚父者，范增也；沛公北向坐；张良西向侍。范增数目项王，举所佩玉玦以示之者三，项王默然不应。范增起，出，召项庄，谓曰："君王为人不忍。若入前为寿，寿毕，请以剑舞，因击沛公于坐，杀之。不者，若属皆且为所虏！"庄则入为寿。寿毕，曰："君王与沛公饮，军中无以为乐，请以剑舞。"项王曰："诺。"项庄拔剑起舞。项伯亦拔剑起舞，常以身翼蔽沛公，庄不得击。

（《项羽本纪》节选）

译

At this, still by night, Hsiang Po left, went back to his camp, and reported to King Hsiang in full what the Magistrate of P'ei had said. With this Hsiang Po said: "If the Magistrate of P'ei had not defeated the lands within the Pass first, how would you have dared to enter? Now he has great merit, and you would set upon him. This is unprincipled. It would be better to treat him well." King Hsiang gave his promise. At sunrise, the Magistrate of P'ei, accompanied by over one hundred horsemen, came to see King Hsiang. When he arrived at Hung-men, he apologized: "You and I joined forces and attacked Ch'in, General. You fought north of the Ho, I fought south of the Ho. But I never expected that I could enter the Pass first, vanquish Ch'in, and see you again here. Now, the words of petty men have caused a rift between us." King Hsiang said: "This was what Ts'ao Wu-shang, your Left Marshal, told me. If not [for this], how could I have come to [doubt you]?" King Hsiang took the opportunity to invite the Magistrate of P'ei to stay and drink with him that day. King Hsiang and Hsiang Po sat facing east; Ya-fu sat facing south (Ya Fu was Fan Tseng); the Magistrate of P'ei sat facing north; and Chang Liang, waiting upon them, sat facing west. Fan Tseng several times glanced at King Hsiang, thrice lifting up the horseshoe-shaped jade disc hung from his girdle to show him. King Hsiang was silent and did not respond. Fan Tseng rose and left to summon Hsiang Chuang, telling him: "Our king is too kind a person. Go in and proceed to offer a toast. After the toast, ask to do a sword dance and seize the opportunity to attack the Magistrate of P'ei on his mat and kill him.

Otherwise，all of you will be his captives.＂ Hsiang Chuang thus entered and offered a toast． After the toast，he said：＂My King and the Magistrate of P'ei are drinking，but there is nothing in camp with which to entertain you． Allow me to do a sword dance.＂ King Hsiang said：＂You have permission.＂ Hsiang Chuang drew his sword and began to dance． Hsiang Po likewise drew his sword and began to dance，constantly shielding the Magistrate of P'ei with his own body so that Hsiang Chuang was not able to strike him?

二、《阿Q正传》节选

优胜记略

阿Q不独是姓名籍贯有些渺茫，连他先前的"行状"也渺茫。因为未庄的人们之于阿Q，只要他帮忙，只拿他玩笑，从来没有留心他的"行状"的。而阿Q自己也不说，独有和别人口角的时候，间或瞪着眼睛道：

"我们先前——比你阔的多啦！你算是什么东西！"

阿Q没有家，住在未庄的土谷祠里；也没有固定的职业，只给人家做短工，割麦便割麦，舂米便舂米，撑船便撑船。工作略长久时，他也或住在临时主人的家里，但一完就走了。所以，人们忙碌的时候，也还记起阿Q来，然而记起的是做工，并不是"行状"；一闲空，连阿Q都早忘却，更不必说"行状"了。只是有一回，有一个老头子颂扬说："阿Q真能做！"这时阿Q赤着膊，懒洋洋的瘦伶仃的正在他面前，别人也摸不着这话是真心还是讥笑，然而阿Q很喜欢。

阿Q又很自尊，所有未庄的居民，全不在他眼神里，甚而至于对于两位"文童"也有以为不值一笑的神情。夫文童者，将来恐怕要变秀才者也；赵太爷钱太爷大受居民的尊敬，除有钱之外，就因为都是文童的爹爹，而阿Q在精神上独不表格外的崇奉，他想：我的儿子会阔得多啦！加以进了几回城，阿Q自然更自负，然而他又很鄙薄城里人，譬如用三尺三寸宽的木板做成的凳子，未庄人叫"长凳"，他也叫"长凳"，城里人却叫"条凳"，他想：这是错的，可笑！油煎大头鱼，未庄都加上半寸长的葱叶，城里却加上切细的葱丝，他想：这也是错的，可笑！然而未庄人真是不见世面的可笑的乡下人呵，他们没有见过城里的煎鱼！

阿Q"先前阔"，见识高，而且"真能做"，本来几乎是一个"完人"了，但可惜他体质上还有一些缺点。最恼人的是在他头皮上，颇有几处不知于何时的癞疮疤。这虽然也在他身上，而看阿Q的意思，倒也似乎以为不足贵的，因为他讳说"癞"以及一切近于"赖"的音，后来推而广之，"光"也讳，"亮"也讳，再后来，连"灯""烛"都讳了。一犯讳，不问有心与无心，阿Q便全疤通红的发起怒来，估量了对手，口讷的他便骂，气力小的他便打；然而不知怎么一回事，总还是阿Q吃亏的时候多。于是他渐渐的变换了方针，大抵改为怒目而视了。

谁知道阿Q采用怒目主义之后，未庄的闲人们便愈喜欢玩笑他。一见面，他们便假作吃惊的说：

"唉，亮起来了。"

阿Q照例的发了怒，他怒目而视了。

"原来有保险灯在这里！"他们并不怕。

阿Q没有法，只得另外想出报复的话来：

"你还不配……"这时候，又仿佛在他头上的是一种高尚的光荣的癞头疮，并非平常的癞头疮了；但上文说过，阿Q是有见识的，他立刻知道和"犯忌"有点抵触，便不再往底下说。

闲人还不完，只撩他，于是终而至于打。阿Q在形式上打败了，被人揪住黄辫子，在壁上碰了四五个响头，闲人这才心满意足的得胜的走了，阿Q站了一刻，心里想，"我总算被儿子打了，现在的世界真不像样……"于是也心满意足的得胜的走了。

阿Q想在心里的，后来每每说出口来，所以凡是和阿Q玩笑的人们，几乎全知道他有这一种精神上的胜利法，此后每逢揪住他黄辫子的时候，人就先一着对他说：

"阿Q，这不是儿子打老子，是人打畜生。自己说：人打畜生！"

阿Q两只手都捏住了自己的辫根，歪着头，说道：

"打虫豸，好不好？我是虫豸——还不放么？"

但虽然是虫豸，闲人也并不放，仍旧在就近什么地方给他碰了五六个响头，这才心满意足的得胜的走了，他以为阿Q这回可遭了瘟。然而不到十秒钟，阿Q也心满意足的得胜的走了，他觉得他是第一个能够自轻自贱的人，除了"自轻自贱"不算外，余下的就是"第一个"。状元不也是"第一个"么？"你算是什么东西"呢！？

阿Q以如是等等妙法克服怨敌之后，便愉快的跑到酒店里喝几碗酒，又和别人调笑一通，口角一通，又得了胜，愉快的回到土谷祠，放倒头睡着了。假使有钱，他便去押牌宝，一推人蹲在地面上，阿Q即汗流满面的夹在这中间，声音他最响：

"青龙四百！"

"咳～～～开～～～啦！"庄家揭开盒子盖，也是汗流满面的唱。"天门啦～～～角回啦～～～！人和穿堂空在那里啦～～～！阿Q的铜钱拿过来～～～！"

"穿堂一百——一百五十！"

阿Q的钱便在这样的歌吟之下，渐渐的输入别个汗流满面的人物的腰间。他终于只好挤出堆外，站在后面看，替别人着急，一直到散场，然后恋恋的回到土谷祠，第二天，肿着眼睛去工作。

但真所谓"塞翁失马安知非福"罢，阿Q不幸而赢了一回，他倒几乎失败了。

这是未庄赛神的晚上。这晚上照例有一台戏，戏台左近，也照例有许多的赌摊。做戏的锣鼓，在阿Q耳朵里仿佛在十里之外；他只听得庄家的歌唱了。他赢而又赢，铜钱变成角洋，角洋变成大洋，大洋又成了叠。他兴高采烈得非常：

"天门两块！"

他不知道谁和谁为什么打起架来了。骂声打声脚步声，昏头昏脑的一大阵，他才爬起来，赌摊不见了，人们也不见了，身上有几处很似乎有些痛，似乎也挨了几拳几脚似的，几个人诧异的对他看。他如有所失的走进土谷祠，定一定神，知道他的一堆洋钱不见了。赶赛会的赌摊多不是本村人，还到那里去寻根柢呢？

很白很亮的一堆洋钱！而且是他的——现在不见了！说是算被儿子拿去了罢，总还是忽忽不乐；说自己是虫豸罢，也还是忽忽不乐：他这回才有些感到失败的苦痛了。但他立刻转败为胜了。他擎起右手，用力的在自己脸上连打了两个嘴巴，热剌剌的有些痛；打完之后，便心平气和起来，似乎打的是自己，被打的是别一个自己，不久也就仿佛是自己打了别个一般，——虽然还有些热剌剌，——心满意足的得胜的躺下了。

他睡着了。

译

A Brief History of Ah-Q's Victories

It was not only Ah-Q's name and place of origin that were shrouded in mystery—but also the details of his early life. Because the good people of Weizhuang called upon him only to help out with odd jobs, or to serve as the butt of jokes, no one ever paid much attention to such niceties. Neither was Ah-Q himself particularly forthcoming on the subject, except when he got into arguments, viz.:

"My ancestors were much richer than yours! Scum!"

Ah-Q had no home of his own in Weizhuang, he lodged in the Temple of the God of the Earth and the God of the Five Grains. Neither, as the village odd-job man, did he have a fixed profession. If someone was needed to harvest wheat, he harvested wheat; if called upon to husk rice, he husked rice; if a boat wanted poling, that's what he did. If a job was likely to take a while, he lodged with his employer; but once it was over, he left. When people were in a hurry to get something done, therefore, they remembered Ah-Q—but only the odd jobs he could do for them, and not his life history. And as soon as they were no longer in such a hurry, Ah-Q and his elusive biographical details were quickly forgotten. "He puts his back into it, that Ah-Q!" an old man once admiringly remarked, considering our hero's bare, torpidly scrawny torso—that was the closest anyone ever got to constructing a personality profile of him. Those who overheard him couldn't make out whether his eulogizer was being genuine or sarcastic; but Ah-Q, at least, was delighted.

Ah-Q had a robust sense of his own self-worth, placing the rest of Weizhuang far beneath him in the social scale. Even the village's two aspiring young scholars—the Zhao and Qian sons—he considered with haughty contempt. In time, they could both reasonably be expected to get through at least the lowest rung of the official examinations—the path to power and riches. Their fathers, the venerable Mr Zhao and Mr Qian, therefore received the village's craven respect not just for their personal wealth, but also for their sons' academic prospects. Only Ah-Q remained invulnerable to the glamour of their future promise: My son will be much richer than them! he thought to himself. A few trips into town further bolstered Ah-Q's amour propre, adding townspeople to his already abundant store of subjects of scorn. People in town couldn't get anything right: they said "narrow benches" for the wooden trestles, three feet long by three inches wide, that the people of Weizhuang—him included—quite correctly called "long benches". How stupid can people be! he thought. Or when frying fish, the people of Weizhuang cut their spring onions into halfinch lengths, while townspeople shredded them. How stupid can people be! he thought again. Though the people of Weizhuang, of course, were still village idiots: think of it—they didn't even know how people fried fish in town!

This Ah-Q of ours—with his wealthy forebears, his urban sophistication, his laudable application to his chosen career—would have been the embodiment of perfection, had it not been for his regrettable possession of a few constitutional defects. The most annoying of which was the perfidious emergence on his scalp of a number of gleaming ringworm scars. Although they were of his own revered body's making, Ah-Q felt them unworthy of him and for this reason came to view as taboo the word "ringworm", or anything that sounded like it. In time, the scope of this linguistic prohibition steadily broadened: first to "shiny", then "bright", extending a little later on to "lamp" or "candle". Any flaunting of the taboo—whether deliberate or accidental—provoked first the controversial scars to glow a furious red. Ah-Q would then size up his adversary: the dull-witted he would subject to a tongue-lashing; the weak he would punch in the nose. The curious thing, though, was how often—in fact, almost always—Ah-Q came off worse. In time, then, he pared his strategy down to an Angry Glare.

Another curious thing: after Ah-Q began practising the Art of the Angry Glare, Weizhuang's idlers took to provoking him with ever greater relish.

"Bit bright, isn't it?" they would remark, in deliberate surprise, on encountering him.

Cue the Angry Glare.

"Oh ... a lamp!" they would shamelessly continue.

Ah-Q struggled to find an appropriate riposte.

"You're not worth a ..." At moments such as these, Ah-Q's ringworm suddenly struck him as a badge of honour for which no sacrifice was too great; far superior to your average, run-of-the-mill dermatological defect. As has been amply demonstrated, however, Ah-Q was a man of exceptional prescience: sensing an imminent breaking of his cherished taboo, he said no more.

But his interlocutors wouldn't let it lie. On they went needling him, until the whole thing ended in blows, and Ah-Q's formal submission: with the seizing of his sallow queue and the robust knocking of his head four or five times against a wall. After which, his adversaries would at last depart, their hearts fairly singing with the joys of victory. "Beaten again by that scum," Ah-Q would stand there, thinking to himself. "It's like a father getting thrashed by his sons. What's the world coming to ..." Then he, too, would jubilantly leave the scene of his triumph.

In time, whenever something like this happened, Ah-Q began to say out loud what at first he had only thought. In this way, Ah-Q's tormentors learnt of his habit of declaring moral victory over the ashes of defeat, and added their own revisions while yanking on his queue.

"Or how about," Ah-Q would twist his head back round, trying to protect the base of his queue, "a slug? I'm a slug! A slug! Now will you let me go?"

They would not, and went on to give his head the time-honoured bashing against the nearest hard surface, before swinging off, their hearts again singing with the joys of victory, thinking this time their point had been well and truly made. And yet within ten seconds, Ah-Q had set jubilantly off on his own way. He was now the top self-abaser in China, and once you'd discarded the inconvenient "self-abaser", you were left with "top" — "top" as in "top in the civil service examinations". "Ha! Scum!"

Once Ah-Q's enemies had been trounced by such ingenious means, he would trot happily off to the tavern, down a few bowls of wine, crack a few jokes, start a few arguments and, victorious again, return happily to the Temple of Earth and Grain, where he would lay his head down and go straight to sleep. If he had money in his pocket, he would go off to gamble, sweatily squeezing his way in among a crowd of other chancers squatted down on the ground.

"Four hundred on the Green Dragon!" he would roar, louder than anyone else.

"There ... we ... go!" the banker would sing out, lifting the lid on his box, his face also swimming in sweat. "Heaven's Gate wins ... Evens on the Corner ... Nothing on the Passage ... Over here with Ah-Q's stake!"

"One hundred on the Passage—one hundred and fifty!"

And so Ah-Q's money was sung away into the pockets of others, their faces equally slippery with sweat, until there was nothing left for him to do but push his way back from the front line, and watch from the back, feeling anxious on other people's behalf. When everyone else scattered he, too, would take himself reluctantly back to his temple, appearing for work the next day with puffy eyes.

But every silver lining has its cloud, to paraphrase the proverb, and the one time that Ah-Q was unfortunate enough to win, he lost almost everything.

It was the evening of Weizhuang's Festival of the Gods. There was opera, as usual, with gambling stalls set up near the stage. The drums and gongs buzzed only faintly in Ah-Q's ears, as if the musicians were miles away. All he could hear was the banker's singsong. He won, and he won again, his coppers turning silver, his silver turning into dollars-a great pile of shiny dollars. He was dizzy with euphoria.

"Two dollars on Heaven's Gate!"

He didn't know who started the fighting, or why. The sounds of cursing, of blows, of footsteps blurred into a single confused roar; and when finally he clambered to his feet, stalls and gamblers had disappeared. His body seemed to hurt in various places, as if it had been hit or kicked, and people were looking curiously at him. After taking himself back, rather nonplussed, to the Temple of Earth and Grain, he recovered his wits sufficiently to discover his pile of money was gone. How was he to get to the bottom of it? Most of the gamblers that night had come from outside the village.

That shiny pile of silver dollars! Once it had been all his—but where was it now? He tried telling himself his son had stolen it; his discontent continued to simmer. He told himself he was a slug-still no peace of mind. Now, only now, did he feel the bitterness of defeat.

And yet victory, as ever, was close at hand. His right hand soared upwards, to deliver one—two forceful slaps to the face. He then got up, his cheeks burning with pain, his good humour fully restored. Soon enough, he was perfectly convinced that he had hit someone else entirely—even though his cheeks continued to sting rather. He lay down, his heart easy with victory.

And fell asleep.

(translated by Julia Lovell)

三、《围城》节选

这位张先生是浙江沿海人，名叫吉民，但他喜欢人唤他 Jimmy。他在美国人花旗洋行里做了二十多年的事，从"写字"（小书记）升到买办，手里着实有钱。只生一个女儿，不惜工本地栽培，教会学校里所能传授熏陶的洋本领、洋习气，美容院理发铺所能制造的洋时髦、洋姿态，无不应有尽有。这女儿刚十八岁，中学尚未毕业，可是张先生夫妇保有他们家乡的传统思想，以为女孩子到二十岁就老了，过二十还没嫁掉，只能进古物陈列所供人凭吊了。张太太择婿很严，说亲的虽多，都没成功。有一个富商的儿子，也是留学生，张太太颇为赏识，婚姻大有希望，但一顿饭后这事再不提起。吃饭时大家谈到那几天因战事关系，租界封锁，蔬菜来源困难，张太太便对那富商儿子说："府上人多，每天伙食账不会小罢？"那人说自己不清楚，想来是多少钱一天。张太太说："那么府上的厨子一定又老实，又能干！像我们人数不到府上一半，每天厨房开销也要那个数目呢！"那人听着得意，张太太等他饭毕走了，便说："这种人家排场太小了！只吃那么多钱一天的菜！我女儿舒服惯的，过去吃不来苦！"婚事从此作罢。夫妇俩磋商几次，觉得宝贝女儿嫁到人家去，总不放心，不如招一个女婿到自己家里来。那天张先生跟鸿渐同席，回家说起，认为颇合资格：家世头衔都不错，并且现在没真做到女婿已住在挂名丈人家里，将来招赘入门，易如反掌。更妙是方家经这番战事，摆不起乡绅人家臭架子，这女婿可以服服帖帖地养在张府上。结果张太太要鸿渐来家相他一下。

方鸿渐因为张先生请他早到谈谈，下午银行办公完毕就去。马路上经过一家外国皮货铺子看见獭绒西装外套，新年廉价，只卖四百元。鸿渐常想有这样一件外套，留学时不敢买。譬如在伦敦，男人穿皮外套而没有私人汽车，假使不像放印子钱的犹太人或打拳的黑人，人家就疑心是马戏班的演员，再不然就是开窑子的乌龟；只有在维也纳，穿皮外套是常事，并且有现成的皮里子卖给旅客衬在外套里。他回国后，看穿的人很多，现在更给那店窗里的陈列撩得心动。可是盘算一下，只好叹口气。银行里薪水一百块钱已算不薄，零用尽够。丈人家供吃供住，一个钱不必贴，怎好向周经理要钱买奢侈品？回国所余六十多镑，这次孝敬父亲四十镑添买些家具，剩下不过折合四百余元。东凑西挪，一股脑儿花在这件外套上面，不大合算。国难时期，万事节约，何况天气不久回暖，就省了罢。到了张家，张先生热闹地欢迎道："Hello! Doctor 方，好久不见！"张先生跟外国人来往惯了，说话有个特征——也许在洋行、青年会、扶轮社等圈子里，这并没有什么奇特——喜欢中国话里夹无谓的英文字。他并无中文难达的新意，需要借英文来讲；所以他说话里嵌的英文字，还比不得嘴里嵌的金牙，因为金牙不仅妆点，尚可使用，只好比牙缝里嵌的肉屑，表示饭菜吃得好，此外全无用处。他仿美国人读音，惟妙惟肖，也许鼻音学得太过火了，不像美国人，而像伤风塞鼻子的中国人。他说 "very well" 二字，声音活像小洋狗在咕噜——"vurry wul"。可惜罗马人无此耳福，否则决不单说 R 是鼻音的狗字母。当时张先生跟鸿渐拉手，问他是不是天天 "go downtown"。鸿渐寒暄已毕，瞧玻璃橱里都是碗、瓶、碟子，便说："张先生喜欢收藏磁器？"

"Sure! have a look see!"张先生打开橱门，请鸿渐赏鉴。鸿渐拿了几件，看都是 "成化""宣德""康熙"，也不识真假，只好说："这东西很值钱罢？"

"Sure! 值不少钱呢，Plenty of dough。并且这东西不比书画。买书画买了假的，一文不值，只等于 waste paper。磁器假的，至少还可以盛菜盛饭。我有时请外国 friends 吃饭，就用那个康熙窑'油底蓝五彩'大盘做 salad dish，他们都觉得古色古香，菜的味道也有点 old-time。"

方鸿渐道："张先生眼光一定好，不会买假东西。"

张先生大笑道："我不懂什么年代花纹，事情忙，也没工夫翻书研究。可是我有 hunch；看见一件东西，忽然 what d'you call 灵机一动，买来准 O. K.。他们古董掮客都佩服我，我常对他们说：'不用拿假货来 fool 我。O yeah，我姓张的不是 sucker，休想骗我！'"关上橱门，又说："咦，headache——"便揿电铃叫用人。

鸿渐不懂，忙问道："张先生不舒服，是不是？"

张先生惊奇地望着鸿渐道："谁不舒服？你？我？我很好呀！"

鸿渐道："张先生不是说'头痛'么？"

张先生呵呵大笑，一面分付进来的女佣说："快去跟太太小姐说，客人来了，请她们出来。make it snappy！"说时右手大拇指从中指弹在食指上"啪"的一响。他回过来对鸿渐笑道："headache 是美国话，指'太太'而说，不是'头痛'！你没到 States 去过罢！"

方鸿渐正自惭寡陋，张太太张小姐出来了，张先生为鸿渐介绍。张太太是位四十多岁的胖女人，外国名字是小巧玲珑的 Tessie。张小姐是十八岁的高大女孩子，着色鲜明，穿衣紧俏，身材将来准会跟她老太爷那洋行的资本一样雄厚。鸿渐没听清她名字，声音好像"我你他"，想来不是 Anita，就是 Juanita，她父母只缩短叫她 Nita。张太太上海话比丈夫讲得好，可是时时流露本乡土音，仿佛罩褂太小，遮不了里面的袍子。张太太信佛，自说天天念十遍"白衣观世音咒"，求菩萨保佑中国军队打胜；又说这观音咒灵验得很，上海打仗最紧急时，张先生到外滩行里去办公，自己在家里念咒，果然张先生从没遭到流弹。鸿渐暗想，享受了最新的西洋科学设备，而竟抱这种信仰，坐在热水管烘暖的客堂里念佛，可见"西学为用，中学为体"并非难事。他和张小姐没有多少可谈，只好问她爱看什么电影。跟着两个客人来了，都是张先生的结义弟兄。一个叫陈士屏，是欧美烟草公司的高等职员，大家唤他 Z. B.，仿佛德文里"有例为证"的缩写。一个叫丁讷生，外国名字倒不是诗人 Tennyson 而是海军大将 Nelson，也在什么英国轮船公司做事。张太太说，人数凑得起一桌麻将，何妨打八圈牌再吃晚饭。方鸿渐赌术极幼稚，身边带钱又不多，不愿参加，宁可陪张小姐闲谈。经不起张太太再三怂恿，只好入局。没料到四圈之后，自己独赢一百余元，心中一动，想假如这手运继续不变，那獭绒大衣便有指望了。这时候，他全忘了在船上跟孙先生讲的法国迷信，只要赢钱。八圈打毕，方鸿渐赢了近三百块钱。同局的三位，张太太、"有例为证"和"海军大将"一个子儿不付，一字不提，都站起来准备吃饭。鸿渐唤醒一句道："我今天运气太好了！从来没赢过这许多钱。"

张太太如梦初醒道："咱们真糊涂了！还没跟方先生清账呢。陈先生，丁先生，让我一个人来付他，咱们回头再算得了。"便打开钱袋把钞票一五一十点交给鸿渐。

吃的是西菜。"海军大将"信基督教，坐下以前，还向天花板眨白眼，感谢上帝赏饭。方鸿渐因为赢了钱，有说有笑。饭后散坐抽烟喝咖啡，他瞧见沙发旁一个小书架，猜来都是张小姐的读物。一大堆《西风》、原文《读者文摘》之外，有原文小字白文《莎士比亚全集》、《新旧约全书》、《家庭布置学》、翻版的《居里夫人传》、《照相自修法》、《我国与我民》等不朽大著，以及电影小说十几种，里面不用说有《乱世佳人》。一本小蓝书，背上金字标题道：《怎样去获得丈夫而且守住他》（How to Gain a Husband and Keep Him）。鸿渐忍不住抽出一翻，只见一节道："对男人该温柔甜蜜，才能在他心的深处留下好印象。女孩子们，别忘了脸上常带光明的笑容。"看到这里，这笑容从书上移到鸿渐脸上了。再看书面作者是个女人，不知出嫁没有，该写明"某某夫人"，这书便见得切身阅历之谈，想着笑容更廓大了。抬头忽见张小姐注意自己，忙把书放好，收敛笑容。"有例为证"要张小姐弹钢琴，大家同声附和。张小姐弹完，鸿渐要补救这令她误解的笑容，抢先第一个称"好"，求她再弹一曲。他又坐一会，才告辞出门。洋车到半路，他想起那书名，不禁失笑。丈夫是女人的职业，没有丈夫就等于失业，所以该牢牢捧住这饭碗。哼！我偏不愿意女人读了那本书当我是饭碗，我宁可他们瞧不起我，骂我饭桶。"我你他"小姐，咱们没有"举碗齐眉"的缘分，希望另有好运气的人来爱上您。想到这里，鸿渐顿足大笑，把天空月亮当作张小姐，向她挥手作别。洋车夫疑心他醉了，回头叫他别动，车不好拉。

客人全散了，张太太道："这姓方的不合式，气量太小，把钱看得太重，给我一试就露出本相。他那时候好像怕我们赖账不还的，可笑不可笑？"

张先生道："德国货总比不上美国货呀。什么博士！还算在英国留过学，我说的英文，他好多听不懂。欧战以后，德国落伍了。汽车、飞机、打字机、照相机，哪一件不是美国花样顶新！我不爱欧洲留学生。"

张太太道："Nita，你看这姓方的怎么样？"

张小姐不能饶恕方鸿渐看书时的微笑，干脆说："这人讨厌！你看他吃相多坏！全不像在外国住过的。他喝汤的时候，把面包去蘸！他吃铁排鸡，不用刀叉，把手拈了鸡腿起来咬！我全看在眼睛里。吓！这算什么礼貌？我们学校里教社交礼节的 Miss Prym 瞧见了准会骂他猪猡相 piggy wiggy！"

当时张家这婚事一场没结果，周太太颇为扫兴。可是方鸿渐小时是看《三国演义》、《水浒》、《西游记》那些不合教育原理的儿童读物的；他生得太早，还没福气捧读《白雪公主》、《木偶奇遇记》这一类好书。他记得《三国演义》里的名言："妻子如衣服"，当然衣服也就等于妻子；他现在新添了皮外套，损失个把老婆才不放在心上呢。

译

Mr. Chang was from the coastal area of Chekiang. His given name was Chimin, but he preferred people to call him Jimmy. For over twenty years he had worked for an American firm, the Stars and Stripes Company, rising from a clerk to become a comprador, and he had amassed a sizable fortune. He had but one daughter and had not spared any expense in her upbringing. She had acquired all the foreign skills and ways that the church schools could teach or instill, and all the foreign hairstyles and makeup that beauty salons and hairdressers could create. She was just eighteen and had not yet graduated from high school, but Mr. and Mrs. Chang, who held to the traditional view of their hometown, thought that a girl was old by the time she was twenty, and if she passed this age still unwed, she could only be put in a museum of old relics to be viewed with nostalgia.

Mrs. Chang was very strict in her choice of a son-in-law, and though many people had proposed matches, none of them had made it. One of these was the son of a well-to-do businessman and a returned student to boot. Mrs. Chang was favorably impressed with him and held high hopes for a marriage, but after one dinner, she never mentioned the matter again. During the meal they began talking about the fact that because of the war the concessions were under a blockade and vegetables were hard to get. Mrs. Chang turned to the son of the well-to-do businessman and said, "With so many people in your family, the daily cost for food must be quite high, I should think."

He replied that he was not quite sure, but thought it was so much money per day.

Mrs. Chang exclaimed, "Then your cook must be both honest and resourceful. Our family isn't half as large as yours, yet our cook spends the same amount every day!"

He was quite pleased at hearing this, but after dinner was over and he had left, Mrs. Chang said, "That family lives on peanuts! They spend so little on food a day! Since my daughter is used to comfort, she couldn't take such hardship!" The question of marriage was dropped at this point.

After a few deliberations, the husband and wife decided that they could never rest easy about marrying their precious daughter into another family. It would be far better to adopt a son-in-law into their own. The day Mr. Chang met Hung-chien at the party he mentioned him later at home, saying he found him well qualified: the family background and qualifications were quite good. Furthermore, since he was now already living at the home of his nominal father-in-law without ever having actually become his son-in-law, taking him into the family would be as easy as turning the palm. What made it even better was that since the Fangs had lost so much in the war, they couldn't put on any of the presumptuous airs of a country squire, and the son-in-law would live submissively at the Changs. In the end, Mrs. Chang wanted Hung-chien to dine with them, so she could take a look at him.

Since Mr. Chang had invited him to come early for a chat, Fang Hung-chien went over in the afternoon right after work at the bank. Along the way he passed a foreign fur goods store where he saw in the window a Western-style fur overcoat. It was on sale at only $400 during New Year's. He had always wanted an overcoat like that but had never dared buy one when he was studying abroad. In London, for instance, a man who wore such an overcoat but did not own a private car, unless he looked like a Jewish usurer or a Negro boxer, would be suspected of being a circus performer, or else a pimp who ran a brothel. It was only in Vienna that fur coats were commonly worn, and ready-made fur linings were sold to travelers to line their coats. After returning to China, he had seen many people wearing fur, and now he was even more stirred by the display in the window. After some calculations, however, he could only heave a sigh. His $100 salary at the bank was already considered handsome and ample spending money, and since his father-in-law was providing both room and board and he didn't have to pay a cent, how could he ask Mr. Chou for money to buy a luxury item? He had dutifully presented forty of the sixty-odd pounds left after his return home to his father to buy furniture. The rest had been converted into a little over $400. It would hardly do to sink all his money at once into that coat. In a time of national austerity, one had to economize in everything, and since the weather would be warming up soon, he might as well forget it.

When he arrived at the Changs, Mr. Chang gave him a hearty welcome, "Hello, Dr. Fang! Haven't seen you for a long time!"

Mr. Chang was used to dealing with foreigners and his speech had a special characteristic—perhaps in a foreign firm, the YMCA, the Rotary Club, or other such places, this was nothing unusual—he liked to sprinkle his Chinese with meaningless English expressions. It wasn't that he had new ideas, which were difficult to express in Chinese and required the use of English. The English words inlaid in his speech could not thus be compared with the gold teeth inlaid in one's mouth, since gold teeth are not only decorative but functional as well. A better comparison would be with the bits of meat stuck between the teeth—they show that one has had a good meal but are otherwise useless. He imitated the American accent down to the slightest inflection, though maybe the nasal sound was a little overdone, sounding more like a Chinese with a cold and a stuffy nose, rather than an American speaking. The way he said "Very well" sounded just like a dog growling— "Vurry wul". A pity the Romans never had a chance to hear it, for otherwise the Latin poet Persius would not have been the only one to say that "r" was a nasal in the dog's alphabet (sonat hic de nare canina litera).

As Mr. Chang shook hands with Hung-chien, he asked him if he had to go downtown every day. When the pleasantries were over, Hung-chien noticed a glass cupboard filled with bowls, jars, and plates and asked, "Do you collect porcelain, Mr. Chang?"

"Sure! Have a look-see. " Mr. Chang opened the cupboard and invited Hung-chien to inspect them. Hung-chien picked up a few pieces and noticed they were all marked with such reign periods as "Ch-eng-hua", "Hsüan-te", or "K-anghsi. " Unable to tell whether they were genuine or fake, he merely said, "These must be quite valuable. "

"Sure! Worth quite a lot of money, plenty of dough. Besides, these things aren't like calligraphy or paintings. If you buy calligraphy or paintings which turn out to be fakes, they aren't worth a cent. They just amount to wastepaper. If the porcelain is fake, at least it can hold food. Sometimes I invite foreign friends over for dinner and use this big K'ang-hsi 'underglaze-blue-and-col ored ware' plate for a salad dish. They all think the ancient colors and odor make the food taste a little old time. "

Fang Hung-chien said, "I'm sure you have a good eye. You wouldn't ever buy a fake. "

Mr. Chang laughed heartily and said, "I don't know anything about period designs. I'm too busy to have time to sit down and study it. But I have a hunch when I see something, and a sudden—what d'you call? —inspiration comes to me. Then I buy it and it turns out to be quite OK. Those antique dealers all respect me. I always say to them, 'Don't try to fool me with fakes. Oh yeah, Mr. Chang here is no sucker. Don't think you can cheat me!'" He closed the cupboard and said, "Oh, headache," then pressed an electric bell to summon the servant.

Puzzled, Hung-chien asked quickly, "Aren't you feeling well, Mr. Chang?"

Mr. Chang looked at Hung-chien in astonishment and said, "Who's not feeling well? You? Me? Why, I feel fine!"

"Didn't you say you had a headache?" asked Hung-chien.

Mr. Chang roared with laughter. At the same time he instructed the maid who entered, "Go and tell my wife and daughter the guest is here. Ask them to come out. Make it snappy!" At this he snapped his fingers. Turning to Hung-chien, he said with a laugh, " 'Headache' is an American expression for 'wife', not 'pain in head!' I guess you haven't been to the States!"

Just as Fang Hung-chien was feeling ashamed of his ignorance, Mrs. Chang and Miss Chang came out. Mr. Chang introduced them to Hung-chien. Mrs. Chang was a portly woman of forty or more with the dainty little foreign name of "Tessie". Miss Chang was a tall girl of eighteen with a fresh complexion, trim-fitting clothes, and a figure which promised to be just as ample as the capital in her father's foreign company. Hung-chien did not quite catch her name. It sounded like Wo-Ni-Ta (I-You-He). He guessed that it was either "Anita" or "Juanita". Her parents called her "Nita" for short. Mrs. Chang spoke Shanghainese better than her husband, but her native accent often showed through like an undersized jacket that doesn't cover up the gown underneath. Mrs. Chang was a Buddhist and said that she recited the "Goddess of Mercy Chant" ten times a day to beg the Bodhissattva to protect China's army in its fight for victory. This chant, she said, was very efficacious. When the fighting in Shanghai was at its worst, Mr. Chang had gone to the export company to work while she stayed at home reciting incantations and, sure enough, Mr. Chang had come through without being hit by any stray bullets.

Hung-chien thought to himself, Mrs. Chang enjoys the latest gadgets of Western science and yet she still holds to such beliefs, sitting in the living room heated by hot water pipes to recite Buddhist chants. Apparently "Western learning for practical application; Chinese learning as a base" was not so hard to implement after all.

Miss Chang and Hung-chien had little to talk about, so he could only ask her which movies she liked best. Two guests arrived next, both of whom were Mr. Chang's sworn brothers. One of them, Ch'en Shih-p'ing, held a high position in the Euro-American Tobacco Company. Everyone called him Z. B., like the abbreviation in German for the words, "for example," zum Beispiel. The other, Ting Na-sheng, whose foreign name was not Tennyson, the poet, but Nelson, the admiral, worked in a British steamship company. Mrs. Chang said that since there were enough people for a game of mahjong, why not play eight rounds before dinner? Fang Hung-chien was quite an amateur at gambling, and since he had little money with him, didn't care to join in. He would have preferred to chat with Miss Chang, but unable to withstand Mrs. Chang's repeated prodding, he finally agreed to play. Contrary to his expectations, by the end of the fourth round, he alone had won over a hundred dollars. He suddenly thought that if his luck held out, there was hope for the fur coat yet. By this time he had completely forgotten the French superstition he had told Mr. Sun on the boat. All he wanted was to win money. At the end of the eighth round, Fang Hung-chien had won nearly three hundred dollars. The three other players, Mrs. Chang, "For Example," and "Admiral Nelson," all stood up and got ready to eat without paying a cent or mentioning a word about paying. Hung-chien reminded them with the remark, "How lucky I've been today. I've never won so much money before."

As though waking from a dream, Mrs. Chang said, "Why, how stupid of us! We haven't settled with Mr. Fang yet. Mr. Ch'en, Mr. Ting, let me pay him, and we can settle it among ourselves later on." She then opened her purse and handed the notes over to Hung-chien, counting them out one by one.

They had Western food. "Admiral Nelson," who was a Christian, rolled his eyes up toward the ceiling and thanked God for bestowing the food before he sat down. Because he had won so much money, Fang Hung-chien was full of talk and banter. After the meal everyone sat about smoking and drinking coffee. He noticed a little bookcase next to the sofa and supposed it contained Miss Chang's reading material. Besides a big stack of *West Wind* and *Reader's Digest* in the original, there was an unannotated, small-type edition of *The Complete Works of Shakespeare* in the original, the *Bible*, *Interior Decorating*, a reprint of *The Biography of Madame Curie*, *Teach Yourself Photography*, *My Country and My People* [by Lin Yutang], and other immortal classics, as well as an anthology of a dozen screen plays, one of which, needless to say, was *Gone with the Wind*.

There was one small blue volume with the title in gilt letters on the spine: How to Gain a Husband and Keep Him. Hung-chien could not resist taking it out and skimming through it. He came across a paragraph which read: "You must be sweet and gentle to the man in order to leave a good impression deep in his heart. Girls, never forget always to have a bright smile on your face." As he read this, the smile transferred itself from the book to his own face. When he looked again at the cover, he noticed the author was a woman and wondered if she were married. She should have written "Mrs. So-and-So", then the book would have obviously been the voice of experience. At this thought his smile broadened. Raising his head, he suddenly noticed Miss Chang's gaze on him and hastily replaced the book and wiped the smile from his face.

"For Example" asked Miss Chang to play the piano, and they all echoed the request in unison. When Miss Chang had finished playing, in order to rectify the misunderstanding which had caused his smile, Hung-chien was first to say "Wonderful", and called for an encore. He stayed for a while longer, then said goodbye. Halfway home in the rickshaw, he remembered the title of the book and burst out laughing. Husbands are women's careers. Not having a husband is like being unemployed, so she has to hold tightly to her "rice bowl". Well, I don't happen to want any woman to take me as her "rice bowl" after reading that book. I'd rather have them scorn me and call me a "rice bucket". Miss Wo-Ni-Ta, we just weren't meant to "raise the bowl to the eyebrows". I hope some other lucky guy falls in love with you. At this thought Hung-chien stamped his foot and laughed loudly. Pretending the moon in the sky was Miss Chang, he waved goodbye to her. Suspecting he was drunk, the rickshaw puller turned his head and asked him to keep still, for it was hard to pull the rickshaw.

After all the guests had left, Mrs. Chang said, "That Fang fellow isn't suitable. He's too small-minded and values money too highly. He showed his true colors the moment I tested him. He acted as if he were afraid we weren't going to pay him off. Isn't that funny?"

Mr. Chang said, "German goods don't measure up to American ones. Some doctor! He's supposed to have studied in England, but he didn't even understand a lot of the English I spoke. After the first World War, Germany fell behind. All the latest designs of cars, airplanes, typewriters, and cameras are American made. I don't care for returned students from Europe."

"Nita, what do you think of that Fang fellow?" asked Mrs. Chang.

Miss Chang, who could not forgive Fang Hung-chien for his smile while reading the book, replied simply, "He's obnoxious! Did you see the way he ate? Does he look like someone who's ever been abroad! When he drank his soup, he dipped his bread in it! And when he ate the roast chicken, instead of using a fork and knife, he picked a leg up with his fingers! I saw it all with my own eyes. Huh! What kind of manners is that? If Miss Prym, our etiquette teacher, ever saw that, she'd certainly call him a piggy-wiggy!"

When the affair of marriage with the Changs came to naught, Mrs. Chou was greatly disappointed. But when Fang Hung-chien was young he was brought up on the Romance of the Three Kingdoms, the Tale of the Marshes, Monkey, and other such children's literature that were not in line with basic educational principles for children. He was born too soon to have had the good fortune to take up such fine books as Snow White and Pinocchio. He remembered the famous saying from the Romance of the Three Kingdoms, "A wife is like a suit of clothes," and of course clothes also meant the same as wife. He now had himself a new fur coat. The loss of a wife or two wasn't about to worry him.

(Translated by Jeanne Kelly and Nathan K. Mao)

四、*Pride and Prejudice* 节选

It is a truth universally acknowledged, that a single man in possession of a good fortune, must be in want of a wife.

However little known the feelings or views of such a man may be on his first entering a neighbourhood, this truth is so well fixed in the minds of the surrounding families, that he is considered the rightful property of some one or other of their daughters.

"My dear Mr. Bennet," said his lady to him one day, "have you heard that Netherfield Park is let at last?"

Mr. Bennet replied that he had not.

"But it is," returned she; "for Mrs. Long has just been here, and she told me all about it."

Mr. Bennet made no answer.

"Do you not want to know who has taken it?" cried his wife impatiently.

"You want to tell me, and I have no objection to hearing it."

This was invitation enough.

"Why, my dear, you must know, Mrs. Long says that Netherfield is taken by a young man of large fortune from the north of England; that he came down on Monday in a chaise and four to see the place, and was so much delighted with it, that he agreed with Mr. Morris immediately; that he is to take possession before Michaelmas, and some of his servants are to be in the house by the end of next week."

"What is his name?"

"Bingley."

"Is he married or single?"

"Oh! Single, my dear, to be sure! A single man of large fortune; four or five thousand a year. What a fine thing for our girls!"

"How so? How can it affect them?"

"My dear Mr. Bennet," replied his wife, "how can you be so tiresome! You must know that I am thinking of his marrying one of them."

"Is that his design in settling here?"

"Design! Nonsense, how can you talk so! But it is very likely that he may fall in love with one of them, and therefore you must visit him as soon as he comes."

"I see no occasion for that. You and the girls may go, or you may send them by themselves, which perhaps will be still better, for as you are as handsome as any of them, Mr. Bingley may like you the best of the party."

"My dear, you flatter me. I certainly have had my share of beauty, but I do not pretend to be anything extraordinary now. When a woman has five grown-up daughters, she ought to give over thinking of her own beauty."

"In such cases, a woman has not often much beauty to think of."

"But, my dear, you must indeed go and see Mr. Bingley when he comes into the neighbourhood. "

"It is more than I engage for, I assure you. "

"But consider your daughters. Only think what an establishment it would be for one of them. Sir William and Lady Lucas are determined to go, merely on that account, for in general, you know, they visit no newcomers. Indeed you must go, for it will be impossible for us to visit him if you do not. "

"You are over-scrupulous, surely. I dare say Mr. Bingley will be very glad to see you; and I will send a few lines by you to assure him of my hearty consent to his marrying whichever he chooses of the girls; though I must throw in a good word for my little Lizzy. "

"I desire you will do no such thing. Lizzy is not a bit better than the others; and I am sure she is not half so handsome as Jane, nor half so good-humoured as Lydia. But you are always giving her the preference. "

"They have none of them much to recommend them," replied he; "they are all silly and ignorant like other girls; but Lizzy has something more of quickness than her sisters. "

"Mr. Bennet, how can you abuse your own children in such a way? You take delight in vexing me. You have no compassion for my poor nerves. "

"You mistake me, my dear. I have a high respect for your nerves. They are my old friends. I have heard you mention them with consideration these last twenty years at least. "

"Ah, you do not know what I suffer. "

"But I hope you will get over it, and live to see many young men of four thousand a year come into the neighbourhood. "

"It will be no use to us, if twenty such should come, since you will not visit them. "

"Depend upon it, my dear, that when there are twenty, I will visit them all. "

Mr. Bennet was so odd a mixture of quick parts, sarcastic humour, reserve, and caprice, that the experience of three-and-twenty years had been insufficient to make his wife understand his character. Her mind was less difficult to develop. She was a woman of mean understanding, little information, and uncertain temper. When she was discontented, she fancied herself nervous. The business of her life was to get her daughters married; its solace was visiting and news.

译

译文一

有钱的单身汉总要娶位太太，这是一条举世公认的真理。

这条真理还真够深入人心的，每逢这样的单身汉新搬到一个地方，四邻八舍的人家尽管对他的性情一无所知，却把他视为自己某一个女儿的合法财产。

"亲爱的贝内特先生，"一天，贝内特太太对丈夫说道，"你有没有听说内瑟菲尔德庄园终于租出去了？"

贝内特先生回答道，没有听说。

"的确租出去了，"太太说道。"朗太太刚刚来过，她把这事一五一十地全告诉我了。"

贝内特先生没有答话。

"难道你不想知道是谁租去的吗？"太太不耐烦地嚷道。

"既然你想告诉我，我听听也无妨。"

这句话足以逗引太太讲下去了。

"哦，亲爱的，你应该知道，朗太太说，内瑟菲尔德让英格兰北部的一个阔少爷租去了；他星期一那天乘坐一辆驷马马车来看房子，看得非常中意，当下就和莫里斯先生讲妥了；他打算赶在米迦勒节①以前搬进新居，下周末以前打发几个佣人先住进来。"

"他姓什么？"

"宾利。"

"成亲了还是单身？"

"哦！单身，亲爱的，千真万确！一个有钱的单身汉，每年有四五千镑的收入。真是女儿们的好福气！"

"这是怎么说？跟女儿们有什么关系？"

"亲爱的贝内特先生，"太太答道，"你怎么这么令人讨厌！告诉你吧，我正在思谋他娶她们中的一个做太太呢。"

"他搬到这里就是为了这个打算？"

"打算！胡扯，你怎么能这么说话！他兴许会看中她们中的哪一个，因此，他一来你就得去拜访他。"

"我看没有那个必要哦。你带着女儿们去就行啦，要不你索性打发她们自己去，这样或许更好些，因为你的姿色并不亚于她们中的任何一个，你一去，宾利先生倒作兴看中你呢。"

"亲爱的，你太抬举我啦。我以前确实有过美貌的时候，不过现在却不敢硬充有什么出众的地方了。一个女人家有了五个成年的女儿，就不该对自己的美貌再转什么念头了。"

"这么说来，女儿家对自己的美貌也转不了多久的念头啦。"

"不过，亲爱的，宾利先生一搬到这里，你可真得去见见他，那会是多好的一门亲事。威廉爵士夫妇打定主意要去，还不就是为了这个缘故，因为你知道，他们通常是不去拜访新搬来的邻居的。你真应该去一次，要不然，我们母女就没法去见他了。"②

"你实在过于多虑了。宾利先生一定会很高兴见到你的。我可以写封信让你带去，

---

① 米迦勒节：9月29日，英国四个结账日之一。雇用用人多在此日，租约也多于此日履行。
② 按英国当时的习俗，拜访新迁来的邻居，先得由家中男主人登门拜访之后，女眷才可以去走访。

102

就说他随便想娶我哪位女儿，我都会欣然同意。不过，我要为小莉齐①美言两句。"

"我希望你别做这种事。莉齐丝毫不比别的女儿强，我敢说，论漂亮，她远远及不上简；论性子，她远远及不上莉迪亚。可你总是偏爱她。"

"她们哪一个也没有多少好称道的"，贝内特先生答道。"她们像别人家的姑娘一样，一个个又傻又蠢，倒是莉齐比几个姐妹们伶俐些。"

"贝内特先生，你怎么能这样糟蹋自己的孩子？你就喜欢气我，压根儿不体谅我那脆弱的神经。"

"你错怪我了，亲爱的。我非常尊重你的神经。它们是我的老朋友啦。至少在这二十年里，我总是听见你郑重其事地说起它们。"

"唉！你不知道我受多大的罪。"

"我希望你会好起来，亲眼看见好多每年有四千镑收入的阔少爷搬到这一带。"

"既然你不肯去拜访，即使搬来二十个，那对我们又有什么用。"

"放心吧，亲爱的，等搬来二十个，我一定去挨个拜访。"

贝内特先生是个古怪人，一方面乖觉诙谐，好挖苦人，另一方面又不苟言笑，变幻莫测，他太太积二三十年之经验，还摸不透他的性格。这位太太的脑子就不那么难捉摸了。她是个智力贫乏、孤陋寡闻、喜怒无常的女人。一踫到不称心的时候，就自以为神经架不住，她人生的大事，是把女儿们嫁出去；她平生的慰藉，是访亲拜友和打听消息。

（孙致礼　译，1990 年）

译文二

拥有了丰厚财产的单身汉一定会娶位太太，这早已是举世公认的真理。

这种人每逢新搬到一个地方，尽管他的性情丝毫不为邻居们所了解，他也会总被四邻八舍看成是自己某个女儿应该得到的一笔财产。因为，"有钱单身汉定会娶太太"这条真理早已深入人心。

一天，班内特太太对丈夫说："我亲爱的老爷，你听说了吗，尼尔菲庄园还是租出去了？"

班内特先生回答说他没听说过。

"确实租出去了，"她又说，"刚才朗格尔太太来过，她把这事儿前前后后都跟我说了。"

班内特先生没作声。

"难道你不想知道谁租下来了吗？"班内特太太急得大叫起来。

"你既然想告诉我，我听听也可以。"

这足以使她勇气十足地继续讲了。

"哦，亲爱的，你要知道，朗格尔太太说了，租尼尔菲庄园的是从英格兰本部来的一个阔少爷；他星期一那天来看房子时，乘的是一辆驷马大车，听说他看得非常满意，当场就和莫里斯先生谈妥了；他打算米迦勒节以前搬进来，听说下周末他的几个佣人就

---

① 莉齐系二女儿伊丽莎白的昵称，伊莱扎也是她的昵称。

先住进来。"

"他叫什么名字？"

"他姓宾格莱。"

"有太太了，还是单身？"

"啊，是单身，亲爱的，的确单身！没错儿，一个家产丰厚的单身汉，每年能收入四五千镑呢，这对咱们女儿来说真是件好事。"

"为什么？与女儿们有什么关系？"

"亲爱的老爷，"太太大叫，"你真傻！你想，他要是看中了我们的一个女儿该多好！"

"难道他来这儿住就因为有这想法吗？"

"会有这种想法？真是胡说！不过，或许他会看中一个的，所以，他一搬进来你就得去他那里拜访。"

"没必要。要去你就带女儿们去吧。或者你让她们自己去，这倒更好了——你比咱们每个女儿都好看，如果你去了，宾格莱先生看中你可怎么办？"

"亲爱的老爷，可别取笑我了。以前我确实也年轻漂亮过，可现在不行了。一个有了五个成年姑娘的女儿早不该在自己美貌上费工夫了。"

"这么说，一个女儿特别在意自己美貌的好时候并不多喽。"

"我亲爱的老爷，宾格莱先生如果真搬到这里，你不能不去看看他呀。"

"但是，我没必要非得去吧。"

"你就想想咱们的女儿吧。你想，不论她们哪一个能嫁到这样的人家，都够好的。威廉姆爵士夫妇决定了要去拜访他的，也是为这个。要知道，他们一般可不会去拜访新邻居的。你真得去一趟，否则，我和女儿们可怎么能去！"

"你想得过分周到啦。我觉得，宾格莱先生看到你们会非常高兴；或者，我写封信你们带去，让他知道无论他看中我们哪个女儿，我都会痛快地答应把她嫁过去；我还会特意夸赞我的小丽琪几句。"

"你千万别这样。丽琪哪儿也不比她们几个更好。我敢说，论相貌，她赶不上简一半；论脾气，她赶不上莉蒂娅一半儿，可你总偏向她。"

"她们没什么值得夸的，"他答道，"跟别人家的姑娘一样，又傻又物质；而丽琪却比她们有主见。"

"亲爱的老爷，你竟这样作践自己的亲生女儿呀！你是以我生气为代价使自己高兴吧。你从来不会想到我患有神经衰弱。"

"你真误会我了，亲爱的。我特别尊重你的神经，他们已是我的老朋友了。至少最近二十年里，我经常听到你语气沉重地提起它们。"

"唉！你真体会不到我天天是怎样熬过来的！"

"我倒真希望看你这毛病好起来。这样，你就会看到每年有四千英镑收入的阔少爷们都慢慢搬来与你为邻了。"

"既然你不喜欢拜访他们，那么，虽有二十个搬到这里，对我们也没用。"

"放心吧，亲爱的太太，果真有了二十个时，我肯定会一个一个地拜访。"

　　班内特先生很是刁钻古怪。他擅长戏谑，且能不露声色，思维敏捷，经常突发奇想，以致与他已有二三十年生活经历的太太都摸不透他的脾气。班内特太太倒是头脑比较简单。她毫无灵气，见识短浅，并且常无定准地发脾气，一遇到不如意的事，她就以神经衰弱为借口聊以自慰。她这一生的使命似乎就是嫁女儿，她乐此不疲地走亲访友，不辞辛苦地探听新闻。

评

①What are the major differences between these two versions?

②Compare the two versions above. Which one is closer to the original as far as the style is concerned?

五、*The Scarlet Letter* 节选

Hester Prynne's term of confinement was now at an end. Her prison door was thrown open, and she came forth into the sunshine, which, falling on all alike, seemed, to her sick and morbid heart, as if meant for no other purpose than to reveal the scarlet letter on her breast. Perhaps there was a more real torture in her first unattended footsteps from the threshold of the prison, than even in the procession and spectacle that have been described, where she was made the common infamy, at which all mankind was summoned to point its finger. Then, she was supported by an unnatural tension of the nerves, and by all the combative energy of her character, which enabled her to convert the scene into a kind of lurid triumph. It was, moreover, a separate and insulated event, to occur but once in her lifetime, and to meet which, therefore, reckless of economy, she might call up the vital strength that would have sufficed for many quiet years. The very law that condemned her—a giant of stern features, but with vigor to support, as well as to annihilate, in his iron arm—had held her up, through the terrible ordeal of her ignominy. But now, with this unattended walk from her prison-door, began the daily custom, and she must either sustain and carry it forward by the ordinary resources of her nature, or sink beneath it. She could no longer borrow from the future, to help her through the present grief. Tomorrow would bring its own trial with it; so would the next day, and so would the next; each its own trial, and yet the very same that was now so unutterably grievous to be borne. The days of the far-off future would toil onward, still with the same burden for her to take up, and bear along with her, but never to fling down; for the accumulating days, and added years, would pile up their misery upon the heap of shame. Throughout them all, giving up her individuality, she would become the general symbol at which the preacher and moralist might point, and in which they might vivify and embody their images of woman's frailty and sinful passion. Thus the young and pure would be taught to look at her, with the scarlet letter flaming on her breast, —at her, the child of honorable parents, —at her, the mother of a babe, that would hereafter be a woman, —at her, who had once been innocent, —as the figure, the body, the reality of sin. And over her grave, the infamy that she must carry thither would be her only monument.

It may seem marvellous, that, with the world before her, —kept by no restrictive clause of her condemnation within the limits of the Puritan settlement, so remote and so obscure, —free to return to her birthplace, or to any other European land, and there hide her character and identity under a new exterior, as completely as if emerging into another state of being, —and having also the passes of the dark, inscrutable forest open to her, where the wildness of her nature might assimilate itself with a people whose customs and life were alien from the law that had condemned her, —it may seem marvellous, that this woman should still call that place her home, where, and where only, she must needs be the type of shame. But there is a fatality, a feeling so irresistible and inevitable that it has the force of doom, which almost invariably compels human beings to linger around and haunt, ghostlike, the spot where some great and marked event has given the color to their lifetime; and still the more irresistibly, the darker the tinge that saddens it. Her sin, her ignominy, were the roots which she had struck into the soil. It was as if a new birth, with stronger assimilations than the first, had converted the forest-land, still so uncongenial to every other pilgrim and wanderer, into Hester Prynne's wild and dreary, but life-long home. All other scenes of earth— even that village of rural England, where happy infancy and stainless maidenhood seemed yet to be in her mother's keeping, like garments put off long ago—were foreign to her, in comparison. The chain that bound her here was of iron links, and galling to her inmost soul, but never could be broken.

It might be, too, —doubtless it was so, although she hid the secret from herself, and grew pale whenever it struggled out of her heart, like a serpent from its hole, —it might be that another feeling kept her within the scene and pathway that had been so fatal. There dwelt, there trode the feet of one with whom she deemed herself connected in a union, that, unrecognized on earth, would bring them together before the bar of final judgment, and make that their marriage-altar, for a joint futurity of endless retribution. Over and over again, the tempter of souls had thrust this idea upon Hester's contemplation, and laughed at the passionate and desperate joy with which she seized, and then strove to cast it from her. She barely looked the idea in the face, and hastened to bar it in its dungeon. What she compelled herself to 64 The Scarlet Letter believe, —what, finally, she reasoned upon, as her motive for continuing a resident of New England, —was half a truth, and half a self delusion. Here, she said to herself, had been the scene of her guilt, and here should be the scene of her earthly punishment; and so, perchance, the torture of her daily shame would at length purge her soul, and work out another purity than that which she had lost; more saint-like, because the result of martyrdom.

Hester Prynne, therefore, did not flee. On the outskirts of the town, within the verge of the peninsula, but not in close vicinity to any other habitation, there was a small thatched cottage. It had been built by an earlier settler, and abandoned, because the soil about it was too sterile for cultivation, while its comparative remoteness put it out of the sphere of that social activity which already marked the habits of the emigrants. It stood on the shore, looking across a basin of the sea at the forest-covered hills, towards the west. A clump of scrubby trees, such as alone grew on the peninsula, did not so much conceal the cottage from view, as seem to denote that here was some object which would fain have been, or at least ought to be, concealed. In this little, lonesome dwelling, with some slender means that she possessed, and by the license of the magistrates, who still kept an inquisitorial watch over her, Hester established herself, with her infant child. A mystic shadow of suspicion immediately attached itself to the spot. Children, too young to comprehend wherefore this woman should be shut out from the sphere of human charities, would creep nigh enough to behold her plying her needle at the cottage-window, or standing in the door-way, or laboring in her little garden, or coming forth along the pathway that led townward; and, discerning the scarlet letter on her breast, would scamper off, with a strange, contagious fear.

Lonely as was Hester's situation, and without a friend on earth who dared to show himself, she, however, incurred no risk of want. She possessed an art that sufficed, even in a land that afforded comparatively little scope for its exercise, to supply food for her thriving infant and herself. It was the art—then, as now, almost the only one within a woman's grasp-of needle-work. She bore on her breast, in the curiously embroidered letter, a specimen of her delicate and imaginative skill, of which the dames of a court might gladly have availed themselves, to add the richer and more spiritual adornment of human ingenuity to their fabrics of silk and gold. Here, indeed, in the sable simplicity that generally characterized the Puritanic modes of dress, there might be an infrequent call for the finer productions of her handiwork. Yet the taste of the age, demanding whatever was elaborate in compositions of this kind, did not fail to extend its influence over our stern progenitors, who had cast behind them so many fashions which it might seem harder to dispense with. Public ceremonies, such as ordinations, the installation of magistrates, and all that could give majesty to the forms in which a new government manifested itself to the people, were, as a matter of policy, marked by a stately and well-conducted ceremonial, and a sombre, but yet a studied magnificence. Deep ruffs, painfully wrought bands, and gorgeously embroidered gloves, were all deemed necessary to the official state of men assuming the reins of power; and were readily allowed to individuals dignified by rank or wealth, even while sumptuary laws forbade these and similar extravagances to the plebeian order. In the array of funerals, too, —whether for the apparel of the dead body, or to typify, by manifold emblematic devices of sable cloth and snowy lawn, the sorrow of the survivors, —there was a frequent and characteristic demand for such labor as Hester Prynne could supply. Baby-linen-for babies then wore robes of state—afforded still another possibility of toil and emolument.

译

海丝特·白兰的监禁期满了。牢门打开，她走到阳光下。那普照众生的日光，在她那病态的心灵看来，似乎只是为了暴露她胸前的红字。这是她第一次独自走出牢门，比起之前众目睽睽之下走上千夫所指的示众受辱台，这才是真正的折磨。当时，她神经异常紧张，个性不屈，竟将那种场面变成一种惨淡的胜利。毕竟，那样的事在她的一生中仅此一次，接下来便无需耗费太多精力。就惩办她示众的法律而论，那是一个外貌狰狞的巨人，其铁腕既可以消灭她，也可以支撑她，扶持着她挺过了示众的煎熬。然而此时此刻，走出狱门后，她就要开始日复一日的正常生活了。要么好好活下去，要么就永远沉沦。她再也无法预支未来，渡过眼前的悲痛悲伤。明天有明天的考验，后天又有后天的考验，再下一天仍会如此。每天都有每天的考验，然而在忍受难以言喻的痛苦这一点上又都是那样的遥远的未来的时日，仍有其要由她承载的重荷，需要她一步步走下去，终生背负着，永远不得抛却。日复一日，年复一年，耻辱之上复堆积层层苦难。她将在长年累月之中，放弃她的个性，而成为布道师和道学家们交相指责的反面女性人物，用她的存在形象地说明，女性不过是脆弱与罪孽的情欲的象征。他们将教育纯洁的年轻人好好看看她——这个胸前佩戴着耀眼的红字的女人；看看她——这个父母受人敬重却堕落至此的孩子；看看她——这个要抚养女婴的母亲；看看她——这个原本是纯洁无辜的女人；看看这个人，这个罪恶的实体。那个耻辱将伴她入土，并成为她坟上的唯一墓碑。

（选译）

六、*Mrs. Dalloway* 节选

In many ways, her mother felt, she was extremely immature, like a child still, attached to dolls, to old slippers; a perfect baby; and that was charming. But then, of course, there was in the Dalloway family the tradition of public service. Abbesses, principals, head mistresses, dignitaries, in the republic of women—without being brilliant, any of them, they were that. She penetrated a little further in the direction of St. Paul's. She liked the geniality, sisterhood, motherhood, brotherhood of this uproar. It seemed to her good. The noise was tremendous; and suddenly there were trumpets (the unemployed) blaring, rattling about in the uproar; military music; as if people were marching; yet had they been dying—had some woman breathed her last and whoever was watching, opening the window of the room where she had just brought off that act of supreme dignity, looked down on Fleet Street, that uproar, that military music would have come triumphing up to him, consolatory, indifferent.

It was not conscious. There was no recognition in it of one fortune, or fate, and for that very reason even to those dazed with watching for the last shivers of consciousness on the faces of the dying, consoling. Forgetfulness in people might wound, their ingratitude corrode, but this voice, pouring endlessly, year in year out, would take whatever it might be; this vow; this van; this life; this procession, would wrap them all about and carry them on, as in the rough stream of a glacier the ice holds a splinter of bone, a blue petal, some oak trees, and rolls them on.

But it was later than she thought. Her mother would not like her to be wandering off alone like this. She turned back down the Strand.

A puff of wind (in spite of the heat, there was quite a wind) blew a thin black veil over the sun and over the Strand. The faces faded; the omnibuses suddenly lost their glow. For although the clouds were of mountainous white so that one could fancy hacking hard chips off with a hatchet, with broad golden slopes, lawns of celestial pleasure gardens, on their flanks, and had all the appearance of settled habitations assembled for the conference of gods above the world, there was a perpetual movement among them. Signs were interchanged, when, as if to fulfil some scheme arranged already, now a summit dwindled, now a whole block of pyramidal size which had kept its station inalterably advanced into the midst or gravely led the procession to fresh anchorage. Fixed though they seemed at their posts, at rest in perfect unanimity, nothing could be fresher, freer, more sensitive superficially than the snow-white or gold-kindled surface; to change, to go, to dismantle the solemn assemblage was immediately possible; and in spite of the grave fixity, the accumulated robustness and solidity, now they struck light to the earth, now darkness.

Calmly and competently, Elizabeth Dalloway mounted the Westminster omnibus.

译

很多时候，她母亲都觉得她太不成熟，像个孩子似的，离不开布娃娃，喜欢穿旧拖鞋。一个十足的婴儿，还挺有魅力的。

当然啦，在达洛维家族也有一个从事公共服务的传统，女修道院院长、公立学校校长和私立学校校长，还有一些其他女性领域的显要人物——她们都不太聪明，但都有魅力。她又往圣保罗大教堂方向走了一小段路，她喜欢亲近感，喧闹钟声中的姐妹、母女还有兄弟们。这对她有好处。噪音很大，不知从哪突然传来嘹亮的小号（是失业者们），穿透喧哗声，应该是军乐，似乎有人在游行（齐步前进）。如果有人即将离世，一名女人正在弥留之际，她身旁的守护人，无论是谁，在她去世的神圣时刻，若打开房间窗户，往舰队街上看，逼近的军乐的喧闹声，无疑是种安慰，因为它对这一切一无所知。

声响并无意识。看不出是运气，或是命运，即便是见了垂危之人最后颤抖的那一幕，也觉得欣慰。忘却让人伤心，忘恩负义也具有腐蚀性，但这种无休止的声音，年复一年，日复一日，将带走一切——誓言，车厢，生活，还有这个队列——将把它们裹起，卷走，就像冰川的激流挟着一块碎骨，一片蓝花瓣，还有几棵橡树，滚滚前行。

时间比她想象的要晚了。母亲不喜欢她这样漫游。她沿着河岸街往回走。

一阵清风吹来（尽管天气炎热，还是有好一阵风），太阳和河岸街都罩上了一层薄薄的黑纱。那些脸庞渐渐看不清了，公交车也失去了光泽。云朵如大山般，一片雪白，似乎是用斧头在中间削下硬条，两侧是金色的斜坡，天堂般的草地，仿佛天上集会的场所，众神隐约其中。还有一些记号，大概是在完成原定的会议章程吧。过了一会儿，山峰渐渐消失了，又过了一会儿，金字塔般大小的云挪到中间或庄严地驶入新的停靠点。这些云看起来都停留在原地，表面雪白、金黄，没有比这更新鲜、更自在、更有灵性的了。忽而又变了形，消失了，庄严的集会解散了。肃穆，稳固，却又不失活力。光线射到地面，天暗下来了。

伊丽莎白·达洛维登上了威斯敏斯特的公交车，镇静而自信。

第三节 翻译练习

一、《红楼梦》节选

黛玉方进入房时，只见两个人搀着一位鬓发如银的老母迎上来，黛玉便知是他外祖母。方欲拜见时，早被他外祖母一把搂入怀中，心肝儿肉叫着大哭起来。当下地下侍立之人，无不掩面涕泣，黛玉也哭个不住。一时众人慢慢解劝住了，那黛玉方拜见了外祖母。……当下贾母一一指与黛玉道："这是你大舅母。这是你二舅母。这是你先珠大哥的媳妇珠大嫂子。"黛玉一一拜见过。贾母又说："请姑娘们来。今日远客才来，可以不必上学去了。"众人答应了一声，便去了两个。

不一时，只见三个奶嬷嬷并五六个丫鬟，簇拥着三个姊妹来了。第一个肌肤微丰，合中身材，腮凝新荔，鼻腻鹅脂，温柔沉默，观之可亲。第二个削肩细腰，长挑身材，鸭蛋脸儿，俊眼修眉，顾盼神飞，文彩精华，见之忘俗。第三个身量未足，形容尚小。其钗环裙袄，三人皆是一样的妆饰。黛玉忙起身迎上来见礼，互相厮认过，大家归了坐。丫鬟斟上茶来。不过说些黛玉之母如何得病，如何请医服药，如何送死发丧。不免贾母又伤感起来，因说："我这些儿女，所疼者独有你母亲。今日一旦先舍我而去，连面也不能一见，今见了你，我怎不伤心！"说着，搂了黛玉在怀，又呜咽起来。众人忙都宽慰解释，方略略止住。

……

一语未了，只听后院中有人笑声，说："我来迟了，不曾迎接远客！"黛玉纳罕道："这些人个个皆敛声屏气，恭肃严整如此，这来者系谁，这样放诞无礼？"心下想时，只见一群媳妇丫鬟拥着一人从后房门进来。这个人打扮与姑娘们不同，彩绣辉煌，恍若神妃仙子。头上戴着金丝八宝攒珠髻，绾着朝阳五凤挂珠钗，项上戴着赤金盘螭缨珞圈，裙边系着豆绿宫绦双衡比目玫瑰佩；身上穿着缕金百蝶穿花大红云缎窄褃袄，外罩五彩刻丝石青银鼠褂；下着翡翠撒花洋绉裙。一双丹凤三角眼，两弯柳叶吊梢眉，身量苗条，体格风骚，粉面含春威不露，丹唇未启笑先闻。黛玉连忙起身接见。贾母笑道："你不认得他。他是我们这里有名的一个泼皮破落户儿，南省俗谓作'辣子'，你只叫他'凤辣子'就是了。"

黛玉正不知以何称呼，只见众姊妹都忙告诉他道："这是琏二嫂子。"黛玉虽不识，也曾听见母亲说过，大舅贾赦之子贾琏，娶的就是二舅母王氏的内侄女；自幼假充男儿教养的，学名王熙凤。黛玉忙陪笑见礼，以"嫂"呼之。

这熙凤携着黛玉的手，上下细细打谅了一回，仍送至贾母身边坐下，因笑道："天下真有这样标致人物！我今日才算看见了！况且这通身的气派，竟不像老祖宗的外孙女儿，竟是个嫡亲孙女，怨不得老祖宗天天口头心头一时不忘。只可怜我这妹妹这么命苦，怎么姑妈偏就去世了！"说着，便用帕拭泪。贾母笑道："我才好了，你又来招我。你妹妹远路才来，身子又弱，也才劝住了，快再休提前话。"这熙凤听了，忙转悲为喜道："正是呢！我一见了妹妹，一心都在他身上了，又是喜欢，又是伤心，竟忘了老祖宗。该打，该打！"又忙携黛玉之手，问："妹妹几岁了？可也上过学？现吃什么药？在这里不要想家，想要什么吃的、什么玩的，只管告诉我；丫头老婆们不好了，也只管告诉我。"一面又问婆子们："林姑娘的行李东西可搬进来了？带了几个人来？你们赶早打扫两间屋子，叫他们去歇歇。"

说话时，已摆了果茶上来。熙凤亲为捧茶捧果。又见二舅母问他："月钱放过不曾？"熙凤道："月钱已放完了。才刚带着人到后楼上找缎子，找了这半日，也并没见昨日太太说的那样的，想是太太记错了。"王夫人道："有没有，什么要紧。"因又说道："该随手拿出两个来给你这妹妹裁衣裳的，等晚上想着叫人再去拿罢，可别忘了。"熙凤道："这倒是我先料着了，知道妹妹不过这两日到的，我已预备下了，等太太回去过了目好送来。"王夫人一笑，点头不语。

二、《活着》节选

和福贵相遇，使我对以后收集民谣的日子充满快乐的期待，我以为那块肥沃茂盛的土地上福贵这样的人比比皆是。在后来的日子里，我确实遇到了许多像福贵那样的老人，他们穿得和福贵一样的衣裤，裤裆都快耷拉到膝盖了。他们脸上的皱纹里积满了阳光和泥土，他们向我微笑时，我看到空洞的嘴里牙齿所剩无几。他们时常流出混浊的眼泪，这倒不是因为他们时常悲伤，他们在高兴时甚至是在什么事都没有的平静时刻，也会泪流而出，然后举起和乡间泥路一样粗糙的手指，擦去眼泪，如同掸去身上的稻草。

可是我再也没遇到一个像福贵这样令我难忘的人了，对自己的经历如此清楚，又能如此精彩地讲述自己。他是那种能够看到自己过去模样的人，他可以准确地看到自己年轻时走路的姿态，甚至可以看到自己是如何衰老的。这样的老人在乡间实在难以遇上，也许是困苦的生活损坏了他们的记忆，面对往事他们通常显得木讷，常常以不知所措的微笑搪塞过去。他们对自己的经历缺乏热情，仿佛是道听途说般的只记得零星几点，即便是这零星几点也都是自身之外的记忆，用一两句话表达了他们所认为的一切。在这里，我常常听到后辈们这样骂他们：

"一大把年纪全活到狗身上去了。"

福贵就完全不一样了，他喜欢回想过去，喜欢讲述自己，似乎这样一来，他就可以一次一次地重度此生了。他的讲述像鸟爪抓住树枝那样紧紧抓住我。

家珍走后，我娘时常坐在一边偷偷抹眼泪，我本想找几句话去宽慰宽慰她，一看到她那副样子，就什么话也说不出来了。倒是她常对我说：

"家珍是你的女人，不是别人的，谁也抢不走。"

我听了这话，只能在心里叹息一声，我还能说什么呢？好端端的一个家成了砸破了的瓦罐似的四分五裂。到了晚上，我躺在床上常常睡不着，一会儿恨这个，一会恨那个，到头来最恨的还是我自己。夜里想得太多，白天就头疼，整日无精打采，好在有凤霞，凤霞常拉着我的手问我：

"爹，一张桌子有四个角，削掉一个角还剩几个角？"

也不知道凤霞是从哪里去听来的，当我说还剩三个角时，凤霞高兴的格格乱笑，她说：

"错啦，还剩五个角。"

听了凤霞的话，我想笑却笑不出来，想到原先家里四个人，家珍一走就等于是削掉了一个角，况且家珍肚里还怀着孩子，我就对凤霞说：

"等你娘回来了，就会有五个角了。"

家里值钱的东西都变卖光了以后，我娘就常常领着凤霞去挖野菜，我娘挎着篮子小脚一扭一扭地走去，她走得还没有凤霞快。她头发都白了，却要学着去干从没干过的体力活。

看着我娘拉着凤霞看一步走一步，那小心的样子让我眼泪都快掉出来了。

我想想再不能像从前那样过日子了，我得养活我娘和凤霞。我就和娘商量着到城里亲友那里去借点钱，开个小铺子，我娘听了这话一声不吭，她是舍不得离开这里，人上了年纪都这样，都不愿动地方。我就对娘说：

"如今屋子和地都是龙二的了，家安在这里跟安在别处也一样。"

我娘听了这话，过了半晌才说：

"你爹的坟还在这里。"

我娘一句话就让我不敢再想别的主意了，我想来想去只好去找龙二。

龙二成了这里的地主，常常穿着丝绸衣衫，右手拿着茶壶在田埂上走来走去，神气得很。镶着两颗大金牙的嘴总是咧开笑着，有时骂看着不顺眼的佃户时也咧着嘴，我起先还以为他对人亲热，慢慢地就知道他是要别人都看到他的金牙。

龙二遇到我还算客气，常笑嘻嘻地说：

"福贵，到我家来喝壶茶吧。"

我一直没去龙二家是怕自己心里发酸，我两脚一落地就住在那幢屋子里了，如今那屋子是龙二的家，你想想我心里是什么滋味。

其实人落到那种地步也就顾不上那么多了，我算是应了人穷志短那句古话了。那天我去找龙二时，龙二坐在我家客厅的太师椅子里，两条腿搁在凳子上，一手拿茶壶一手拿着扇子，看到我走进来，龙二咧嘴笑道：

"是福贵，自己找把凳子坐吧。"

他躺在太师椅里动都没动，我也就不指望他泡壶茶给我喝。我坐下后龙二说：

"福贵，你是来找我借钱的吧？"

我还没说不是，他就往下说道：

"按理说我也该借几个钱给你，俗话说是救急不救穷，我啊，只能救你的急，不会救你的穷。"

我点点头说："我想租几亩田。"

龙二听后笑眯眯地问：

"你要租几亩？"

我说："租五亩。"

"五亩？"龙二眉毛往上吊了吊，问："你这身体能行吗？"

我说："练练就行了。"

他想一想："我们是老相识了，我给你五亩好田。"

龙二还是讲点交情的，他真给了我五亩好田。我一个人种五亩地，差点没累死。我从没干过农活，学着村里人的样子干活，别说有多慢了。看得见的时候我都在田里，到了天黑，只要有月光，我还要下地。庄稼得赶上季节，错过一个季节就全错过啦。到那时别说是养活一家人，就是龙二的租粮也交不起。俗话说是笨鸟先飞，我还得笨鸟多飞。

我娘心疼我，也跟着我下地干活，她一大把年纪了，脚又不方便，身体弯下去才一会儿工夫就直不起来了，常常是一屁股坐在了田里。我对她说：

"娘，你赶紧回去吧。"

我娘摇摇头说："四只手总比两只手强。"

我说："你要是累成病，那就一只手都没了，我还得照料你。"

我娘听了这话，才慢慢回到田埂上坐下，和凤霞呆在一起。凤霞是天天坐在田埂上陪我，她采了很多花放在腿边，一朵一朵举起来问我叫什么花，我哪知道是什么花，就说：

"问你奶奶去。"

我娘坐到田埂上，看到我用锄头就常喊：

"留神别砍了脚。"

我用镰刀时，她更不放心，时时说：

"福贵，别把手割破了。"

我娘老是在一旁提醒也不管用，活太多，我得快干，一快就免不了砍了脚割破手。

手脚一出血，可把我娘心疼坏了，扭着小脚跑过来，捏一块烂泥巴堵住出血的地方，嘴里一个劲儿地数落我，一说得说半晌，我还不能回嘴，要不她眼泪都会掉出来。

我娘常说地里的泥是最养人的，不光是长庄稼，还能治病。那么多年下来，我身上那儿弄破了，都往上贴一块湿泥巴。我娘说得对，不能小看那些烂泥巴，那可是治百病的。

人要是累得整天没力气，就不会去乱想了。租了龙二的田以后，我一挨到床就呼呼地睡去，根本没工夫去想别的什么。说起来日子过得又苦又累，我心里反倒踏实了。我想着我们徐家也算是有一只小鸡了，照我这么干下去，过不了几年小鸡就会变成鹅，徐家总有一天会重新发起来的。

从那以后，我是再没穿过绸衣了，我穿的粗布衣服是我娘亲手织的布，刚穿上那阵子觉得不自在，身上的肉被磨来磨去，日子一久也就舒坦了。前几天村里的王喜死了，王喜是我家从前的佃户，比我大两岁，他死前嘱咐儿子把他的旧绸衣送给我，他一直没忘记我从前是少爷，他是想让我死之前穿上绸衣风光风光。我啊，对不起王喜的一片好心，那件绸衣我往身上一穿就赶紧脱了下来，那个难受啊，滑溜溜的像是穿上了鼻涕做的衣服。

三、*Jane Eyre* 节选

I rose; I dressed myself with care: obliged to be plain—for I had no article of attire that was not made with extreme simplicity—I was still by nature solicitous to be neat. It was not my habit to be disregardful of appearance or careless of the impression I made: on the contrary, I ever wished to look as well as I could, and to please as much as my want of beauty would permit. I sometimes regretted that I was not handsomer; I sometimes wished to have rosy cheeks, a straight nose, and small cherry mouth; I desired to be tall, stately, and finely developed in figure; I felt it a misfortune that I was so little, so pale, and had features so irregular and so marked. And why had I these aspirations and these regrets? It would be difficult to say: I could not then distinctly say it to myself; yet I had a reason, and a logical, natural reason too. However, when I had brushed my hair very smooth, and put on my black frock—which, Quakerlike as it was, at least had the merit of fitting to a nicety—and adjusted my clean white tucker, I thought I should do respectably enough to appear before Mrs. Fairfax, and that my new pupil would not at least recoil from me with antipathy. Having opened my chamber window, and seen that I left all things straight and neat on the toilet table, I ventured forth.

Traversing the long and matted gallery, I descended the slippery steps of oak; then I gained the hall: I halted there a minute; I looked at some pictures on the walls (one, I remember, represented a grim man in a cuirass, and one a lady with powdered hair and a pearl necklace), at a bronze lamp pendent from the ceiling, at a great clock whose case was of oak curiously carved, and ebon black with time and rubbing. Everything appeared very stately and imposing to me; but then I was so little accustomed to grandeur.

四、"The Fall of the House of Usher" 节选

DURING the whole of a dull, dark, and soundless day in the autumn of the year, when the clouds hung oppressively low in the heavens, I had been passing alone, on horseback, through a singularly dreary tract of country, and at length found myself, as the shades of the evening drew on, within view of the melancholy House of Usher. I know not how it was—but, with the first glimpse of the building, a sense of insufferable gloom pervaded my spirit. I say insufferable; for the feeling was unrelieved by any of that half-pleasurable, because poetic, sentiment, with which the mind usually receives even the sternest natural images of the desolate or terrible. I looked upon the scene before me—upon the mere house, and the simple landscape features of the domain—upon the bleak walls—upon the vacant eye-like windows—upon a few rank sedges—and upon a few white trunks of decayed trees—with an utter depression of soul which I can compare to no earthly sensation more properly than to the after-dream of the reveller upon opium—the bitter lapse into every-day life—the hideous dropping off of the veil. There was an iciness, a sinking, a sickening of the heart—an unredeemed dreariness of thought which no goading of the imagination could torture into aught of the sublime. What was it—I paused to think—what was it that so unnerved me in the contemplation of the House of Usher? It was a mystery all insoluble; nor could I grapple with the shadowy fancies that crowded upon me as I pondered. I was forced to fall back upon the unsatisfactory conclusion, that while, beyond doubt, there are combinations of very simple natural objects which have the power of thus affecting us, still the analysis of this power lies among considerations beyond our depth. It was possible, I reflected, that a mere different arrangement of the particulars of the scene, of the details of the picture, would be sufficient to modify, or perhaps to annihilate its capacity for sorrowful impression; and, acting upon this idea, I reined my horse to the precipitous brink of a black and lurid tarn that lay in unruffled lustre by the dwelling, and gazed down—but with a shudder even more thrilling than before—upon the remodelled and inverted images of the gray sedge, and the ghastly tree-stems, and the vacant and eye-like windows.

第三章　戏剧的翻译

戏剧既可以阅读，也可以用来演出，这种双重特征决定了戏剧翻译与诗歌、小说的翻译有着一些根本的区别。下文在介绍戏剧的基本特点后，通过一些经典剧作的翻译，如中国传统戏剧《牡丹亭》以及莎士比亚的剧本的翻译，来说明戏剧翻译的主要特征。

第一节　文体特征

戏剧具有可读性、可视性和可听性，是文字、图像和声音等多种媒介的结合，具有多模态性和表演性两大主要特征。

一、多模态

Drama as a Multimedial Form of Presentation
The dramatic text as a scenically enacted text.
The criteria outlined in the previous sections, namely the omission of the mediating communication system and performative speech, are indispensable, though in themselves still rather inadequate preconditions for a model of dramatic communication. Taken on their own, these criteria would force us to identify as dramatic texts such historical forms as, for example, the Victorian "dramatic monologue" of Tennyson and Browning or novels written entirely in dialogue form. There is, however one criterion which enables us to distinguish between such literary forms and drama: the multimedial nature of dramatic text presentation. As a "performed" text, drama, in contrast to purely literary texts, makes use not only of verbal, but also of acoustic and visual codes. It is a synaesthetic text. This important criterion provides the starting point for any semiotic analysis of drama. ... Both definitions correctly regard the dramatic text as the scenically enacted text, one of whose components is the verbally manifested text. These two levels may be distinguished by their differing degrees of stability and/or variability, for whilst the verbally manifested text is normally fixed orthographically, and thus remains historically more or less stable, the scenic component of the stage enactment is variable—a fact clearly demonstrated in modern productions of the classics,

even in those that do not alter the written text in any significant way.

The scenic level itself may be divided into two components by implementing the same criterion of stability versus variability. First, there are those elements of the stage enactment which are either explicitly demanded by the literary text, or at least clearly implied by it, and secondly, there are those which are the "ingredients" added by the production. Such ingredients are always present, even in the most "authentic" productions, since the very physical presence of the multimedial text always adds a surplus of information to the literary text. This dual-layered aspect of dramatic texts has resulted in two often strongly diverging types of interpretation: the purely literary interpretations of the verbally fixed text substrata, and the various productions and enactments of the texts on stage.

The repertoire of codes and channels

Dramatic texts have the potential to activate all channels of the human senses. Over the centuries, of course, dramatic productions have been restricted almost exclusively to texts employing acoustic and visual codes alone. Exceptions to this are more recent developments such as happenings or ritualist theatre, which also experiment with haptic (physical contact between actors and audience), olfactory and even gustatory effects.

The dominant acoustic sign system is usually language, but this may be accompanied or replaced by non-verbal acoustic codes such as realistic noises, conventionalised sound effects (bells, thunder etc.) and music. Similarly, the visual component of the supersign "dramatic text" presents itself as a structured complex of individual visual codes. The most important of these are the stature and physiognomy of the actors, choreography and the grouping of characters, mime and gesture, mask, costume and properties, the size and form of the stage itself, the set and, finally, lighting. This set of components is integrated into the dramatic text as a system of interdependent structural elements. The relationships that exist between these various components will be the subject of the following paragraphs.

We have presented, in the form of a diagram (3.1), the repertoire of the codes and channels that are employed in dramatic texts. Our first classification criterion has been derived from the structure of human sensual perception—that is, from the five senses as channels for conveying information. As we remarked above, the vast majority of dramatic texts has exhibited a clear preference for the visual and acoustic channels, whilst the remaining senses of smell, touch and taste have been activated extremely sporadically, and then almost exclusively in the modern theatre of the avant-garde. An example of the use of touch was given in Paradise Now (1968) by the "living theatre" of Julian and Judith Beck, in which the audience was invited to join the actors for the great love-scene and then to be carried into the street on the actors'shoulders. Since these channels are activated so rarely, however, they have been placed in brackets in the diagram, and further classification of information mediated by them has been omitted.

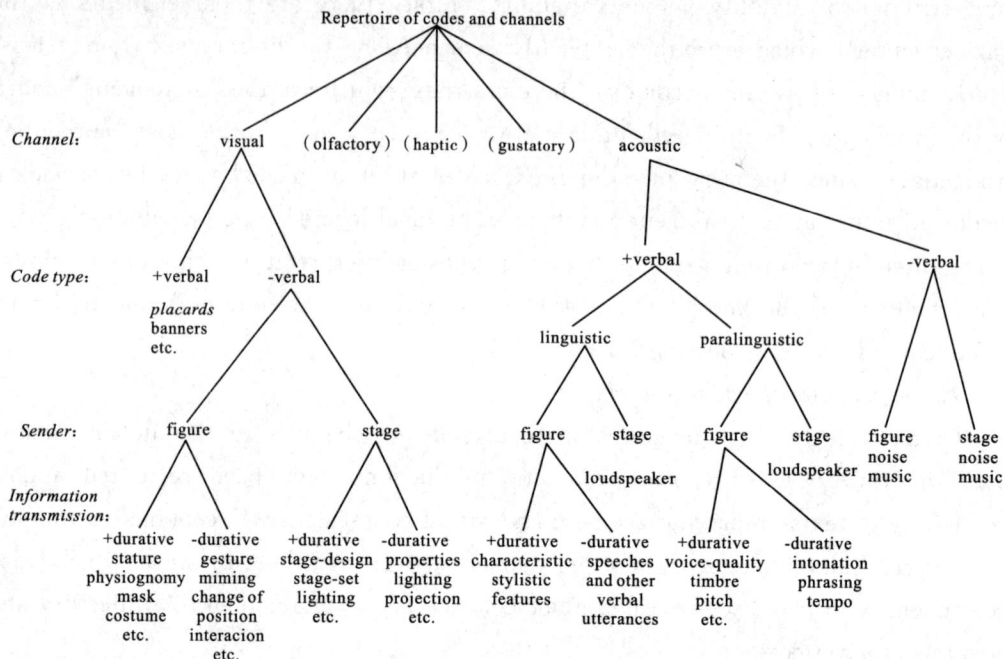

Repertoire of codes and channels

Channel: visual （olfactory） （haptic） （gustatory） acoustic

Code type: +verbal -verbal +verbal -verbal

placards banners etc.

linguistic paralinguistic

Sender: figure stage figure stage figure stage figure stage

loudspeaker loudspeaker noise noise music music

Information transmission:

+durative	-durative	+durative	-durative	+durative	-durative	+durative	-durative
stature physiognomy mask costume etc.	gesture miming change of position interacion etc.	stage-design stage-set lighting etc.	properties lighting projection etc.	characteristic stylistic features	speeches and other verbal utterances	voice-quality timbre pitch etc.	intonation phrasing tempo

图 3.1　戏剧文本符码

The second classification criterion is the type of code used. Of particular semiotic relevance in this context is the distinction between verbal and non-verbal codes and the further subdivision of the verbal codes into linguistic and paralinguistic codes. Generally speaking, the linguistic code is a "symbolic code", whose signs are based on an arbitrary set of conventions. This means that the relationship between the sign and the signified object is unmotivated. At the same time, however, the majority of signs belonging to the paralinguistic and non-verbal codes are either "indices" that are related to the signified object physically or contiguously or "icons" which represent the signified object by being similar to it.

Thus, within the supersign of the dramatic text, codes of varying degrees of standardisation operate together. Whilst the linguistic code represents a strictly standardised system of rules that guarantees a relatively high level of explicitness in the decoding process, the non-verbal indices and icons are much more ambiguous. As a result, this frequently leads to marked differences of interpretation.

In the external communication system, however, this horizontal juxtaposition of the various code-types is transformed into a vertically arranged hierarchy. The text appears as an iconic supersign, within which even the transmission of symbolic and indexical signs has been iconicised into a fictional model of real communication. This iconic supersign is itself determined by comprehensive secondary codes—i. e. the numerous literary and dramatic conventions and genres—and is transmitted by the distributive channels open to dramatic texts. It has not been possible to show this process directly on our diagram, simply because it takes place on a more comprehensive plane.

The third classification criterion derives from the fictional sender of information. Put rather simply, we distinguish between character and non-character—i. e. the stage. Thus, costume is related to character as the properties are to the stage, for example. However, shifts in these relationships may occur, as a result of which a property might be so strongly associated with a particular character that it becomes a part of his or her costume, or, conversely—as in a masquerade or travesty—a character might become so far removed from his or her costume that it becomes a property.

Our final classification criterion refers to the characteristics that apply to the various ways of transmitting information. In this context, we distinguish between durative and non-durative elements, according to whether the same single piece of information is being transmitted over an extended period of time or whether new pieces of information are continually being transmitted. The difference is merely relative, however, and the decision to allocate a particular sign to one or another of these categories depends on the length of the observation period. Thus, the transmission of information by the set within a closed scenic context is generally durative, whereas in the course of the text as a whole, with set-changes between scenes and/or acts, it is generally non-durative. The structuring of this part of our diagram was therefore based on relative values and general tendencies alone and would have to be revised before it could apply to certain individual texts or historical text-types. In a large number of modern texts, for example, developments in stage technology have made it possible for the set, lighting and even stage-design to change from durative to non-durative.

Listing these criteria has underlined and clarified our thesis that the multimedial dramatic text contains more information than the literary text. Not even the purely verbal component of the supersign "dramatic text" can be determined from the orthographically fixed text alone, since there are a number of unpredictable, paralinguistic variables of both a durative—such as the voice-quality of the particular actor—and nondurative kind—such as intonation, tempo and the use of pauses etc. —which are introduced into the oral enactment of the text by the actor. As far as non-verbal, acoustic and visual codes are concerned, this information differential is generally even greater, for even the most detailed description of a dramatic figure, his actions and sphere of action must, of necessity, be subordinate to the physical presence, mimetic skills and gestures of each individual actor, and the physical presence of each individual set.

(From *The Theory and Analysis of Drama*，有删改)

二、表演性

Drama in the Context of Public Performance Activities

Structurally speaking, the features associated with dramatic texts that we analysed in the preceding sections (the overlapping of internal and external communication systems, relative autonomy, multimediality and the collective nature of production and reception) are all qualities that also apply to non-literary performance activities. Indeed, if "performance" can be described as "the doing of an activity by an individual or group largely for the pleasure of another individual or group", then drama clearly belongs to this category as much as games with fixed rules, sporting competition, ritual and unstructured forms of "play". What all of these share is the indirect nature of their relationship with the real world. In all cases, this has been brought about by embedding the internal communication system in the external system (which, in drama, provides the specific link between "fictionality" and reality), by clearly distinguishing between performers and spectators, by emphasising the differences between drama and more specifically economic forms of productivity, by suspending the temporal and spatial relationships of ordinary everyday life, and, finally, by implementing special rules and conventions.

These structurally related performance activities are partly connected to each other as progressive steps in the context of a general process of development. Thus, unstructured play may serve as the ontogenetic source of all the other activities in the development of the individual, and, historically speaking, ritual may be interpreted as a phylogenetic precursor of drama. The weakest structural affinity exists between drama and unstructured play, since the latter is not necessarily public, does not require an audience and is not preprogrammed with fixed rules. More recent developments, such as those in the sphere of the happening, have nonetheless often come close to unstructured play in so far as the distinction between performers and spectators tends to disappear, and the execution of the text is not completely determined in advance.

...

The literary historian is not always quite as sharply aware of the importance of non-verbal codes for the dramatic text as the dramatist. Poring over his printed texts, the former tends to neglect the multimedia! aspect of theatrical performance, whereas the latter regards this as a crucial component of the literary text. For, in the words of Max Frisch: Whoever appears on the stage and does not make proper use of the stage will find it working against him. Making use of the stage means: not being just on it, but with it.

Like Frisch, Ionesco is another to emphasise the unity of the multimedial dramatic text, maintaining that to strip it down to the bare minimum would be an inexcusable aberration and abbreviation ...

Statements such as these seem particularly important at a time when，for various socio-cultural reasons，plays—at least the non-trivial ones—are more often read than seen in the theatre. They apply particularly to the institutionalised study of dramatic texts at schools and universities，where they are frequently stripped of their theatrical qualities. Dr Johnson's neoclassical dictum："A play read affects the mind like a play acted"，can only be true of the reader who is able to bring the numerous explicit and implicit signs and signals inherent in the literary text to life in his imagination.

(From *The Theory and Analysis of Drama*)

第二节 赏·译·评

下文主要选《牡丹亭》和《罗密欧与朱丽叶》两部作品进行评析。

一、《牡丹亭》（节选）

译

译文一

第一出　标目	Scene One Prelude
	(Entre Announcer)
【蝶恋花】	Announcer：
〔末上〕忙处抛人闲处住，	(To the tune of *Die Lian Hua*)
百计思量，	All the men prefr remaining free;
没个为欢处。	Yet howe'er they try,
白日消磨肠断句，	They are as worried as can be.
世间只有情难诉。	Among the sentimental tales I write,
玉茗堂前朝复暮，	Love is as mysterious as the sea.
红烛迎人，俊得江山助。	I write the tale from morning till night,
但是相思莫相负，	With candles burning bright,
牡丹亭上三生路。	Englightening me in the brightest ray.
	when a beauty falls in love with a man.
	The Peony Pavilion sees her ardent way.

杜宝黄堂， 生丽娘小姐， 爱踏春阳。 感梦书生折柳， 竟为情伤。 写真留纪， 葬梅花道院凄凉。 三年上， 有梦梅柳子， 于此赴高唐。 果尔回生定配。 赴临安取试， 寇起淮扬。 整把杜公围困， 小姐惊惶。 教柳郎行探， 反遭疑激恼平章。 风流况， 施行正苦，报中状元郎。	"Du Bao，the magistrate, Has a daughter by the name of Liniang, Who strolls in a sunny springtime date. When she dreams of a scholar breaking willows, She's thrown into a grievous state. She draws a self-potrait And pines away lamenting o'er her fate. When three years have passed by， Liu Mengmei comes along To meet her in the garden once again. Du Liniang gains her second life. When Liu is about to seek office in Lin'an, There arrives a mob of rebellieous men. As Du Bao is besieged inside the town, His daughter is in a panic then. Liu Mengmei goes to seek information, But his good will is beyond Du's ken. When his love affair is in great trouble, News comes that Liu is allotted office And Liu at last fulfills his yen."
杜丽娘梦写丹青记。 陈教授说下梨花枪。 柳秀才偷载回生女。 杜平章刁打状元郎。	Du Liniang draws a portrait true to life; Chen Zuiliang brings about the peach once more; Liu Mengmei meets his resurrected wife; Du Bao give tortures to his son-in-law.

（汪榕培　译）

译文二

牡丹亭	
第一出 标目 【蝶恋花】 [末上] 忙处抛人闲处住， 百计思量， 没个为欢处。 白日消磨肠断句， 世间只有情难诉。 玉茗堂前朝复暮， 红烛迎人， 俊得江山助。 但是相思莫相负， 牡丹亭上三生路。	Translated by Cyril Birch PROLOGUE−SPEAKER：① By busy world rejected，in my own world of retreat I pondered a hundred schemes finding joy in none. All day I spent polishing verses of heart-rending sadness For the telling of "love，in all life hardest to tell"② Dawns warmed and twilights shadowed my Hall of Limpid Tea Till "with red candle I welcomed friends" —and always "the hills and streams raised high my powers." Let my only keep faith with the history of this longing, Of the road which led Through three incarnations③ to the Peony Pavilion.

---

① The player of the role of Ch'en Tsui-ling，the old tutor who first appears in Scene Four. Here he speaks in the voice of the author himself. Usually it is the player of a less prominent "older male" role who is given the prologue.

② Quotation, slightly altered to suit the present rhyme-scheme，from a poet of the T'ang dynasty. Quotations are extremely frequent throughout the play and are mostly from the T'ang poets. The 1958 Peking edition gives the sources: here I shall simply mark them as quotes.

③ The history of the girl who died and through the power of love returned to life. "Three incantations" is an exaggeration born of the belief that it required three lifetimes for a perfect love to attain consummation. There is probably a reference here to the "rock of three incarnations": during the T'ang period a strong friendship grew between Li Yuan and the monk Yuan-kuan (or Yuan-tse). Approaching death，Yuan-kuan told Li that in twelve years' time they would meet before the Tien-chu Temple in Hangchou. When in time came Li Yuan found there，by the "rock of three incarnations"，a herd-boy who was the reincarnation of Yuan-luan. (*Tai-p'ing kuang-chi*)

杜宝黄堂， 生丽娘小姐， 爱踏春阳。 感梦书生折柳， 竟为情伤。 写真留纪， 葬梅花道院凄凉。 三年上， 有梦梅柳子， 于此赴高唐。 果尔回生定配。 赴临安取试， 寇起淮扬。 正把杜公围困， 小姐惊惶。 教柳郎行探， 反遭疑激恼平章。	To the Perfect To Pao Was born a daughter Li-niang Who longed to walk in the spring light. Roused by a dream of a young scholar who broke off a branch from the willow She pined and died of love, but left her portrait memorial In the Pium-blossom Shrine where her cold grave lay. Three years passed and a scholar, named Liu, for "willow", Meng-mei, for "dreaming of plum-flower" Found at this Kao-t'ang his dream of love. ① Then in truth she returned to life and became his bride. But when the examinations took him to Lin-an bandit arouse at Huai-yang Besieged Perfect Tu and filled Li-niang with fear. Sent by her to seek news Liu raised doubts and anger in the mind of Tu Bao, now First Minister.
风流况， 施行正苦， 报中状元郎。	A romantic tale, But a tale whose execution② Almost caused the execution Of Prize Candidate③ Liu Meng mei, announced in the nick of time.
杜丽娘梦写丹青记。 陈教授说下梨花枪。 柳秀才偷载回生女。 杜平章刁打状元郎。	Tu Li-niang takes colored inks To portray herself after dreaming, Tutor Ch'en used his tongue To subdue the "pear-blossom spear," The graduate Liu escorts by stealth A girl returned to the living, Minister Tu strings up and flogs The young Prize Candidate. ④

Notes:

评

①Compare and contrast: What is the major difference between Wang's version and

① According to the Kao-t'ang Fu by the Han poet Sung Yü, the mountain Wu-shan at Ka-t'ang was where Prince Huei of Ch'u made love in a dream to a beautiful woman who told him, "At dawn I am the morning clouds, at dust the driving rain."

② Pun on the phrase *shih-hsing*, "put into practice/ apply punishment". So far as possible such puns will be retained in translation, at the risk of some prolixity and occasional inventions.

③ *Chuang-yuan*, winner of first place for the entire country in the examination held in the palace for the final proving of scholars.

④ The *tsa-chü* drama of the Yuan period concluded with hisa-ch'ang shih. These verses however are merely cleverly-arranged pastiches of appropriate lines from earlier (usually T'ang) poets, and all are omitted from the present translation.

Birch's version? Are the detailed annotations of the latter necessary? Why?

②In translating Chinese classical literature, what should be taken as the first priority, faithfulness, expressiveness or elegance? Why?

③What are their respective target audience? In translating of classics, how should reception be taken into consideration?

④Some dramas are translated to be read, while others are translated so to be performed，How about the above two different versions of *The Peony Pavilion*?

二、*Romeo and Juliet*（节选）

ROMEO   She speaks：
O，speak again，bright angel! for thou art
As glorious to this night，being o'er my head
As is a winged messenger of heaven
Unto the white-upturned wondering eyes
Of mortals that fall back to gaze on him
When he bestrides the lazy-pacing clouds
And sails upon the bosom of the air.

JULIETO   Romeo，Romeo! wherefore art thou Romeo?
Deny thy father and refuse thy name；
Or，if thou wilt not，be but sworn my love，
And I'll no longer be a Capulet.

ROMEO   [Aside] Shall I hear more, or shall I speak at this?

JULIET   Tis but thy name that is my enemy；
Thou art thyself，though not a Montague.
What's Montague? it is nor hand，nor foot，
Nor arm，nor face，nor any other part
Belonging to a man. O，be some other name!
What's in a name? that which we call a rose
By any other name would smell as sweet；
So Romeo would，were he not Romeo call'd，
Retain that dear perfection which he owes
Without that title. Romeo，doff thy name，
And for that name which is no part of thee
Take all myself.

ROMEOI   Take thee at thy word：
Call me but love，and I'll be new baptized；
Henceforth I never will be Romeo.

125

JULIET	What man art thou that thus be screen'd in night
	So stumblest on my counsel?
ROMEO	By a name
	I know not how to tell thee who I am:
	My name, dear saint, is hateful to myself,
	Because it is an enemy to thee;
	Had I it written, I would tear the word.
JULIET	My ears have not yet drunk a hundred words
	Of that tongue's utterance, yet I know the sound:
	Art thou not Romeo and a Montague?
ROMEO	Neither, fair saint, if either thee dislike.
JULIET	How camest thou hither, tell me, and wherefore?
	The orchard walls are high and hard to climb,
	And the place death, considering who thou art,
	If any of my kinsmen find thee here.
ROMEO	With love's light wings did I o'er-perch these walls;
	For stony limits cannot hold love out,
	And what love can do that dares love attempt;
	Therefore thy kinsmen are no let to me.
JULIET	If they do see thee, they will murder thee.
ROMEO	Alack, there lies more peril in thine eye
	Than twenty of their swords: look thou but sweet,
	And I am proof against their enmity.
JULIET	I would not for the world they saw thee here.
ROMEO	I have night's cloak to hide me from their sight;
	And but thou love me, let them find me here:
	My life were better ended by their hate,
	Than death prorogued, wanting of thy love.
JULIET	By whose direction found'st thou out this place?
ROMEO	By love, who first did prompt me to inquire;
	He lent me counsel and I lent him eyes.
	I am no pilot; yet, wert thou as far
	As that vast shore wash'd with the farthest sea,
	I would adventure for such merchandise.
JULIET	Thou know'st the mask of night is on my face,
	Else would a maiden blush bepaint my cheek
	For that which thou hast heard me speak to-night
	Fain would I dwell on form, fain, fain deny

What I have spoke: but farewell compliment!
Dost thou love me? I know thou wilt say "Ay",
And I will take thy word: yet if thou swear'st,
Thou mayst prove false; at lovers' perjuries
Then say, Jove laughs. O gentle Romeo,
If thou dost love, pronounce it faithfully:
Or if thou think'st I am too quickly won,
I'll frown and be perverse an say thee nay,
So thou wilt woo; but else, not for the world.
In truth, fair Montague, I am too fond,
And therefore thou mayst think my 'havior light:
But trust me, gentleman, I'll prove more true
Than those that have more cunning to be strange.
I should have been more strange, I must confess,
But that thou overheard'st, ere I was ware,
My true love's passion: therefore pardon me,
And not impute this yielding to light love,
Which the dark night hath so discovered.

ROMEO Lady, by yonder blessed moon I swear
That tips with silver all these fruit-tree tops—

JULIET O, swear not by the moon, the inconstant moon,
That monthly changes in her circled orb,
Lest that thy love prove likewise variable.

ROMEO What shall I swear by?

JULIET Do not swear at all;
Or, if thou wilt, swear by thy gracious self,
Which is the god of my idolatry,
And I'll believe thee.

ROMEO If my heart's dear love—

JULIET Well, do not swear: although I joy in thee,
I have no joy of this contract to-night:
It is too rash, too unadvised, too sudden;
Too like the lightning, which doth cease to be
Ere one can say "It lightens". Sweet, good night!
This bud of love, by summer's ripening breath,
May prove a beauteous flower when next we meet.
Good night, good night! as sweet repose and rest
Come to thy heart as that within my breast!

译

| 罗密欧 | 她说话了。啊！再说下去吧，光明的天使！因为我在这夜色之中仰视着你，就像一个尘世的凡人，张大了出神的眼睛，瞻望着一个生着翅膀的天使，驾着白云缓缓地驰过了天空一样。 |

罗密欧　她说话了。啊！再说下去吧，光明的天使！因为我在这夜色之中仰视着你，就像一个尘世的凡人，张大了出神的眼睛，瞻望着一个生着翅膀的天使，驾着白云缓缓地驰过了天空一样。

朱丽叶　罗密欧啊，罗密欧！为什么你偏偏是罗密欧呢？否认你的父亲，抛弃你的姓名吧；也许你不愿意这样做，那么只要你宣誓做我的爱人，我也不愿再姓凯普莱特了。

罗密欧　（旁白）我还是继续听下去呢，还是现在就对她说话？

朱丽叶　你是什么人，在黑夜里躲躲闪闪地偷听人家的话？

罗密欧　我没法告诉你我叫什么名字。敬爱的神明，我痛恨我自己的名字，因为它是你的仇敌；要是把它写在纸上，我一定把这几个字撕成粉碎。

朱丽叶　我的耳朵里还没有灌进从你嘴里吐出来的一百个字，可是我认识你的声音；你不是罗密欧，蒙太古家里的人吗？

罗密欧　不是，美人，要是你不喜欢这两个名字。

朱丽叶　告诉我，你怎么会到这儿来，为什么到这儿来？花园的墙这么高，是不容易爬上来的；要是我家里的人瞧见你在这儿，他们一定不让你活命。

罗密欧　我借着爱的轻翼飞过园墙，因为砖石的墙垣是不能把爱情阻隔的；爱情的力量所能够做到的事，它都会冒险尝试，所以我不怕你家里人的干涉。

朱丽叶　要是他们瞧见了你，一定会把你杀死的。

罗密欧　唉！你的眼睛比他们二十柄刀剑还厉害；只要你用温柔的眼光看着我，他们就不能伤害我的身体。

朱丽叶　我怎么也不愿让他们瞧见你在这儿。

罗密欧　朦胧的夜色可以替我遮过他们的眼睛。只要你爱我，就让他们瞧见我吧；与其因为得不到你的爱情而在这世上捱命，还不如在仇人的刀剑下丧生。

朱丽叶　谁叫你找到这儿来的？

罗密欧　爱情怂恿我探听出这一个地方；他替我出主意，我借给他眼睛。我不会操舟驾舵，可是倘使你在辽远的海滨，我也会冒着风波寻访你这颗珍宝。

朱丽叶　幸亏黑夜替我罩上了一重面罩，否则为了我刚才被你听去的话，你一定可以看见我脸上羞愧的红晕。我真想遵守礼法，否认已经说过的言语，可是这些虚文俗礼，现在只好一切置之不顾了！你爱我吗？我知道你一定会说"是的"；我也一定会相信你的话；可是也许你起的誓只是一个谎，人家说，对于恋人们的寒盟背信，天神是一笑置之的。温柔的罗密欧啊！你要是真的爱我，就请你诚意告诉我；你要是嫌我太容易降心相从，我也会堆起怒容，装出倔强的神气，拒绝你的好意，好让你向我婉转求情，否则我是无论如何不会拒绝你的。俊秀的蒙太古啊，我真的太痴心了，所以也许你会觉得我的举动有点轻浮；可是相信我，朋友，总有一天你会知道我的忠心远胜过那些善于矜持作态的人。我必须承认，倘不是你乘我不备的时候偷听去了我的真情的表白，我一定会更加矜持一点的；所以原谅我吧，是黑夜泄漏了我心底的秘密，不要把我的允诺看作无耻的轻狂。

罗密欧	姑娘，凭着这一轮皎洁的月亮，它的银光涂染着这些果树的梢端，我发誓——
朱丽叶	啊！不要指着月亮起誓，它是变化无常的，每个月都有盈亏圆缺；你要是指着它起誓，也许你的爱情也会像它一样无常。
罗密欧	那么我指着什么起誓呢？
朱丽叶	不用起誓吧；或者要是你愿意的话，就凭着你优美的自身起誓，那是我所崇拜的偶像，我一定会相信你的。
罗密欧	要是我的出自深心的爱情——
朱丽叶	好，别起誓啦。我虽然喜欢你，却不喜欢今天晚上的密约；它太仓促、太轻率、太出人意料了，正像一闪电光，等不及人家开一声口，已经消隐了下去。好人，再会吧！这一朵爱的蓓蕾，靠着夏天的暖风的吹拂，也许会在我们下次相见的时候，开出鲜艳的花来。晚安，晚安！但愿恬静的安息同样降临到你我两人的心头！

（朱生豪　译）

第三节　翻译练习

一、《牡丹亭》（节选）

第三出　训女
【满庭芳】
［外扮杜太守］西蜀名儒，
南安太守，
几番廊庙江湖。
紫袍金带，
功业未全无。
华发不堪回首。

意抽簪万里桥西，

还只怕君恩未许，

五马欲踟蹰。

"一生名宦守南安，莫作寻常太守看。到来只饮官中水，归去惟看屋外山。"自家南安太守杜宝，表字子充，乃唐朝杜子美之后。流落巴蜀，年过五旬。想廿年登科，三年出守，清名惠政，播在人间。内有夫人甄氏，乃魏朝甄皇后嫡派。此家峨眉山，见世出贤德。夫人单生小女，才貌端妍，唤名丽娘，未议婚配。看起自来淑女，无不知书。今日政有余闲，不免请出夫人，商议此事。正是："中郎学富单传女，伯道官贫更少儿。"

【绕池游】

［老旦上］甄妃洛浦，

嫡派来西蜀，

封大郡南安杜母。

［见介］

［外］"老拜名邦无甚德，

［老旦］妾沾封诰有何功！

［外］春来闺阁闲多少？

［老旦］也长向花阴课女工。"

［外］女工一事，想女儿精巧过人。看来古今贤淑，多晓诗书。他日嫁一书生，不枉了谈吐相称。你意下如何？

［老旦］但凭尊意。

【前腔】

［贴持酒台，随旦上］娇莺欲语，

眼见春如许。

寸草心，

怎报的春光一二！

［见介］爹娘万福。

［外］孩儿，后面捧着酒肴，是何主意？

［旦跪介］近日春光明媚，爹娘宽坐后堂，女孩阿尔敢进三爵之觞，少效千春之祝。

［外笑介］生受你。

【玉山颓】

［旦进酒介］爹娘万福，

女孩儿无限欢娱。

生黄堂百岁春光，

进美酒一家天禄。

祝萱花椿树，

虽则是子生迟暮，

守得见这蟠桃熟。

〔合〕且提壶，花间竹下长引着凤凰雏。

〔外〕春香，酌小姐一杯。

【前腔】

吾家杜甫，为飘零老愧妻孥。

〔泪介〕夫人，我比子美公公更可怜也。他还有念老夫诗句男儿，俺则有学母氏画眉娇女。

〔老旦〕相公休焦，倘然招得好女婿，与儿子一般。

〔外笑介〕可一般呢！

〔老旦〕"做门楣"古语，

为甚的这叨叨絮絮，才到中年路。……

〔外〕适问春香，你白日眠睡，是何道理？假如刺绣余闲，有架上图书，可以寓目。他日到人家，知书知礼，父母光辉。这都是你娘亲失教也。

【玉抱肚】

宦囊清苦，也不曾诗书误儒。你好些时做客为儿，有一日把家当户。是为爹的疏散不儿拘，道的个为娘是女模。

【前腔】

〔老旦〕眼前儿女，俺为娘心苏体劬。娇养他掌上明珠，出落的人中美玉。儿呵，爹三分说话你自心模，难道八字梳头做目呼。

【前腔】

〔旦〕黄堂父母，倚娇痴惯习如愚。刚打的秋千画图，闲榻着鸳鸯绣谱。从今后茶余饭饱破工夫，玉镜台前插架书。

〔老旦〕虽然如此，要个女先生讲解才好。

〔外〕不能够。

【前腔】

后堂公所，请先生则是黉门腐儒。

〔老旦〕女儿呵，怎念遍的孔子诗书，但略识周公礼数。

〔合〕不枉了银娘玉姐只做个纺砖儿，谢女班姬女校书。

〔外〕请先生不难，则要好生管待。

【尾声】说与你夫人爱女休禽犊，馆明师茶饭须清楚。你看俺治国齐家、也则是数卷书。

二、《过客》

时：

或一日的黄昏。

地：

或一处。

人：

老翁——约七十岁，白须发，黑长袍。

女孩——约十岁，紫发，乌眼珠，白底黑方格长衫。

过客——约三四十岁，状态困顿倔强，眼光阴沉，黑须，乱发，黑色短衣裤皆破碎，赤足著破鞋，胁下挂一个口袋，支着等身的竹杖。

东，是几株杂树和瓦砾；西，是荒凉破败的丛莽；其间有一条似路非路的痕迹。一间小土屋向这痕迹开着一扇门；门侧有一段枯树根。

（女孩正要将坐在树根上的老翁搀起。）

翁——孩子。喂，孩子！怎么不动了呢？

孩——（向东望着，）有谁走来了，看一看罢。

翁——不用看他。扶我进去罢。太阳要下去了。

孩——我，——看一看。

翁——唉，你这孩子！天天看见天，看见土，看见风，还不够好看么？什么也不比这些好看。你偏是要看谁。太阳下去时候出现的东西，不会给你什么好处的。……还是进去罢。

孩——可是，已经近来了。阿阿，是一个乞丐。

翁——乞丐？不见得罢。

（过客从东面的杂树间跄踉走出，暂时踌躇之后，慢慢地走近老翁去。）

客——老丈，你晚上好？

翁——阿，好！托福。你好？

客——老丈，我实在冒昧，我想在你那里讨一杯水喝。我走得渴极了。这地方又没有一个池塘、一个水洼。

翁——唔，可以可以。你请坐罢。（向女孩）孩子，你拿水来，杯子要洗干净。

（女孩默默地走进土屋去。）

翁——客官，你请坐。你是怎么称呼的。

客——称呼？——我不知道。从我还能记得的时候起，我就只一个人。我不知道我本来叫什么。我一路走，有时人们也随便称呼我，各式各样地，我也记不清楚了，况且相同的称呼也没有听到过第二回。

翁——阿阿。那么，你是从那里来的呢？

客——（略略迟疑，）我不知道。从我还能记得的时候起，我就在这么走。

翁——对了。那么，我可以问你到那里去么？

客——自然可以。——但是，我不知道。从我还能记得的时候起，我就在这么走，要走到一个地方去，这地方就在前面。我单记得走了许多路，现在来到这里了。我接着就要走向那边去，（西指，）前面！

（女孩小心地捧出一个木杯来，递去。）

客——（接杯，）多谢，姑娘。（将水两口喝尽，还杯，）多谢，姑娘。这真是少有的好意。我真不知道应该怎样感激！

翁——不要这么感激。这于你是没有好处的。

客——是的，这于我没有好处。可是我现在很恢复了些力气了。我就要前去。老丈，你大约是久住在这里的，你可知道前面是怎么一个所在么？

翁——前面？前面，是坟。

客——（诧异地，）坟？

孩——不，不，不的。那里有许多许多野百合、野蔷薇，我常常去玩、去看他们的。

客——（西顾，仿佛微笑，）不错。那些地方有许多许多野百合，野蔷薇，我也常常去玩过，去看过的。但是，那是坟。（向老翁，）老丈，走完了那坟地之后呢？

翁——走完之后？那我可不知道。我没有走过。

客——不知道?!

孩——我也不知道。

翁——我单知道南边、北边、东边，你的来路。那是我最熟悉的地方，也许倒是于你们最好的地方。你莫怪我多嘴，据我看来，你已经这么劳顿了，还不如回转去，因为你前去也料不定可能走完。

客——料不定可能走完？……（沉思，忽然惊起，）那不行！我只得走。回到那里去，就没一处没有名目，没一处没有地主，没一处没有驱逐和牢笼，没一处没有皮面的笑容，没一处没有眶外的眼泪。我憎恶他们，我不回转去！

翁——那也不然。你也会遇见心底的眼泪，为你的悲哀。

客——不。我不愿看见他们心底的眼泪，不要他们为我的悲哀！

翁——那么，你，（摇头，）你只得走了。

客——是的，我只得走了。况且还有声音常在前面催促我，叫唤我，使我息不下。可恨的是我的脚早经走破了，有许多伤，流了许多血。（举起一足给老人看，）因此，我的血不够了；我要喝些血。但血在那里呢？可是我也不愿意喝无论谁的血。我只得喝些水，来补充我的血。一路上总有水，我倒也并不感到什么不足。只是我的力气太稀薄了，血里面太多了水的缘故罢。今天连一个小水洼也遇不到，也就是少走了路的缘故罢。

翁——那也未必。太阳下去了，我想，还不如休息一会的好罢，像我似的。

客——但是，那前面的声音叫我走。

翁——我知道。

客——你知道？你知道那声音么？

翁——是的。他似乎曾经也叫过我。

客——那也就是现在叫我的声音么？

翁——那我可不知道。他也就是叫过几声，我不理他，他也就不叫了，我也就记不清楚了。

客——唉唉，不理他。……（沉思，忽然吃惊，倾听着，）不行！我还是走的好。我息不下。可恨我的脚早经走破了。（准备走路。）

孩——给你！（递给一片布，）裹上你的伤去。

客——多谢，（接取，）姑娘。这真是……这真是极少有的好意。这能使我可以走更多的路。（就断砖坐下，要将布缠在踝上，）但是，不行！（竭力站起，）姑娘，还了你罢，还是裹不下。况且这太多的好意，我没法感激。

翁——你不要这么感激。这于你没有好处。

客——是的，这于我没有什么好处。但在我，这布施是最上的东西了。你看，我全身上可有这样的。

翁——你不要当真就是。

客——是的。但是我不能。我怕我会这样：倘使我得到了谁的布施，我就要像兀鹰看见死尸一样，在四近徘徊，祝愿她的灭亡，给我亲自看见；或者咒诅她以外的一切全都灭亡，连我自己，因为我就应该得到咒诅。但是我还没有这样的力量；即使有这力量，我也不愿意她有这样的境遇，因为她们大概总不愿意有这样的境遇。我想，这最稳当。（向女孩，）姑娘，你这布片太好，可是太小一点了，还了你罢。

孩——（惊惧，退后，）我不要了！你带走！

客——（似笑，）哦哦，……因为我拿过了？

孩——（点头，指口袋，）你装在那里，去玩玩。

客——（颓唐地退后，）但这背在身上，怎么走呢？……

翁——你息不下，也就背不动。——休息一会，就没有什么了。

客——对咧，休息……（默想，但忽然惊醒，倾听。）不，我不能！我还是走好。

翁——你总不愿意休息么？

客——我愿意休息。

翁——那么，你就休息一会罢。

客——但是，我不能……

翁——你总还是觉得走好么？

客——是的。还是走好。

翁——那么，你也还是走好罢。

客——（将腰一伸，）好，我告别了。我很感谢你们。（向着女孩，）姑娘，这还你，请你收回去。

（女孩惊惧，敛手，要躲进土屋里去。）

翁——你带去罢。要是太重了，可以随时抛在坟地里面的。

孩——（走向前，）阿阿，那不行！

客——阿阿，那不行的。

翁——那么，你挂在野百合野蔷薇上就是了。

孩——（拍手，）哈哈！好！

客——哦哦……

（极暂时中，沉默。）

翁——那么，再见。祝你平安。（站起，向女孩，）孩子，扶我进去罢。你看，太阳早已下去了。（转身向门。）

客——多谢你们。祝你们平安。（徘徊，沉思，忽然吃惊，）然而我不能！我只得走。我还是走好罢……

（即刻昂了头，奋然向西走去。）

（女孩扶老人走进土屋，随即阖了门。过客向野地里跄踉地闯进去，夜色跟在他后面。）

三、*Julius Caesar* 节选

Act Ⅲ Scene 2

(The Forum. Brutus and Cassius enter, along with a crowd of citizens.)

CITIZENS　　We will be satisfied!

BRUTUS　　　Then listen to me, friends.

　　　　　　　I will tell you the reasons for Caesar's death.

　　　　　　　(Brutus goes to the pulpit.)

CITIZEN 1　　Brutus will speak. Silence!

BRUTUS　　　Be patient until the end. Romans, countrymen, and friends! Be silent, so you may hear my words. Believe me because of my honor, and have respect for my honor, so you may believe. Judge me by your wisdom, and awaken your senses so you may judge wisely. If anyone in this crowd was a friend of Caesar's, I say to him that Brutus's love of Caesar was no less than his. If that friend asks why Brutus rose against Caesar, this is my answer: Not that I loved Caesar less, but that I loved Rome more. Would you rather that Caesar were living, and we all died slaves? Or would you rather have Caesar dead, and live as free men? As Caesar loved me, I weep for him. As he was lucky, I rejoice for him. As he was brave, I honor him. But as he was ambitious—I killed him. Who here is so low that he would be a slave? If any, speak out, for I have offended him. Who here is so vile that he will not love his country? If any, speak out, for I have offended him. I pause for a reply.

ALL　　　　　None, Brutus, none.

BRUTUS	Then none have I offended.
	(Antony and others enter, with Caesar's body.)
	Here comes his body, mourned by Mark
	Antony, who had no hand in his death,
	but shall receive benefit from it. He, like
	all of you, shall have a place in the ruling
	of our country. With this I end: As I
	killed my best friend for the good of
	Rome, I have the same dagger for myself
	when it shall please my country to
	require my death.
ALL	Live, Brutus, live, live!
CITIZEN 1	Bring him to his house with honor.
CITIZEN 2	Give him a statue.
CITIZEN 3	Let him be Caesar.
CITIZEN 4	Caesar's better parts
	Shall be crowned in Brutus.
BRUTUS	My countrymen—
CITIZEN 2	Peace! Silence! Brutus speaks.
BRUTUS	Good people, allow me to leave alone.
	For my sake, stay here with Antony,
	Honor Caesar's corpse, and hear the speech
	Which, by our permission, Mark Antony
	Is allowed to make. I beg you, no one leave,
	Except me, until Antony has spoken.

(Brutus exits.)

CITIZEN 1	Let us hear Mark Antony.
CITIZEN 3	Yes! Let him go up into the pulpit.
	We'll hear him. Noble Antony, go up!
ANTONY	For Brutus's sake, I owe this to you.
	(Antony goes to the pulpit.)
CITIZEN 4	What did he say about Brutus?
CITIZEN 3	For Brutus's sake, he owes us.
CITIZEN 4	It would be best that he speak no
	harm of Brutus here.
CITIZEN 1	This Caesar was a tyrant.
CITIZEN 3	Yes, that's certain.
	We are blessed that Rome is rid of him.

ANTONY	You gentle Romans—
ALL	Quiet! Let us hear him.
ANTONY	Friends，Romans，countrymen，lend me your ears!

I come to bury Caesar，not to praise him.

The evil that men do lives after them，

The good is often buried with their bones.

So let it be with Caesar.　The noble Brutus

Has told you Caesar was ambitious.

If it were so，it was a serious fault，

And seriously has Caesar answered for it.

Here，by permission of Brutus and the rest—

For Brutus is an honorable man；

So are they all，all honorable men—

I come to speak at Caesar's funeral.

He was my friend，faithful and just to me.

But Brutus says he was ambitious，

And Brutus is an honorable man.

Caesar brought many captives to Rome，

Whose ransoms filled the public treasury.

Did this in Caesar seem ambitious?

When the poor have cried，Caesar has wept.

Ambition should be made of sterner stuff.

Yet Brutus says he was ambitious，

And Brutus is an honorable man.

You all saw，on the feast of Lupercal，

Three times I presented him a kingly crown，

Which he three times refused.　Was this ambition?

Yet Brutus says he was ambitious，

And surely he is an honorable man.

I speak not to disprove what Brutus said，

But only to speak of what I do know.

All of you loved Caesar at one time，

not without cause.

What cause now stops you，then，

from mourning for him?

Oh judgment，you have fled to brutish beasts，

And men have lost their reason!

(He cries.) Bear with me.

	My heart is in the coffin there with Caesar,
	And I must pause until it returns to me.
CITIZEN 1	I think he makes a lot of sense.
CITIZEN 2	You heard his words?
	Caesar would not take the crown.
	Therefore, it is certain he was not ambitious.
CITIZEN 3	It seems Caesar has been wronged.
CITIZEN 4	If so, someone must pay for it!
CITIZEN 2	Poor Antony! Look—his sore eyes
	are as red as fire with weeping.
CITIZEN 3	There's not a nobler man in Rome than Antony.
CITIZEN 4	Listen. He begins again to speak.
ANTONY	Only yesterday Caesar's word
	Stood against the world. Now here he lies.
	Where is proper respect?
	Oh, masters! If I wanted to stir your rage,
	I would do Brutus and Cassius wrong,
	Who, you all know, are honorable men.
	I will not do them wrong. I would prefer to
	Wrong the dead, to wrong myself and you,
	Than to wrong such honorable men.
	But here's a paper with the seal of Caesar.
	I found it in his closet. It is his will.
	If the common people heard it, they would
	Rush to kiss dead Caesar's wounds and
	Dip their handkerchiefs in his blood—
	Yes, and beg a hair of his for memory and,
	Dying, mention it in their wills, passing it on
	As a rich treasure to their children.
CITIZEN 4	Read the will, Mark Antony!
ALL	The will! Let's hear Caesar's will.
ANTONY	Patience, friends, I must not read it.
	You are not wood, not stones, but men.
	Hearing the will of Caesar will inflame you.
	It will make you mad. It is good that
	You don't know that you are his heirs,
	For if you did, then what would come of it?
CITIZEN 4	Read the will. We'll hear it, Antony.

138

ANTONY	I've gone too far to tell you of it.
	I fear I wrong the honorable men
	Whose daggers have stabbed Caesar.
CITIZEN 4	Traitors all, not honorable men!
ALL	The will! The testament!
CITIZEN 2	They were villains, murderers!
	The will! Read the will!
ANTONY	You will force me then to read it?
	Make a ring around the corpse of Caesar,
	Look closely at him who made the will.
	Shall I come down? Have I your permission?
ALL	Come down!
	(Antony comes down from the pulpit.)
CITIZEN 3	Make a ring. Gather around.
CITIZEN 4	Stand back from the body.
CITIZEN 2	Make room for the noble Antony.
ANTONY	If you have tears, prepare to shed them now.
	You all know this cloak. I remember
	The first time Caesar ever wore it.
	It was on a summer's evening, in his tent,
	On a day he won a great battle.
	Look, in this place ran Cassius's dagger.
	See what a tear the envious Casca made,
	And here his best friend Brutus stabbed.
	As he pulled his cursed steel away,
	See how the blood of Caesar followed it,
	As if rushing outside to see for sure
	If Brutus so unkindly knocked, for
	Brutus, as you know, was Caesar's angel.
	Oh, you gods, how dearly Caesar loved him!
	This was the unkindest cut of all.
	For when the noble Caesar saw him stab,
	It burst his mighty heart. Great Caesar fell.
	Oh, what a fall there was, my countrymen!
	Then I, and you, and all of us fell down,
	While bloody treason rose up over us.
	Oh, now you weep, and I know that you feel
	The force of pity. These are gracious drops.

	Kind souls, why do you weep when
	All you see is Caesar's wounded clothing?
	Look here. (He lifts Caesar's cloak.)
	Here is the man himself—
	Stabbed, you see, by traitors.
CITIZEN 1	Oh, pitiful sight!
CITIZEN 2	Oh, noble Caesar!
CITIZEN 3	Oh, day of woe!
CITIZEN 4	Oh, most bloody sight!
CITIZEN 1	We will get our revenge.
ALL	Revenge! Let's find them! Burn!
	Kill! Let not a traitor live!
ANTONY	Stay, countrymen.
CITIZEN 1	Quiet, there! Hear the noble Antony.
CITIZEN 2	We'll hear him, we'll follow him,
	we'll die with him!
ANTONY	Good friends, let me not stir you up.
	They who have done this deed are honorable.
	I do not know what made them do it.
	As they are wise and honorable, they
	Will, no doubt, give you good reasons.
	I did not come to steal away your hearts.
	I am no fine speaker, as Brutus is.
	As you all know, I am a plain, blunt man
	Who loved my friend. My poor words
	Only tell you what you already know.
	I must ask these wounds,
	poor dumb mouths,
	To speak for me. But if I were Brutus, and
	Brutus were Antony, there would be an
	Antony who would stir your spirits until
	Every wound of Caesar would cry out,
	And move the very stones of Rome to rise and mutiny.
ALL	We'll have revenge!
CITIZEN 1	We'll burn the house of Brutus!
CITIZEN 3	Let's go. Seek the conspirators!
ANTONY	Please let me speak, countrymen.
	You have forgotten the will I mentioned.

ALL	The will! Let's stay and hear the will.
ANTONY	Here is the will, under Caesar's seal.
	It grants every Roman citizen 75 drachmas.
CITIZEN 2	Noble Caesar! We'll avenge you!
ANTONY	He's also left you all his walks,
	His private arbors, and new-planted orchards
	Along the Tiber River. He has left them
	For you and your heirs to enjoy forever.
	Here was a Caesar! When comes another
	like him?
CITIZEN 1	Never, never! Come, away, away!
	We'll burn his body in the holy place,
	And with the burning sticks set fire
	To the traitors' houses. Take up the body!
CITIZEN 2	Go fetch fire.
CITIZEN 3	Tear down their houses, benches,
	windows—everything!
	(Citizens exit with the body.)
ANTONY	Now let it work.
	Trouble, you're loose. Go where you want.
	(A servant enters.)
	What is it, fellow?
SERVANT	Sir, Octavius is in Rome.
	He and Lepidus are at Caesar's house.
ANTONY	I'll go straight there.
SERVANT	He said that Brutus and Cassius
	Rode like madmen away from Rome.
ANTONY	They probably heard about how I had
	Moved the people. Bring me to Octavius.
	(They exit.)

第四章　散文的翻译

从广义上说，散文是有别于讲求韵律的诗歌的文学作品；从狭义上看，散文是指除小说、诗歌和戏剧等文学体裁之外的其他文学作品。

第一节　文体特征

下面选择《论散文》和《散文的语言》两篇文章来探讨散文的基本特征。

一、散文的风格

一切的散文都是一种翻译。把我们脑子里的思想情绪想象译成语言文字。古人说，言为心声，其实文也是心声。头脑笨的人，说出来是蠢，写成散文也是拙劣的，说话固然沉挚，写成散文必定情致缠绵；思路清晰的人，说话自然有条不紊，写成散文更能澄清澈底。散文是没有一定的格式的，是最自由的，同时也是最不容易处置的，因为一个人的人格思想，在散文里绝无隐饰的可能，提起笔来便把作者整个的性格纤毫毕现地表示出来。

一个人便有一种散文，喀赖尔翻译莱辛的作品的时候说："没人有他自己的文调，就如同他自己的鼻子一般。"布丰说："文调就是那个人。"文调的美纯粹是作者的性格的流露，所以有一种不可形容的妙处：或如奔涛澎湃，能令人惊心动魄；或是委婉流利，有飘逸之致；或是简练雅洁，如斩钉截铁……总之，散文的妙处真可说是气象万千，变化无穷。

散文的调虽是作者内心的流露，其美妙虽是不可捉摸，而散文的艺术仍是所不可少的。散文的艺术便是作者的自觉的选择，只有一个形容词能够描写他心中的一种特色，只有一个动词能够表示他心中的一个动作。在万千的辞字中他要去寻求那一个——只有那一个个——合适的字，绝无一字的敷衍将就。他的一篇文字是经过这样的苦痛的步骤写成的，所以才能有纯洁无疵的功效。平常人的语言文字只求能达，艺术的散文要求其能真实——对于作者心中的意念的真实。福楼拜致力于字句的推敲，也不过是要求把自己的意念确切地表示出来罢了。

散文的美妙多端，然而最高的理想也不过是"简单"二字而已。简单就是经过选择删芟以后的完美的状态。普通一般的散文，在艺术上的毛病，大概全是与这个简单的理想相反的现象。散文的艺术之中最根本的原则，就是"割爱"。一句有趣的俏皮话，一个漂亮的字眼，凡是与原意不甚洽和者，都要割爱。散文的美，不在乎你能写出多少旁征博引的故事穿插，亦不在乎多少典丽的辞句，而在能把心中的情思干干净净直截了当表现出来。散文的美，美在适当。不肯割爱的人，在文章的大体上是要失败的。

散文的问答应该是活泼的，而不是堆砌的——应该是像一泓流水那样的活泼流动。要免除堆砌的毛病，相当的自然是必须保持的。用字用典要求其美，但是要忌其僻。文字要保持相当的自然，同时也必须显示作者个人的心情，散文要写得亲切，即是要写得自然。

（梁实秋《论散文》，有删改）

二、散文的语言

Most people who bother with the matter at all would admit that the English language is in a bad way, but it is generally assumed that we cannot by conscious action do anything about it. Our civilization is decadent and our language—so the argument runs—must inevitably share in the general collapse. It follows that any struggle against the abuse of language is a sentimental archaism, like preferring candles to electric light or hansom cabs to aeroplanes. Underneath this lies the half-conscious belief that language is a natural growth and not an instrument which we shape for our own purposes.

Now, it is clear that the decline of a language must ultimately have political and economic causes: it is not due simply to the bad influence of this or that individual writer. But an effect can become a cause, reinforcing the original cause and producing the same effect in an intensified form, and so on indefinitely. A man may take to drink because he feels himself to be a failure, and then fail all the more completely because he drinks. It is rather the same thing that is happening to the English language. It becomes ugly and inaccurate because our thoughts are foolish, but the slovenliness of our language makes it easier for us to have foolish thoughts. The point is that the process is reversible. Modern English, especially written English, is full of bad habits which spread by imitation and which can be avoided if one is willing to take the necessary trouble. If one gets rid of these habits one can think more clearly, and to think clearly is a necessary first step toward political regeneration: so that the fight against bad English is not frivolous and is not the exclusive concern of professional writers. I will come back to this presently, and I hope that by that time the meaning of what I have said here will have become clearer. Meanwhile, here are five specimens of the English language as it is now habitually written.

These five passages have not been picked out because they are especially bad—I could have quoted far worse if I had chosen—but because they illustrate various of the mental vices from which we now suffer. They are a little below the average, but are fairly representative examples. I number them so that I can refer back to them when necessary:

(1) I am not, indeed, sure whether it is not true to say that the Milton who once seemed not unlike a seventeenth-century Shelley had not become, out of an experience ever more bitter in each year, more alien [sic] to the founder of that Jesuit sect which nothing could induce him to tolerate.

(2) Above all, we cannot play ducks and drakes with a native battery of idioms which prescribes egregious collocations of vocables as the basic put up with for tolerate, or put at a loss for bewilder.

(3) On the one side we have the free personality: by definition it is not neurotic, for it has neither conflict nor dream. Its desires, such as they are, are transparent, for they are just what institutional approval keeps in the forefront of consciousness; another institutional pattern would alter their number and intensity; there is little in them that is natural, irreducible, or culturally dangerous. But on the other side, the social bond itself is nothing but the mutual reflection of these self-secure integrities. Recall the definition of love. Is not this the very picture of a small academic? Where is there a place in this hall of mirrors for either personality or fraternity?

(4) All the "best people" from the gentlemen's clubs, and all the frantic Fascist captains, united in common hatred of Socialism and bestial horror at the rising tide of the mass revolutionary movement, have turned to acts of provocation, to foul incendiarism, to medieval legends of poisoned wells, to legalize their own destruction of proletarian organizations, and rouse the agitated petty-bourgeoise to chauvinistic fervor on behalf of the fight against the revolutionary way out of the crisis.

(5) If a new spirit is to be infused into this old country, there is one thorny and contentious reform which must be tackled, and that is the humanization and galvanization of the B. B. C. Timidity here will bespeak canker and atrophy of the soul. The heart of Britain may be sound and of strong beat, for instance, but the British lion's roar at present is like that of Bottom in Shakespeare's *A Midsummer Night's Dream*—as gentle as any sucking dove. A virile new Britain cannot continue indefinitely to be traduced in the eyes or rather ears, of the world by the effete languors of Langham Place, brazenly masquerading as "standard English". When the Voice of Britain is heard at nine o'clock, better far and infinitely less ludicrous to hear aitches honestly dropped than the present priggish, inflated, inhibited, school-ma'amish arch braying of blameless bashful mewing maidens!

Each of these passages has faults of its own, but, quite apart from avoidable ugliness, two qualities are common to all of them. The first is staleness of imagery; the other is lack of precision. The writer either has a meaning and cannot express it, or he inadvertently says something else, or he is almost indifferent as to whether his words mean anything or not. This mixture of vagueness and sheer incompetence is the most marked characteristic of modern English prose, and especially of any kind of political writing. As soon as certain topics are raised, the concrete melts into the abstract and no one seems able to think of turns of speech that are not hackneyed: prose consists less and less of words chosen for the sake of their meaning, and more and more of phrases tacked together like the sections of a prefabricated hen-house. I list below, with notes and examples, various of the tricks by means of which the work of prose-construction is habitually dodged.

DYING METAPHORS. A newly invented metaphor assists thought by evoking a visual image, while on the other hand a metaphor which is technically "dead" (e. g. iron resolution) has in effect reverted to being an ordinary word and can generally be used without loss of vividness. But in between these two classes there is a huge dump of worn-out metaphors which have lost all evocative power and are merely used because they save people the trouble of inventing phrases for themselves. Examples are: Ring the changes on, take up the cudgel for, toe the line, ride roughshod over, stand shoulder to shoulder with, play into the hands of, no axe to grind, grist to the mill, fishing in troubled waters, on the order of the day, Achilles' heel, swan song, hotbed. Many of these are used without knowledge of their meaning (what is a "rift", for instance?), and incompatible metaphors are frequently mixed, a sure sign that the writer is not interested in what he is saying. Some metaphors now current have been twisted out of their original meaning without those who use them even being aware of the fact. For example, toe the line is sometimes written as tow the line. Another example is the hammer and the anvil, now always used with the implication that the anvil gets the worst of it. In real life it is always the anvil that breaks the hammer, never the other way about: a writer who stopped to think what he was saying would avoid perverting the original phrase.

OPERATORS OR VERBAL FALSE LIMBS. These save the trouble of picking out appropriate verbs and nouns, and at the same time pad each sentence with extra syllables which give it an appearance of symmetry. Characteristic phrases are render inoperative, militate against, make contact with, be subjected to, give rise to, give grounds for, have the effect of, play a leading part (role) in, make itself felt, take effect, exhibit a tendency to, serve the purpose of, etc. The keynote is the elimination of simple verbs. Instead of being a single word, such as break, stop, spoil, mend, kill, a verb becomes a phrase, made up of a noun or adjective tacked on to some general-purpose verb such as prove, serve, form, play, render. In addition, the passive voice is wherever possible used in preference to the active, and noun constructions are used instead of gerunds (by examination of instead of by examining). The range of verbs is further cut down by means of the -ize and de- formations, and the banal statements are given an appearance of profundity by means of the not un-formation. Simple conjunctions and prepositions are replaced by such phrases as with respect to, having regard to, the fact that, by dint of, in view of, in the interests of, on the hypothesis that; and the ends of sentences are saved by anticlimax by such resounding commonplaces as greatly to be desired, cannot be left out of account, a development to be expected in the near future, deserving of serious consideration, brought to a satisfactory conclusion, and so on and so forth.

PRETENTIOUS DICTION. Words like phenomenon, element, individual (as noun), objective, categorical, effective, virtual, basic, primary, promote, constitute, exhibit, exploit, utilize, eliminate, liquidate, are used to dress up a simple statement and give an air of scientific impartiality to biased judgements. Adjectives like epoch-making, epic, historic, unforgettable, triumphant, age-old, inevitable, inexorable, veritable, are used to dignify the sordid process of international politics, while writing that aims at glorifying war usually takes on an archaic colour, its characteristic words being: realm, throne, chariot, mailed fist, trident, sword, shield, buckler, banner, jackboot, clarion. Foreign words and expressions such as cul de sac, ancien regime, deus ex machina, mutatis mutandis, status quo, gleichschaltung, weltanschauung, are used to give an air of culture and elegance. Except for the useful abbreviations i. e. , e. g. and etc. , there is no real need for any of the hundreds of foreign phrases now current in the English language. Bad writers, and especially scientific, political, and sociological writers, are nearly always haunted by the notion that Latin or Greek words are grander than Saxon ones, and unnecessary words like expedite, ameliorate, predict, extraneous, deracinated, clandestine, subaqueous, and hundreds of others constantly gain ground from their Anglo-Saxon numbers. The jargon peculiar to Marxist writing (hyena, hangman, cannibal, petty bourgeois, these gentry, lackey, flunkey, mad dog, White Guard, etc.) consists largely of words translated from Russian, German, or French; but the normal way of coining a new word is to use Latin or Greek root with the appropriate affix and, where necessary, the size formation. It is often easier to make up words of this kind (deregionalize, impermissible, extramarital, non-fragmentary and so forth) than to think up the English words that will cover one's meaning. The result, in general, is an increase in slovenliness and vagueness.

MEANINGLESS WORDS. In certain kinds of writing, particularly in art criticism and literary criticism, it is normal to come across long passages which are almost completely lacking in meaning. Words like romantic, plastic, values, human, dead, sentimental, natural, vitality, as used in art criticism, are strictly meaningless, in the sense that they not only do not point to any discoverable object, but are hardly ever expected to do so by the reader. When one critic writes, "The outstanding feature of Mr. X's work is its living quality", while another writes, "The immediately striking thing about Mr. X's work is its peculiar deadness", the reader accepts this as a simple difference opinion. If words like black and white were involved, instead of the jargon words dead and living, he would see at once that language was being used in an improper way. Many political words are similarly abused. The word Fascism has now no meaning except in so far as it signifies "something not desirable". The words democracy, socialism, freedom, patriotic, realistic, justice have each of them several different meanings which cannot be reconciled with one another. In the case of a word like democracy, not only is there no agreed definition, but the attempt to make one is resisted from all sides. It is almost universally felt that when we call a country democratic we are praising it: consequently the defenders of every kind of regime claim that it is a democracy, and fear that they might have to stop using that word if it were tied down to any one meaning. Words of this kind are often used in a consciously dishonest way. That is, the person who uses them has his own private definition, but allows his hearer to think he means something quite different. Statements like Marshal Petain was a true patriot, The Soviet press is the freest in the world, The Catholic Church is opposed to persecution, are almost always made with intent to deceive. Other words used in variable meanings, in most cases more or less dishonestly, are: class, totalitarian, science, progressive, reactionary, bourgeois, equality.

Now that I have made this catalogue of swindles and perversions, let me give another example of the kind of writing that they lead to. This time it must of its nature be an imaginary one. I am going to translate a passage of good English into modern English of the worst sort. Here is a well-known verse from Ecclesiastes:

I returned and saw under the sun, that the race is not to the swift, nor the battle to the strong, neither yet bread to the wise, nor yet riches to men of understanding, nor yet favour to men of skill; but time and chance happeneth to them all.

Here it is in modern English:

Objective considerations of contemporary phenomena compel the conclusion that success or failure in competitive activities exhibits no tendency to be commensurate with innate capacity, but that a considerable element of the unpredictable must invariably be taken into account.

This is a parody, but not a very gross one. Exhibit (3) above, for instance, contains several patches of the same kind of English. It will be seen that I have not made a full translation. The beginning and ending of the sentence follow the original meaning fairly closely, but in the middle the concrete illustrations—race, battle, bread—dissolve into the vague phrases "success or failure in competitive activities". This had to be so, because no modern writer of the kind I am discussing—no one capable of using phrases like "objective considerations of contemporary phenomena" — would ever tabulate his thoughts in that precise and detailed way. The whole tendency

147

of modern prose is away from concreteness. Now analyze these two sentences a little more closely. The first contains forty-nine words but only sixty syllables, and all its words are those of everyday life. The second contains thirty-eight words of ninety syllables: eighteen of those words are from Latin roots, and one from Greek. The first sentence contains six vivid images, and only one phrase ("time and chance") that could be called vague. The second contains not a single fresh, arresting phrase, and in spite of its ninety syllables it gives only a shortened version of the meaning contained in the first. Yet without a doubt it is the second kind of sentence that is gaining ground in modern English. I do not want to exaggerate. This kind of writing is not yet universal, and outcrops of simplicity will occur here and there in the worst-written page. Still, if you or I were told to write a few lines on the uncertainty of human fortunes, we should probably come much nearer to my imaginary sentence than to the one from Ecclesiastes.

As I have tried to show, modern writing at its worst does not consist in picking out words for the sake of their meaning and inventing images in order to make the meaning clearer. It consists in gumming together long strips of words which have already been set in order by someone else, and making the results presentable by sheer humbug. The attraction of this way of writing is that it is easy. It is easier—even quicker, once you have the habit—to say, In my opinion it is not an unjustifiable assumption that than to say I think. If you use ready-made phrases, you not only don't have to hunt about for the words; you also don't have to bother with the rhythms of your sentences since these phrases are generally so arranged as to be more or less euphonious. When you are composing in a hurry—when you are dictating to a stenographer, for instance, or making a public speech—it is natural to fall into a pretentious, Latinized style. Tags like a consideration which we should do well to bear in mind or a conclusion to which all of us would readily assent will save many a sentence from coming down with a bump. By using stale metaphors, similes, and idioms, you save much mental effort, at the cost of leaving your meaning vague, not only for your reader but for yourself. This is the significance of mixed metaphors. The sole aim of a metaphor is to call up a visual image. When these images clash—as in The Fascist octopus has sung its swan song, the jackboot is thrown into the melting pot—it can be taken as certain that the writer is not seeing a mental image of the objects he is naming; in other words he is not really thinking. Look again at the examples I gave at the beginning of this essay. Professor Laski (1) uses five negatives in fifty three words. One of these is superfluous, making nonsense of the whole passage, and in addition there is the slip—alien for akin—making further nonsense, and several avoidable pieces of clumsiness which increase the general vagueness. Professor Hogben (2) plays ducks and drakes with a battery which is able to write prescriptions, and, while disapproving of the everyday phrase put up with, is unwilling to look egregious up in the dictionary and see what it means; (3), if one takes an uncharitable attitude towards it, is simply meaningless: probably one could work out its intended meaning by reading the whole of the article in which it occurs. In (4), the writer knows more or less what he wants to say, but an accumulation of stale phrases chokes him like tea leaves blocking a sink. In (5), words and meaning have almost parted company. People who write in this manner usually have a general emotional meaning—they dislike one thing and want to express solidarity with another—but they are not interested in the detail of what they are saying. A scrupulous writer, in every sentence that he writes, will ask himself at least four questions, thus: What am I trying to say? What words will express it? What image or idiom will make it clearer? Is this image fresh enough to have an effect? And he will probably ask himself two more: Could I put it more shortly? Have I said anything that is avoidably ugly? But you are not obliged to go to all this trouble. You can shirk it by simply throwing your mind open and letting the ready-made phrases come crowding in. The will constructs your sentences for you—even think your thoughts for you, to a certain extent—and at need they will perform the important service of partially concealing your meaning even from yourself. It is at this point that the special connection between politics and the debasement of language becomes clear.

In our time it is broadly true that political writing is bad writing. Where it is not true, it will generally be found that the writer is some kind of rebel, expressing his private opinions and not a 'party line'. Orthodoxy, of whatever colour, seems to demand a lifeless, imitative style. The political dialects to be found in pamphlets, leading articles, manifestos, White papers and the speeches of undersecretaries do, of course, vary from party to party, but they are all alike in that one almost never finds in them a fresh, vivid, homemade turn of speech. When one watches some tired hack on the platform mechanically repeating the familiar phrases—bestial, atrocities, iron heel, bloodstained tyranny, free peoples of the world, stand shoulder to shoulder—one often has a curious feeling that one is not watching a live human being but some kind of dummy: a feeling which suddenly becomes stronger at moments when the light catches the speaker's spectacles and turns them into blank discs which seem to have no eyes behind them. And this is not altogether fanciful. A speaker who uses that kind of phraseology has gone some distance toward turning himself into a machine. The appropriate noises are coming out of his larynx, but his brain is not involved, as it would be if he were choosing his words for himself. If the speech he is making is one that he is accustomed to make over and over again, he may be almost unconscious of what he is saying, as one is when one utters the responses in church. And this reduced state of consciousness, if not indispensable, is at any rate favourable to political conformity.

...

But if thought corrupts language, language can also corrupt thought. A bad usage can spread by tradition and imitation even among people who should and do know better. The debased language that I have been discussing is in some ways very convenient. Phrases like a not unjustifiable assumption, leaves much to be desired, would serve no good purpose, a consideration which we should do well to bear in mind, are a continuous temptation, a packet of aspirins always at one's elbow. Look back through this essay, and for certain you will find that I have again and again committed the very faults I am protesting against. By this morning's post I have received a pamphlet dealing with conditions in Germany. The author tells me that he "felt impelled" to write it. I open it at random, and here is almost the first sentence I see: "〔The Allies〕have an opportunity not only of achieving a radical transformation of Germany's social and political structure in such a way as to avoid a nationalistic reaction in Germany itself, but at the same time of laying the foundations of a co-operative and unified Europe." You see, he "feels impelled" to write—feels, presumably, that he has something new to say—and yet his words, like cavalry horses answering the bugle, group themselves automatically into the familiar dreary pattern. This invasion of one's mind by ready-made phrases (lay the foundations, achieve a radical transformation) can only be prevented if one is constantly on guard against them, and every such phrase anaesthetizes a portion of one's brain.

I said earlier that the decadence of our language is probably curable. Those who deny this would argue, if they produced an argument at all, that language merely reflects existing social conditions, and that we cannot influence its development by any direct tinkering with words and constructions. So far as the general tone or spirit of a language goes, this may be true, but it is not true in detail. Silly words and expressions have often disappeared, not through any evolutionary process but owing to the conscious action of a minority. Two recent examples were explore every avenue and leave no stone unturned, which were killed by the jeers of a few journalists. There is a long list of flyblown metaphors which could similarly be got rid of if enough people would interest themselves in the job; and it should also be possible to laugh the not un-formation out of existence, to reduce the amount of Latin and Greek in the average sentence, to drive out foreign phrases and strayed scientific words, and, in general, to make pretentiousness unfashionable. But all these are minor points. The defence of the English language implies more than this, and perhaps it is best to start by saying what it does not imply.

To begin with it has nothing to do with archaism, with the salvaging of obsolete words and turns of speech, or with the setting up of a "standard English" which must never be departed from. On the contrary, it is especially concerned with the scrapping of every word or idiom which has outworn its usefulness. It has nothing to do with correct grammar and syntax, which are of no importance so long as one makes one's meaning clear, or with the avoidance of Americanisms, or with having what is called a "good prose style". On the other hand, it is not concerned with fake simplicity and the attempt to make written English colloquial. Nor does it even imply in every case preferring the Saxon word to the Latin one, though it does imply using the fewest and shortest words that will cover one's meaning. What is above all needed is to let the meaning choose the word, and not the other way around. In prose, the worst thing one can do with words is surrender to them. When you think of a concrete object, you think wordlessly, and then, if you want to describe the thing you have been visualising you probably hunt about until you find the exact words that seem to fit it. When you think of something abstract you are more inclined to use words from the start, and unless you make a conscious effort to prevent it, the existing dialect will come rushing in and do the job for you, at the expense of blurring or even changing your meaning. Probably it is better to put off using words as long as possible and get one's meaning as clear as one can through pictures and sensations. Afterward one can choose—not simply accept—the phrases that will best cover the meaning, and then switch round and decide what impressions one's words are likely to make on another person. This last effort of the mind cuts out all stale or mixed images, all prefabricated phrases, needless repetitions, and humbug and vagueness generally. But one can often be in doubt about the effect of a word or a phrase, and one needs rules that one can rely on when instinct fails. I think the following rules will cover most cases:

Ⅰ. Never use a metaphor, simile, or other figure of speech which you are used to seeing in print.

Ⅱ. Never use a long word where a short one will do.

Ⅲ. If it is possible to cut a word out, always cut it out.

Ⅳ. Never use the passive where you can use the active.

Ⅴ. Never use a foreign phrase, a scientific word, or a jargon word if you can think of an everyday English equivalent.

Ⅵ. Break any of these rules sooner than say anything outright barbarous.

These rules sound elementary, and so they are, but they demand a deep change of attitude in anyone who has grown used to writing in the style now fashionable. One could keep all of them and still write bad English, but one could not write the kind of stuff that I quoted in those five specimens at the beginning of this article.

I have not here been considering the literary use of language, but merely language as an instrument for expressing and not for concealing or preventing thought. Stuart Chase and others have come near to claiming that all abstract words are meaningless, and have used this as a pretext for advocating a kind of political quietism. Since you don't know what Fascism is, how can you struggle against Fascism? One need not swallow such absurdities as this, but one ought to recognise that the present political chaos is connected with the decay of language, and that one can probably bring about some improvement by starting at the verbal end. If you simplify your English, you are freed from the worst follies of orthodoxy. You cannot speak any of the necessary dialects, and when you make a stupid remark its stupidity will be obvious, even to yourself. Political language—and with variations this is true of all political parties, from Conservatives to Anarchists—is designed to make lies sound truthful and murder respectable, and to give an appearance of solidity to pure wind. One cannot change this all in a moment, but one can at least change one's own habits, and from time to time one can even, if one jeers loudly enough, send some worn-out and useless phrase — some jackboot, Achilles' heel, hotbed, melting pot, acid test, veritable inferno, or other lump of verbal refuse—into the dustbin where it belongs.

(From George Orwell, "Politics and the English Language", 1946)

第二节　赏·译·评

一、《归去来兮辞》

归去来兮，田园将芜胡不归？既自以心为形役，奚惆怅而独悲？悟已往之不谏，知来者之可追。实迷途其未远，觉今是而昨非。舟遥遥以轻飏，风飘飘而吹衣。问征夫以前路，恨晨光之熹微。乃瞻衡宇，载欣载奔。僮仆欢迎，稚子候门。三径就荒，松菊犹存。携幼入室，有酒盈樽。引壶觞以自酌，眄庭柯以怡颜。倚南窗以寄傲，审容膝之易安。园日涉以成趣，门虽设而常关。策扶老以流憩，时矫首而遐观。云无心以出岫，鸟倦飞而知还。景翳翳以将入，抚孤松而盘桓。归去来兮，请息交以绝游。世与我而相违，复驾言兮焉求？悦亲戚之情话，乐琴书以消忧。农人告余以春及，将有事于西畴。或命巾车，或棹孤舟。既窈窕以寻壑，亦崎岖而经丘。木欣欣以向荣，泉涓涓而始流。善万物之得时，感吾生之行休。已矣乎！寓形宇内复几时？曷不委心任去留？胡为乎遑遑欲何之？富贵非吾愿，帝乡不可期。怀良辰以孤往，或植杖而耘耔。登东皋以舒啸，临清流而赋诗。聊乘化以归尽，乐夫天命复奚疑！

译

Ah, Homeward Bound I Go!

Ah, homeward bound I go!

Why not go home, seeing that my field and gardens with weeds are overgrown?

Myself have made my soul serf to my body:

why have vain regrets and mourn alone?

Fret not over bygones and the forward journey take.

Only a short distance have I gone astray,

and I know today I am right,

if yesterday was a complete mistake.

Lightly floats and drifts the boat,

and gently flows and flaps my gown.

I inquire the road of a wayfarer,

and sulk at the dimness of the dawn.

Then when I catch sight of my old roofs,

joy will my steps quicken.

Servants will be there to bid me welcome,

and waiting at the door are the greeting children.

Gone to seed, perhaps, are my garden paths,

but there will still be

the chrysanthemums and the pine!

I shall lead the youngest boy in by the hand,

and on the table there stands a cup full of wine!

Holding the pot and cup, I give myself a drink,

happy to see in the courtyard the hanging bough.

I lean upon the southern window with an immense satisfaction,

and note that the little place is cosy enough to walk around.

The garden grows more familiar

and interesting with the daily walks.

What if no one knocks at the always closed door!

Carrying a cane I wander at peace,

and now and then look aloft to gaze at the blue above.

There the clouds idle away from their mountain recesses

without any intent or purpose,

and birds, when tired of their wandering flights,

will think of home.

Darkly then fall the shadows and, ready to come home,

I yet fondle the lonely pines and loiter around.

Ah, homeward bound I go!

Let me from now on learn to live alone!

The world and I are not made for one another,

and why go round like one looking for what he has not found?

Content shall I be with conversations with my own kin,

and there will be music and books

to while away the hours.

The farmers will come and tell me that spring is here

and there will be work to do at the western farm.

Some order covered wagons;

some row in small boats.

Sometimes we explore quiet, unknown ponds,

and sometimes we climb over steep, rugged mounds.

There the trees, happy of heart, grow marvelously green,

and spring water gushes forth with a gurgling sound.

I admire how things grow and prosper

according to their seasons,

and feel that thus, too, shall my life go its round.

Enough!

How long yet shall I this mortal shape keep?

Why not take life as it comes,

and why hustle and bustle like one on an errand bound?

Wealth and power are not my ambitions,

and unattainable is the abode of the gods!

I would go forth alone on a bright morning,

or perhaps, planting my cane,

begin to pluck the weeds and till the ground.

Or I would compose a poem beside a clear stream,

or perhaps go up to Tungkao

and make a long-drawn call on top of the hill.

So would I be content to live and die,

and without questionings of the heart,

gladly accept Heaven's will.

(From *The Importance of Living*, by Lin Yutang)

二、《醉翁亭记》

环滁皆山也。其西南诸峰，林壑尤美，望之蔚然而深秀者，琅琊也。山行六七里，渐闻水声潺潺，而泻出于两峰之间者，酿泉也。峰回路转，有亭翼然临于泉上者，醉翁亭也。作亭者谁？山之僧智仙也。名之者谁？太守自谓也。太守与客来饮于此，饮少辄醉，而年又最高，故自号曰醉翁也。醉翁之意不在酒，在乎山水之间也。山水之乐，得之心而寓之酒也。

若夫日出而林霏开，云归而岩穴暝，晦明变化者，山间之朝暮也。野芳发而幽香，佳木秀而繁阴，风霜高洁，水落而石出者，山间之四时也。朝而往，暮而归，四时之景不同，而乐亦无穷也。

至于负者歌于途，行者休于树，前者呼，后者应，伛偻提携，往来而不绝者，滁人游也。临溪而渔，溪深而鱼肥，酿泉为酒，泉香而酒冽，山肴野蔌，杂然而前陈者，太守宴也。宴酣之乐，非丝非竹，射者中，弈者胜，觥筹交错，起坐而喧哗者，众宾欢也。苍颜白发，颓然乎其间者，太守醉也。

已而夕阳在山，人影散乱，太守归而宾客从也。树林阴翳，鸣声上下，游人去而禽鸟乐也。然而禽鸟知山林之乐，而不知人之乐；人知从太守游而乐，而不知太守之乐其乐也。醉能同其乐，醒能述以文者，太守也。太守谓谁？庐陵欧阳修也。

译

译文一

The Roadside Hut of the Old Drunkard

The District of Chu is enclosed all around by hills, of which those in the southwest boast the most lovely forests and dales. In the distance, densely wooded and possessed of a rugged beauty, is Mt. Langya. When you penetrate a mile or two into this mountain you begin to hear the gurgling of a stream, and presently the stream—the Brewer's Spring—comes into sight cascading between two peaks. Rounding a bend you see a hut with a spreading roof by the stream, and this is the Roadside Hut of the Old Drunkard. This hut was built by the monk Zhixian. It was given its name by the governor, referring to himself. The governor, coming here with his friends, often gets tipsy after a little drinking; and since he is the most advanced in years, he calls himself the Old Drunkard. He delights less in drinking than in the hills and streams, taking pleasure in them and expressing the feeling in his heart through drinking.

Now at dawn and dusk in this mountain come the changes between light and darkness: when the sun emerges, the misty woods become clear; when the clouds hang low, the grottoes are wrapped in gloom. Then in the course of the four seasons, you find wild flowers burgeoning and blooming with a secret fragrance, the stately trees put on their mantle of leaves and give a goodly shade, until wind and frost touch all with austerity, the water sinks low and the rocks at the bottom of the stream emerge. A man going there in the morning and returning in the evening during the changing pageant of the seasons can derive endless pleasure from the place.

And the local people may be seen making their way there and back in an endless stream, the old and infirm as well as infants in arms, men carrying burdens who sing as they go, passersby stopping to rest beneath the trees, those in front calling out and those behind answering. There the governor gives a feast with a variety of dishes before him, mostly wild vegetables and mountain produce. The fish are freshly caught from the stream, and since the stream is deep and the fish are fat; the wine is brewed with spring water, and since the spring is sweet the wine is superb. There they feast and drink merrily with no accompaniment of strings or flutes; when someone wins a game of touhu or chess, when they mark up their scores in drinking games together, or raise a cheerful din sitting or standing, it can be seen that the guests are enjoying themselves. The elderly man with white hair in the middle, who sits utterly relaxed and at his ease, is the governor, already half drunk.

Then the sun sinks towards the hills, men's shadows begin to flit about and scatter; and now the governor leaves, followed by his guests. In the shade of the woods birds chirp above and below, showing that the men have gone and the birds are at peace. But although the birds enjoy the hills and forests, they cannot understand the men's pleasure in them; and although men enjoy accompanying the governor there, they cannot understand his pleasure either. The governor is able to share his enjoyment with others when he is in his cups, and sober again can write an essay about it. Who is this governor? Ouyang Xiu of Luling.

（杨宪益、戴乃迭　译）

译文二

The Old Drunkard's Arbour

The district of Ch'u is entirely surrounded by hills, and the peaks to the south-west are clothed with a dense and beautiful growth of trees, over which the eye wanders in rapture away to the confines of Shantung.

A walk of two or three miles on those hills brings one within earshot of the sound of falling water which gushes forth from a ravine, and is known as the Wine-Fountain; while hard by in a nook at a bend in the road stands a kiosque, commonly spoken of as the Old Drunkard's Arbour.

It was built by a Buddhist priest, called Deathless Wisdom, who lived among these hills; and who received the above name from the Governor himself. For the latter used to bring his friends hither to take wine; and as he personally was incapacitated by a very few cups, and was, moreover, well stricken in years, he gave himself the sobriquet of the Old Drunkard.

But it was not wine that attracted him to this spot; it was the charming scenery which wine enabled him to enjoy.

The sun's rays, peeping at dawn through the trees, by-and-by to be obscured behind gathering clouds, leaving naught but gloom around, give to this spot the alternations of morning and night.

The wild flowers that exhale their perfume from the darkness of some shady dell; the luxuriant foliage of the dense forest of beautiful trees; the clear frosty wind; and the naked boulders of the lessening torrent; —these are the indications of spring, summer, autumn, and winter.

Morning is the time to go thither, returning with the shades off night; and although the place presents a different aspect with the changes of the season, its charms are subject to no interruption, but continue always.

Burden-carriers sing their way along the road，travellers rest awhile under the trees；shouts from one，responses from another；old people hobbling along；children in arms，children dragged along by hand；backwards and forwards all day long without a break；—these are the people of Ch'u.

A cast in the stream，and a fine fish taken from some spot where the eddying pools begin to deepen；a draught of cool wine from the fountain；and a few such dishes of meats and fruits as the hills are able to provide；—these，nicely spread out beforehand，constitute the Governor's feast.

And in the revelry of the banquet hour there is no thought of toil or trouble. Every archer hits his mark，and every player wins his partie；goblets flash from hand to hand，and a buzz of conversation is heard as the guests move unconstrainedly about. Among them is an old man with white hair，bald at the top of his head. This is the drunken Governor，who，when the evening sun kisses the tips of the hills，and the falling shadows are drawn out and blurred，bends his steps homewards in company with his friends. Then in the growing darkness are heard sounds above and below：the beasts of the field and the birds of the air are rejoicing at the departure of man. They，too，can rejoice in hills and trees，but they cannot rejoice as man rejoices.

So also the Governor's friends. They rejoice with him，though they know not at what it is that he rejoices. Drunk，he can rejoice with them；sober，he can discourse with them；—such is the Governor. And should you ask who is the Governor，I reply，"Ou-yang Hsiu of Lu-ling."

（Herbert A. Giles 译）

评

① What is the major difference between the two versions? Which one is better? Why?

②What do you know about the translators?

三、《匆匆》

燕子去了，有再来的时候；杨柳枯了，有再青的时候；桃花谢了，有再开的时候。但是，聪明的，你告诉我，我们的日子为什么一去不复返呢？——是有人偷了他们罢：那是谁？又藏在何处呢？是他们自己逃走了罢：现在又到了哪里呢？我不知道他们给了我多少日子；但我的手确乎是渐渐空虚了。在默默里算着，八千多日子已经从我手中溜去；像针尖上一滴水滴在大海里，我的日子滴在时间的流里，没有声音，也没有影子。

我不禁头涔涔而泪潸潸了。去的尽管去了，来的尽管来着；去来的中间，又怎样地匆匆呢？早上我起来的时候，小屋里射进两三方斜斜的太阳。太阳他有脚啊，轻轻悄悄地挪移了；我也茫茫然跟着旋转。于是——洗手的时候，日子从水盆里过去；吃饭的时候，日子从饭碗里过去；默默时，便从凝然的双眼前过去。我觉察他去的匆匆了，伸出手遮挽时，他又从遮挽着的手边过去，天黑时，我躺在床上，他便伶伶俐俐地从我身上跨过，从我脚边飞去了。

等我睁开眼和太阳再见，这算又溜走了一日。我掩着面叹息。但是新来的日子的影儿又开始在叹息里闪过了。在逃去如飞的日子里，在千门万户的世界里的我能做些什么呢？只有徘徊罢了，只有匆匆罢了；在八千多日的匆匆里，除徘徊外，又剩些什么呢？过去的日子如轻烟，被微风吹散了，如薄雾，被初阳蒸融了；我留着些什么痕迹呢？我何曾留着像游丝样的痕迹呢？我赤裸裸来到这世界，转眼间也将赤裸裸的回去罢？但不能平的，为什么偏要白白走这一遭啊？你聪明的，告诉我，我们的日子为什么一去不复返呢？

译

Swallows may have gone, but there is a time of return; willow trees may have died back, but there is a time of regreening; peach blossoms may have fallen, but they will bloom again. Now, you the wise, tell me, why should our days leave us, never to return? —If they had been stolen by someone, who could it be? Where could he hide them? If they had made the escape themselves, then where could they stay at the moment?

I don't know how many days I have been given to spend, but I do feel my hands are getting empty. Taking stock silently, I find that more than eight thousand days have already slid away from me. Like a drop of water from the point of a needle disappearing into the ocean, my days are dripping into the stream of time, soundless, traceless. Already sweat is starting on my forehead, and tears welling up in my eyes.

Those that have gone have gone for good, those to come keep coming; yet in between, how swift is the shift, in such a rush? When I get up in the morning, the slanting sun marks its presence in my small room in two or three oblongs. The sun has feet, look, he is treading on, lightly and furtively; and I am caught, blankly, in his revolution. Thus—the day flows away through the sink when I wash my hands, wears off in the bowl when I eat my meal, and passes away before my day-dreaming gaze as reflect in silence. I can feel his haste now, so I reach out my hands to hold him back, but he keeps flowing past my withholding hands. In the evening, as I lie in bed, he strides over my body, glides past my feet, in his agile way. The moment I open my eyes and meet the sun again, one whole day has gone. I bury my face in my hands and heave a sigh. But the new day begins to flash past in the sigh.

What can I do, in this bustling world, with my days flying in their escape? Nothing but to hesitate, to rush. What have I been doing in that eight-thousand-day rush, apart from hesitating? Those bygone days have been dispersed as smoke by a light wind, or evaporated as mist by the morning sun. What traces have I left behind me? Have I ever left behind any gossamer traces at all? I have come to the world, stark naked; am I to go back, in a blink, in the same stark nakedness? It is not fair though: why should I have made such a trip for nothing!

You the wise, tell me, why should our days leave us, never to return?

(朱纯深 译)

四、*Nature* 节选

To speak truly, few adult persons can see nature. Most persons do not see the sun. At least they have a very superficial seeing. The sun illuminates only the eye of the man, but shines into the eye and the heart of the child. The lover of nature is he whose inward and outward senses are still truly adjusted to each other; who has retained the spirit of infancy even into the era of manhood. His intercourse with heaven and earth, becomes part of his daily food. In the presence of nature, a wild delight runs through the man, in spite of real sorrows. Nature says, he is my creature, and mangre all his impertinent griefs, he shall be glad with me. Not the sun or the summer alone, but every hour and season yields its tribute of delight; for every hour and change corresponds to and authorizes a different state of mind, from breathless noon to grimmest midnight. Nature is a setting that fits equally well a comic and or a mourning piece. In good health, the air is a cordial of incredible virtue. Crossing a bare common, in snow puddles, at twilight under a clouded sky, without having in my thoughts any occurrence of social good fortune, I have enjoyed a perfect exhilaration.

...

In the woods too, a man casts off his years, as the snake his slough, and at what period soever of life, is always a child. In the woods, is perpetual youth. Within these plantations of God, a decorum and sanctity reign, a perennial festival is dressed, and the guest sees not how he should tire of them in a thousand years. In the woods, we return to reason and faith. There I feel that nothing can befall me in life, —no disgrace, no calamity, (leaving me my eyes,) which nature cannot repair. Standing on the bare ground, —my head bathed by the blithe air, and uplifted into infinite space, —all mean egotism vanishes. I become a transparent eye-ball; I am nothing; I see all; the currents of the Universal Being circulate through me; I am part or particle of God. The name of the nearest friend sounds then foreign and accidental: to be brothers, to be acquaintances, —master or servant, is then a trifle and a disturbance. I am the lover of uncontained and immortal beauty. In the wilderness, I find something more dear and connate than in streets or villages. In the tranquil landscape, and especially in the distant line of the horizon, man beholds somewhat as beautiful as his own nature.

译

说实话，很少有成年人看到自然，大多数人看不到太阳。至少他们看得很肤浅。太阳光只能照亮成人的眼睛，但对孩子来说，却还能照进他们的心灵。爱好自然的人，内在感觉和外部感官是相互协调的，就算已经成年，还依然保持童稚之心。与自然的交流，是他每天不可或缺的精神滋养。一看到自然，即便还在痛苦之中，喜悦之情也可以遍及全身。自然会说，他是我的孩子，尽管他很难过，跟我在一起，他将快乐无比。除了太阳和夏天，每一个时刻和季节，都能带给他快乐，因为每一个时辰，每一个变化，从无声的正午到可怕的子夜，都暗合着不同的心境。自然就是一个大背景，上演喜剧和上演悲剧一样适宜。在身心爽朗的日子，空气如同醇美的甜酒，令人难以置信。暮色中，在乌云密布的天空下，穿过平滑的广场，踏着雪泥，脑子里没有好运突临的杂念，欣欣然如入梦幻之境。我几乎不敢想象自己有多么快乐。

......

在树林里，人们挣脱岁月羁绊，就像蛇蜕去表皮一样，重新成为孩子；在树林里，他永远年轻。在上帝的御苑里，充溢着礼仪和圣洁，一年四季都装点得如节日，客人在这呆上一千年，也不觉疲倦；在树林里，我们回归理性和信仰，感觉不到生活的一切不幸，没有耻辱，没有灾难，这些是自然无法修复的。我漫不经心地徜徉在空气中，宛如升华到无穷的宇宙时空中——一切卑微自私的想法都随风而去。我化作透明的眼球，虽然无影无形，却看到了一切。宇宙之流在我周身循环不止，我成了上帝的一部分。最亲近的朋友的名字，此刻听起来也显得那么遥远，那么突然。是成为兄弟，成为熟人，还是成为主人、仆人——这一切都变得无足轻重。我爱上了无止境的永恒之美。在旷野中，我看到了比城镇或村庄里更宝贵、更亲切的东西。在静谧的景色中，尤其是在远处的地平线上，人们看到了跟他本性一样美好的东西。

评

①What does "reign" mean in "a decorum and sanctity reign"?
②What are the stylish features of Emerson's prose?

五、"How to Grow Old"

In spite of the title, this article will really be on how not to grow old, which, at my time of life, is a much more important subject. My first advice would be to choose your ancestors carefully. Although both my parents died young, I have done well in this respect as regards my other ancestors. My maternal grandfather, it is true, was cut off in the flower of his youth at the age of sixty-seven, but my other three grandparents all lived to be over eighty. Of remoter ancestors I can only discover one who did not live to a great age, and he died of a disease which is now rare, namely, having his head cut off.

A great grandmother of mine, who was a friend of Gibbon, lived to the age of ninety-two, and to her last day remained a terror to all her descendants. My maternal grandmother, after having nine children who survived, one who died in infancy, and many miscarriages, as soon as she became a widow, devoted herself to woman's higher education. She was one of the founders of Girton College, and worked hard at opening the medical profession to women. She used to relate how she met in Italy an elderly gentleman who was looking very sad. She inquired the cause of his melancholy and he said that he had just parted from his two grandchildren. "Good gracious", she exclaimed, "I have seventy-two grandchildren, and if I were sad each time I parted from one of them, I should have a dismal existence!" "Madre snaturale," he replied. But speaking as one of the seventy-two, I prefer her recipe. After the age of eighty she found she had some difficulty in getting to sleep, so she habitually spent the hours from midnight to 3 a. m. in reading popular science. I do not believe that she ever had time to notice that she was growing old. This, I think, is proper recipe for remaining young. If you have wide and keen interests and activities in which you can still be effective, you will have no reason to think about the merely statistical fact of the number of years you have already lived, still less of the probable brevity of your future.

As regards health I have nothing useful to say since I have little experience of illness. I eat and drink whatever I like, and sleep when I cannot keep awake. I never do anything whatever on the ground that it is good for health, though in actual fact the things I like doing are mostly wholesome.

Psychologically there are two dangers to be guarded against in old age. One of these is undue absorption in the past. It does not do to live in memories, in regrets for the good old days, or in sadness about friends who are dead. One's thoughts must be directed to the future and to things about which there is something to be done. This is not always easy: one's own past is gradually increasing weight. It is easy to think to oneself that one's emotions used to be more vivid than they are, and one's mind keener. If this is true it should be forgotten, and if it is forgotten it will probably not be true.

The other thing to be avoided is clinging to youth in the hope of sucking vigor from its vitality. When your children are grown up they want to live their own lives, and if you continue to be as interested in them as you were when they were young, you are likely to become a burden to them, unless they are unusually callous. I do not mean that one should be without interest in them, but one's interest should be contemplative and, if possible, philanthropic, but not unduly emotional. Animals become indifferent to their young as soon as their young can look after themselves, but human beings, owing to the length of infancy, find this difficult.

I think that a successful old age is easiest for those who have strong impersonal interests involving appropriate activities. It is in this sphere that long experience is really fruitful，and it is in this sphere that the wisdom born of experience can be exercised without being oppressive．It is no use telling grown-up children not to make mistakes，both because they will not believe you，and because mistakes are an essential part of education．But if you are one of those who are incapable of impersonal interests，you may find that your life will be empty unless you concern yourself with you children and grandchildren．In that case you must realize that while you can still render them material services，such as making them an allowance or knitting them jumpers，you must not expect that they will enjoy your company．

Some old people are oppressed by the fear of death．In the young there is a justification for this feeling．Young men who have reason to fear that they will be killed in battle may justifiably feel bitter in the thought that they have been cheated of the best things that life has to offer．But in an old man who has known human joys and sorrows，and has achieved whatever work it was in him to do，the fear of death is somewhat abject and ignoble．The best way to overcome it—so at least it seems to me—is to make your interests gradually wider and more impersonal，until bit by bit the walls of the ego recede，and your life becomes increasingly merged in the universal life．An individual human existence should be like a river-small at first，narrowly contained within its banks，and rushing passionately past rocks and over waterfalls．Gradually the river grows wider，the banks recede，the waters flow more quietly，and in the end，without any visible break，they become merged in the sea，and painlessly lose their individual being．The man who，in old age，can see his life in this way，will not suffer from the fear of death，since the things he cares for will continue．And if，with the decay of vitality，weariness increases，the thought of rest will not be unwelcome．I should wish to die while still at work，knowing that others will carry on what I can no longer do and content in the thought that what was possible has been done．

译

如何平静老去

虽然有这样一个标题，这篇文章真正要谈的却是怎样才能不老。在我这个年纪，这实在是一个至关重要的问题。我的第一个忠告是，要仔细选择你的祖先。尽管我的双亲皆属早逝，但是考虑到我的其他祖先，我的选择还是很不错的。是的，我的外祖父六十七岁时去世，正值盛年，可是另外三位祖父辈的亲人都活到八十岁以上。至于稍远些的亲戚，我只发现一位没能长寿的，他死于一种现已罕见的病症：被杀头。我的一位曾祖母是吉本的朋友，她活到九十二岁高龄，一直到死，她始终是让子孙们全都感到敬畏的人。我的外祖母，一辈子生了十个孩子，活了九个，还有一个早年夭折，此外还有过多次流产。可是守寡以后，她马上就致力于妇女的高等教育事业。她是格顿学院的创办人之一，力图使妇女进入医疗行业。她总好讲起她在意大利遇到过的一位面容悲哀的老年绅士。她询问他忧郁的缘故，他说他刚刚同两个孙儿女分离。"天哪！"她叫道，"我有七十二个孙儿孙女，如果我每次分离就要悲伤不已，那我早就没法活了！""奇怪的母亲。"他回答说。但是，作为她的七十二个孙儿孙女的一员，我却要说我更喜欢她的见地。上了八十岁，她开始感到有些难以入睡，她便经常在午夜时分至凌晨三时这段时间里阅读科普方面的书籍。我想她根本就没有功夫去留意她在衰老。我认为，这就是保持年轻的最佳方法。如果你的兴趣和活动既广泛又浓烈，而且你又能从中感到自己仍然精力旺盛，那么你就不必去考虑你已经活了多少年这种纯粹的统计学情况，更不必去考虑你那也许不很长久的未来。

至于健康，由于我这一生几乎从未患过病，也就没有什么有益的忠告。我吃喝均随心所欲，醒不了的时候就睡觉。我做事情从不以它是否有益健康为依据，尽管实际上我喜欢做的事情通常都是有益健康的。

从心理角度讲，老年需防止两种危险。一是过分沉湎于往事。人不能生活在回忆当中，不能生活在对美好往昔的怀念或对去世的友人的哀念之中。一个人应当把心思放在未来，放到需要自己去做点什么的事情上。要做到这一点并非轻而易举，往事的影响总是在不断增加。人们总认为自己过去的情感要比现在强烈得多，头脑也比现在敏锐。假如真的如此，就该忘掉它；而如果可以忘掉它，那你自以为是的情况就可能并不是真的。

另一件应当避免的事是依恋年轻人，期望从他们的勃勃生气中获取力量。子女们长大成人以后，都想按照自己的意愿生活。如果你还想像他们年幼时那样关心他们，你就会成为他们的包袱，除非他们是异常迟钝的人。我不是说不应该关心子女，而是说这种关心应该是含蓄的，假如可能的话，还应是宽厚的，而不应该过分地感情用事。动物的幼子一旦自立，大动物就不再关心它们了。人类则因其幼年时期较长而难于做到这一点。

我认为，对于那些具有强烈的爱好，其活动又都恰当适宜，并且不受个人情感影响的人们，成功地度过老年决非难事。只有在这个范围里，长寿才真正有益；只有在这个范围里，源于经验的智慧才能得到运用而不令人感到压抑。告诫已经成人的孩子别犯错误是没有用处的，因为一来他们不会相信你，二来错误原本就是教育所必不可少的要素之一。但是，如果你是那种受个人情感支配的人，你就会感到，不把心思都放在子女和孙儿女身上，你就会觉得生活很空虚。假如事实确实如此，那么你必须明白，虽然你还能为他们提供物质上的帮助，比如支援他们一笔钱或者为他们编织毛线外套的时候，决不要期望他们会因为你的陪伴而感到快乐。

有些老人因害怕死亡而苦恼。年轻人害怕死亡是可以理解的。有些年轻人担心他们会在战斗中丧身。一想到会失去生活能够给予他们的种种美好事情，他们就感到痛苦。这种担心并不是无缘无故的，也是情有可原的。但是，对于一位经历了人世的悲欢、履行了个人职责的老人，害怕死亡就有些可怜且可耻了。克服这种恐惧的最好办法是——至少我是这样看的——逐渐扩大你的兴趣范围并使其不受个人情感的影响，直至包围自我的围墙一点点地离开你，而你的生活则越来越融合于大家的生活之中。每一个人的生活都应该像河水一样——开始是细小的，被限制在狭窄的两岸之间，然后热烈地冲过巨石，滑下瀑布。渐渐地，河道变宽了，河岸扩展了，河水流得更平稳了。最后，河水流入了海洋，不再有明显的间断和停顿，而后便毫无痛苦地摆脱了自身的存在。能够这样理解自己一生的老人，将不会因害怕死亡而痛苦，因为他所珍爱的一切都将继续存在下去。而且，如果随着精力的衰退，疲倦之感日渐增加，长眠并非不受欢迎的念头。我渴望死于尚能劳作之时，同时知道他人将继续我所未竟的事业，我大可因为已经尽了自己之所能而感到安慰。

第三节　翻译练习

一、《项脊轩志》

项脊轩，旧南阁子也。室仅方丈，可容一人居。百年老屋，尘泥渗漉，雨泽下注；每移案，顾视无可置者。又北向，不能得日，日过午已昏。余稍为修葺，使不上漏；前辟四窗，垣墙周庭，以当南日，日影反照，室始洞然。又杂植兰桂竹木于庭，旧时栏楯，亦遂增胜。借书满架，偃仰啸歌，冥然兀坐，万籁有声；而庭阶寂寂，小鸟时来啄食，人至不去。三五之夜，明月半墙，桂影斑驳，风移影动，珊珊可爱。然余居于此，多可喜，亦多可悲。

先是，庭中通南北为一。迨诸父异爨，内外多置小门墙，往往而是。东犬西吠，客逾庖而宴，鸡栖于厅。庭中始为篱，已为墙，凡再变矣。家有老妪，尝居于此。妪，先大母婢也，乳二世，先妣抚之甚厚。室西连于中闺，先妣尝一至。妪每谓余曰："某所，而母立于兹。"妪又曰："汝姊在吾怀，呱呱而泣；娘以指叩门扉曰：'儿寒乎？欲食乎？'吾从板外相为应答。"语未毕，余泣，妪亦泣。

余自束发读书轩中，一日，大母过余曰："吾儿，久不见若影，何竟日默默在此，大类女郎也？"比去，以手阖门，自语曰："吾家读书久不效，儿之成，则可待乎！"顷之，持一象笏至，曰："此吾祖太常公宣德间执此以朝，他日，汝当用之！"瞻顾遗迹，如在昨日，令人长号不自禁。

轩东故尝为厨，人往，从轩前过。余扃牖而居，久之，能以足音辨人。轩凡四遭火，得不焚，殆有神护者。

项脊生曰："蜀清守丹穴，利甲天下，其后秦皇帝筑女怀清台；刘玄德与曹操争天下，诸葛孔明起陇中。方二人之昧昧于一隅也，世何足以知之，余区区处败屋中，方扬眉瞬目，谓有奇景。人知之者，其谓与坎井之蛙何异？"

余既为此志，后五年，吾妻来归。时至轩中，从余问古事，或凭几学书。吾妻归宁，述诸小妹语曰："闻姊家有阁子，且何谓阁子也？"其后六年，吾妻死，室坏不修。其后二年，余久卧病无聊，乃使人复葺南阁子，其制稍异于前。然自后余多在外，不常居。

庭有枇杷树，吾妻死之年所手植也，今已亭亭如盖矣。

二、"A Meditation upon a Broomstick"

This single stick, which you now behold ingloriously lying in that neglected corner, I once knew in a flourishing state in a forest. It was full of sap, full of leaves, and full of boughs; but now in vain does the busy art of man pretend to vie with nature, by tying that withered bundle of twigs to its sapless trunk; it is now at best but the reverse of what it was, a tree turned upside-down, the branches on the earth, and the root in the air; it is now handled by every dirty wench, condemned to do her drudgery, and, by a capricious kind of fate, destined to make other things clean, and be nasty itself; at length, worn to the stumps in the service of the maids, it is either thrown out of doors or condemned to the last use—of kindling a fire. When I behold this I sighed, and said within myself, "Surely mortal man is a broomstick!" Nature sent him into the world strong and lusty, in a thriving condition, wearing his own hair on his head, the proper branches of this reasoning vegetable, till the axe of intemperance has lopped off his green boughs, and left him a withered trunk; he then flies to art, and puts on a periwig, valuing himself upon an unnatural bundle of hairs, all covered with powder, that never grew on his head; but now should this our broomstick pretend to enter the scene, proud of those birchen spoils it never bore, and all covered with dust, through the sweepings of the finest lady's chamber, we should be apt to ridicule and despise its vanity. Partial judges that we are of our own excellencies, and other men's defaults!

But a broomstick, perhaps you will say, is an emblem of a tree standing on its head; and pray what is a man but a topsy-turvy creature, his animal faculties perpetually mounted on his rational, his head where his heels should be, grovelling on the earth? And yet, with all his faults, he sets up to be a universal reformer and corrector of abuses, a remover of grievances, rakes into every slut's corner of nature, bringing hidden corruptions to the light, and raises a mighty dust where there was none before, sharing deeply all the while in the very same pollutions he pretends to sweep away. His last days are spent in slavery to women, and generally the least deserving; till, worn to the stumps, like his brother besom, he is either kicked out of doors, or made use of to kindle flames for others to warm themselves by.

三、"The Author's Account of Himself"

I am of this mind with Homer, that as the snaile that crept out of her shel was turned eftsoones into a toad, and thereby was forced to make a stoole to sit on; so the traveller that stragleth from his owne country is in a short time transformed into so monstrous a shape, that he is faine to alter his mansion with his manners, and to live where he can, not where he would.

——Lyly's Euphues

I was always fond of visiting new scenes, and observing strange characters and manners. Even when a mere child I began my travels, and made many tours of discovery into foreign parts and unknown regions of my native city, to the frequent alarm of my parents, and the emolument of the town crier. As I grew into boyhood, I extended the range of my observations. My holiday afternoons were spent in rambles about the surrounding country. I made myself familiar with all its places famous in history or fable. I knew every spot where a murder or robbery had been committed, or a ghost seen. I visited the neighboring villages, and added greatly to my stock of knowledge, by noting their habits and customs, and conversing with their sages and great men. I even journeyed one long summer's day to the summit of the most distant hill, whence I stretched my eye over many a mile of terra incognita, and was astonished to find how vast a globe I inhabited.

This rambling propensity strengthened with my years. Books of voyages and travels became my passion, and in devouring their contents, I neglected the regular exercises of the school. How wistfully would I wander about the pier-heads in fine weather, and watch the parting ships, bound to distant climes; with what longing eyes would I gaze after their lessening sails, and waft myself in imagination to the ends of the earth!

Further reading and thinking, though they brought this vague inclination into more reasonable bounds, only served to make it more decided. I visited various parts of my own country; and had I been merely a lover of fine scenery, I should have felt little desire to seek elsewhere its gratification, for on no country had the charms of nature been more prodigally lavished. Her mighty lakes, her oceans of liquid silver; her mountains, with their bright aerial tints; her valleys, teeming with wild fertility; her tremendous cataracts, thundering in their solitudes; her boundless plains, waving with spontaneous verdure; her broad, deep rivers, rolling in solemn silence to the ocean; her trackless forests, where vegetation puts forth all its magnificence; her skies, kindling with the magic of summer clouds and glorious sunshine; —no, never need an American look beyond his own country for the sublime and beautiful of natural scenery.

But Europe held forth all the charms of storied and poetical association. There were to be seen the masterpieces of art, the refinements of highly cultivated society, the quaint peculiarities of ancient and local custom. My native country was full of youthful promise; Europe was rich in the accumulated treasures of age. Her very ruins told the history of the times gone by, and every mouldering stone was a chronicle. I longed to wander over the scenes of renowned achievement—to tread, as it were, in the footsteps of antiquity—to loiter about the ruined castle—to meditate on the falling tower—to escape, in short, from the commonplace realities of the present, and lose myself among the shadowy grandeurs of the past.

I had, besides all this, an earnest desire to see the great men of the earth. We have, it is true, our great men in America: not a city but has an ample share of them. I have mingled among them in my time, and been almost withered by the shade into which they cast me; for there is nothing so baleful to a small man as the shade of a great one, particularly the great man of a city. But I was anxious to see the great men of Europe; for I had read in the works of various philosophers, that all animals degenerated in America, and man among the number. A great man of Europe, thought I, must therefore be as superior to a great man of America, as a peak of the Alps to a highland of the Hudson; and in this idea I was confirmed by observing the comparative importance and swelling magnitude of many English travellers among us, who, I was assured, were very little people in their own country. I will visit this land of wonders, thought I, and see the gigantic race from which I am degenerated.

It has been either my good or evil lot to have my roving passion gratified. I have wandered through different countries and witnessed many of the shifting scenes of life. I cannot say that I have studied them with the eye of a philosopher, but rather with the sauntering gaze with which humble lovers of the picturesque stroll from the window of one print-shop to another; caught sometimes by the delineations of beauty, sometimes by the distortions of caricature, and sometimes by the loveliness of landscape. As it is the fashion for modern tourists to travel pencil in hand, and bring home their portfolios filled with sketches, I am disposed to get up a few for the entertainment of my friends. When, however, I look over the hints and memorandums I have taken down for the purpose, my heart almost fails me, at finding how my idle humor has led me astray from the great object studied by every regular traveller who would make a book. I fear I shall give equal disappointment with an unlucky landscape-painter, who had travelled on the Continent, but following the bent of his vagrant inclination, had sketched in nooks, and corners, and by-places. His sketch-book was accordingly crowded with cottages, and landscapes, and obscure ruins; but he had neglected to paint St. Peter's, or the Coliseum, the cascade of Terni, or the bay of Naples, and had not a single glacier or volcano in his whole collection.

第五章　儿童文学的翻译

儿童文学指的是可供儿童阅读的任何材料，如人文、历史、传统文化、科普读物、卡通等。由于儿童的心理特点和思维方式与成人有比较显著的不同，面向他们的文学作品在语言、风格和内容上与成人文学相比，也有所不同。

第一节　文体特征

下面从"何为儿童文学""儿童文学何为"等维度对这一文体的基本特征进行介绍。

一、儿童的文学

今天所讲儿童的文学，换一句话便是"小学校里的文学"。美国的斯喀特尔（Scudder）、麦克林托克（Maclintock）诸人都有这样名称的书，说明文学在小学教育上的价值，他们以为儿童应该读文学的作品，不可单读那些商人杜撰的读本。读了读本，虽然说是识字了，却不能读书，因为没有读书的趣味。这话原是不错，我也想用同一的标题，但是怕要误会，以为是主张叫小学儿童读高深的文学作品，所以改作今称，表明这所谓文学，是单指"儿童的"文学。

以前的人对于儿童多不能正当理解，不是将他当作缩小的成人，拿"圣经贤传"尽量地灌下去，便将他看作不完全的小人，说小孩懂得甚么，一笔抹杀，不去理他。近来才知道儿童在生理心理上，虽然和大众有点不同，但他仍是完全的个人，有他自己的内外两面的生活。儿童期的二十几年的生活，一面固然是成人生活的预备，但一面也自有独立的意义与价值；因为全生活只是一个生长，我们不能指定那一截的时期，是真正的生活。我以为顺应自然生活各期，——生长，成熟，老死，都是真正的生活。所以我们对于误认儿童为缩小的成人的教法，固然完全反对，就是都不承认儿童的独立生活的意见，我们也不以为然。那全然蔑视的不必说了，在诗歌里鼓吹合群，在故事里提倡爱国，专为将来设想，不顾现在儿童生活的需要的办法，也不免浪费了儿童的时间，缺损了儿童的生活。我想儿童教育，是应当依了他内外两面的生活的需要，恰如其分的供给他，使他生活满足丰富，至于因了这供给的材料与方法而发生的效果，那是当然有的副产物，不必是供给时的唯一目的物。换一句话说，因为儿童生活上有文学的需要，我们供给他，便利用这机会去得一种效果——与儿童将来生活上有益的一种思想或习性，当作副产物，并不因为要得这效果，便不管儿童的需要如何，供给一种食料，强迫他吞下去。所以小学校里的文学的教材与教授，第一须注意于"儿童的"这一点，其次才是效果，如读书的趣味，智情与想象的修养等。

儿童生活上何以有文学的需要？这个问题，只要看文学的起源的情形，便可以明白。儿童那里有自己的文学？这个问题，只要看原始社会的文学的情形，便可以明白。照进化说讲来，人类的个体发生原来和系统发生的程序相同：胚胎时代经过生物进化的历程，儿童时代又经过文明发达的历程；所以儿童学（Paidologie）上的许多事项，可以借了人类学（Anthropologie）上的事项来作说明。文学的起源，本由于原人的对于自然的畏惧与好奇，凭了想象，构成一种感情思想，借了言语行动表现出来，总称是歌舞，分起来是歌、赋与戏曲小说。儿童的精神生活本与原人相似，他的文学是儿歌、童话，内容形式多不但与原人的文学相同，而且有许多还是原始社会的遗物，常含有野蛮或荒唐思想。儿童与原人的比较，儿童的生物学与原始的文学的比较，现在已有定论，可以不必多说；我们所要注意的，只是在于怎么样能够适当的将"儿童的"文学供给与儿童。

近来有许多人对于儿童的文学，不免怀疑，因为他们觉得儿歌童话时机多有荒唐乖谬的思想，恐于儿童有害。这个疑惧本也为无理，但我们有这两种根据，可以解释他。

第一，我们承认儿童有独立的生活，就是说他们内面的生活与大人不同，我们应当客观地理解他们，并加以相当的尊重。婴儿不会吃饭，只能给他乳吃；不会走路，只好抱他：这是大家都知道的。精神上的情形，也正同这个一样。儿童没有一个不是拜物教的，他相信草木能思想，猫狗能说话，正是当然的事；我们要纠正他，说草木是植物猫狗是动物，不会思想或说话，这事不但没有什么益处，反是有害的，因为这样使他们的生活受了伤了。即使不说儿童的权利那些话，但不自然的阻遏了儿童的想象力，也就所失很大了。

第二，我们又知道儿童的生活，是转变的、生长的。因为这一层，所以我们可以放胆供给儿童需要的歌谣故事，不必愁他有什么坏影响，但因此我们又更须细心斟酌，不要使他停滞，脱了正当的轨道。譬如婴儿生了牙齿可以吃饭，脚力强了可以走路了，却还是哺乳提抱，便将使他的胃肠与脚的筋肉反变衰弱了。儿童相信猫狗能说话的时候，我们便同他们讲猫狗说话的故事，不但要使得他们喜悦，也因为知道这过程是跳不过的——然而又自然的会推移过去的，所以相当的对付了，等到儿童要知道猫狗是什么东西的时候到来，我们再可以将生物学的知识供给他们，倘若不问儿童生活的转变如何，只是始终同他们讲猫狗说话的事，那时这些荒唐乖谬的弊害才真要出来了。

据麦克托林克说，儿童的想象如被迫压，他将失了一切的兴味，变成枯燥的唯物的人；但如被放纵，又将有变成梦想家，他的心力都不中用了。所以小学校里的正当的文学教育，有这种三种作用：（1）顺应满足儿童之本能的兴趣与趣味，（2）培养并指导那些趣味，（3）唤起以前没有的新的兴趣与趣味。这（1）便是我们所说的供给文学的本意，（2）与（3）是利用这机会去得一种效果。但怎样才能恰当的办到呢？依据儿童心理发达的程序与文学批评的标准，于教材选择与教授方法上，加以注意，当然可以得到若干效果。教授方法的话可以不必多说了，现在只就教材选择上，略略说明以备参考。

儿童学上的分期，大约分作四期，一、婴儿期（一至三岁），二、幼儿期（三至十），三、少年期（十至十五），四、青年期（十五至二十）。我们现在所说的是学校里一年至六年的儿童，便是幼儿期及少年期的前半，至于七年以上所谓中学程度的儿童，这回不暇说及，当俟另外有机会再讲了。

幼儿期普遍又分作前后两期，三到六岁为前期，又称幼稚园时期，六至十岁为后期，又称初等小学时期。前期的儿童，心理的发达上最旺盛的是感觉作用，其他感情意志的发动也多以感觉为本，带着冲动的性质，这时期的想象，也只是所动的，就是联想的及模仿的两种，对于现实与虚幻，差不多没有什么区别。到了后期，观察与记忆作用逐渐发达，得了各种现实的经验，想象作用也就受了限制，须与现实不相冲突，才能容纳；若表现上面，也变了主动的，就是所谓构成的想象了，少年期的前半大抵也是这样，不过自我意识更为发达，关于社会道德等的观念，也渐明白了。

约略根据了这个程序，我们将各期的儿童的文学分配起来，大略如下：

幼儿前期

（1）诗歌　这时期的诗歌，第一要注意的是声调。最好是用现有的儿歌，如北平的"水牛儿""小耗子"都可以用，就是那趁韵而成的如"忽听门外人咬狗"，咒语一般的抉择歌如"铁脚斑斑"，只要音节有趣，也是一样可用的，因为幼儿唱歌只好听，内容意义不甚紧要，但是粗俗的歌词也应该排斥，所以选择诗歌不必积极的罗致名著，只须消极加以别择便好了。古今诗里有适宜的，当然可用；但特别新做的儿歌，我反不大赞成，因为这是极难的，难得成功的。

（2）寓言　寓言实在只是童话的一种，不过略为简短，又多含着教训的意思，普通就称作寓言。在幼儿教育上，他的价值单在故事的内容，教训实是可有可无；倘这意义是自明的，儿童自己能够理会，原也很好，如借此去教修身的大道理，便不免谬了。这不但因为在这时期教了不能了解，且恐要养成曲解的癖，于将来颇有弊病。象征的著作须得在少年期的后期（第六七年学）去读，才有益处。

（3）童话　童话也最好利用原有的材料，但现在的尚未有人收集，古书里的须待修订，没有恰好的童话集可用。翻译别国的东西，也是一法，只须稍加审择便好。本来在童话里，保存着原始的野蛮的思想制度，比别处更多。虽然我们说过儿童是小野蛮，喜欢荒唐乖谬的故事，本是当然，但有几种也不能不注意：就是凡过于悲哀、苦痛、残酷的，不宜采用。神怪的事只要不过恐怖的限度，总还无妨；因为将来理智发达，儿童自然会不再相信这些，若是过于悲哀或痛苦，便永远在脑里留下一个印象，不会消灭，于后来思想上很有影响；至于残酷的害，更不用说了。

幼儿后期

（1）诗歌　这期间的诗歌不只是形式重要，内容也很重要了；读了固然要好听，还要有意思，有趣味。儿歌也可应用，前期读过还可以重读，前回听他的音，现在认他的文字与意义，别有一种兴趣。文学的作品倘有可采用的，极为适宜，但恐不多。如选取新诗，须择叶韵而声调和谐的；但有词调小曲调的不取，抽象描写或讲道理的也不取。儿童是最能分行而又最是保守的；他们所喜欢的诗歌，恐怕还是五七言以前的声调，所以普通的诗难得受他们的赏鉴；将来的新诗人能够超越时代，重新寻到自然的音节，那时真正的新的儿歌才能出现了。

（2）童话　小学的初年还可以用普通的童话，但是以后儿童辨别力渐强，对于现实与虚幻已经分出界限，所以童话里的想象也不可太与现实分离；丹麦安兑尔然（Hans C. Andersen）作的童话集里，有许多适用的材料。传说也可以应用，但应当注意，不可过量的鼓动崇拜英雄的心思；或助长粗暴残酷的行为。中国小说里的《西游记》讲神怪的事，却与《封神传》不同，也算纯朴率真，有几节可以当童话用。《今古奇观》等书里边，也有可取的地方，不过须加以修订才能适用罢了。

（3）天然故事　这是寓言的一个变相；以前读寓言是为他的故事，现在却是为他所讲的动物生活。儿童在这时期，好奇心很是旺盛，又对于牲畜及园艺极热心，所以给他读这些故事，随后引到记述天然的著作，便很容易了。但中国这类著作非常缺少，不得不取材于译书，如《万物一览》等书了。

少年期

（1）诗歌　浅探的文言可以应用，如唐代的乐府及古诗里多有好的材料；中国缺少叙事的民歌（Ballad），只有《孔雀东南飞》等几篇可以算得佳作，《木兰行》便不大适用。这时期的儿童对于普通的儿歌，大抵已经没有什么趣味了。

（2）传说　传说与童话相似，只是所记的是有名英雄，虽然也含有空想分子，比较的近于现实。在自我意识团体精神渐渐发达的时期，这类故事，颇为合宜；但容易引起不适当的英雄崇拜与爱国心，极须注意，最好采用各国的材料，使儿童知道人性里共通的地方，可以免去许多偏见。奇异而有趣味的，或真切而合乎人情的，都可采用；但讲明太祖那颇仑①等的故事，还以不用为宜。

（3）写真实的故事　这与现代的写实小说不同，单指多含现实分子的故事，如欧洲的《鲁滨孙》（Robinson Crusoe）或《吉诃德先生》②（Don Quixote）而言。中国的所谓社会小说里，也有可取的地方，如《儒林外史》及《老残游记》之类，纪事叙景都可，只不要有玩世的口气，也不可有夸张或感伤的"杂剧的"气味。《官场现形记》与《广陵潮》没有什么可取，便因为这个缘故。

（4）寓言　这时期的教寓言，可以注意在意义，助成儿童理智发达。希腊及此外欧洲寓言作家的作品都可选用；中国古文及佛经里也有许多很好的譬喻。但寓言的教训，多是从经验出来，不是凭理论的，所以尽有顽固或悖谬的话，用时应当注意，又篇末大抵附有训语，可以删去，让儿童自己去想，指定了反妨害他们的活动了。滑稽故事此时也可以用，童话里本有这一部类，不过用在此刻也偏重意义罢了。古书如《韩非子》等的里边，颇有可用的材料，大都是属于理智的滑稽，就是所谓机智。感情的滑稽实例很少；世俗大多数的滑稽都是感觉的，没有文学的价值了。

（5）戏曲　儿童的游戏中本含有戏曲的原质，现在不过伸张综合了，适应他们的需要。在这里边，他们能够发扬模仿的及构成的想象作用，得到团体游戏的快乐，这虽然是指实演而言，但诵读也别有兴趣，不过这类著作，中国一点都没有，还须等人去研究

---

① 拿破仑。
② 《堂吉诃德》。

创作；能将所读的传说去戏剧化，原是最好，却又极难，所以也只好先从翻译入手了。

以上约略就儿童的各期，分配应用的文学种类，还只是理论上的空谈，须经过实验，才能确实的编成一个详表。以前所说多偏重"儿童的"，但关于"文学的"这一层，也不可将他看轻；因为儿童所需要的是文学，并不是商人杜撰的各种文章，所以选用的时候还应当注意文学的价值。所谓文学的，却也并非要引了文学批评的条例，细细的推敲，只是说须有文学趣味罢了。文章单纯、明了、匀整；思想真实、普遍：这条件便已完备了。麦克林托克说，小学校里的文学有两种重要的作用：①表现具体的影像，②造成组织的全体；文学之所以能培养指导及唤起儿童的新的兴趣与趣味，大抵由于这个作用。所以这两条件，差不多就可以用作儿童文学的艺术上的标准了。

中国向来对于儿童，没有正当的理解，又因为偏重文学，所以在文学中可以供儿童之用的，实在绝无仅有；但是民间口头流传的也不少，古书中也有可用的材料，不过没有人采集或修订了，拿来应用。坊间有几种唱歌和童话，却多是不合条件，不适于用。我希望有热心人，结合一个小团体，起手研究，逐渐收集各地歌谣故事，修订古书里的材料，翻译外国的著作，编成几部书，供家庭学校的用，一面又编成儿童用的小册，用了优美的装帧，刊印出去，于儿童教育有许多的功效。我以前因为汉字困难，怕这事不大容易成功，现在有了注音字母，可以不必多愁了。但插画一事，仍是为难。现今中国画报上的插画，几乎没有一张过得去的，要寻能够为儿童书作插画的，自然更不易得了，这真是一件可惜的事。

（周作人，《1920 年 10 月 26 日在北平孔德学校讲演》）

二、"How Does Children's Literature Exist"

Just as there are competing histories of children's literature, so there are of children's literature criticism—and the two are interlinked. Most of these histories set the beginnings of children's literature in the eighteenth century—sometimes dated as precisely as 1744 with John Newbery's *A Little Pretty Pocket-Book*, as it is in Harvey Darton—and most draw on the tension between instruction and entertainment, often explicitly, *Fantasy and Reason* (1984), which is seen as a battle eventually won by entertainment. Harvey Darton, again, dates this precisely, to Carroll's *Alice* (1865), which he speaks of as the first appearance "in print ... of liberty of thought in children's books", instigating a golden age in children's literature. However, we need to be aware that such "grand narratives" about the area's development are only that. Through them children's literature critics frequently construct a "story" of a movement from darkness to light—just as developmental psychologists, like Piaget, envisage the child growing from an original, autistic state to adult rationality. The notion of a Bildungsroman is, therefore, often implicit, celebrating the discipline as having recently "come of age". But there are other stories, querying this. At one extreme, Gillian Adams (1986) takes children's literature texts back some 4,000 years, to

Sumer; at the other, Jacqueline Rose (1984) argues that the whole enterprise is impossible anyway-something that Karín Lesnik-Oberstein (1994) extends to its criticism. In this chapter, I shall try to get behind these various stories, to see what "regimes of truth" they draw on, in order to tease out what I shall term the conditions of possibility of children's literature and its criticism—and, particularly, to revisit those who see it as impossible.

This will involve steering a course between, on the one hand, notions that there is an underlying "essential" child whose nature and needs we can know and, on the other, the notion that the child is nothing but the product of adult discourse (as some social constructionists argue). I shall suggest that neither of these positions is tenable: that the problematic of children's literature lies in the gap between the "constructed" and the "constructive" child, in what I shall term a "hybrid", or border area.

Let me begin with Jacqueline Rose's provocative suggestion that, despite the possessive apostrophe in the phrase "children's literature", it has never really been owned by children:

Children's fiction rests on the idea that there is a child who is simply there to be addressed and that speaking to it might be simple . If children's fiction builds an image of the child inside the book, it does so in order to secure the child who is outside the book, the one who does not come so easily within its grasp.

Adults, she argues, evoke this child for their own purposes (desires, in fact), as a site of plenitude to conceal the fractures that trouble us all: concerns over a lack of coherent subjectivity, over the instabilities of language and, ultimately, existence itself. Barrie's *Peter Pan* texts are seen as perfect examples of this, purporting to be about the eternal child, but actually acknowledging the problems of such a construction, especially in the way that Barrie himself had problems producing a final, definitive version of his text.

Rose's book remains a revolutionary work, opening up children's literature to wider debates in cultural studies. However, her insight into the power of the child as a cultural trope (standing for innocence, the natural, the primitive, and so on) has led to a neglect of the child as a social being, with a voice. Rose herself does not deny the existence of the child "outside the book", on whom she actually draws at times, conceding that things are indeed different "at the point of readership"; her emphasis is simply elsewhere, just as is James Kincaid's in his related work, *Child Loving* (1992), which details how the figure of the child, constructed as innocent, a site of purity, thereby became, in the Victorian period, an erotic lure for adults. However, Kincaid's work has been misread in similar ways to that of Rose; Carolyn Steedman thus laments that

James Kincaid's conclusion . that the child "is not, in itself, anything", is very easy to reach

(and quite irresponsible proposals may follow on it) . children were both the repositories of adults' desires (or a text, to be "written" and "rewritten", to use a newer language), and social beings who lived in social worlds.

Like Rose, Kincaid does not deny the child as a social being; indeed, he too draws on what he terms "children with quite ordinary child needs". But Steedman's point is still valid: that the thrust of much of this criticism has tended to make the child appear voiceless. Lesnik-Oberstein goes further, arguing that this must be so for, unlike other disempowered groups such as women, who can speak for themselves, "Children, in culture and history, have no such voice".

Ironically, even to make such a claim is to have already separated out "the child" as a special being, subject to its own rules, distinct from other social groups. Furthermore, such a universal claim effectively adulterates (forgive the pun) a social constructionist perspective; for if children are merely constructions, social conditions might construct them otherwise. In effect, in order to make such a wide-sweeping claim, it would seem that Lesnik-Oberstein is, tacitly at least, invoking more enduring qualities, such as, to quote Allison James and Alan Prout, the "different physical size of children and their relative muscular weakness compared to adults"; however, as they continue, it would be absurd were it otherwise, exempting "human beings from the rest of the animal kingdom by denying any effects of our biological and physical being". This, as they say, is "cultural determinism", as problematic as its opposite: a humanistic essentialism.

The claim, therefore, "that the 'child' has no 'voice' within the hierarchies of our society, because 'adults' either silence or create that voice", actually helps construct the child as a helpless, powerless being, and contributes to the culturally hegemonic norm. As Rex and Wendy Stainton Rogers put it, "To model the child as constructed but not as constructive ... permits us to see the young person as having their identity constructed by outside forces but not the young person constructing their identity out of the culturally available." They, therefore, are of the opinion that the child's voice "should be heard".

(From *Understanding Children's Literature*，有删改)

第二节　赏·译·评

一、《呼兰河传》节选

呼兰河这小城里边住着我的祖父。

我生的时候，祖父已经六十多岁了，我长到四五岁，祖父就快七十了。

我家有一个大花园，这花园里蜂子、蝴蝶、蜻蜓、蚂蚱，样样都有。蝴蝶有白蝴蝶、黄蝴蝶。这种蝴蝶极小，不太好看。好看的是大红蝴蝶，满身带着金粉。

蜻蜓是金的，蚂蚱是绿的，蜂子则嗡嗡地飞着，满身绒毛，落到一朵花上，胖圆圆的就和一个小毛球似的不动了。

花园里边明晃晃的，红的红，绿的绿，新鲜漂亮。

据说这花园，从前是一个果园。祖母喜欢吃果子就种了果园。祖母又喜欢养羊，羊就把果树给啃了。果树于是都死了。到我有记忆的时候，园子里就只有一棵樱桃树，一棵李子树，因为樱桃和李子都不大结果子，所以觉得它们是并不存在的。小的时候，只觉得园子里边就有一棵大榆树。

这榆树在园子的西北角上，来了风，这榆树先啸，来了雨，大榆树先就冒烟了；太阳一出来，大榆树的叶子就发光了，它们闪烁得和沙滩上的蚌壳一样了。

祖父一天都在后园里边，我也跟着祖父在后园里边。祖父戴一个大草帽，我戴一个小草帽，祖父栽花，我就栽花；祖父拔草，我就拔草。当祖父下种，种小白菜的时候，我就跟在后边，把那下了种的土窝，用脚一个一个地溜平，哪里会溜得准，东一脚的，西一脚的瞎闹。有的菜种不单没被土盖上，反而把菜籽踢飞了。

小白菜长得非常之快，没有几天就冒了芽了。一转眼就可以拔下来吃了。

祖父铲地，我也铲地；因为我太小，拿不动那锄头杆，祖父就把锄头杆拔下来，让我单拿着那个锄头的"头"来铲。其实哪里是铲，也不过爬在地上，用锄头乱勾一阵就是了。也认不得哪个是苗，哪个是草。往往把韭菜当做野草一起地割掉，把狗尾草当做谷穗留着。

等祖父发现我铲的那块满留着狗尾草的一片，他就问我：

"这是什么？"

我说：

"谷子。"

祖父大笑起来，笑得够了，把草摘下来问我：

"你每天吃的就是这个吗？"

我说：

"是的。"

我看着祖父还在笑，我就说：

"你不信，我到屋里拿来你看。"

我跑到屋里拿了鸟笼上的一头谷穗，远远地就抛给祖父了，说：

"这不是一样的吗？"

祖父慢慢地把我叫过去，讲给我听，说谷子是有芒针的，狗尾草则没有，只是毛嘟嘟的真像狗尾巴。

祖父虽然教我，我看了也并不细看，也不过马马虎虎承认下来就是了。一抬头看见了一个黄瓜长大了，跑过去擒下来，我又去吃黄瓜去了。

黄瓜也许没有吃完，又看见了一个大蜻蜓从旁飞过，于是丢了黄瓜又去追蜻蜓。蜻蜓飞得多么快，哪里会追得上。好在一开初也没有存心一定追上，所以站起来，跟了蜻蜓跑了几步就又去做别的去了。

采一个倭瓜花心，捉一个大绿豆青蚂蚱，把蚂蚱腿用线绑上，绑了一会儿，也许把蚂蚱腿就绑掉了，线头上只拴了一只腿，而不见蚂蚱了。

玩腻了，又跑到祖父那里去乱闹一阵，祖父浇菜，我也抢过来浇，奇怪的就是并不往菜上浇，而是拿着水瓢，拼尽了力气，把水往天空里一扬，大喊着：

"下雨了，下雨了。"

太阳在园子里是特大的，天空是特别高的，太阳的光芒四射，亮得使人睁不开眼睛，亮得蚯蚓不敢钻出地面来，蝙蝠不敢从什么黑暗的地方飞出来。是凡在太阳下的，都是健康的、漂亮的，拍一拍连大树都会发响的，叫一叫就是站在对面的土墙都会回答似的。

花开了，就像花睡醒了似的。鸟飞了，就像鸟上天了似的。虫子叫了，就像虫子在说话似的。一切都活了，都有无限的本领，要做什么，就做什么。要怎么样，就怎么样，都是自由的。倭瓜愿意爬上架就爬上架，愿意爬上房就爬上房。黄瓜愿意开一个谎花，就开一个谎花，愿意结一个黄瓜，就结一个黄瓜。若都不愿意，就是一个黄瓜也不结，一朵花也不开，也没有人问它。玉米愿意长多高就长多高，它若愿意长上天去，也没有人管。蝴蝶随意地飞，一会儿从墙头上飞来一对黄蝴蝶，一会儿又从墙头上飞走了一个白蝴蝶。它们是从谁家来的，又飞到谁家去？太阳也不知道这个。

只是天空蓝悠悠的，又高又远。

可是白云一来了的时候，那大团的白云，好像洒了花的白银似的，从祖父的头上经过，好像要压到了祖父的草帽那么低。

我玩累了，就在房子底下找个阴凉的地方睡着了。不用枕头，不用席子，就把草帽遮在脸上就睡了。

译

The town of Hulan River is where my granddad lived. When I was born, Granddad was already past sixty, and by the time I was four or five, he was approaching seventy.

Our house had a large garden that was populated by insects of all types: bees, butterflies, dragonflies and grasshoppers. There were white butterflies and yellow ones; but these varieties were quite small and not very pretty. the really attractive butterflies were the scarlet ones whose entire bodies were covered with a fine golden powder.

The dragonflies were gold in color, the grasshoppers green. The bees buzzed everywhere, their bodies covered with a fine layer of down, and when they landed on flowers, their plump little round bodies appeared to be motionless balls of fur.

The garden was bright and cheerful, deriving its freshness and beauty from all the reds and greens. I heard it had once been a fruit orchard that was planted because of Grandmother's fondness for fruit. But Grandmother had also been fond of raising goats, and they had stripped the bark from her fruit trees, killing them. From the time of earliest recollection, the garden had only a single cherry tree and a single plum tree, and since neither bore much fruit, I wasn't really aware of their existence. When I was a child I felt that a tall elm was the only tree in our garden. This tree, which was in the northwest corner of the garden, was their first to rustle in the wind and the first to give off clouds of mist when it rained. Then when the sun came out, its leaves shone radiantly, sparkling like the mother-of-pearl found on a sandbar.

Granddad spent most of the day in the rear garden, and I spent my time there with him. Granddad wore a large stray hat, I wore a small one; when Granddad planted flower, so did I, and when Granddad pulled weeds, that's what I did too. When he planted cabbage seeds, I tagged along behind him filling in each of the little holes with my foot. But with my random and careless foot work, there was no way in the world I could have made a neat job of it. Some of the tome not only did I fail to cover the seeds with dirt, I actually sent them flying with my foot.

The Chinese cabbages grew so quickly that sprouts began appearing within a few days, and in no time they were ready to be picked and eaten.

When Granddad hoed the ground, so did I, but since I was too small to manage the long handle of the hoe, Granddad removed it and let me do my hoeing using only the head. Actually, there wasn't much hoeing involved in it, as I just crawled along on the ground chopping and digging at will with the head of hoe, not bothering to differentiate between the sprouts and the grass. Invariably, I mistook leeks for weeds and pulled them all out together by their roots, leaving the foxtails, discovered that the plot of the found I'd been hoeing was covered only with foxtails, he asked me:

"What's all that?"

"Grain," I answered.

He started to laugh, and when he'd finished, he pulled a foxtail and asked me:

"Is this what you've been eating every day?"

"Yes. "

Seeing that he was still laughing, I added:

"If you don't believe me, I'll go inside and get some to show you. "

So I ran inside and got a handful of grain from the birdcage, which I threw to Granddad from a distance, saying:

"Isn't this the same thing?"

Granddad called me over and explained patiently that the grain stalks have beards, while the foxtails have only cluster tat look very much like real foxes' tails. But although he was teaching me something new, I wasn't really paying any attention, and only make a cursory acknowledgement for what he way saying. Then, raising my head, I spotted a ripe cucumber and ran over, picked it, and began to eat. But before

I'd finished, a large dragon fly darting past me caught my eye, so I threw down the cucumber and chased after it. Really, how could I expect to catch a dragonfly that flew that fast? The nice part about it was, I never really had any intention of catching it, and only got to my feet, ran a few steps, then started doing something else.

At such times I'd pluck a pumpkin flower or catch a big green grasshopper and tie one of its legs with a piece of thread. After a while, the leg might snap off, so there'd be a leg dangling from the piece of thread, while the grasshopper from which it had come was nowhere to be found.

After I grew tired of playing, I'd run back over to where Granddad was and dash about noisily for a while. If he was watering the plants, I'd grab the watering gourd away from him and do it myself, though in a peculiar fashion: instead of sprinkling water on the vegetables themselves, I'd fling the water into the air with all my might and shout.

"It's raining, it's raining!"

The sun was particularly strong in the garden, and there was a very high sky above. The sun's rays beat down so brightly I could barely keep my eyes open; it was so bright that worms dared not bore up through the round, and bats dared not emerge from their dark hiding places. Everything touched by the sunlight was healthy and beautiful and when I smacked the trunk of the big elm tree with my hand, it resounded; when I shouted, it seemed as if even the earthen wall standing opposite me was answering my shouts.

When the flowers bloomed, its was as if they were awakening from a slumber. When the birds flew, it was as if they were climbing up the heavens. When the insects chirped, it was as if they were talking to each other. All these things were alive. There was no limit to their abilities, and whatever they wanted to do, they had the power to do it. They did as they wiled in complete freedom.

If the pumpkins felt like climbing up the trellis, they did so and if they felt like climbing up the side of the house, they did that. If the cucumber plant wanted to bring fourth an abortive flower, it did so, and it wanted to bear a cucumber, it did that; if it wanted none of these, then not a single cucumber nor a flower appeared, and no one would question its decision. The cornstalks grew as tall as they wished and if they felt like reaching up to the heavens, no one would give it a second thought. Butterflies flew wherever they desired, one moment there'd be a pair of yellow butterflies flying over from the other side of the wall, the next moment a solitary white butterfly flying off from this side of the wall. Whose house had they just left? Whose house were they flying to? Even the sun didn't know the answers to such questions.

There was only the deep bule sky, lofty and far, far away.

But when white clouds drew near they looked like great etched silver ingot, and as they passed over Grandad's head they were so low they seemed about to press down and touch his straw hat. When I'd grow tired from all my playing I search for a cool shady place near the house and went to sleep. I didn't need a pillow or a grass mat, but simply covered my face with my stray hat and fell asleep.

(translated by Howard Goldblatt)

二、*Charlotte's Web* 节选

Bad News

Wilbur liked Charlotte better and better each day. Her campaign against insects seemed sensible and useful. Hardly anybody around the farm had a good word to say for a fly. Flies spent their time pestering others. The cows hated them. The horses detested them. The sheep loathed them. Mr. and Mrs. Zuckerman were always complaining about them, and putting up screens.

Wilbur admired the way Charlotte managed. He was particularly glad that she always put her victim to sleep before eating it.

"It's real thoughtful of you to do that, Charlotte," he said.

"Yes," she replied in her sweet, musical voice, "I always give them an anaesthetic so they won't feel pain. It's a little service I throw in." As the days went by, Wilbur grew and grew. He ate three big meals a day. He spent long hours lying on his side, half asleep, dreaming pleasant dreams. He enjoyed good health and he gained a lot of weight. One afternoon, when Fern was sitting on her stool, the oldest sheep walked into the barn, and stopped to pay a call on Wilbur.

"Hello!" she said. "Seems to me you're putting on weight."

"Yes, I guess I am," replied Wilbur. "At my age it's a good idea to keep gaining."

"Just the same, I don't envy you," said the old sheep. "You know why they're fattening you up, don't you?"

"No," said Wilbur.

"Well, I don't like to spread bad news," said the sheep, "but they're fattening you up because they're going to kill you, that's why."

"They're going to what?" screamed Wilbur. Fern grew rigid on her stool.

"Kill you. Turn you into smoked bacon and ham," continued the old sheep. "Almost all young pigs get murdered by the farmer as soon as the real cold weather sets in. There's a regular conspiracy around here to kill you at Christmastime. Everybody is in the plot—Lurvy, Zuckerman, even John Arable."

"Mr. Arable?" sobbed Wilbur. "Fern's father?"

"Certainly. When a pig is to be butchered, everybody helps. I'm an old sheep and I see the same thing, same old business, year after year. Arable arrives with his. 22

179

shoots the ..."

"Stop!" screamed Wilbur. "I don't want to die! Save me, somebody! Save me!" Fern was just about to jump up when a voice was heard.

"Be quiet, Wilbur!" said Charlotte, who had been listening to this awful conversation.

"I can't be quiet," screamed Wilbur, racing up and down. "I don't want to be killed. I don't want to die. Is it true what the old sheep says, Charlotte? Is it true they are going to kill me when the cold weather comes?"

"Well," said the spider, plucking thoughtfully at her web, "the old sheep has been around this barn a long time. She has seen many a spring pig come and go. If she says they plan to kill you, I'm sure it's true. It's also the dirtiest trick I ever heard of. What people don't think of!"

Wilbur burst into tears. "I don't want to die," he moaned. "I want to stay alive, right here in my comfortable manure pile with all my friends. I want to breathe the beautiful air and lie in the beautiful sun."

"You're certainly making a beautiful noise," snapped the old sheep.

"I don't want to die!" screamed Wilbur, throwing himself to the ground.

"You shall not die," said Charlotte, briskly.

"What? Really?" cried Wilbur. "Who's going to save me?"

"I am," said Charlotte.

"How?" asked Wilbur.

"That remains to be seen. But I am going to save you, and I want you to quiet down immediately. You're carrying on in a childish way. Stop your crying! I can't stand hysterics."

译

坏消息

威尔伯一天比一天喜欢夏洛。它和昆虫作战似乎是有道理的，是有用的。农场没有谁会说苍蝇好话。苍蝇一辈子都在骚扰别人。牛恨它们。马讨厌它们。羊憎恶它们。朱克曼先生和太太一直抱怨它们，还装上了纱窗。

威尔伯佩服夏洛的做法，特别欣赏它在吃它们之前先让它们睡着。

"你这样做实在有头脑，夏洛。"它说。

"是的，"夏洛用它唱歌似的甜美的声音说，"我一直先麻醉它们，让它们不感到痛苦。这是我能帮的一点小小的忙。"

日子一天天过去，威尔伯越长越大。它一天大吃三顿。它舒舒服服地侧身躺上很长时间，半睡半醒，做着美梦。它身体很棒，胖了许多。一天下午，当弗恩正坐在她的凳子上时，最老的那只羊走进谷仓，停下来看威尔伯。

"你好，"它说，"我觉得你发福了。"

"是的，我想是的，"威尔伯回答说，"在我这个岁数，不断长胖是件好事。"

"不过我不羡慕你，"那老羊说，"你知道他们为什么让你长胖吗？"

"不知道，"威尔伯说。

"唉，我不想当小广播。"老羊说，"不过他们让你长胖只为了要杀你，就是这么回事。"

"他们要做什么？"威尔伯尖叫起来。弗恩在她的凳子上呆住了。

"杀你，把你变成熏肉火腿，"老羊说下去，"一到天气变得实在太冷时。几乎所有的猪年纪轻轻地就都被农民杀了。在这里，圣诞节杀你们是一种固定的阴谋活动。人人参与——勒维，朱克曼，甚至约翰·阿拉布尔。"

"阿拉布尔先生？"威尔伯哭起来，"弗恩的爸爸？"

"当然，杀猪人人帮忙。我是只老羊，一年又一年，这同样的事情看多了，都是老一套。那个阿拉布尔拿着他那支点二二口径步枪到这里，一枪……"

"别说了！"威尔伯尖叫，"我不要死！救救我，你们哪一位！救救我！"弗恩正要跳起来，听见了一个声音。

"安静点，威尔伯！"一直在听这番可怕谈话的夏洛说。

"我没法安静，"威尔伯跑过来跑过去，尖叫着说，"我不要给一枪射死。我不要死。老羊说的是真的吗，夏洛？天冷了他们要杀我，这是真的吗？"

"这个嘛，"蜘蛛弹拨着它的网，动着脑筋，"老羊在这谷仓里很久了。它看到许多春猪来了又走了。如果它说他们打算杀你，我断定这是真的。这也是我听到过的最肮脏的勾当。有什么事人想不出来啊！"

威尔伯哇哇大哭。"我不要死，"它呻吟说，"我要活，我要活在这舒服的肥料堆上，和我所有的朋友在一起。我要呼吸美丽的空气，躺在美丽的太阳底下。"

"你发出的吵闹声实在够美丽。"老羊厉声对它说。

"我不要死！"威尔伯扑倒在地上尖叫。

"你不会死。"夏洛轻快地说。

"什么？真的吗？"威尔伯叫道。"谁来救我？"

"我救你。"夏洛说。

"怎么救？"威尔伯问道。

"这得走着瞧。不过我要救你的，你给我马上安静下来。你太孩子气了。你马上停止，别哭了！这种歇斯底里我受不了。"

（任溶溶　译）

评

①What do you think about the language of *Charlotte's Web*?

②Is it appropriate to translate "It's real thoughtful of you to do that, Charlotte" as "你这样做实在有头脑？" Do you have a better translation?

第三节　翻译练习

一、《青铜葵花》节选

七岁女孩葵花走向大河边时，雨季已经结束，多日不见的阳光，正像清澈的流水一样，哗啦啦漫泻于天空。一直低垂而阴沉的天空，忽然飘飘然扶摇直上，变得高远而明亮。

草是潮湿的，花是潮湿的，风车是潮湿的，房屋是潮湿的，牛是潮湿的，鸟是潮湿的……世界万物都还是潮湿的。

葵花穿过潮湿的空气，不一会儿，从头到脚都潮湿了。她的头发本来就不浓密，潮湿后，薄薄地粘在头皮上，人显得更清瘦，而那张有点儿苍白的小脸，却因为潮湿，倒显得比往日要有生气。

一路的草，叶叶挂着水珠。她的裤管很快就被打湿了。路很泥泞，她的鞋几次被粘住后，索性脱下，一手抓了一只，光着脚丫子，走在凉丝丝的烂泥里。

经过一棵枫树下，正有一阵轻风吹过，摇落许多水珠，有几颗落进她的脖子里，她一激灵，不禁缩起脖子，然后仰起面孔，朝头上的枝叶望去，只见那叶子，一片片皆被连日的雨水洗得一尘不染，油亮亮的，让人心里很喜欢。

不远处的大河，正用流水声吸引着她。

她离开那棵枫树，向河边跑去。

她几乎天天要跑到大河边，因为河那边有一个村庄。那个村庄有一个很好听的名字：大麦地。

大河这边，就葵花一个孩子。

葵花很孤独，是那种一只鸟拥有万里天空而却看不见另外任何一只鸟的孤独。这只鸟在空阔的天空下飞翔着，只听见翅膀划过气流时发出的寂寞声。苍苍茫茫，无边无际。各种形状的云彩，浮动在它的四周。有时，天空干脆光光溜溜，没有一丝痕迹，像巨大的青石板。实在寂寞时，它偶尔会鸣叫一声，但这鸣叫声，直衬得天空更加的空阔，它的心更加的孤寂。

大河这边，原是一望无际的芦苇，现在也还是一望无际的芦苇。

那年的春天，一群白鹭受了惊动，从安静了无数个世纪的芦苇丛中呼啦啦飞起，然后在芦荡的上空盘旋，直盘旋到大麦地的上空，嘎嘎鸣叫，仿佛在告诉大麦地人什么。它们没有再从它们飞起的地方落下去，因为那里有人——许多人。

许多陌生人，他们一个个看上去，与大麦地人有明显的区别。

他们是城里人。他们要在这里盖房子、开荒种地、挖塘养鱼。

他们唱着歌，唱着城里人唱的歌，用城里的唱法唱。歌声嘹亮，唱得大麦地人一个个竖起耳朵来听。

几个月过去，七八排青砖红瓦的房子，鲜鲜亮亮地出现在了芦荡里。

不久竖起一根高高的旗杆，那天早晨，一面红旗升上天空，犹如一团火，静静地燃烧在芦荡的上空。

这些人与大麦地人似乎有联系，似乎又没有联系，像另外一个品种的鸟群，不知从什么地方落脚到这里。他们用陌生而好奇的目光看大麦地人，大麦地人也用陌生而好奇的目光看他们。

他们有自己的活动范围，有自己的话，有自己的活，干什么都有自己的一套。白天干活，夜晚开会。都到深夜了，大麦地人还能远远地看到这里依然亮着灯光。四周一片黑暗，这些灯光星星点点，像江上、海上的渔火，很神秘。

这是一个相对独立的世界。

不久，大麦地的人对它就有了称呼：五七干校。

后来，他们就"干校干校"地叫着："你们家那群鸭子，游到干校那边了。""你家的牛，吃了人家干校的庄稼，被人家扣了。""干校鱼塘里的鱼，已长到斤把重了。""今晚上，干校放电影。"……

那时，在这片方圆三百里的芦荡地区，有好几所干校。

那些人，都来自于一些大城市。有些大城市甚至离这里很远。也不全都是干部，还有作家、艺术家。他们主要是劳动。

大麦地人对什么叫干校、为什么要有干校，一知半解。他们不想弄明白，也弄不明白。这些人的到来，似乎并没有给大麦地带来什么不利的东西，倒使大麦地的生活变得有意思了。干校的人，有时到大麦地来走一走，孩子们见了，就纷纷跑过来，或站在巷子里傻呆呆地看着，或跟着这些人。人家回头朝他们笑笑，他们就会忽地躲到草垛后面或大树后面。干校的人觉得大麦地的孩子很有趣，也很可爱，就招招手，让他们过来。胆大的就走出来，走上前去。干校的人，就会伸出手，抚摸一下这个孩子的脑袋。有时，干校的人还会从口袋里掏出糖果来。那是大城市里的糖果，有很好看的糖纸。孩子们吃完糖，舍不得将这些糖纸扔掉，抹平了，宝贝似的夹在课本里。干校的人，有时还会从大麦地买走瓜果、蔬菜或是咸鸭蛋什么的。大麦地的人，也去河那边转转，看看那边的人在繁殖鱼苗。大麦地四周到处是水，有水就有鱼。大麦地人不缺鱼。他们当然不会想起去繁殖鱼苗。他们也不会繁殖。可是这些文文静静的城里人，却会繁殖鱼苗。他们给鱼打针，打了针的鱼就很兴奋，在水池里撒欢一般闹腾。雄鱼和雌鱼纠缠在一起，弄得水池里浪花飞溅。等它们安静下来了，他们用网将雌鱼捉住。那雌鱼已一肚子籽，肚皮圆鼓鼓的。他们就用手轻轻地捋它的肚子。那雌鱼好像肚子胀得受不了了，觉得捋得很舒服，就乖乖地由他们捋去。捋出的籽放到一个翻着浪花的大水缸里。先是无数亮晶晶的白点，在浪花里翻腾着翻腾着，就变成了无数亮晶晶的黑点。过了几天，那亮晶晶的黑点，就变成了一尾一尾的小小的鱼苗。这景象让大麦地的大人小孩看得目瞪口呆。

在大麦地人的心目中，干校的人是一些懂魔法的人。

干校让大麦地的孩子们感到好奇，还因为干校有一个小女孩。

他们全都知道她的名字：葵花。

二、*Charlie and the Chocolate Factory* 节选

Mr Willy Wonka's Factory

In the evenings, after he had finished his supper of watery cabbage soup, Charlie always went into the room of his four grandparents to listen to their stories, and then afterwards to say good night.

Every one of these old people was over ninety. They were as shrivelled as prunes, and as bony as skeletons, and throughout the day, until Charlie made his appearance, they lay huddled in their one bed, two at either end, with nightcaps on to keep their heads warm, dozing the time away with nothing to do. But as soon as they heard the door opening, and heard Charlie's voice saying, "Good evening, Grandpa Joe and Grandma Josephine, and Grandpa George and Grandma Georgina," then all four of them would suddenly sit up, and their old wrinkled faces would light up with smiles of pleasure—and the talking would begin. For they loved this little boy. He was the only bright thing in their lives, and his evening visits were something that they looked forward to all day long. Often, Charlie's mother and father would come in as well, and stand by the door, listening to the stories that the old people told; and thus, for perhaps half an hour every night, this room would become a happy place, and the whole family would forget that it was hungry and poor.

One evening, when Charlie went in to see his grandparents, he said to them, "Is it really true that Wonka's Chocolate Factory is the biggest in the world?"

True? "cried all four of them at once. " Of course it's true! Good heavens, didn't you know that? It's about fifty times as big as any other!'

"And is Mr Willy Wonka really the cleverest chocolate maker in the world?"

"My dear boy," said Grandpa Joe, raising himself up a little higher on his pillow, Mr. Willy Wonka is the most amazing. the most fantastic, the most extraordinary chocolate maker the world has ever seen! I thought everybody knew that!"

"I knew he was famous, Grandpa Joe, and I knew he was very clever ..." "Clever!" cried the old man. "He's more than that! He's a magician with chocolate! He can make anything—anything he wants! Isn't that a fact, my dears?"

The other three old people nodded their heads slowly up and down, and said, "Absolutely true. Just as true as can be. "

And Grandpa Joe said, "You mean to say I've never told you about Mr Willy Wonka and his factory?"

"never," answered little Charlie.

"Good heavens above! I don't know what's the matter with me!"

"Will you tell me now, Grandpa Joe, please?"

"I certainly will. Sit down beside me on the bed, my dear, and listen carefully. "

Grandpa Joe was the oldest of the four grandparents. He was ninety-six and a half, and that is just about as old as anybody can be. Like all extremely old people, he was delicate and weak, and throughout the day he spoke very little. But in the evenings, when Charlie, his beloved grandson, was in the room, he seemed in some marvellous way to grow quite young again. All his tiredness fell away from him, and he became as eager and excited as a young boy.

"Oh, what a man he is, this Mr. Willy Wonka!" cried Grandpa Joe. "did you know, for example, that he has himself invented more than two hundred new kinds of chocolate bars, each with a different centre, each far sweeter and creamier and more delicious than anything the other chocolate factories can make!"

"Perfectly true!" cried Grandma Josephine. "And he sends them to all the four corners of the earth! Isn't that so, Grandpa Joe?"

"It is, my dear, it is. And to all the kings and presidents of the world as well. But it isn't only chocolate bars that he makes. Oh, dear me, no! He has some really fantastic inventions up his sleeve, Mr. Willy Wonka has! Did you know that he's invented a way of making chocolate ice cream so that it stays cold for hours and hours without being in the refrigerator? You can even leave it lying in the sun all morning on a hot day and it won't go runny!"

"But that's impossible!" said little Charlie, staring at his grandfather.

"Of course it's impossible!" cried Grandpa Joe. "It's completely absurd! But Mr. Willy Wonka has done it!"

"Quite right!" the others agreed, nodding their heads. "Mr. Wonka has done it. "

"And then again," Grandpa Joe went on speaking very slowly now so that Charlie wouldn't miss a word, "Mr. Willy Wonka can make marshmallows that taste of violets, and rich caramels that change colour every ten seconds as you suck them, and little feathery sweets that melt away deliciously the moment you put them between your lips. He can make chewing-gum that never loses its taste, and sugar balloons that you can blow up to enormous sizes before you pop them with a pin and gobble them up. And, by a most secret method, he can make lovely blue birds eggs with black spots on them, and when you put one of these in your mouth, it gradually gets smaller and smaller until suddenly there is nothing left except a tiny little pink sugary baby bird sitting on the tip of your tongue. "

Grandpa Joe paused and ran the point of his tongue slowly over his lips. "It makes my mouth water just thinking about it," he said.

"Mine, too," said little Charlie. "But please go on. "

While they were talking, Mr and Mrs Bucket, Charlie's mother and father, had come quietly into the room, and now both were standing just inside the door, listening.

"Tell Charlie about that crazy Indian prince," said Grandma Josephine. "He'd like to hear that."

"You mean Prince Pondicherry?" said Grandpa Joe, and he began chuckling with laughter.

"Completely dotty!" said Grandpa George.

"But very rich," said Grandma Georgina.

"What did he do?" asked Charlie eagerly.

"Listen," said Grandpa Joe, "and I'll tell you."

第六章　影视字幕的翻译

随着影视行业的繁荣发展，影视作品文化内涵也越来越丰富。好的字幕翻译，关涉文化对等和转换等问题，同时也需要注意口语性和表演性等与纸质文本不同的影视语言特征。下面在介绍电影字幕的基本特征后，再选取近年来比较热门的影视作品的翻译进行译介。

第一节　文体特征

荧屏上的"语言"，既有文字的，也有"非文字"声音语言和图片语言。在介绍了电影的特殊语言特征后，本部分从视听性和瞬时性等角度对字幕进一步展开探讨。

一、影视"语言"

Cinematic Language

By cinematic language—a phrase that we have already used a few times in this book—we mean the accepted systems, methods, or conventions by which the movies communicate with the viewer. To fully understand cinema as a language, let's compare it with another, more familiar form of language—the written one you're engaged with this instant. Our written language is based, for the purpose of this explanation, on words. Each of those words has a generally accepted meaning; but when juxtaposed and combined with other words into a sentence and presented in a certain context, each can convey meaning that is potentially far more subtle, precise, or evocative than that implied by its standard "dictionary" definition.

Instead of arranging words into sentences, cinematic language combines and composes a variety of elements—for example, lighting, movement, sound, acting, and a number of camera effects—into single shots. As you work your way through this book, you will learn that most of these individual elements carry conventional, generalized meanings. But when combined with any number of other elements and presented in a particular context, that element's standardized meaning grows more individuated and complex. And the integrated arrangement of all of a shot's combined elements provides even greater expressive potential. So, in cinema, as in the written word, the whole is greater than the sum of its parts. But the analogy doesn't end there. Just as authors arrange sentences into paragraphs and chapters, filmmakers derive still more accumulated meaning by organizing shots into a system of larger components: sequences and scenes. Furthermore, within sequences and scenes a filmmaker can juxtapose shots to create a more complex meaning than is usually achieved in standard prose. As viewers, we analyze cinematic language and its particular resources of expression and meaning. If your instructor refers to the text of a movie or asks you to read a particular shot, scene, or movie, she is asking you to apply your understanding of cinematic language.

The conventions that make up cinematic language are flexible, not rules; they imply a practice that has evolved through film history, not an indisputable or "correct" way of doing things. In fact, cinematic conventions represent a degree of agreement between the filmmaker and the audience about the mediating element between them: the film itself. Although filmmakers frequently build upon conventions with their own innovations, they nonetheless understand and appreciate that these conventions were themselves the result of innovations. For example, a dissolve between two shots usually indicates the passing of time but not the extent of that duration, so in the hands of one filmmaker it might mean two minutes, and in the hands of another, several years. Thus you will begin to understand and appreciate that the development of cinematic language, and therefore the cinema itself, is founded on this tension between convention and innovation.

In all of this, we identify with the camera lens. The filmmaker (here in this introduction, we use that generic term instead of the specific terms screenwriter, director, cinematographer, editor, and so on that we'll use as we proceed) uses the camera as a maker of meaning, just as the painter uses the brush or the writer uses the pen: the angles, heights, and movements of the camera function both as a set of techniques and as expressive material, the cinematic equivalent of brushstrokes or of nouns, verbs, and adjectives. From years of looking at movies, you are already aware of how cinematic language creates meaning: how close-ups have the power to change our proximity to a character or low camera angles usually suggest that the subject of the shot is superior or threatening.

Looking at this single image (见图 6.1), without even knowing what movie it is from or anything about the various characters pictured in the frame, we can immediately infer layers of meaning and significance. If we think of cinematic language as akin to written language, we can think of this single image from Cary Fukunaga's *Jane Eyre* (2011) as a richly layered "sentence" that communicates by combining and arranging multiple visual elements (or "words" in this analogy) that include lighting, composition，depth，design，cinematography，and performance.

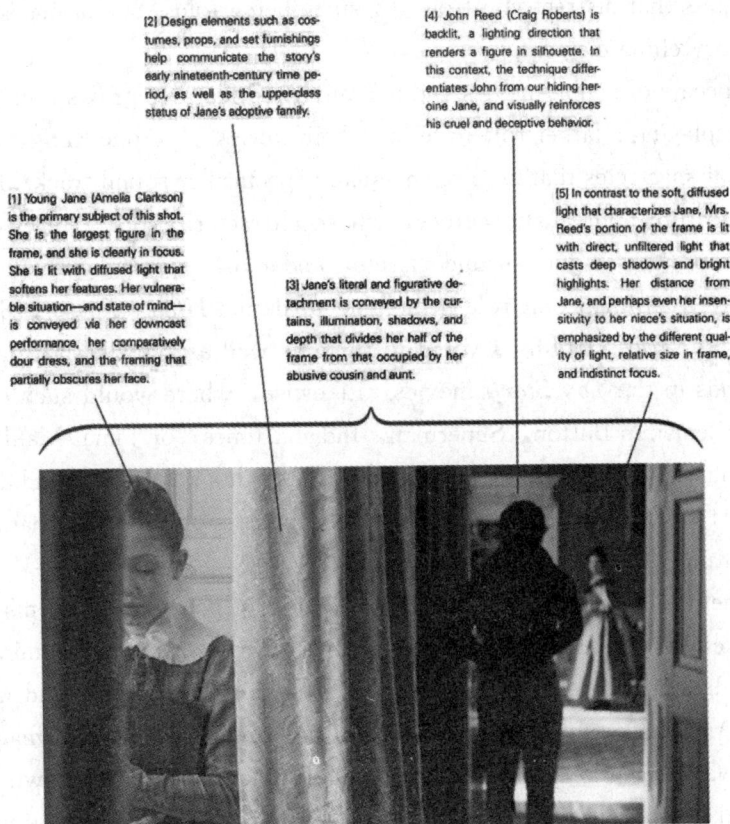

[2] Design elements such as costumes, props, and set furnishings help communicate the story's early nineteenth-century time period, as well as the upper-class status of Jane's adoptive family.

[4] John Reed (Craig Roberts) is backlit, a lighting direction that renders a figure in silhouette. In this context, the technique differentiates John from our hiding heroine Jane, and visually reinforces his cruel and deceptive behavior.

[1] Young Jane (Amelia Clarkson) is the primary subject of this shot. She is the largest figure in the frame, and she is clearly in focus. She is lit with diffused light that softens her features. Her vulnerable situation—and state of mind—is conveyed via her downcast performance, her comparatively dour dress, and the framing that partially obscures her face.

[3] Jane's literal and figurative detachment is conveyed by the curtains, illumination, shadows, and depth that divides her half of the frame from that occupied by her abusive cousin and aunt.

[5] In contrast to the soft, diffused light that characterizes Jane, Mrs. Reed's portion of the frame is lit with direct, unfiltered light that casts deep shadows and bright highlights. Her distance from Jane, and perhaps even her insensitivity to her niece's situation, is emphasized by the different quality of light, relative size in frame, and indistinct focus.

图 6.1　A Scene from *Jane Eyre*

（From *Looking at Movies：An Introduction to Film*，有删改）

二、视听性

What Is Sound

The movies engage two senses：vision and hearing. Although some viewers and even filmmakers assume that the cinematographic image is paramount，what we hear from the screen can be at least as significant as what we see on it，and sometimes what we hear is more significant. Director Steven Spielberg says，"The eye sees better when the sound is great." Sound—talking，laughing，singing，music，and the aural effects of objects and settings—can be as expressive as any of the other narrative and stylistic elements of cinematic form. What we hear in a movie is often technologically more complicated to produce than what we see. In fact，because of the constant advances in digital technology，sound may be the most intensively creative part of contemporary moviemaking. Spielberg，for one，has also said that，since the 1970s，breakthroughs in sound have been the movie industry's most important technical and creative innovations. He does not mean "using the technology to show off" by producing gimmicky sounds that distract you from the story being told, but rather sound used as an integral storytelling element.

As the success of action movies and 3-D animated features grows each year, sound and music are playing a larger role in telling their stories. For one thing, these movies are often visual spectacles that require an equally spectacular sound track. For another, they usually feature nonrealistic heroes, whose characterization requires every sound element—narration, dialogue, sound effects, and music—to make them come alive. Sound has played an important role in helping to define *Harry Potter*, *Spider-Man*, and *Shrek* in the series of films devoted to them as well as Woody and Buzz Lightyear and their friends in the *Toy Story* movies. Likewise, where would such characters as James Bond, Benjamin Button, Superman, Indiana Jones, or Jamal Malik be without sound to establish their worlds and adventures? Without a powerful sound design that is an integral part of the movie's artistic vision, both the story and the characters would be less fascinating.

Christopher Nolan's *Inception* (2010) is a case in point[①]. As seems appropriate for a science-fiction action movie about the creative powers of the human mind—how our thoughts and dreams create imaginary worlds—the story is complex and intellectually challenging. And the sound design, which shifts seamlessly between imagination and reality, and our perceptions of them, is equally caught up in its own intricacies. Richard King is responsible for the memorable sound editing of Inception and many other distinguished movies, including *War of the Worlds* (2005). His style produces sound that is multilayered and deeply textured, incorporating a bold and aggressive mix of sounds and music that complement the vivid visual and special effects. Virtually all of the sounds were produced in the studio, including the incredible sounds of the weapons, vehicles, explosions, and scenes of destruction.

Stanley Kubrick's *The Shining* (1980, sound by Dino Di Campo, Jack T. Knight, and Winston Ryder) opens with a series of helicopter point-of-view shots that,

---

① *Inception* is about an illegal espionage project that enters the subconscious minds of its targets to gain valuable information. Dominic Cobb (Leonardo DiCaprio, *right*), the leader of the team, has hired Ariadne (Ellen Page, *left*), a gifted young architecture student, to design labyrinthine dreamscapes for this work, but she (like the viewer) is still in the learning stage. In this image, they sit in a Parisian café that is part of a larger street scene exploding all around them. Ariadne (like the viewer) is astonished to see that they sit unhurt while the perceivable world is destroyed around them, but then Ariadne awakens in the design studio to realize that she has been dreaming this episode. The action is crafted with such visual and aural detail that everything we see—flower pots, people, wine glasses, tables, chairs, automobiles—explodes in its own unique way and with its own unique sound. Every sight and sound image has been created and implanted in Ariadne's dream to show her (and the viewer) the power of the "dreams within dreams" project in which she is now a key player. Richard King, the sound designer and editor, and his sound mixers (Lora Hirschberg, Gary A. Rizzo, and Ed Novick) won Oscars for the movie's richly textured sound design.

without the accompanying sound, might be mistaken for a TV commercial. In these shots, we see a magnificent landscape, a river, and then a yellow Volkswagen driving upward into the mountains on a winding highway. Whereas we might expect to hear a purring car engine, car wheels rolling over asphalt, or the passengers' conversation, instead we hear music: an electronic synthesis by composers Wendy Carlos and Rachel Elkind of the *Dies Irae*, one of the most famous Gregorian chants, which became the fundamental music of the Roman Catholic Church. The Dies Irae (literally, "the day of wrath") is based on *Zephaniah* 1: 14—16, a reflection on the Last Judgment. It is one section of the *Requiem Mass*, or *Mass for the Dead*. Experiencing the shots together with the sound track, we wonder about the location, the driver, and the destination. What we hear gives life to what we see and offers some clues to its meaning. The symbolic import and emotional impact of this music transforms the footage into a movie pulsating with portentous energy and dramatic potential. Once we identify this music, we suspect it is warning us that something ominous is going to happen before the movie ends. Thus forewarned, we are neither misled nor dissatisfied.

The sound in the scenes just described (or in any movie scene) operates on both physical and psychological levels. For most narrative films, sound provides cues that help us form expectations about meaning; in some cases, sound actually shapes our analyses and interpretations. Sound calls attention not only to itself but also to silence, to the various roles that each plays in our world and in the world of a film. The option of using silence is one crucial difference between silent and sound films; a sound film can emphasize silence, but a silent film has no option. As light and dark create the image, so sound and silence create the sound track. Each property—light, dark, sound, silence—appeals to our senses differently.

In film history, the transition to sound began in 1927. It brought major aesthetic and technological changes in the way movies were written, acted, directed, and screened to the public. After the first few sound movies, where sound was more of a novelty than a formal element in the telling of the story, a period of creative innovation helped integrate sound—vocal sounds, environmental sounds, music, and silence—into the movies. The results of this innovation can be seen and heard in some of the great movies of the 1930s, including King Vidor's *Hallelujah*! (1929; sound by Douglas Shearer), Rouben Mamoulian's *Applause* (1929; sound by Ernest Zatorsky), G. W. Pabst's Westfront 1918 (1930; sound by W. L. Bagier Jr.), Fritz Lang's M (1931; sound by Adolf Jansen), and Ernst Lubitsch's Trouble in *Paradise* (1932; no sound credit). Comparing one or more of these movies to several silent classics will help you to understand how profoundly sound changed the movies.

Like every other component of film form, film sound is the product of specific decisions by the filmmakers. The group responsible for the sound in movies, the sound crew, generates and controls the sound physically, manipulating its properties to produce the effects that the director desires. Let's look more closely at the various aspects of sound production controlled by the sound crew.

(From *Looking at Movies*: *An Introduction to Film*)

三、时空性

Change in Mode

The shift of mode from speech to writing presents the subtitler with yet more challenges. Characteristics of spontaneous speech, such as slips of the tongue, pauses, false starts, unfinished sentences, ungrammatical constructions, etc., are difficult to reproduce in writing. The same goes for dialectal, idiolectal and pronunciation features that contribute to the moulding of screen characters. The use of a pseudo-phonetic transcription to reproduce a regional or social dialect in the subtitles, for instance, would not be helpful as it would hinder the readability of the text by adding to the reading time of the subtitle, and also hinder the comprehension of the message by obscuring the style.

What then is the subtitler to do? Certain spoken features may need to be rendered in the subtitles if their function is to promote the plot. But rather than reproducing mistakes in an uneducated character's speech, a subtitler can make use of appropriate, usually simpler, vocabulary in order to indicate education, regional dialect or social class of the character. Or the decision may be taken not to reproduce the stuttering in a character's speech since viewers have resource to this information already from the feedback effect of the soundtrack. For the subtitler, it is a matter of deciding in each case what priority needs to be given to certain features of each sequence of speech. ...

All know what subtitles are: condensed written translations of original dialogue which appear as lines of text, usually positioned towards the foot of the screen. Subtitles appear and disappear to coincide in time with the corresponding portion of the original dialogue and are almost always added to the screen image at a later date as a post-production activity.

Interlingual subtitling is a type of language transfer in which the translation, that is the subtitles, do not replace the original Source Text (ST), but rather, both are present in synchrony in the subtitled version. Subtitles are said to be most successful when not noticed by the viewer. For this to be achieved, they need to comply with certain levels of readability and be as concise as necessary in order not to distract the viewer's attention from the programme. So, what are the techniques used to make subtitles unobtrusive? And what is the subtitler's role? The answers to these questions can be found if we take a closer look at the technical, textual and linguistic constraints of subtitling.

Technical Constraints

The technical spatial and temporal constraints of audiovisual programmes relate directly to the format of subtitles.

Space. In the limited space allowed for a subtitle there is no room for long explanations. Two lines of text are usually the norm, and the number of characters per line depends on a number of factors, including the subtitling workstation used. Since readability of the text is of paramount importance, it has been suggested that an ideal subtitle is a sentence long, with the clauses of which it consists placed on separate lines.

Time. The length of a subtitle is directly related to its on-air time. Accurate in and out timing is very important and the text in the subtitles should always be in balance with the appropriate reading time setting. No matter how perfect a subtitle is in terms of format and content, it will always fail to be successful if viewers do not have enough time to read it. A lower word per minute (wpm) or character per minute (cpm) setting is applied, for example, when subtitling children's programmes, as children cannot reach adult reading speeds.

Presentation. Subtitles can take up to 20% of screen space. Important factors for their legibility are the size of the characters, their position on screen, as well as the technology used for the projection of subtitles in the cinema (DTS or Dolby), TV broadcast, DVD emulation, etc., as it affects their definition. In our digital age, most of these problems have been solved. In DVD subtitling, for instance, the choice of any font and font size supported by Windows is possible, unlike teletext subtitling for television, where this is not the case. These technical constraints determine subtitlers' work practice and their linguistic choices.

Textual Constraints

In subtitling, language transfer operates across two modes, from speech to writing, from the soundtrack to the written subtitles. This shift of mode creates a number of processing and cohesion issues that make it difficult to maintain the filmic illusion in the target product.

Oral-aural Processing

Since in subtitling both source and target texts are present simultaneously (see Gottlieb, 1994: 265 for details on the four channels that compose the audiovisual text), the viewer of a subtitled programme has at least two different types of information on which to concentrate: the action on the screen, and the translation of the dialogue, that is the subtitles. This adds to the verbal information that might appear in the original programme in the form of inserts and which the viewers have to process through the visual channel, making it more difficult for them to relax and enjoy the programme. The situation becomes more difficult when the timing of the subtitles is not satisfactorily done. When a subtitle is continued over a shot change, for example, the viewer may think that it is a new subtitle and re-read it, losing precious viewing time. Also, the temporal succession of subtitles is quite different from the linear succession of sentences in a book; it does not allow the eye to move backwards or forwards to clarify misunderstandings, recapitulate the basic facts or see what will happen next. This can be done, however, when watching a film or a programme on video or DVD by using the rewind function.

As a result, in order for the subtitled text to be successful, it needs to preserve the "sequence of speech acts ... in such a way as to relay the dynamics of communication". A few rough rules are usually observed by subtitlers to help minimise the potentially negative effects of these extra processing demands made by the viewer.

(a) When the visual dimension is crucial for the comprehension of a particular scene, subtitlers should offer only the most basic linguistic information, leaving the eyes of the viewers free to follow the images and the action.

(b) Conversely, when important information is not in the images but in the soundtrack, subtitlers should produce the fullest subtitles possible, to ensure that the viewers are not left behind.

(c) The presentation of the subtitles, the way in which the words of each subtitle are arranged on the screen, and on each subtitle line, can help enhance readability.

This last point relates to the role of grammar and word order in subtitling. The simpler and more commonly used the syntactic structure of a subtitle, the least effort needed to decipher its meaning. For example, in all the subtitled versions of the following text from Hitchcock's *Psycho*, the main and subordinate clauses of the sentence are placed in separate subtitle lines and the syntax is through a re-arrangement of the original phrase as shown in the English subtitle.

表 6.1　Example 1

Original dialogue 01h19′21″04—01h19′24″22.	
One thing people never ought to be when they're buying used cars is in a hurry.	
English subtitle	*French subtitle*
People never ought to be in a hurry when buying used cars.	On ne devrait pas être pressé quand on achète une voiture d'occasion.
Italian subtitle	*German subtitle*
Non si dovrebbe mai andare di fretta quando si compra una macchina.	Beim Gebrauchtwagenkauf sollte man es nie eilig haben.

Even appropriate line breaks within a single subtitle can facilitate comprehension and increase reading speed if segmentation is done into noun or verb phrases, rather than smaller units of a sentence or clause. In the example below from Weird Science it is possible, within the time allowed, to read the text of both subtitles, which are identical from a semantic point of view. However, of the two solutions in Example 2, the subtitle format in Option 2 is easier to read as the text is broken up after the noun phrase 'your parents'.

表 6.2　Example 2

Original dialogue 01h03′53″01—01h03′57″11	
I don't understand. How come your parents trust you all of a sudden?	
Option 1	Option 2
I don't understand why your parents trust you all of a sudden.	I don't understand why your parents trust you all of a sudden.

Finally, in this example from the audio-commentary of Hitchcock's Vertigo, we can see how long sentences are split up into shorter ones in an obvious attempt to increase reading speed. As in this case, conjunctions usually provide a natural split for subtitle breaks.

表 6.3　Example 3

Original dialogue	English subtitles
Option 1	Option 2
I met with him, talked to him, I've told him the whole story and he started the painting and one day he said he must meet Vera Miles to keep on going.	01h26′31″07—01h26′34″08 Met with him, told him the whole story and he started the painting.
	01h26′35″06—01h26′38″23′ One day he said he must meet Vera Miles to keep on going.

Textuality Issues

Because of the limited space generally available for subtitles, certain elements of the soundtrack have to be omitted, and the obvious solution is to do away with redundant elements of speech. Redundancy helps participants in a conversation grasp its intended meaning more easily and its elimination from film dialogue may, therefore, weaken cohesion in the subtitled text. The question then is to what extent the predictability of discourse is affected by the systematic deletion of redundant features and the impact this may have on the viewers' understanding of the narrative. There is, however, a strong link between the dialogue of a film and the context in which it takes place. Apart from linguistic redundancy in audiovisual programmes, there is also situational redundancy that usually works in favour of the translator.

The visual information often helps viewers process the subtitles, and to a certain extent this compensates for the limited verbal information they contain. For example, aspects of interpersonal communication may be found in intonation, rhythm and the facial and kinesic movements that accompany the dialogue which are, to an extent, universal. When, in *Braveheart*, Mel Gibson cries out "Hold! Hold! Hold! Now!" at the moment when the British cavalry is about to attack the frontline of the Scottish army, the viewers can easily understand what is happening, even without a translation. This is also known as the "feedback effect" of films.

(From *Audiovisual Translation Language Transfer on Screen*，有删改)

第二节　赏·译·评

一、《卧虎藏龙》片段

赏

2000 年，李安导演的《卧虎藏龙》在中外电影界大放异彩，荣获第 73 届奥斯卡最佳外语片等 4 项大奖，也是华语电影历史上第一部荣获奥斯卡金像奖的影片。在非英语影片中，其斩获的提名奖项数目之多，是前所未有的，这一纪录一直维持到 2018 年的影片《罗马》（*Roma*）的出现。

《卧虎藏龙》主要讲述了有退出江湖之意的一代大侠李慕白，托付红颜知己俞秀莲将自己的青冥剑带到京城，作为礼物送给贝勒爷收藏，不想这一举动却惹来更多的江湖恩怨。在影片中，中国传统古典美学和情感理念开拓到了新的高度。影片中带有思辨哲理的对白、具有意象境界的场景以及充满韵律美感的动作等各种艺术元素和视听语言，无一不展现导演细腻深沉的艺术风格和对东西方文化的深刻理解与把握。对于这样集娱乐、审美和哲理于一身的影片，其字幕翻译工作势必也十分考验译者的水平，下文将选取其中一个场景的字幕翻译，在课堂上结合电影视频进行分析解读。

译

秀莲，慕白来啦！	Shu Lien, Mu Bai is here!
家里好吗？	How's everything?
挺好的，请进。	Fine. Please come in.
秀：慕白兄，好久不见。	Mu Bai, it's been too long.

慕：是啊。 镖局的生意怎么样？	It has. How's business?
秀：还行，你好吗？	Good.　And how are you?
慕：好。	Fine.
秀：道元真人年初从武当山路过这里， 说起你正在闭关修炼。 有时候我真羡慕你， 我光是忙着镖局的生意，静不下来。	Monk Zhen said you were at Mount Wudang.　He said you were practicing deep meditation. The mountain must be so peaceful. I envy you. My work keeps me so busy.　I hardly get any ease.
慕：我破了戒，提早出关。	I left the training early.
秀：为什么？道人说这次的闭关对你非常重要。	Why?　Mond Zhen said it was important for you.
慕：这次闭关静坐的时候， 我一度进入了一种很深的寂静， 我的周围只有光， 时间、空间都不存在了， 我似乎碰到了师父们从未指点过的境地。	During my meditation ... I fell into a profound silence. There was only light around. Both time and space disappeared. I was in a state that my master never told me about.
秀：你得道了？	You were enlightened?
慕：嗯， 我没有这种感觉， 因为我并没有得道的喜乐， 相反的，却被一种寂灭的悲哀环绕。 这悲哀超过了我能承受的极限， 我出了定，没办法再继续， 有些事……我需要想想。	No. I didn't feel the bliss of enlightenment. Instead，I was surrounded by an endless sorrow. I couldn't bear it. I broke off my meditation. I couldn't go on. There was something... pulling me back.
秀：什么事？	What was it?
慕：一些心里放不下的事。 你要出门了吗？	Something I can't let go off. You're leaving soon?
秀：有一趟镖要到，已经收拾好了，就要上路。	We're preparing a convoy for a delivery to Peking.
慕：有件东西…… 烦劳你替我带给贝勒爷。	Perhaps I could ask you to deliver something for Sir Te for me.
秀：青冥剑！把它送给贝勒爷？	The Green Destiny sword?　You're giving it to Sir Te?
慕：贝勒爷一直是最关心我们的人。	I am.　He has always been our greatest protector.
秀：我还是不明白， 这是你随身的佩剑， 这么多年它一直跟着你。	I don't quite understand. How can you part with it? It has always been with you.

慕：跟着我惹来不少的江湖恩怨。你看它干干净净的，因为它杀人不沾。	Too many men have died at its edge. It only looks pure because blood goes so easily from its blade.
秀：你不是个滥杀无辜的人。所以你才配用这把剑。	You use it justly. You're worthy of it.
慕：该是离开这些恩怨的时候了。	It's time for me to leave it behind.
秀：离开？ 之后呢？ 干脆和我一起去， 我觉得你应该亲手把剑交给贝勒爷。 记得我们以前经常结伴去吗？	So what will you do now? Why not come with me? You can give the sword to Sir Te yourself. It'll be just like old times.
慕：我这趟下山，想去给恩师扫墓。 恩师遭碧眼狐狸暗算…… 这么多年了，师仇还没报， 我竟然萌生了退出江湖的念头。	First I must visit my master's grave. It's been many years since... Jade Fox murdered him. I have to avenge his death. And yet I'm thinking of quitting.
秀：既然是这样， 办完了事，你到时跟我会合，我就等你。	Join me once you have finished. I can wait for you in Peking.
慕：也许吧。	Perhaps.

评

①How are the culturally-loaded words and phrases dealt with?

②In the video-clip of *Crouching Tiger Hidden Dragon*，what are the differences between the written text above and the scripts on the screen?

二、*Little Women* 片段

译

Jo：Excuse me. I was looking for the *Weekly Volcano* office. I wish to see Mr. Dashwood. A friend of mine desired me to offer a story by her. She ... She wrote it. She'd be glad to write more if this suits.	请问，我在找《火山周报》办公室。 我想见戴斯伍先生， 有位朋友让我帮她投稿， 若适合刊载，她很乐意多写。
Editor：Not a first attempt, I take it.	不是第一次投稿。
Jo：No, sir. She has sold to Olympic and Scandal, and she got a prize for a tale at the Blarneystone Banner.	不是，先生。 她还曾给《奥林匹克》和《丑闻》投过， 还获得了"巧言石"文学奖。

Editor：A prize?	得过奖？
Jo：Yes.	是的。
Editor：Sit. We'll take this.	请坐。 我们会出版。
Jo：You will?	真的？
Editor：With alternations.　It's too long.	不过要修改一下，太长了。
Jo：But you've cut ... I took care to have a few of my sinners repent.	但你删掉了…… 我已让文中的一些罪人痛改前非了。
Editor：The country just went through a war. People want to be amused，not preached at. Morals don't sell nowadays. Perhaps mention that to your friend.	国家经历战乱， 人们想寻欢，不想听训， 这年头道德不卖钱了， 可以跟你朋友提一下。
Jo：What compensation ...?　How do you ...?	请问酬劳……贵社怎么……
Editor：We pay 25 to 30 for things of this sort. We'll pay 20 for that.	这类作品 25 块到 30 块， 那篇 20 块。
Jo：You can have it.　Make the edits. Should I tell my ... un，my friend You'll take another if she had done better than this?	成交，删改吧。 我能跟朋友说，如果有更好的作品， 你们也会刊载吗？
Editor：We'll look at it.　Tell her to make it short and spicy. And if the main character's a girl， make sure she's married by the end. Or dead.　Either way.　—Excuse me? What name would she like to put to the story?	看看再说，叫她写短一点，要有看头。 如果主角是女生， 结局一定要嫁人， 去世也行。 你说什么？ 她想用什么笔名？
Jo：Yes.　None at all，if you please. ...	匿名，麻烦你。 ……
Editor：Just as she likes，of course.	好的，如她所愿。
Good afternoon，Miss March.	午安。
Jo：Good afternoon. You're on fire.	午安， 你着火了。
Jo：Thank you.	谢谢
You're on fire!	你着火了！

评

①Without pictures and sound，how do you feel about the dialogues above?

②What does "sb.　be on fire" mean in English? It appears twice in the above-mentioned dialogue.　According to the context，is it appropriate to translate both as "你着火了"? What lesson should be learnt from this screenplay translation practice?

③What do you think about the language style of the original and the translated?

第三节　翻译练习

一、《琅琊榜》片段

再加上今天送到的北燕这份国书
差不多周边各国
也都表示过有意
向霓凰公主求婚了吧

是
除了南楚

霓凰可是执掌云南王府
十万铁骑的一军统领
威慑南楚近十年
就算再借他们一百个胆子
只怕是也不敢厚颜到金陵来
求娶郡主

那可不是吗
郡主不仅是陛下您
亲封的一品君侯
她那名头还上了琅琊高手榜呢
这样的人物品格
这一般的人谁配得上啊
可不就得陛下您
为她多操点心了

霓凰在南境十年
边陲安定
十万铁骑对她是忠心不二啊
只怕时间再久了
南境大军
只知穆王 不知梁王
这南境嘛

怕就变成南国喽
穆青既已成年
正是从他姐姐手里
接手长官云南王府的时机
霓凰嘛
是该歇歇了

二、*The Flipped* 片段

JULl　　The first day I met Bryce Loski，I flipped.

It was those eyes，

something in those dazzling eyes.

You wanna push this one together?

JULl　　His family had just moved

into the neighborhood ...

... and I'd gone over to help them.

I'd been in the van all of two minutes

when his dad sent him off to help his mom.

I could see he didn't wanna go.

So I chased after him to see if we could

play a little before he got trapped inside.

The next thing I know，

he's holding my hand ...

... and looking right into my eyes.

My heart stopped.

Was this it?

Would this be my first kiss?

But then his mother came out.

Well，hello.

JULl　　And he was so embarrassed，

his cheeks turned completely red.

I went to bed that night thinking

of the kiss that might have been.

I mean，it was clear he had feelings for me，

but he was just too shy to show them.

My mother said boys were like that.

So I decided to help him out.

Bryce? You're here.

JULI   I would give him plenty

of opportunity to get over his shyness.

By the sixth grade,

I'd learned to control myself.

Then Sherry Stalls entered the picture.

Sherry Stalls was nothing but a whiny,

gossipy，backstabbing flirt.

All hair and no substance.

And there she was ...

... holding hands with Bryce. My Bryce.

The one who was walking around

with my first kiss.

My solution was to ignore her.

I knew a boy of Bryce's caliber ...

... would eventually see through

a shallow conniver like Sherry Stalls.

It took all of a week.

They broke up at recess.

She didn't take it well.

Now that Bryce was out of Sherry's

evil clutches，he started being nicer to me.

JULI   He was so shy and so cute ...

... and his hair，

it smelled like watermelon.

I couldn't get enough of it.

I spent the whole year

secretly sniffing watermelon ...

... and wondering if I was ever going to get my kiss.

第七章 歌曲的翻译

歌曲翻译，确切地说，应该是歌曲的"译配"，因为它不仅涉及歌词的准确对应，还要考虑译文如何与音响、韵律和节奏等外在形式的相互协调和配合，即如何让诗性、音乐性与表演性三大要素和谐统一，从而达到原曲的意境。

第一节 文体特征

无论在东方，还是在西方，音乐都被看作是与人的内心灵魂相通的。在进行具体的歌曲翻译之前，有必要从古典文献出发，先厘清一下关于"何为音乐"这一本质问题。

一、"音者，生于人心"

先王之济五味，和五声也，以平其心，成其政也。声亦如味，一气、二体、三类、四物、五声、六律、七音、八风、九歌以相成也。清浊、大小、短长、疾徐、哀乐、刚柔、迟速、高下、出入、周疏以相济也。君子听之，以平其心，心平德和。故《诗》曰："德音不瑕。"今据不然，君所谓可，据亦曰可；君所谓否，据亦曰否。若以水济水，谁能食之？若琴瑟之专一，谁能听之？同之不可也如是。

（《左传·昭公二十年》节选）

凡音之起，由人心生也。人心之动，物使之然也。感于物而动，故形于声；声相应，故生变；变成方，谓之音；比音而乐之，及干戚羽旄，谓之乐也。乐者，音之所由生也，其本在人心感于物也。是故其哀心感者，其声噍以杀；其乐心感者，其声啴以缓；其喜心感者，其声发以散；其怒心感者，其声粗以厉；其敬心感者，其声直以廉；其爱心感者，其声和以柔。六者非性也，感于物而后动，是故先王慎所以感之。故礼以导其志，乐以和其声，政以壹其行，刑以防其奸。礼乐刑政，其极一也，所以同民心而出治道也。

凡音者，生人心者也。情动于中，故形于声，声成文谓之音。是故治世之音安以乐，其正和；乱世之音怨以怒，其正乖；亡国之音哀以思，其民困。声音之道，与正通矣。宫为君，商为臣，角为民，徵为事，羽为物。五者不乱，则无恬懘之音矣。宫乱则荒，其君骄；商乱则捶，其臣坏；角乱则忧，其民怨；徵乱则哀，其事勤；

羽乱则危，其财匮。五者皆乱，迭相陵，谓之慢。如此则国之灭亡无日矣。郑卫之音，乱世之音也，比于慢矣。桑间濮上之音，亡国之音也，其政散，其民流，诬上行私而不可止。

凡音者，生于人心者也；乐者，通于伦理者也。是故知声而不知音者，禽兽是也；知音而不知乐者，众庶是也。唯君子为能知乐。是故审声以知音，审音以知乐，审乐以知政，而治道备矣。是故不知声者不可与言音，不知音者不可与言乐。知乐则几于礼矣。礼乐皆得，谓之有德。德者得也。是故乐之隆，非极音也；食飨之礼，非极味也。清庙之瑟，朱弦而疏越，一倡而三叹，有遗音者矣。大飨之礼，尚玄酒而俎腥鱼，大羹不和，有遗味者矣。是故先王之制礼乐也，非以极口腹耳目之欲也，将以教民平好恶而反人道之正也。

（《史记·乐书》节选）

二、"Music is a Moral Law"

Greek myths and legends tell of the wondrous effects of music. Traditionally, in ancient Greece, music was included in education and was part of religious and civic ceremonies. Music was an integral part of men's lives and readily accepted by them. Yet, when Greek philosophers attempted to go beyond the levels of myth and custom, they discovered, as Aristotle says, that it is not easy to determine the nature of music or why anyone should have a knowledge of it. Not only is a musical piece intrinsically complex, but when it is seen as related to man and his life even greater complexities enter into the picture.

Plato and Aristotle, the first Greek philosophers to examine the ends of music, recognized this and placed most of their discussions of music in their political works. There they examined the relationship which music has to the common good, particularly its place in education. They saw music as allied to the intricacies of man's nature and the perfection of nature.

For Plato man's first education is aimed at forming the whole person, with gymnastics directed primarily towards a child's body, and music directed principally toward his soul. Working together, they help establish and maintain the proper order in man 's nature. Not only does education begin by forming the fundamental parts of man, the body and the soul, but it also begins with movements which are natural to man. Plato explicitly indicates this with respect to choric training, which is identical with a child's education through gymnastics and music:

All young creatures are naturally full of tire, and can keep neither their limbs nor their voices quiet. They are perpetually breaking into disorderly cries and jumps, but whereas no other animal develops a sense of order of either kind, mankind forms a solitary exception.

Order in movement is called rhythm, order in articulation—the blending of acute with grave—pitch, and the name for the combination of the two is choric art. (Laws)

Choric art begins with natural movements which are so easy that even a baby can perform them. Using these movements, music helps prepare the soul for acting. Just as gymnastics, based on spontaneous physical movements, helps prepare the body for easily performing complicated maneuvers.

This first formation of the soul is called "education" by Plato to distinguish it from virtue. Education refers to the molding of the soul along good lines with regard, to pleasure and pain; virtue adds understanding to good habits of pleasure and pain. Plato speaks of music as educating through habits, by imparting by the melody a certain harmony of spirit that is not science, and by rhythm, measure and graces Music puts order in the child's soul by training him to feel pleasure and pain properly, even though he may not understand what the proper way to feel them would be.

According to Plato, music is a useful instrument for education "because more than anything else rhythm and harmony find their way into the inmost soul and take strongest hold upon it". Music begins by striking the senses and then passing through the senses, it goes more deeply into the soul. Musical education, in turn, can go as far as the music itself goes, Plato insists that it should not just give dexterity to the fingers or strength to the voice; musical education should measure and order the movements of the soul by training the child to feel pleasure and pain in the right way. In reaching out and touching the soul, music should move the soul toward goodness, It can happen, however, that the soul is badly trained and deformed by music. In these instances musical training is carried to a wrong end: music must penetrate the soul but it must not push it toward vice. One uses of music suggested by Plato, then, is to mold the soul along good lines, that is, dispose it toward moral virtue.

The question now arises as to why Plato thinks that music can move the soul toward goodness or its contrary. He says that music prepares the young for virtue by familiarizing them with well-ordered emotion. To understand how music can do this we should look at what Plato says about lullabies:

This course (of rocking) is adopted and its usefulness recognized both by those who nurse small children and by those who administer remedies in cases of Corybantism. Thus when mothers have children suffering from sleeplessness, and want to pull them to rest, the treatment they apply is to give them not quiet but motion, for they rock them constantly in their arms; and instead of silence, they use a kind of crooning noise; and thus they literally cast a spell upon the children (like the victims of Bacchic frenzy) by employing the combined movement of dance and song as a remedy.

So whenever one applies an external shaking to affections of this kind, the external motion thus applied over-powers the internal motion of fear and frenzy, and by thus overpowering it, brings about a manifest calm in the soul and a cessation of the grievous palpitations of the heart which had existed in each case. Thus it produces very satisfactory results. The children it puts to sleep; the Bacchants, who are awake, it puts into a sound state of mind instead of a frenzied condition, by means of dancing and playing . (Laws)

When a child is too excited for his own good, his mother tempers his emotion by slowly rocking and singing to him. The baby picks up the rhythm of this movement and he relaxes. Thus the mother counteracts the action of one emotion by substituting another emotion for it. A lullaby makes a baby feel all right by making him feel the way he should feel, that is, inducing a calm, balanced movement in him.

There are two important points contained in Plato's comment on lullabies. The first is that music moves the listener emotionally, and the second is that music can make him feel right. These two facts taken together explain why music can dispose a child toward virtue.

Plato states in several places that music reproduces or imitates the emotions. In the *Laws* he remarks that "rhythm and music generally are a reproduction expressing the moods of better and worse men". In the *Republic* he says that we can recognize in music different types of emotional movements such as "soberness, courage, liberality, and high-mindedness, and all their kindred and their opposites, too, in all the combinations that contain and convey them". For Plato music's power over emotional states is founded on its force as an imitation of emotion. When someone listens to a piece, he picks up its emotional movement and begins to move in the open way. To paraphrase Plato, musical movement, containing an expression of emotion, conveys this emotion to the listener.

Since music moves the listener emotionally, by repetition it can familiarize him with certain emotional states. Plato explains that when music familiarizes someone with a disposition appropriate to a particular circumstance, it makes him feel right. This is how it disposes him toward virtue. The rightness of music is judged by the fittingness of the emotion reproduced in the listener. The best music is not only a good imitation in the sense that it is effective in moving the listener, but it is also an imitation of a good or well-ordered emotion. Music can also put an improper order in the emotions, stirring up the listener too much in some circumstances and not enough in others. Plato sees unsuitable music as disposing toward vice when "by gradual infiltration it softly overflows upon the character and pursuits of men".

According to Plato, whether it is for weal or woe, music naturally forms the soul according to its own image in a subtle and powerful way. It penetrates deeply and directly, pushing its way into the soul of the listener, moving his emotions and giving them its shape. The music departs, but it leaves its mark on the listener.

Once a child has become accustomed, through music, to letting his emotions run away with him, he will continue to find excessive emotion pleasing. On the other hand, if he has become familiar with measured emotion, he will find that pleasing. This is the basis of Plato's attitude toward music as an instrument of moral formation: music can dispose a child toward virtue because it directly moves him on the emotional level. This imitation of emotion, then, is the second, and the most fundamental end of music suggested by Plato. Not only can music dispose toward virtue, but it is very effective in doing so. The reason for this leads us to the third end which Plato assigns to music, that of giving pleasure ...

Furthermore, Plato places great value on music's ability to develop habits of taste because these habits are extended to other areas. When a good musical education puts the right measure in a child's emotions, it instills in him an almost natural attraction toward what is good and aversion to anything bad before he can understand why things are good or bad. At first the child judges the goodness and badness of things by their affinity with his own state and the consequent pleasure which they bring. If the child has been well-formed, he may eventually become able to understand why something is good or bad because "when reason came the man thus nurtured would be the first to give her welcome, by this affinity he would know her". When a man has been properly molded by music, his emotions will present no obstacle to his understanding of virtue.

For Plato musical pleasure is not an end in itself: it should be subordinated to another end, fostering virtue in the soul. Unless reason enters in to determine what music will bring harmony to the emotions, the listener risks falling under the sway of music that brings irrational pleasure and disposes him toward vice instead of virtue. Plato accepts pleasure as an end of music but insists that it be used at the service of virtue.

There is a fourth end of music which Plato indicates, that of indirectly preparing the intellect for learning. He suggests that music does this in two ways. First, it does this by disposing the listener toward moral virtue and so predisposing him for learning. In the *Protagoras* Plato urges children to study music so that they "become more balanced, more capable in whatever the y say or do, for rhythms and harmonious adjustment are essential to the whole of human life. Music's influence extends to all man's activities inasmuch as the acquisition of moral virtue is a prerequisite to the acquisition of intellectual virtue.

Secondly, he indicates that music prepares the intellect for learning "in the way of liberal education", which does not give the child any specialized training or knowledge. A musical education neither trains a child to be a skillful musician nor teaches him a science. What Plato says about all the fine arts as fostering learning can be applied to music in particular，he speaks of these arts as preparing the mind for understanding by providing a cultural formation. They do this first by arousing and feeding man's love of knowledge and secondly by purifying and sharpening his perceptions. For Plato music directly touches the emotions and remotely prepares the intellect for learning，so that this end which refers to the intellectual life is consequent upon its effect in the moral order.

Plato，then，assigns four ends to music，and he sees a certain order between them：first，music moves the emotions：second，it gives pleasure：third，it disposes toward moral goodness；and fourth，it disposes toward learning. The most fundamental end of music is the moving of the emotions. This is the reason why music pleases and can dispose toward virtue. Musical pleasure is subordinated to moral goodness：it can，but should not，be used to encourage badly ordered emotions in the listener. Finally，the art of music has a remote influence over the intellect which follows from its ability to introduce the listener to well-ordered emotions.

(From "Plato and Aristotle on the Ends of Music"，1978，有删改)

第二节　赏·译·评

一、《义勇军进行曲》

起来！

不愿做奴隶的人们！

把我们的血肉，筑成我们新的长城！

中华民族到了最危险的时候，

每个人被迫着发出最后的吼声。

起来！

起来！

起来！

我们万众一心，冒着敌人的炮火，

前进！

冒着敌人的炮火，

前进！

前进！

前进！进！

译

译文一	译文二
Arise Ye who refuse to be slave with our flesh and blood build up our new Great Wall China masses have met the day of all danger Indignation fill the hearts of our countrymen Arise Arise Arise	Arise You who refuse to be bound slaves Let's stand up and fight for Liberty and true democracy All the world is facing The change of tyranny Everyone who wants freedom is now crying Arise Arise Arise All of us in one heart With the torch of freedom March on With the torch of freedom March on March on and on

评

上面第一个版本的翻译，忠实于原文，但在用英文演唱的时候，还需要考虑节奏、换气和重音等问题，由于中文和英文的差异，很可能在实际效果上，就要减弱很多。而译文二保罗·罗伯逊演绎的《义勇军进行曲》，充分考虑了歌曲的现场演唱效果，淋漓尽致地展现了原曲中铿锵有力、不卑不亢的精神。

二、《捉泥鳅》节选

池塘里水满了，雨也停了，
田边的稀泥里到处是泥鳅。
天天我等着你，等着你捉泥鳅；
大哥哥好不好，咱们去捉泥鳅？

赏

《捉泥鳅》是一首富有浓郁的田园风味及生活情趣的台湾校园歌曲。歌曲通过对雨后孩子要去捉泥鳅的急切心情的描写，展示了一幅活泼动人的田间嬉戏图。全曲由六个乐句组成，自然小调式，一、三、五等单数小节的节奏基本相同，双数小节的节奏略有变化。旋律在逐渐变化中层层递进，推向高潮，生动地描绘出孩童在田间嬉戏的形象。在翻译成英文的时候，需要注意节奏和韵律，尽量保持原作的意境。

译

Yelling to all my friends gather around the field，

Inside the muddy field hiding many eels，

Wait for you every day just to catch the eels.

Since the rain has stopped，now let's go catch the eels

三、《夫妻双双把家还》节选

女：树上的鸟儿成双对

男：绿水青山带笑颜

随手摘下花一朵

我于娘子戴发间

女：从今不再受那奴役苦

男：夫妻双双把家还

女：你耕田来我织布

男：我挑水来你浇园

女：寒窑虽破能避风雨

男：夫妻恩爱苦也甜

女：你我好比鸳鸯鸟

男：好比鸳鸯鸟

女：比翼双飞

合：在人间

译

Birds in the trees are playing happily in pairs.

Green hills and clear streams all give us a happy smile.

From the roadside I pick a beautiful flower.

I fix it in the hair of my beautiful wife.

From now on we'll never suffer from slavery.

We are now going home as husband and wife.

You plough our fields and I weave cloth for us.

I fetch water；you water our crops.

Our cottage is humble，but it keeps us from storms.

Love between husband and wife can turn bitterness into honey.

You and I，like a pair of lovebirds，always fly side by side in the human world.

In the human world.

（纪玉华　译）

评

①It is pleasing to read the translation，while can you sing it to the original tune?

②What are the differences between "translating to sing" and "translating to read"?

③What modifications can be made to make the translation better?

四、"Old Man River"

There's an old man called the Mississippi
That's the old man I don't like to be!
What does he care if the world's got troubles?
What does he care if the land ain't free?

That old man river
That old man river
He must know sumpin'
But don't say nothin'
He just keeps rollin'
He keeps on rollin' along

He don't plant taters
He don't plant cotton
And them that plants' em is soon forgotten
But old man river
He just keeps rollin' along

You and me，we sweat and strain,
Body all achin' and racked with pain,
Tote that barge，and lift that bale
You show a little grit
And you lands in jail

But I keeps laughin'
Instead of cryin'
I must keep fightin'
Until I'm dyin'

And old man river

He'll just keep rollin' along

赏

这是一首反映美国黑人悲惨生活的歌曲，以美国著名黑人歌唱家保罗·罗伯逊（Paul Robeson）在 1936 年发行的电影《演船》（*Showboat*）中的演唱最为经典。那深厚的男低音充满了感人肺腑的力量，激发了阵阵如雷般的掌声，演唱者也一举成名。1937 年，在英国举行了支持西班牙共和国的群众大会，罗伯逊将《老人河》的歌词改为"我们要乐观地继续战斗下去，直到死为止"，表达了人们维护和平与正义的呼声，激起到会群众震耳欲聋的欢呼声。这首反映美国黑人悲惨生活的歌曲，迅速传遍了全世界，至今常在音乐会上演出。

译

黑人劳动在密西西比河上，
黑人劳动白人来享乐，
黑人工作到死不得休息。
从早推船直到太阳落，
白人工头多凶恶，
切莫乱动招灾祸，
弯下腰、低下头，
我拉起纤绳把船拖。
让我快快离开白人工头，
快快离开密西西比河。
请你告诉我那个地方，
我要渡过古老的约旦河。
老人河，啊，老人河！
你知道一切，
但总是沉默，
你滚滚奔流，
你总是不停地流过。
他不种番薯也不种棉花，
那耕种的人早被人遗忘。
但老人啊，
你总是不停地流过。
我们流血又流汗，
浑身酸痛受折磨，
为了免得坐监牢，
还要拉船扛包裹。
我们这样地痛苦疲倦，

既害怕死亡，
又厌倦生活。
但老人河啊！
你总是不停地流过。

（邓映易　译）

五、“Down by the Salley Gardens”

Down by the salley gardens my love and I did meet;
She passed the salley gardens with little snow-white feet.
She bid me take love easy, as the leaves grow on the tree;
But I, being young and foolish, with her would not agree.
In a field by the river my love and I did stand,
And on my leaning shoulder she laid her snow-white hand.
She bid me take life easy, as the grass grows on the weirs;
But I was young and foolish, and now am full of tears.

译

译文一
在莎莉花园深处，吾爱与我曾相遇。
她穿越莎莉花园，纤足如雪般皎白。
她嘱咐我要爱得轻松，就像新叶在枝椏萌芽。
但我当年年幼无知，不予轻率苟同。
在河边的田野，吾爱与我曾驻足。
她搭靠在我的肩膀上，用她那嫩白小手。
她嘱咐我要活得轻松，就像青草在堤岸滋长。
但我当年年幼无知，而今热泪盈眶。
在莎莉花园深处，吾爱与我曾经相遇。
她穿越莎莉花园，纤足如雪般皎白。
她嘱咐我要爱得轻松，就像新叶在枝椏萌芽。
但我当年年幼无知，不予轻率苟同。

译文二
在莎莉花园深处，吾爱与我曾经相遇。她雪花般的纤足，向着花园尽头走去。
她嘱我爱得简单，如枝上萌发的新绿。但当年年少无知，不愿接受她的心语。
在远方河畔旷野，吾爱与我并肩伫立。在我微倾的肩上，她搭起纯白的手臂。
她嘱我活得淡然，像青草滋长于岸堤。但当年年少无知，如今早已泪满衣裳。

译文三

斯遇佳人，仙苑重深。玉人雪趾，往渡穿林。
嘱我适爱，如叶逢春。我愚且顽，负此明言。
斯水之畔，与彼曾伫。比肩之处，玉手曾拂。
嘱我适世，如荇随堰。惜我愚顽，唯余泣叹。

评

以爱尔兰诗人威廉·巴特勒·叶芝（William Butler Yeats）创作的《莎莉花园》一诗改编的歌曲为例，叶芝曾说，这首诗的创作灵感来自一位老农妇唱的不太完整的一首歌，它只有短短如下几行：

Down by yon flowery garden my love and I we first did meet.
I took her in my arms and to her I gave kisses sweet
She bade me take life easy just as the leaves fall from the tree.
But I being young and foolish, with my darling did not agree.

该诗经叶芝改编后，成为一首完整的诗，之后又添加了音乐元素，多个歌唱家都演唱过，其中以藤田惠美的版本流传最为广泛。

就诗歌的翻译而言，无论风格还是语言、意象，译文三无疑是比较经典的。从风格上看，四字构造也是中国最古老的爱情诗集《诗经》的形式。同时，译文中还有一些中国古典爱情诗中的意象，如"如荇随堰"一句，也很容易就让我们想起《关雎》中类似的意象："参差荇菜，左右采之。窈窕淑女，琴瑟友之。"还有许多中英文对应的意象，也是信手拈来，如"如叶逢春""玉手"等等，可谓真正做到了"化境"。相比之下，译文二虽然也用了整齐的句式，所有句子都是七字的，右边所有句子都是八字的，但却显得刻意、不自然，如"像青草滋长于岸堤"一句，"滋长"有"滋生"之意，给人的联想是杂草丛生，丧失了原文自然、随意之感，美感也大打折扣。而"在我微倾的肩上，她搭起纯白的手臂"一句，不仅不太自然，甚至还稍显累赘了。至于译文一，除"不予轻率苟同"两句，在文体上与全文的风格有一些出入外，其他则主要是用日常的语言进行直译。

这是诗歌语言层面的，但如果谱了曲，配上了画面，译文三就未必是最佳的选择了。古香古色的四字文言译文，在纸面上可以反复品读。但因为视频的瞬间性特点，每一屏只出现一句歌词，听众很可能还没来得及看明白译文，画面就翻过去了。此外，有一些文字看似流畅并符合审美需求，但在歌曲翻译中，有时可能显得画蛇添足。例如："She passed the Salley gardens with little snow-white feet"一句，按照汉语的表达，应该把状语"with little snow-white feet"部分提前，如译文二"她雪花般的纤足，向着花园尽头走去"和译文三"玉人雪趾，往渡穿林"，但在歌曲翻译中，要尽可能保持与原句顺序一致，否则就会出现译文与原文或视频图片不符的情况，造成理解的偏差。在歌曲的翻译中，应尽可能遵循时效性和表演性优先的原则。

第三节 翻译练习

翻译中，注意中英文用词的节奏、韵律以及字幕的长短差异等。

一、《送别》

长亭外，古道边，芳草碧连天。晚风拂柳笛声残，夕阳山外山。
天之涯，地之角，知交半零落。一壶浊酒尽余欢，今宵别梦寒。
长亭外，古道边，芳草碧连天。问君此去几时来，来时莫徘徊。

二、《女驸马》节选

为救李郎离家园
谁料皇榜中状元
中状元着红袍
帽插宫花好哇
好新鲜哪
我也曾赴过琼林宴
我也曾打马御街前
人人夸我潘安貌
原来纱帽照哇
照婵娟哪
我考状元不为把名显
我考状元不为做高官
为了多情的李公子
夫妻恩爱花好月儿圆哪

三、"Silver Hair among the Gold"

Darling, I am growing old,
Silver threads among the gold,
Shine upon my brow today;
Life is fading fast away;
But, my darling, you will be
Always young and fair to me,
Yes! my darling, you will be

Always young and fair to me.

Darling, I am growing old.
Silver threads among the gold,
Shine upon my brow today;
Life is fading fast away.

When your hair is silver white,
And your cheeks no longer bright,
With the roses of the May,
I will kiss your lips, and say
Oh! My darling, mine alone
You have never older grown,
Yes! my darling, mine alone,
You have never older grown!

Love can never more grow old,
Locks may lose their brown and gold;
Cheeks may fade and hollow grow,
But the hearts that love will know,
Never, never winter's frost and chill;
Summer warmth is in them still
Never winter's frost and chill,
Summer warmth is in them still.

Love is always young and fair,
What to us is silver hair;
Faded cheeks, or steps grown slow,
To the heart that beats below?
Since I kissed you mine alone, alone.
You have never older grown
Since I kissed you mine alone,
Your have never older grown.

主要参考文献

一、中文文献

奥斯汀，1990．傲慢与偏见［M］．孙致礼，译．南京：译林出版社．

曹文轩，2013．青铜葵花［M］．北京：天天出版社．

陈平原，2010．中国散文小说史［M］．北京：北京大学出版社．

达尔，2009．查理和巧克力工厂［M］．任溶溶，译．济南：明天出版社．

郭预衡，2011．中国散文史［M］．上海：上海古籍出版社．

胡适，2015．四十自述［M］．北京：民主与建设出版社．

怀特，2013．夏洛的网［M］．任溶溶，译．上海：上海译文出版社．

江枫，2009．江枫论文学翻译自选集［M］．武汉：武汉大学出版社．

林庚，2007．中国文学简史［M］．北京：北京大学出版社．

林海音，2015．城南旧事［M］．北京：北京联合出版公司．

刘勰，2013．文心雕龙［M］．北京：中华书局．

卢卡奇，2013．小说理论［M］．北京：商务印书馆．

孟伟根，2012．戏剧翻译研究［M］．杭州：浙江大学出版社．

普林斯，2013．叙事学：叙事的形式与功能［M］．北京：中国人民大学出版社．

钱穆，2021．中国思想史［M］．北京：九州出版社．

申丹，韩佳明，王丽亚，2005．英美小说叙事理论研究［M］．北京：北京大学出版社．

司马迁，2006．史记［M］．北京：中华书局．

孙康宜，宇文所安，2016．剑桥中国文学史［M］．北京：生活·读书·新知三联书店．

汪曾祺，2018．人间世相［M］．长春：时代文艺出版社．

王宏印，2012．文学翻译批评论稿［M］．上海：上海外语教育出版社．

王佐良，2019．英国文学史［M］．北京：商务印书馆．

韦伯，2018．新教伦理与资本主义精神［M］．阎克文，译．上海：上海人民出版社．

吴翔林，1993．英诗格律及自由诗［M］．北京：商务印书馆．

萧红，2014．呼兰河传［M］．北京：北京联合出版公司．

许渊冲，2016．文学与翻译［M］．北京：北京大学出版社．

杨燕起，陈可清，赖长扬，2005．史记集评［M］．北京：华文出版社．

朱光潜，2017．诗论［M］．上海：华东师范大学出版社．

二、外文文献

BARSAM R，MONAHAN D，2016. Looking at movies：an introduction to film. 5th edition. New York：W. W. Norton & Company.

BAYM N，2007. The norton anthology of American literature. 7th edition. New York & London：W. W. Norton & Company.

BENTLEY E，2010. The playwright as thinker. 4th edition. London：University of Minnesota Press.

BOOTH W，1983. The rhetoric of fiction. Chicago and London：The University of Chicago Press.

BRAUN E，2016. Meyerhold on theatre. 4th edition. London：Bloomsbury.

BROOKS C，ROBERT P W，2004. Understanding poetry. 4th edition. Beijing：Foreign Language Teaching and Research Press.

BUFFAGNI C，Garzelli B，2012. Film translation from east to west：dubbing, subtitling and didactic practice. Bern：Peter Lang.

CHIARO D，Heiss C，Bucaria C，2008. Between text and image：updating research in screen translation. Amsterdam & Philadelphia：John Benjamins Publishing Company.

CINTAS J D，Anderman G，2009. Audiovisual translation：language transfer on screen. New York：Palgrave Macmillan.

DWYER T，2017. Speaking in subtitles：revaluing screen translation. Edinburgh：Edinburgh University Press.

EAGLETON T，2012. The event of literature. New Haven：Yale University Press.

ELLENDER C，2015. Dealing with difference in audiovisual translation：subtitling linguistic variation in films. Bern：Peter Lang.

FOSTER E M，2005. Aspects of the novel. London：Penguin Classics.

FPRSTER T C，2006. How to read novels like a professor. New York：Harper Collins Publishers.

GREENBLATT S，2006. The Norton anthology of American literature. 7th edition. New York & London：W. W. Norton & Company.

HARLAN R，2005. Literary theory from Plato to Barthes. Beijing：Foreign Language Teaching and Research Press.

HUNT P，2005. Understanding children's literature. 2nd edition, New York：Routledge.

LODGE D，1992. The art of fiction：illustrated from classic and modern texts. New York：Penguin Group.

LYNCH-BROWN C，Tomlinson CM，1999. Essentials of children's literature. 3rd

edition. Boston：Allyn and Bacon.

OWEN S，1981. The great age of Chinese poetry：the high tang. New Haven and London：Yale University Press.

PFLISTER M，1993. The theory and analysis of drama. trans. John Halliday. Cambridge：Cambridge University Press.

STYAN J L，1963. The elements of drama. Cambridge：Cambridge University Press.

WILLIAM H N, Jr.，1994. The grand scribe's records. trans. Tsai-fa Cheng，Zongli Lu，William H. Nienhauser，Jr.，et al. Bloomington：Indiana University Press.